Jay Bell Books
www.jaybellbooks.com

Cover art and interior illustrations by Cassy Fallon
www.cassyfallon.com

-=Books by Jay Bell=-

The Something Like... series
#1 Something Like Summer
#2 Something Like Autumn
#3 Something Like Winter
#4 Something Like Spring
#5 Something Like Lightning
#6 Something Like Thunder
#7 Something Like Stories - Volume One
#8 Something Like Hail
#9 Something Like Rain
#10 Something Like Stories - Volume Two
#11 Something Like Forever
#12 Something Like Stories - Volume Three

The Loka Legends series
#1 The Cat in the Cradle
#2 From Darkness to Darkness

Other Novels
Kamikaze Boys
Hell's Pawn
Straight Boy
Out of Time, Into You

Other Short Stories
Language Lessons
Like & Subscribe
The Boy at the Bottom of the Fountain

Thank You!

My sincerest appreciation goes out to the following people who, through their support on Patreon, have empowered me to continue writing and publishing the stories in my heart:

Mark Andrews ♥ Kevin Arvizu ♥ Daniel Attaway ♥ Danny Barson ♥ Emma Beck ♥ Kevin Bowling-Swan ♥ Chris & Kai Burton ♥ The By George Boys ♥ Scott Caldwell ♥ Chad Cazee ♥ Cory Chamberlin ♥ Cort Channon ♥ Josh Chernos ♥ Matthew Christian ♥ Phil Clark ♥ Matthew Cliburn ♥ April Cook ♥ Andy Corvin ♥ Neil Courtney ♥ D-Dee Damiano ♥ Jeff Davault ♥ Ann DeVoy ♥ Chantal de Pessemier ♥ Dicxy ♥ Corey Dobbs ♥ Todd Doty ♥ Andeh DuLac ♥ Mark Edwards ♥ Jeremy Eskelsen ♥ Shaun T. Erickson (AKA "Marcello") ♥ Evy & Lisa ♥ Ilona F. ♥ Travis Falla ♥ Shannon Farnsworth ♥ Tallian Fisher ♥ Zac Ford ♥ Jim Frier ♥ James Gies ♥ Darius Gilbert ♥ Tiffany C. Graham ♥ Luce Graville ♥ Devin Greenlee ♥ David Griffin ♥ Brian H ♥ Nicole Hall ♥ Ashley Hazley ♥ Keith Heathcote ♥ Felisha Height ♥ Florian Heym ♥ Jay Hooks ♥ Dan Hsieh ♥ Stephen Hurwitz ♥ Daniel Hutchinson ♥ Nathan Jackson ♥ Jarter ♥ Leigh Juhlke ♥ Cody Keller ♥ Melissa Kidd ♥ Shaun King ♥ Akshat Krishnan ♥ Eric LaMonte ♥ Kurt Lee ♥ Brittany Rose Lewis ♥ Lisa Lieurance ♥ Felyx Lawson ♥ Cory MacKenzie ♥ David Manfredi ♥ Tony Marquardt ♥ Marc Martinez ♥ Peter Mawer ♥ Susen McBeth ♥ Jini McClelland ♥ Michael & Noah ♥ Carol Molinari ♥ Simon Monroe ♥ Sam Moore ♥ R.T. Mullins ♥ Olivier Ochin ♥ Jim & Gary Omaha ♥ Zara Park ♥ Scott Pearson ♥ Matthew M. Perry ♥ Michael I Pollard ♥ Lydia Poy ♥ Nicholas Quillin ♥ Ossiel Renteria ♥ Matthew Richards ♥ Ryan Riebeling ♥ Russell and Somyos ♥ Stephen Shelton ♥ Urban Andenius Skeppstedt ♥ John Smeallie ♥ Kathie Smestad ♥ Bert Snyers ♥ Heather Somma ♥ Muyang Song ♥ Jo Sowerby ♥ Fabian Stamm ♥ Alex Stark ♥ Stephanie Sullivan ♥ Michael Swearingen ♥ Liz Sweeney ♥ Holly T ♥ Nicole Tapia ♥ Curtis & Richard Terra-Ferguson ♥ Steve Thomas ♥ Stuart Turnbull ♥ Bob Turnure ♥ David Van Zyl ♥ Peter VH ♥ Alan S. Villafana ♥ Kelly Walker ♥ Michael Wallace ♥ Dan Williams ♥ Bob Willower ♥ David Wood ♥ Paige Yodanis ♥

Out of Time, Into You

by JAY BELL

Chapter 1

All my dreams are about to come true. I can almost feel the raw potential crackling in the air. I'm riding a natural high as I cruise down the street with my best friend, our former school receding in the passenger-side mirror. I smirk as it grows increasingly small. And insignificant, because from now on, each action I take will be toward goals that actually matter to me. Such as music.

Needing to find the right tune to match my mood, I browse my favorite music app and settle on one of The Weeknd's older songs, *I Feel it Coming*. Once it's streaming over the car stereo, I look over at Hannah to make sure she approves. She nods, grips the wheel tighter, and starts to move her shoulders to the beat. Encouraged, I crank it up louder and contemplate the bright and shiny future ahead of me. I haven't escaped high school completely. The graduation ceremony isn't until another couple of weeks, and as for tomorrow…

I check my phone again, remembering the text message that came while we were cleaning out our lockers. I didn't have time to read it then, but I give it my full attention now and see a photo of a black tuxedo with a red bowtie laid out on a bed. The text beneath it says, *What are you wearing?*

I snort and send back, *Right now? Nothing.*

Tomorrow I mean. To pram.

I stare at the screen and shake my head in disapproval before turning down the music.

"The boy is about to graduate, and he can't spell prom right?"

"Jacob?" Hannah tears her attention from the road to squint at the screen. "Are you sure autocorrect isn't to blame?"

"I guess we'll find out tomorrow, *if* he picks me up in a stroller."

She laughs but looks a little apprehensive, which is strange because just moments ago we were jumping up and down in the school parking lot and squealing with joy.

"Maybe he's one of those adult baby people," Hannah murmurs.

"That's perfect!" I do a quick image search on the internet, and not surprisingly, I'm spoiled for choice when it comes to grown men dressed in oversized diapers while sucking on pacifiers. I choose the most ridiculous of these and send it to Jacob. He replies with an animated GIF of an actual baby crying, so I send him a photo of the crimson velvet jacket that I ordered for the big occasion.

Jacob responds with: *Wow! You're going to look so hot in that!*

Hopefully, because I plan on wearing it plenty more this summer while playing gigs. My goal is to book as many as I can to keep my skills sharp. When I start at Columbia College Chicago next semester, I want them to mistake me for an artist in residence. And then I want them to teach me everything I don't know, which is plenty. I've always had enough confidence to put myself out there and perform, but I've tried to pair that with the humility necessary to keep learning. And now I'll finally be able to focus on that. No more obligatory classes that won't be useful. Nothing against physics, but all I want is to major in music and minor in entrepreneurship. That should give me a decent chance of finding a way to earn a living from what I love most. I'm lucky to know what that is already. Some people—most of them probably—need more time to figure that out. Like my best friend, for instance.

"You should learn to play the bongos," I say while staring at Hannah. "How hard can it be?"

She laughs and shakes her head. "I don't think there's an instrument in the world that I can coax music out of."

"There's gotta be," I insist. "I've seen you dance. You've got rhythm."

"Not enough for me to enroll in Columbia with you."

"They offer other classes," I say, trying a new tactic. "I'm going to need an agent. And a manager."

"Then it's a good thing I'm getting a business degree," Hannah replies.

"I thought you were going to major in English?"

"That was last week." She looks a little panicked. "Wasn't it?"

I shake my head ruefully. "All I know is that you won't be at school with me, and *that* is a serious problem. So what we're going to do right now is drive this car to the nearest music store and not leave until you've found your instrument. Even if it's something lame like a kazoo."

She smiles before seeming to consider the idea. "I got one for Hanukkah as a kid and loved it."

"There you go," I say as if the matter has been settled. "Maybe we'll start a band." I clear my throat and do my best impression of an emcee. "Ladies and Gentlemen, we have a very special performance for you tonight. Tearing up the piano is none other than our favorite local boy, Mister Reginald Valentine. Accompanying him is an absolute legend—the undisputed *queen* of kazoos—Miss Hannah Watts!"

My fingers are typing on my phone as I say this, and the timing is perfect, because a kazoo solo begins playing over the car speakers. Hannah laughs so hard at this that she nearly has to pull over. I love goofing around with her. That's why I wish things could continue the way they've always been. Not high school or any of that, but us being a part of each other's daily routine. I'm sure we'll still get together in between the demands of our new lives. Isn't that how it ends though? I used to be best friends with Carlos Hernández, but when his family moved across town and he ended up going to Glenbard South High School instead of Glenbard West, suddenly we weren't talking about the same people or events anymore. We still hang out on occasion, but we're not as close. I don't want that to happen with Hannah. She means the world to me.

"No matter where we end up," I tell her, "we have to get together every day. For dinner maybe."

She looks over at me, her expression earnest, and nods. Then she looks back at the road and slams on the brakes. "Crap! Almost missed it."

She means the entrance to a park, Churchill Woods. She manages to make the turn, and I start scanning the parking lot for familiar vehicles, because her driving us here is highly suspicious.

"What's going on?" I ask.

"I told you I need help with something."

"Right, right." I try and fail to fight down a grin. "It's a surprise party, isn't it? Who's coming? Family? Friends?"

"Just us," Hannah says with a humorless chuckle.

Maybe she should aim for a degree in theater, because I nearly believe her. Then again, I don't recognize any of the cars, although they might be parked in the other lot.

"C'mon," I say. "What else could it be?"

"Something important," Hannah says as she puts the car in park.

She opens the door and climbs out before I can ask any more questions. I know she wrote a paper about a crumbling old ruin here, but I don't see why she would need to do further research, or how I could help. No, I'm pretty sure that once we wander into the woods, I'll find a bunch of our friends laughing it up while drinking from a keg. Hannah takes a tote bag from the car's trunk. I consider leaving my backpack in there to keep it safe but decide to take it with me. She calls it my man-purse, although it's more useful than that. Not only does it conveniently hold my stuff, but it also makes a decent cushion to sit on, especially when the ground is still muddy from the recent rain. That'll come in handy soon. And besides, basketball shorts might be comfortable, but load them up with a wallet, phone, and keys, and they'll soon be around my ankles.

"I promise to look surprised," I say as we walk down a paved path that winds between the trees.

"There's no party," Hannah snaps. Then she sighs. "Remember when we used to play here as kids?"

"Of course."

Churchill Park doesn't offer much in the way of amenities. Technically it's a nature preserve, so the absence of baseball diamonds or whatever makes sense. The most exciting feature can be seen as we round a corner and the trees give way, revealing the narrow waters of the DuPage River. Just beyond a stretch of open land, the path we're on becomes a bridge that doesn't cross the river completely but leads instead to a long island in the middle of the water. This place felt so magical when we were young, providing the perfect backdrop for whatever games our imaginations could conjure up. Most often we would pretend to be castaways who were forced to start a new civilization after a shipwreck. I can see why our parents liked bringing us here. Aside from the bridge, there is no other way off the wooded island, so we couldn't have gone too far astray. Mom and Dad would usually relax at one of the nearby picnic benches while we exhausted ourselves by running wild.

"If you want to play Robinson and Mary Crusoe, all you've gotta do is ask," I say drolly. "As long as we revert to our usual roles."

"You still want to be Mary?" she asks.

I smirk and nod. Then I hear a metallic clinking noise coming from the bag she carries. I try to hook a finger to pull it open so I can see inside. Hannah notices my efforts and begins to hustle. Soon we're chasing each other across the bridge while laughing, and it really does feel like we're children again. We stop on the other side to catch our breath. The pavement ends here, the ground beyond so muddy that standing puddles are scattered everywhere.

"We're not actually going into that mess, are we?" I ask.

Hannah turns a pleading expression on me, and I sigh before taking the first step. I'm wearing a pair of Nike Air Max, solid black and in pristine condition. That changes with the next step forward. The muscle shirt I've got on isn't ideal for hiking either, I realize, but I do my best to avoid branches and thorns as the trees close in around us. Our shoes are squelching in unison as we walk down the path toward a familiar destination.

The gate. I've also heard it called the ghost door, or around Halloween, the portal to Hell. Most people in the town of Glen Ellyn, if familiar with it at all, simply call it the gate. The island we're trekking across is long and narrow. At the very tip, where the land rises up and the river splits in two, stands an old archway. Dual pillars made of massive stone slabs stacked on top of each other curve to meet at the top, like the entrance to some forgotten place. There is no surrounding structure. Nobody seems to know why the gate is there, or what its intended purpose was, but plenty have ascribed meaning to it anyway. Including me. When we were younger, it was the front door to our castaway home. My friend Carlos once tried using it as a soccer goal, his ball ending up in the river beyond. First kisses often take place beneath the stone arch, and judging from the burnt-out fires and beer cans scattered everywhere, many have used it as a place to party. Not us. I'm disappointed to see, when the gate comes into view, that Hannah was telling the truth. We're alone out here.

"Remember when Aaron tried building a throne beneath it?" Hannah asks.

"Of course," I say while smiling. My older brother had gathered up all the wood he could find and assembled what *looked* like a chair, but when he tried to sit on it, the entire thing crumbled and his royal ass ended up in the dirt. "I still call him King of the Termites when he gets too bossy. Hey, weren't they supposed to tear this thing down?"

"That's exactly why we're here," Hannah says. "We can't let them!"

We're close enough now to see what a sorry state it's in. The gate skews to one side, which it didn't used to. Not this much anyway. The stone slabs have always been the target of vandals, but the spray paint has gotten so out of control that the surface has become dark and mottled. When we were kids, it had still been possible to read the crap that seriously determined people had chiseled into the surface. Dumb stuff like band names, the initials of lovers, and the occasional year. Someone from the city must have decided to preserve what was left, because at some point, a fence was hastily erected around the gate. Even that is in poor condition, two of the chain-link panels having been wedged open so that it's possible to gain access again.

"Sorry," I say, pinching the bridge of my nose, "but I thought your interest in this was limited to the report you wrote on activism."

"Hashtag save the gate," Hannah says without much enthusiasm. Her expression solidifies with determination as she surveys the damage. "They could at least restore it. This should be a protected historical site!"

"I mean, the tourists *do* flock here all summer long." I glance around the empty clearing pointedly.

Hannah appears wounded. "This place used to be special to us."

"And it always will be," I say, tapping the side of my head. "Up here. They can't take the memories away."

I'm surprised when her chin begins to tremble. Then her eyes fill with hellfire as she pushes through the opening in the fence. "You don't have to agree with me," she says. "I only need your help."

I watch as she marches to one side of the gate. Once there, she drops the tote bag, which lands on the ground with a heavy thud. I stare in disbelief as she starts to pull a long length of chain from it. "What are you doing?"

"Saving the gate," Hannah says.

"Wait, you're going to *chain yourself* to it?"

"They're supposed to tear it down next week. Did you know that?"

"No," I say carefully. "Unless you told me about it, in which case I totally remember. Where did you get a chain that long?"

"From my dad's work."

Her father owns an auto repair shop, which is good, because it means he probably has some sort of tool to cut his daughter free.

"Wait, wait, wait," I say, holding up my hands. "Slow down. At least tell me the plan."

"I'm going to—"

"Chain yourself up, I got that much, but who's going to see? We're the only ones out here."

"That's what I need your help with," Hannah explains. "We're going to livestream my protest!"

"Uh huh. And when the police show up to find a black guy standing in front of a chained up white girl, how do you think they're going to react?"

She stops fussing long enough to glance up in concern. "Do you think they'll shoot you?"

"Does a bear wipe his ass with a rabbit after shitting in the woods? I don't know, but I'm not sticking around to find out!"

"Oh." Hannah frowns in concentration before looking hopeful again. "I've got it! We'll make a video and you can upload it once you're safely at home."

I laugh and shake my head. "I'm not leaving you out here. Listen, if they aren't going to tear this thing down until next week, why are we out here now? Prom is tomorrow."

Hannah scowls and resumes wrapping the chain around herself again.

I watch her for a moment. "This *is* about saving the gate. Right?"

"Of course," she says tersely.

"Then let's come back on Sunday."

"I'm not going to the stupid prom," she snaps. "I don't have a date! I never do!"

That isn't her fault. Hannah is a big girl. The world is full of people who are into that, but in a Midwest high school, all anyone cares about is what other people think. Like the closeted guys who want to do absolutely everything with me as long as it remains a secret.

"I don't have a date either," I tell her.

"You're going with Jacob."

"No, I'm *meeting* him there. I thought I was going with you."

Hannah rolls her eyes. "Sure, but once he shows up, you two will start dancing, and I'll end high school as a pathetic wallflower. And what about afterwards when you two..."

I snort and shake my head. "I'm not hooking up with him. Jacob and I don't have any chemistry. We're the only openly gay guys in our class. Neither of us is bringing someone, but we still want to represent, you know? Show everyone that dances aren't just for straight folks. And it's not just for skinny girls either. Come dance with us."

She lets the chain drop to the ground and sighs. "It's not just prom. Everything is changing and it freaks me out. I'm starting college in three months and have literally no idea what I want to do. I'm clueless! You'll be hanging out with other musicians and won't need me anymore, and if that doesn't kill our friendship, just wait until you start touring."

"Sounds like you've been busy planning my future instead of your own," I say, trying to lighten the mood. "Nobody said anything about me going on tour."

Hannah shakes her head. "You're amazing, Reggie. Even if you don't realize it yet. You'll be famous someday. I'm just a nobody."

"Amazing people have amazing best friends," I say, walking toward her. "You're so much smarter than me." That's no small complement. We've both been in gifted classes for the entirety of high school. Popular kids might worry about having the best car or the latest clothes. For us brainy misfits, status has always come with the highest grade point average, but I adore Hannah for so much more than her intelligence. "*And* you've got a good heart. The way you're always willing to help other people, how you sympathize with them instead of judging... I admire you. And someday you'll meet a straight guy who does too. Until then, you're going to college where you're going to party with me, because this isn't the end for us. Why do you think I want to have dinner together every night? I'm scared too. Like you said, everything is changing. That's just the way it goes. We've gotta keep looking forward. Speaking of which…" I drop to one knee, ignoring the wet squishing sound this makes. "Hannah Watts, would you be my date to prom?"

Her eyes fill with tears, and I know her well enough to tell that they're the happy variety. She pulls me to my feet and into a hug. "I don't want to lose you," she says.

"You won't," I say, surprised by how tight my throat is. "I love you, girl."

"I love you too, Reggie."

We squeeze each other a moment before letting go.

"Are you serious about prom?" she asks sheepishly.

"Uh, yeah! I would have asked sooner if I knew you cared. You kept saying how stupid prom is."

"I still believe that. But I also want to go."

"Is that a 'yes' then?"

I watch her cheeks turn pink before she answers. "Yes."

"Good. Don't you worry about Jacob. I'm not his type anyway. He shot me down sophomore year, remember?"

She looks scandalized by this news. "No! You never told me that."

"Probably because I was too embarrassed. I don't care if Jacob is interested now. He missed his chance. Feel free to remind him of that tomorrow. Really twist the knife and make him regret it."

Hannah laughs, seeming more at ease. "I like what you said about representation. You *should* dance with him. Alone, so there isn't any doubt. I don't mind being a wallflower for a bit. That's where all the good conversations take place anyway." She exhales and looks around, as if seeing it all from a different perspective. "What a crazy plan."

"No kidding! You'd rather get arrested than go stag at a dance?"

"They wouldn't arrest me," Hannah says dismissively. "I'm too white and privileged for that. I figured they'd drive me home and that my mom would ground me from prom."

I think about it and nod. "Sounds like something she would do. Like when she made you quit the Girl Scouts."

"Took her long enough. I kept getting into fist fights, hoping it would happen."

"Love it. That's what your major should be."

"No need," Hannah says as she boxes the air. "Everything

I need to know, I learned from the streets!" She lets her hands drop and glances around once more, this time with affection. "I really will miss this place when they tear it down."

"Me too, but you have to admit, it's not the same anymore."

"No. It's not. Ready to get out of here?"

"No way! This is our last visit to the gate. We've at least gotta take some photos."

She agrees, so we hold out the camera at arm's length to take selfies. Afterwards we balance her phone on a low branch with the timer running so we can get full-body shots of us standing beneath the gate. My own phone remains safely in my backpack, since it's brand new, and I'm not about to let it fall into a muddy puddle. I can't expect my parents to buy me a replacement anymore.

"One more," Hannah says, picking up the fallen chain and draping it over her breasts. "I want people to know that I risked my life to save this place. You can post it online and tell everyone I got arrested. Just make sure I look hot."

"Let's do it!"

We work together to stage the perfect photo. Hannah places herself against one of the gate's pillars and I wrap the chain around her, just like she intended. We even muss her hair and put a little mud on one cheek, like she's been suffering here for days in the name of her noble cause. And yeah, she makes the whole thing work for her. There's only one crucial detail missing.

"Did you bring a padlock?" I ask her.

"Oh." She chuckles to herself. "I kept imagining that you'd tie the chain in a knot. Still think I'm the smartest?"

"You're brilliant," I say, moving close and attempting to tie the chain into a cute bow. The idea is funny, but the end result looks sloppy. "We could use my old combination lock," I say, tugging on the shoulder straps of my backpack. "I've got it with me."

"No, this is perfect." Hannah drapes an arm dramatically over her forehead, resembling the classic damsel in distress. "Hurry up and take a photo. The ground is so wet that I'm sinking."

The mud sucks at my shoes as I move a short distance away. Then I turn and take a few more steps backward, trying to get the entire gate into the frame. I'm surprised by how askew it is. When we first got here, I didn't notice how misaligned the stones of the arch had become, like they've been slowly sliding out of position or… No, I can *see* them move!

My stomach clenches as I look away from the screen. The gate is shifting! The top was slanted before, but now it's lopsided. Hannah notices my panicked expression and glances upward. She reaches the same conclusion and begins tearing at the chains. "Reggie!"

"Hold on!"

I drop her phone and sprint, shoving my way past the half-fallen fence. She's already gotten the bow undone, but the chain is still wrapped around her and the pillar multiple times over.

"Hurry!" she cries.

I grab one end of the chain and begin racing circles around her, noticing how deeply the bottom-most stone has sunk into the mud. They won't need to tear anything down next week. It's all happening now! One last loop to go, but it's tangled up in the back. Hannah keeps pulling on it in panic, which only makes it tighter. My finger gets stuck between links as they come together, and I just barely manage to pull it free, ignoring the pain so I can rip at the chain some more. I finally get it loose enough that it drops to the ground. Hannah starts moving toward the opening in the fence. I'm right behind her, but she must not realize, because she turns around as if worried about me.

"Go!" I say, pushing at her.

Her eyes move upward and widen. I follow her gaze and see a stone slab free-falling in the air. I shove hard, wanting to push her out of harm's way. We're too much alike. Hannah does the same thing. We both end up toppling backward, and as my arms pinwheel, there's no doubt in my mind that I'm about to be crushed to death. The last thing I see is the fear on my best friend's face before the world goes dark. No sound. No visuals. Only the sensation of being squeezed so tight that there isn't room left for thoughts. And then…

Nothing.

Chapter 2

Water strikes my face, cold drops that cause my eyes to shoot open, but there is precious little to see. Night has fallen. I can hear the trees swaying above as they're pummeled by wind. A grumble of thunder sends fear down my spine. Where am I? I squeeze my eyes shut against the rain and take stock of myself. I'm lying on my back, but I'm not completely parallel to the ground. Something is pressing against my spine, like an uncomfortable pillow. When shifting, I feel backpack straps rubbing against the skin of my shoulders. I slip my arms free as I force myself to sit upright, my body stiff as if I've been in the same position for too long. I raise a hand to shield my eyes from the rain just as lightning illuminates a pillar of the gate to my right. That's when it all comes rushing back.

"Hannah!"

I scurry away from the gate, worried that it hasn't finished toppling over yet. My heart is pounding as I blindly search for my best friend. My hands touch nothing but wet grass and mud. Panic rises inside me as I return to my backpack, ripping it open to get at my phone. The glowing screen tells me that it's nearly midnight. There aren't any notifications. Or a signal. I turn on the flashlight and wave it around, but the rain is coming down so hard that it doesn't do much good. I feel woozy, like I've been drinking too much, but I'm still in one piece. The falling stones must have missed me. Not wanting my phone to short out, I turn it off and shove it into my backpack again. I tuck this against the trunk of a nearby tree where I hope it won't get as wet. With my hands free, I do a quick check of my head to make sure the adrenaline coursing through me isn't masking an injury. I don't detect any bruises or blood. How long was I out? And what happened to Hannah? She wouldn't have left me here. Not by choice. Was she hurt? I stumble around in the dark, and even though I'm so lightheaded that I'm on the verge of passing out, I manage another hoarse cry.

"Hannah!"

No answer. Did we both get knocked out? Did someone find her and not me? I squint against the rain in my confusion. Where the hell is the stone slab that I saw falling? Is she pinned beneath it? Or did somebody already clear it away, maybe so she could be airlifted to a hospital or... Oh god, what if she's dead?

"Hannah?" I whimper.

I feel a hand on my shoulder and turn around, nearly crying out in relief, but the sound catches in my throat. I can barely see the person in front of me through the rain. Another flash of lightning changes that, revealing a haggard face surrounded by wild hair and a scraggly beard. Two dark beady eyes stare impassively into my own. The man looks dead. Maybe the rumors were true. The gate really is a doorway to Hell! By the time thunder rumbles through the sky, I'm already running, pumping my arms and legs as fast as they'll go. I don't dare look back, even when I slip and fall, the thought of yellow jagged teeth spurring me on. I can practically feel them biting into my neck. My eyes widen with mad hope when I leave the trees behind. I'm gasping for breath halfway across the bridge, so I stop and grip the rail, ready to jump over the side if I'm still being chased. I don't see anyone behind me, but it's hard to be sure. Without the cover of trees, the rain is even worse here.

Fear propels me onward. The parking lot isn't far. If her car is still there, I'll know that Hannah is in trouble. That means passing through more woods, which I do at breakneck speed, the shadows seeming to close in on me from all sides. The parking lot brings welcome news. Hannah's car is gone. A taxi is waiting there instead. I can see letters on the door and a small sign on top. The interior light is on, a driver behind the wheel. I run straight up to him and hammer on the window, looking back in case a zombie is lurching after me.

"What's all the ruckus?" the driver snarls as he rolls down the window.

The man inside has a creased face and white thinning hair, a half-eaten sandwich balanced on his stomach. I notice the shield-shaped badge pinned to his jacket, and when he reaches over to put on a brimmed hat, I feel a mixture of relief and fear.

"You're a police officer?" I splutter.

"Damn right I am! You better take a step back, boy."

I do as instructed, noticing that the letters on the door aren't for a taxi company. The word POLICE is written above a three-digit number, and below that, the name of my town, Glen Ellyn. What I mistook for a sign on top is a single red dome. The vehicle itself is dark and bulbous with rounded edges. A real classic. I watch, completely confused, as the man climbs out and opens an umbrella while keeping a wary eye on me. The feeling is mutual. I'm not sure he's really a police officer, not in an old car like that, but he certainly has the right vibe as he points a baton at me.

"You better explain yourself!"

"There's someone out there," I try to say between gasping for air. "In the woods."

The officer barks laughter. "Spooked ya, huh? I know what *he's* doin' out there. What about you?"

"The gate fell. I think my friend was hurt. Have you heard about someone being taken to the hospital? Hannah Watts? I was with her."

The officer glances toward the woods, seeming concerned. "There's a girl out there?"

"I don't know."

He rounds on me. "Either there is or there isn't! Did you take a lady friend out there for some necking?"

"Huh?"

He scowls. "Show some respect, boy. I'm losing patience."

"Sorry, *sir*," I say through gritted teeth, "it's just a little hard to concentrate at the moment."

I'm shaking now, either from nerves or the cold rain that continues to beat down on me. He seems to finally realize the condition I'm in and walks around the back of his car. The man opens the trunk and takes out a thick green blanket. I'm thinking he might wrap it around me, but instead he opens the back door of his car and covers one of the seats. Then he steps aside.

"Get in."

I'm tempted, but I hesitate. Something is off. He might be dressed like a police officer, but not a modern one. Maybe he's one of those Civil War reenactors. A version that recreates police history instead. Is that a thing?

"It wasn't a request," the man barks.

Fuck it. At least it'll get me out of the rain. Besides, they usually don't shoot you while you're in their car. Too messy. As soon as I'm seated in the back, he slams the door shut, and I crane my neck to see more of the interior. This is an old car. A spotlight is mounted on the dashboard, and between the front seats, some sort of archaic equipment that I can't make sense of, but there's no sign of a dashcam, GPS, or anything digital. The smell of metal and oil fills my nostrils.

"Let's try this again," the man says after he climbs back in the driver's seat. He tosses the closed umbrella into the footwell of the passenger side before twisting to face me. "What were you doing out there in the woods? Having some fun with your gal?"

I answer with a question of my own. "Why is this car so old?"

He makes a face like I'm an idiot. "Now listen here! I've got better things to do than play games, so I'm going to run you down to the station and lock you up for the night. Maybe tomorrow you'll feel like making sense."

I don't know what to think anymore. Maybe the police thought it would be cute to break out a vintage vehicle. A PR stunt, maybe. I watch as he grabs an old CB receiver and speaks into the handheld microphone. A voice squawks back at him, using police jargon that sounds authentic enough.

"You're really with the police?" I ask.

"I'm sure as shit not with the fire department," he says, shaking his head as he turns the ignition. "What have you been drinking?"

"Nothing. The girl I was with, Hannah Watts, can you ask dispatch if she was taken to the hospital?"

The man looks at me in the rearview mirror and raises an eyebrow. "Why? Did you lose your temper with her?"

"No! That stupid stone gate fell on us!"

He turns in his seat to consider me, his attention lingering on the bright yellow shorts I'm wearing. "Boy oh boy," he says. "Young people dress uglier every year. But you sure don't look like a heap of stones fell on top of ya. Let's see some identification."

I begin to pat myself down, realizing with a jolt that my pockets are empty. Everything I had is in my backpack, including the biggest lifeline back to the people I love and trust.

"My phone! It's still out there in the woods. I need it!"

The man stares at me long and hard. Then he grabs the back of the seat and brings his face close to mine. I can see the white stubble on his sagging jowls and smell mustard on his breath when he says, "Breathe out."

"What?"

"You've been drinking."

"I have not!"

He sniffs and looks confused. "Reefer?"

I snort and shake my head in disbelief. "What century are you from?"

He doesn't take offense at this. Instead he turns back around and puts the car in reverse. "You're not right in the head," he says matter-of-factly. "We'll get you tucked up for the night, don't worry."

"You can't arrest me," I say as the car finishes backing up and starts to roll forward. "I'm a minor." Not true, but my phone isn't the only thing I left in the woods. My wallet is out there too, including my driver's license. He doesn't know how old I am. Or my name. I reach for the door, willing to make a run for it in the rain, but the handle isn't there.

"You aren't under arrest," he responds. "We're just going to put you somewhere safe until we can figure out which loony bin you escaped from."

This isn't cool. Am I being kidnapped or does the Glen Ellyn Police Department really allow a retiree to drive around in this old car? "Can't you take me home? To my parents?"

He grunts as we turn onto the main road. "Where would that be?"

"Six-sixty-five Lenox Road. Please. Sir."

He eyes me in the rearview mirror for a moment before he shrugs. "That's on the way to the station. Let's see what your old man has to say."

That sounds better. I grope around for a seatbelt but never find one. Oh well. We don't have far to go. I could have walked home in nicer weather, which only would have taken half an hour. There isn't much to see on the way, especially in this weather, but I keep my eyes locked on our progress, still not trusting him. He makes the correct turn, but something feels off. We're still the only car on the road. Everything is so dark. I can't see most of the houses. Only when we reach my street does it begin to look more familiar.

"That one," I say when my home comes into view. I yearn to be within the safety of its walls, and to have the protective presence of my parents with me, so I can finally figure out what happened to Hannah. She might still need help. The man I saw out there in the woods, maybe he did something with her.

"This is where you live?" the officer asks, not hiding his disbelief.

I clench my jaw. Our house is one of the most beautiful on the street. The most striking feature is the four white pillars clustered around the front door that stretch two-stories high to support the half-moon roof above. Stately. That's how my mom always describes it. The lot next to ours is unoccupied and filled with trees, and on the other side, an extension has been built onto the house, including a sunroom which overlooks the front yard and the park across the street.

"Yes, sir," I say, masking the animosity in my voice, because I know what the confused expression really means. He can't believe a black family lives somewhere so nice. "My parents must be worried," I say pointedly.

He turns around to look at me again, and I try to show him with my expression how desperate I am to get inside. After a long sigh, he says, "You better come with me," before climbing out of the car and opening the door so I can follow.

As we walk along the cobbled walkway, I'm tempted to make a break for the porch, but I don't want to get shot in the back. As soon as we're close, I can't help it. I rush ahead of him and start pounding on the front door. He catches up and grabs my wrist to stop me, swearing under his breath, but I don't care because it's too late. I made enough noise to wake up the entire house. Sure enough, a light switches on inside. It'll be my dad. I just know it. He'll take one look at who I'm with and start saying that I'm in a world full of trouble. That's okay. I just want to be home again.

The door swings open, and I feel dizzy, because a white guy in pajamas and a bathrobe is standing there. He adjusts his glasses and peers at us both. The man isn't my father. He's old enough to be, but I've never seen him in my life. "Officer O'Brien," the stranger says, fighting off a yawn. "What can I do for you?"

"Sorry to disturb you at such a late hour, Dr. Parker," the officer says, sounding much more respectful in tone, "but I have a bit of a situation here and ahh... Is this one of your patients, by chance?"

The doctor considers me. "Could be. Have we met before?"

"I live here," I say, trying to see past him, because I *know* this is the right house. I was raised here. I have every single detail memorized, like the glass lantern hanging above our heads, which my older brothers broke when they tied a pinata to it and... The lantern is the right kind. But it's no longer broken. My mother lectured us about how old it had been. Irreplaceable. And yet, there it is, looking good as new.

"He's not making a lot of sense," Officer O'Brien says, clamping a hand on my shoulder. "That's why I thought he might be under your care."

"I'm perfectly fine," I growl. "What's going on here? Where's my family?"

"George?" a female voice says from inside. "What's wrong?"

"Everything is fine dear," the doctor says over his shoulder. "Now then, what seems to be—"

I'm done playing around. I push past him, certain that I'll find a camera crew inside. This has to be a YouTube stunt. MrBeast will be inside with a big check, or the revelation that he's moved my family somewhere even better. Our own theme park maybe. That would make more sense than what I discover. The interior is familiar, but as I spin around, the furniture is all wrong. The coats hanging by the door don't belong to my family. I recognize the stairs leading up, having placed my hand on the wooden banister thousands of times, but even the smell in here isn't right. I feel disoriented again. A woman notices me and screams. Feet thud down the stairs, someone my age rushing to her rescue, judging from the way he spreads his arms wide protectively. She's not my mother. He's not one of my brothers.

A hand grabs the back of my neck and squeezes painfully, forcing me to bend over.

"Everybody calm down!" I hear the doctor shout. "No harm has been done. Let's find out what this is about."

All I can do is whimper in pain.

"Officer, please. Let me take a look at him."

I'm finally released. O'Brien has a death grip on my shoulder, but it hurts less than him clawing into my neck.

"I'd better run him down to the station," the officer says.

"I'd rather you didn't," Dr. Parker murmurs, staring into each of my eyes, one at a time. "If he's in shock, or a temporary state of psychosis, locking him up will only make it worse."

"I'm not crazy." I intend to say this with defiance, but my voice trembles. I'm starting to lose it.

"Do you know what day it is?" the doctor asks.

"Friday." I know what he's getting at, and I refuse to play along.

Two little girls rush down the stairs and cluster behind their mother. Their older brother is still standing in front of them, wearing the same pajama and bathrobe combination as his father. His pale-green eyes are locked onto mine, open and earnest instead of accusatory and afraid. Something deep inside of me latches on to them, like a beacon leading back to a safe place. I remember being in my grandmother's bedroom, and how patient she was with my questions as I picked up her possessions or pointed at different objects. *"What's this for? Where did you get that? Who's he?"*

"Daniel," I croak.

The young man looks surprised. His expression matches my own. Of all my grandmother's treasures, my favorite was a black and white photo in a gold frame inlaid with mother of pearl. Even as a little kid, I was drawn to the kindness of his face, or as I grew older, how attractive and even his delicate features were.

"You know my son?" Dr. Parker asks from behind.

"Yeah," I say.

"How?"

"I used to date him," my grandma would answer with a smoky chuckle whenever I asked about the photo. *"But that was a very long time ago."*

My head is spinning. I've seen enough movies like this for the thought to have crossed my mind, but I dismiss the possibility as too ridiculous. Time travel doesn't exist. Does it? Everyone is still watching us as Daniel and I stare each other down.

"You know my gr—," I start to say to him. "Gloria. You know her. Right?"

Daniel nods. His mother breathes a sigh of relief and begins ushering the young girls back upstairs.

"Gloria?" Officer O'Brien repeats.

"The daughter of our housekeeper," Dr. Parker explains. "If

19

we could speak outside for a moment, officer. Danny, would you mind keeping... I'm sorry, what was your name again?"

"Reggie," I say.

"Good. Are you feeling calm enough to sit with my son in the living room for a moment? You'd have to promise not to have any more outbursts." The doctor's tone is warm. He sounds like someone who deals with children on a regular basis.

I'm not a kid anymore, but I nod, since anything is preferable to being carted away by Officer O'Brien. I try not to stare as Dr. Parker has a quiet word with his son. Then the adults step outside, leaving us alone.

Daniel flashes a nervous smile. "Would you like to sit down?"

"Sure." I lead the way to the neighboring living room and flick the light switch, which is where it should be on the wall but made of a heavier material. I fixate on this detail, because it's one thing for all the furniture and decorations to be different. Those could have easily been taken out and swiftly replaced. But to swap out the light switches? The electrical outlets look weird too.

"Would you like a glass of milk?"

I only glance at Daniel, who is standing in the middle of the living room while watching me. I probably seem crazy, but I don't care. I move toward the front of the house, noticing more changes. I have a vague memory of my parents installing energy-saving windows when I was a kid. These are different, the frames wooden instead of plastic. The glass sounds thin when I knock on it.

"Are you okay?"

Daniel again. I turn to face him. "What year is it?"

He seems genuinely surprised by the question. If this was a prank—and I'm starting to have serious doubts—then he would have expected me to ask that. Although he could be an actor or—

"Nineteen fifty-seven."

I search his eyes. They remain on mine for a few seconds before darting away, his face flushing.

"Is this a joke?" I ask, moving toward him. "Please. If it is, just tell me. I'm getting seriously freaked out."

He seems intimidated before he glances at the front door and stands up a little taller. "Everything is going to be all right," he says. "Let's sit down together."

I'm a stranger in their home. If this really is the past... God that sounds stupid! Whatever is going on, I'll handle it better if I calm down. My mom always tried to teach me that. Staying cool and collected gives you the upper hand. Besides, if I'm being punked, they *want* me to freak out. I won't give them the satisfaction. I'll show them how clever I can be. I join him on a lime green couch with wooden legs, still searching the room for anything they missed. A forgotten USB charger plugged into an outlet maybe.

"You know Gloria?" Daniel asks me.

I nod, distracted by the wall surrounding the fireplace, which has been painted canary yellow instead of a rich burgundy. "Yeah."

"How?"

"We're family," I tell him.

"Oh. So what are you doing here?"

I'm about to explain—again—that this is my home, but the truth hasn't gotten me anywhere so far. If this isn't some sort of sick joke, I need a convincing story that won't get me locked up. And a plan to get home again. The front door opens, Daniel rising to confer with his father. I ignore them both and remain seated, trying to think, which isn't easy considering the circumstances. I hear footsteps going upstairs before Dr. Parker returns alone to the living room.

"Would you like a bite to eat?" he asks me with a friendly smile. "You must be hungry."

"Yes. Thank you."

I don't have an appetite, but it gives me more time to think and analyze. The kitchen we enter is completely different. The counters, cabinets, appliances… all of it. I stood in here this very morning and ate a bowl of cereal while browsing my phone. Everything would have needed to be remodeled since then. Even a reality TV show with a huge budget wouldn't be able to do that. The house smells more like baby powder than fresh sawdust or drying paint. I *know* I'm at the right address. Yes, it was dark and rainy outside, but each of the houses along my street are unique, built at a time when neighborhoods weren't so generic, or at least offered more options. Even the products I get a glimpse of in the fridge that Dr. Parker opens look legit. I've never seen milk come in a plain glass bottle before.

I decide to treat the situation as real. If some bleach-toothed host appears to ask how it felt to experience a simulation of the past, I'll laugh at myself along with my friends, but mostly I'll be relieved.

"Hard to go wrong with a roast beef sandwich," Dr. Parker is saying as he works at the counter. "When's the last time you ate?"

"Lunch," I say.

"Oh. A late dinner is better than none at all. I always try to eat three square meals a day. What about you, Reggie?"

"Yeah. Same here."

He looks a little puzzled at this. Maybe I'm being too casual. When he leads me to a Formica-topped kitchen table and puts the food down in front of a chair, I sit and try to show some gratitude. "Thank you, sir."

"My pleasure. You can call me George. George Parker. And you are Reggie…"

"Valentine."

"Reggie Valentine," Dr. Parker repeats. "That has a nice ring to it. Go on and get a couple of bites into you. And some milk. The weather is dismal. I notice you aren't dressed for it."

I shake my head before taking a bite, so my mouth remains as full as possible while I piece together a cover story. That's hard to do when I still don't know what happened.

"Officer O'Brien said he picked you up by Churchill Woods."

"Yes, sir. I must have fallen asleep out there."

"Oh?"

"I was resting and must have nodded off."

He lets me eat a little longer before speaking again. "I know this might sound like a foolish question, but what's the date?"

"May twentieth."

"And the year?"

I feel dumb saying it aloud, certain he'll laugh… but he doesn't. "Nineteen fifty-seven."

"Last one, I promise. Who is the president?"

Damn. They made us memorize the entire lineup back in sophomore year. Or was it even earlier than that? I still know most of the names, but the exact year is harder. Kennedy was the sixties, so it must be Truman. No, wait! "Eisenhower."

He nods as if satisfied. "Good. Sometimes when we go through too much stress, our thoughts can get jumbled, but you seem to be thinking clearly."

"This helps," I say, holding up the sandwich before taking

another bite. The bread is white, flavorless, and spongy. I wish he'd put barbeque sauce on the roast beef instead of mayo.

"You mentioned Gloria earlier," Dr. Parker says.

"Yes, sir. She's my cousin."

"I see! Why did you expect to find her here? In fact, you seemed to think that this was your home. Do you live in the area, Reggie?"

"No." An excuse occurs to me then, but I'm uncomfortable with it. "I'm from Alabama." A state known for being hostile to blacks—a fact that received national thanks to brave people like Claudette Colvin and Rosa Parks, who took a stand rather than remain silent. I might be sketchy on presidents, but I know my civil rights history. I have tremendous respect for those pioneers, and if it wasn't for the extreme circumstances, I would never lie about sharing their struggles. The racism I've experienced during my lifetime would have been *much* worse if not for them. "I was having a rough time down there, and Gloria said I could come live with her family."

"Why did you have this address? She doesn't live here." Dr. Parker's eyebrows shoot up suddenly as if he already knows the answer. "Last winter."

"Huh?"

"When her family stayed with us over the holidays. Their furnace broke down. Gloria spent so much time at Sarah's desk while she was here that we sent it home with them."

I know my grandma likes to write, but I don't understand what that has to do with me.

Dr. Parker notices my blank expression. "She must have used our home as the return address. I believe we received a few responses meant for her."

I'd thank my good fortune if it hadn't dropped me here in the first place. "Where does she live now?"

"Not far, not far. I can take you there tomorrow. All the way from Alabama, huh? That must have been some journey. How did you get here?"

Amtrak? Did that exist back then? Or *now*, I suppose. Greyhound buses are old enough. Right? "I mostly hitchhiked," I say at last, deciding to play it safe.

"I see. Don't you have anything with you? A change of clothes, for instance?"

"I did, but it's all out in the woods. I woke up in the rain and ran off without it." I don't mention the creepy guy who snuck up on me. My story is strange enough already. Dr. Parker seems to accept it though.

"You're welcome to stay with us for the night," he says. "I have to work in the morning, and I'd wager your uncle does too, so I'd rather let him sleep. I wouldn't mind getting back to bed myself. What do you think?"

"I'd appreciate it very much, sir. Thank you." I finish off the sandwich and stand to collect my dishes, intending to bring them to the sink.

Dr. Parker rises and takes them from me. "I'm a pediatrician," he says, "which means I'm a doctor to young people like yourself. I believe you could benefit from a mild sedative that will help you rest easier tonight. Especially after all the excitement."

"Okay," I say.

"Just a moment. I'll be right back."

As soon as he's gone, I consider running. My gut keeps telling me I need to go home, but I'm already there. Instead I wash the dishes he left in the sink, leaving them in the rack to dry. No dishwasher, it would seem. I do open a few drawers, hoping to find an overlooked Pizza Hut flyer or whatever, but everything appears to be from another era.

Dr. Parker returns with a stethoscope around his neck. "Do you mind?" he asks, lifting the metal circle at one end. I already know it's going to be cold.

I shrug and lift my shirt. He presses the drum to different areas of my chest, and then my back as he asks me to breathe in and out. I'm worried I'll have to turn my head and cough, but instead he stares into my pupils before seeming satisfied. I can't help thinking that a reality TV show would worry about getting sued if an unsuspecting contestant had a heart attack. Is that what this is?

"Good news," Dr Parkers says, taking a brown glass bottle from his bathrobe pocket. "You're in excellent health." He twists off the lid and tips a single pill into it. "But I would still recommend taking this."

I'm guessing it's valium or something similar, and that he wants to ensure I won't go ballistic on his family if it turns out that I am crazy. A friend of mine was into pills. Witnessing how it messed up his life was enough to turn me off them forever. I'll make an exception tonight. I *want* to get knocked out. Maybe then I'll wake up where—and when—I'm supposed to be. He watches me as I swallow the pill. I make it easy for him to see that I did.

"I've already spoken to the family about you staying here," Dr. Parker says, "and everyone says you're welcome. You'll be sharing Daniel's room tonight."

"That's fine. Thank you."

He leads me upstairs, my heart lurching with each corner we turn, because no matter what's really going on, this isn't my house anymore. The door leading to the master bedroom no longer has the reassuring presence of my parents behind it. My brothers' rooms, as we pass by them, are most likely being used by little girls. Adding insult to injury, I'm led directly to my old bedroom. Daniel is standing in the doorway with a friendly smile, even if it does look a little forced. I know things were different in the fifties, and that people often left their homes unlocked without fear, but he can't be thrilled about bunking up with a total stranger.

"Danny will help get you settled," Dr. Parker says with a yawn. "I don't want you staying up though. Get to sleep. Understand?"

This is directed at his son, who nods enthusiastically.

Dr. Parker is already trudging toward the master bedroom. "I'm just down the hall if you need me," he says with another yawn.

I look back at Daniel. He gestures toward the bedroom, like he's inviting me in. I'm curious to see how my room has changed, and once I'm in there, it stings worse than I expected. I almost always walk to the far wall when entering to turn on my stereo. Most of my friends are satisfied with a basic Bluetooth speaker or headphones. Me? I have a huge system that includes a digital receiver, CD player, vinyl turntable, and even a tape deck, because some music can't be found on any other format. When cranked up, the speakers are nearly strong enough to shake the teeth from your head. All I see where my precious stereo system should be is a white-paneled dresser. My framed posters of inspiring musicians have been replaced by school pendants and a map of the solar system. His bed is narrower but in the same location as mine; shoved up against a wall to leave the center of the room clear. Daniel chose to put a desk by the window that overlooks the front yard. I considered doing the same, until I noticed there wasn't an electric outlet near enough for my laptop.

"Whenever I have friends spend the night, I always let them have my bed," Daniel is saying from next to it. "I'll sleep on the floor. I'm a Boy Scout, so I'm used to camping."

I notice the sleeping bag that is rolled out next to the bed like the sidecar of a motorcycle and manage not to snort. "My friends usually crash with me in bed," I say.

"Oh." He turns to consider the scene. "I used to do that when I was little, but my bed isn't very big and —"

"I'll take the floor," I say.

"I really don't mind," he presses.

"I do." It comes out gruffer than I mean it to, but I don't like the idea of sleeping in someone else's bed, or smelling them on the sheets, when this is *my room*. Or will be. How many decades from now? Six? Seven? I'm a long way from home.

"Okay, well, I have some pajamas for you." He gestures at a striped pair of cotton pants and a matching shirt that is laid out on the comforter.

"It's fine," I say, already shaking my head. "I usually sleep naked."

His jaw falls open before it snaps shut again. "Even when your friends stay over?"

"Only the ones I really like," I murmur.

Daniel stares. Then he starts laughing. I don't feel like joining him, but I do manage a smile, because it's a nice sound for such a joyless night. Or maybe that pill I took is kicking in. "I'll get changed," I say, grabbing the PJs. My clothes are still damp, my socks especially. I probably tracked mud all over the house. I'll help clean it up tomorrow.

"The bathroom is —"

"Second door on the right," I say before he can finish. "I'll be right back."

Much like the kitchen, the bathroom had been completely renovated by the time I was born, so it looks different than I expect, but the tub, sink, and toilet are in the same places. I notice a dogeared science fiction digest next to the toilet. Daniel had a stack of them in his room. The date on the cover is from two years ago, nineteen-fifty-five, but the paper isn't yellowed or musty from age. I make use of the facilities and then check myself in the mirror, almost relieved that I still look the same. I stand out against the backdrop of pale colors behind me, like somebody Photoshopped me into an image of a vintage home. Even when I strip off the muscle shirt, basketball shorts, and my underwear, I still don't fit in. I look like a scrawny kid who is lost and afraid. The pajamas help, mostly because they make me laugh. I've never worn anything like them. I do a little jig in the mirror, my head swimming. The pill is messing with me for sure. I rub a hand over my short-cropped hair, stare into honey brown eyes that have charmed their fair share of boys, and try to tell myself that it'll all be okay. Except it comes out slurred and sounds more like "It'll bitty oaky."

Gathering up the clothes and shoes I arrived in, I stumble down the hall back to my room. His room. Whatever. I'm past the point of caring. Daniel is already beneath the sheets, his earnest eyes on me as I enter. He really does have the sweetest face. I shake a finger at him and say, "S'not the first time I 'magined you there."

He looks confused, and maybe a little worried. I shut off the light and make my way to the sleeping bag, struggling with the zipper once I'm inside. I can't get the stupid thing to move an inch!

"Here." Daniel, still in bed, leans his torso over the edge of the mattress and takes the zipper from me, his fingers brushing against mine. I'm tempted to grab them, just for the comfort of being close to another warm body. "It always gets stuck," he explains.

"Thanks for that," I mumble as I hear metal teeth buzzing up one side of the bag.

Daniel's sheets rustle as he pulls himself back into his bed. After a beat of silence, he asks, "Are you okay, Reggie?"

"Yeah," I reply. "I just want to go home."

It's the last thing I manage to say, the last clear thought I have, before the sedative really kicks in and I drift away on a sea of white noise.

Chapter 3

Someone is gently shaking me—the hand on my shoulder causing me to rock back and forth. Sunlight warms my face. I clench my eyes shut, partly because I want to sleep in, but also because the dream I had was so upsetting that I'm scared I'll discover it was real.

"Reggie?"

My stomach sinks. I know that voice, but only barely. When I open my eyes, Daniel is squatting next to me. His brown hair has been swept back into a pompadour. He's wearing a collared shirt, light-blue with two vertical navy stripes running down the front. He smells clean and fresh, his pale green eyes alert, making me think I slept the day away. "What time is it?" I grumble.

"Seven," he replies. "You need to get ready for breakfast."

"Fine." I still need a moment to collect myself… and to allow some natural stiffness to subside. When I finally get to my feet, I notice that Daniel is wearing a pair of long beige shorts. He's fully dressed, while in my family, we tend to sit around the breakfast table in our bathrobes. Or sometimes around the TV if it's the weekend. I guess that's not how they do things here.

Daniel starts to explain how the shower works. I wave him into silence and trudge down the hall, relieved when locking the door behind me. I stare for a moment at everything that doesn't look familiar. I guess the sedative is still in my system because I don't feel as upset by it. Only when I'm standing beneath a hissing showerhead does a thought wake me right up.

Hannah! I still don't know what happened to her. What if she's also stuck here in the fifties, eating breakfast with well-meaning strangers? I have to assume the worst. For her sake. By the time I'm drying myself off, I've decided on a course of action.

Daniel is still in his bedroom when I stroll inside. He looks me over before quickly averting his eyes. "Sorry. I should have given you something to wear."

I'm not naked. I have a towel around my waist. People must be more reserved in this era. "Have you seen my clothes?" I ask, looking around for them.

"Mom said that she would wash them. And that I should loan you something."

I check out his outfit again. His socks are pulled up so high that they nearly cover his shins, leaving only a few inches of bare skin beneath the long cloth shorts. This should be fun. "Let's see what you've got."

He opens the closet door and I come up behind to look over his shoulder. I never realized how colorful the fifties were. I'm spoiled for choice now, not only in terms of hues, but patterns as well. Stripes and checks, primarily. Almost every shirt is the same collared style that Daniel is wearing. I notice one that is pale yellow and reach past him to take it.

He seems a little flustered when leading me to the dresser. I choose a pair of white shorts and feel thankful that none of my friends have been born yet. I pull on the shirt, intentionally facing him while I do so. Might as well have a few laughs while I'm here. Daniel quickly moves to the window and keeps his back to me. Just as well. I don't have any underwear to put on, and I'm sure as hell not going to borrow a pair from him. I can freeball it for now. With any luck, I won't be here much longer anyway.

"Uh," I say a few seconds later. "I like long shorts, I really do, but these might as well be pants."

He turns around, expression strained. Then he starts laughing. I'm not sure why, but I can't help doing the same.

"You need to pull them up," Daniel explains.

"I already did," I say, lifting the shirt so he can see. It's not like they're hanging off my hips. I figured that would be too risqué. But even pulled up, the white fabric touches my shins.

Daniel's eyes keep darting to my waistline and away again, like he's torn between politeness and modesty. Bare skin seems to make him uncomfortable. "You have to pull them up higher."

I glance down at myself. "No way."

"Really."

"Show me yours," I say, nodding at his shorts, which cover half his kneecaps.

"Oh." His face turns bright red. Then he lifts his shirt.

I eye the milky white skin of his stomach, wondering where his bellybutton is, when I realize that it's covered by the beige fabric of his shorts. He wasn't kidding! I wince in anticipation as I grab my shorts and hoist them higher, but the crotch doesn't ram into my junk like I feared, although I do wish I had a pair of underwear to help keep things situated. "How do you sit down with these things on?"

"You don't have shorts like this in Alabama?"

"You saw what I was wearing yesterday," I reply.

He's still staring at my waist, so I release the shorts, which slowly begin to descend.

"I'll get you a belt," he says quickly. "I thought we were the same size."

"You must be a little bigger than me," I murmur. "We'll have to compare sometime."

His hands are trembling when he hands me a white belt. The poor kid is going to have nightmares long after I'm gone. I'll be having a few fantasies, but only if I make it home again. That sobers me up. I can flirt with straight guys when I'm back in my own time, and once I've made sure Hannah is safe.

He loans me a pair of knee-high socks, making more faces and noises when I leave them scrunched up around my ankles. I'm given a pair of soft slip-on shoes that match his own, which I'm guessing are for indoor use only. Then I follow him downstairs to the breakfast table.

Dr. Parker is already seated and reading a printed newspaper. Two little girls are next to him, chatting excitedly until they see me. Then they fall silent and stare. I smile broadly at them, causing them to blush and giggle. Daniel leads me to a chair and goes to help his mother, who is working at the stove. An impressive spread is on the table: glasses of orange juice, grapefruit sliced in half, milk, toast, jelly, and a steaming bowl of scrambled eggs.

"How did you sleep last night?" Dr. Parker asks me.

"Like a dream," I say.

"I got a new puppy in mine," one of the girls says to me. "But then its head fell off."

"Drink your milk, Lizzie," Mrs. Parker says as she serves freshly fried bacon onto my plate.

"Thank you," I say, my appetite kicking in.

"It's nothing." Mrs. Parker places a hand on my shoulder. "I'm sorry for reacting the way I did last night."

"I barged into your house," I reply, eager to make peace. "You should have hit me with that frying pan. I would have deserved it!"

The girls laugh at this. Daniel sets a butter tray on the table before sitting next to me. I don't touch my food yet, unsure how families go about breakfast in the fifties. Maybe they pray first, or wait for the father to take a bite. If there's any sort of ritual, I don't notice it. Soon we're all eating, which I like, and talking, which gets tricky.

"George mentioned that you're from Alabama," Mrs. Parker says to me. "Which part?"

"Montgomery."

"Oh! Were you involved in… How old are you, if you don't mind me asking?"

"Eighteen."

This seems to please her. "The same age as Danny. It's a shame you didn't move here sooner. You could have gone to school together."

"Have you graduated already?" I ask him.

"Next week," he says after a swig of juice. "I guess you already did if you were able to come up here."

"Yeah," I say. "School gets out a little earlier in Alabama."

"Why don't you have an accent?" Mrs. Parker asks. "I love how it makes everything sound so charming."

"Let the poor boy eat," Dr. Parker interjects.

"I don't mind," I say. But I also make sure to keep my mouth full so I don't have to answer more questions. Daniel and his father seem to be in a hurry too. The two sisters fill most of the silence, chatting excitedly about their weekend plans, which involve swimming in the lake.

Daniel finishes eating first. "Dad is letting me borrow the car," he says. "After we drop him off at work, I can drive you over to see Gloria."

"That would be great," I say, already beginning to panic. This doesn't mesh with my plan.

"Do you need to call your mother to let her know that you've arrived safely?" Mrs. Parker asks.

"I'll do that from Gloria's place. That way my mom can talk to everyone there, but thank you."

I follow Daniel's lead as the meal comes to an end. He gets up to help clear the table before his mother shoos him away. I'm relieved to be given back my Nikes, especially when I see the loafers Daniel slips on that have leather tassels hanging off them. So hokey.

My stomach sinks when we go outside to the back of the house, and I don't see what I expect to. Not only is the garage separate, but there's only enough room for one car. In my day, the garage has room for three vehicles and is attached directly to the house. That must have been added later. More evidence that I really am in the past. My spirits soar again when the garage door opens, revealing a gorgeous classic car.

"Holy shit!" I say before clamping a hand over my mouth.

Daniel grins. "She's a real beauty, isn't she?"

We watch as Dr. Parker backs the vehicle out. It looks more like a boat, impossibly long with two taillights reminiscent of fins. The white trunk matches the convertible top, the rest of the car's rectangular body covered in sparkling aqua paint. Raised headlights point in our direction as the vehicle swerves around.

"I'm in love," I breathe.

"You'll have to get in line," Daniel retorts as he walks toward it. He opens the passenger-side door for me, which seems excessively chivalrous, until I realize it's the only way for me to climb in the back. I do so eagerly. There's no reason Daniel can't take the passenger seat up front, but he gets in next to me anyway. Dr. Parker arches his eyebrow at this in the rearview mirror. Then he focuses on navigating the driveway so we can turn onto the street.

"I know this is a Chevy," I say. "But what kind? A Bel Air?"

"That's right," Dr. Parker replies. "I bought it as a birthday present to myself a couple of years back. A fifty-five to celebrate my fiftieth."

"Happy belated birthday," I say, running my hands along the vinyl bench seat that matches the dual-tone exterior.

"This car would also make a great graduation present," Daniel says with transparent hope.

"Not a chance," Dr. Parker responds with a dry chuckle.

I turn my attention to the outside world as he drives us

32

through downtown Glen Ellyn, which is small, quaint, and resembles a bygone era, even in my day. So while it doesn't look so different as we cruise down main street, it's difficult to explain away how so many of the business signs could have changed, why everyone is dressed oddly, and where all the classic cars came from. Few are as ostentatious as a turquoise Chevy Bel Air, but none of them look anything like a Honda Civic, that's for sure.

Dr. Parker's office is just off Hillside Avenue. He parks outside and turns around in the seat to face his son. "You'll be here at four o'clock sharp to pick me up? My last appointment is with Ralph Higgins, and you know how his mother likes to talk my ear off. Or anyone who will listen."

"I'll be here right on time, Dad," Daniel promises.

"Good boy. Don't drive anywhere that isn't necessary." He addresses me next. "Say hello to Errol and Harriet."

I nod automatically, which is good, because it takes a second to realize that he's talking about my great-grandparents. "Thank you for taking me in last night."

"No trouble at all. I think you'll enjoy living in the area. We pride ourselves on being progressive thinkers." Dr. Parker checks his watch and excuses himself.

A moment later, I'm standing outside the car with his son.

"Do you need anything while we're downtown?" Daniel asks.

"Sort of," I say, licking my lips nervously. I hope he's not so square as to do everything his parents tell him. If so, I can walk, but I'd rather have company. "I need you to take me to Churchill Woods. I left my things out there last night."

"How come?" he asks.

I'm not sure which aspect he's confused about and I don't care. Now that there aren't any authority figures around to hold me back, I'm eager to get going. I want to figure out what happened to Hannah, and I want to go home, in that order.

"I'll explain on the way," I tell him.

"Okay, but let's put the top down. It's powered!"

Daniel opens the driver-side door and pushes a button. Then we stand back and watch as the white roof accordions and stows behind the rear seat.

"How nifty is that?" Daniel says, grinning at me.

I smile too, mostly because of his word choice. He's a cute

guy. I always thought so when staring at his photo. I didn't always understand why I was so drawn to it, but after I came out, I recognized it as one of the many telltale signs that made me realize I'm into guys. It's fun seeing him like this, so animated and full of color. When we find my phone, I'll record a video to show Grandma. She'll never believe it!

I'm still struggling with that myself, but as the car pulls out and Daniel turns on the radio—do-wop serenading our ride down Main Street—I sure feel like I've been transported to another era. The sky is blue, the sun shining with the same sort of optimism that seems to hang in the air. People smile at each other, stop to talk on street corners, and a few even wave when recognizing who is behind the wheel.

Like a scene out of a movie.

"Turn left here," I say.

Daniel looks surprised but complies. "I thought you wanted to—"

"Just a slight detour." I want to know for sure. It's one thing to redecorate a few blocks downtown to have a more historic vibe, or to speed-renovate the house I live in, but even these unlikely feats would have limits. I urge Daniel to drive away from Glen Ellyn. Eventually I ask him to pull over. He does, and I stare at a field of crops where there should be houses. My friend Carlos lived in one before his family moved. I slept over there more nights than I can count. I know where I am, and where he lived, but it's all gone. Or has yet to exist.

"Is my driving making you nauseous?" Daniel asks me.

"No." I turn to look at him again and accept the truth. I'm in the past, standing next to the guy who used to date my grandma. This isn't a dream, or a TV show, or a prank. It's all real. Not only have I drunk the Kool-Aid, I've guzzled the whole damn pitcher. "I just wanted to see something familiar."

Daniel glances beyond me to the field. "Did you live on a farm in Alabama?"

That works. "Yeah. It was a lot more rural there."

"I'd like to see it," he says. "Maybe we can drive down there together when you return for a visit."

"Sure," I say, hoping that I'll be long gone before that can happen. "Let's keep going."

No more detours. On the way to the woods, I try to take in

every detail of my surroundings, realizing that I'm unlikely to ever have this opportunity again. I should make the most of it and let myself be a tourist in the past before trying to get home. And maybe I would, if not for Hannah.

"What were you doing out here last night?" Daniel asks as we pull into the parking lot of Churchill Woods.

I'm tired of lying. Soon there won't be any point. "You'd never believe me," I reply.

"What if I promised to?"

I ignore him and get out of the car.

Daniel does the same, not giving up so easily. "Where did you leave your things? And why?"

That's a topic I'm willing to discuss as we walk down the path leading to the river. "There was a creepy guy out here. He scared the hell out of me, so I ran off. Any idea who he might be?"

Daniel shakes his head. "Did he attack you?"

"I'm not sure. I was yelling for my friend and he came up behind me."

"Your friend?"

I reply with a question of my own. "You know the stone gate that's out here?"

"The archway?"

"Yeah, exactly. What do you know about it?"

He's silent for a moment as we walk. "I know that it doesn't make sense."

"How so?"

He chews his bottom lip before answering. "Well, if it used to be part of a larger structure, where would it have fit? The river is on one side of the archway, so there wouldn't be room to build anything there. On the other side, the trees are too old."

I furrow my brow, not understanding. "What do you mean?"

"They would have needed to cut down trees to make room for even a small house, but there's no sign of that. Unless something stood there before the settlers came, which can't be right. The Indians didn't build with stone."

"Native Americans," I say automatically.

"Huh?"

"Oh. Umm... They were only called Indians because Columbus thought he had landed in India, so in Alabama, we use 'Native Americans' instead." I clamp my mouth shut and wonder if I'm making history. Daniel might spend the rest of his life enlightening others while spreading the new term around. That doesn't sound like such a bad thing, unless I return to an alternate present and discover that Biff Tannen owns the town and married my mother. I should probably say as little as possible from here on out.

As we're crossing the bridge together, Daniel stops in the middle.

"Look how high the river has swelled!" he says.

"How long did it rain before I got here?" I ask.

"A few days."

"The same as back home." My gaze rises to the trees we're about to enter. "It's going to be muddy. You don't have to come with me."

"I want to!" he insists.

I'm grateful, unsure of what I'll discover but compelled to find out. I resume walking with renewed determination, Daniel hurrying to catch up with me.

"Gloria has to work today," he says quickly. "I thought we could meet her for lunch. Afterwards we could go shopping or catch a matinee. I'm sure my dad will let me give you a ride home with her, once he's off work. How does that sound?"

He finishes with a gasp, like he forgot to breathe. They really need him to let him out of the house more often. Then again, considering that the internet doesn't exist, I'm probably the latest and most exciting news—a mysterious stranger in weird clothes, all the way from politically-correct Alabama. Just wait until I disappear in front of his very eyes! "Sounds like a real gas," I say, hoping I got the usage right.

Daniel smiles as if thrilled.

I nod toward the shadowy interior of the woods as we walk beneath the canopy of leaves. "Keep an eye out in case that creepy guy is still around."

Daniel gets in front of me protectively. Or as it turns out, for an equally noble but much nerdier reason. "I earned the merit badge for tracking on my first try."

"That's right," I say. "You're a Boy Scout.

"Yeah." Daniel squats to check a print. "As of last year, I'm an Eagle Scout."

"That's the highest rank?"

"Sure is. Lift up your shoe, please."

I show him the bottom of it and he nods as if satisfied. "This is the way you came last night."

I could have told him that, but I pretend to be impressed anyway. "Any sign that someone was chasing me?" I ask as we keep walking.

He shakes his head. "Not so far."

"You don't see anyone else out here?" I press, thinking of Hannah.

"No. You mentioned a friend. Is that who you're looking for?"

He's a sharp one. "Yeah. It's a girl, if that helps."

"Did she come with you from Alabama?"

I've always been a relatively honest person, and this is why. Trying to balance so many lies isn't worth the effort. "She's another of my pen pals."

"Oh." He sounds disappointed, maybe even disapproving. "Are you going steady?"

I snort before I catch myself. "No. Nothing like that."

He glances over his shoulder, his forehead crinkling. "Then why were you out here together? At night?"

Damn. I should have used the excuse that he provided. I guess it's not too late. "You don't have to go steady with a girl to spend time alone with her."

He doesn't say anything else until the land begins to rise and we pass through more trees. "Look at this." Daniel hunkers down near the ground. "A boot print!"

"Oh yeah?" I barely even glance at it. The gate has come into view. I move past Daniel, walking so fast that I'm on the verge of breaking into a run.

Compared to how I saw it last, the gate is pristine. The spray paint is gone, the gray stones speckled with moss, revealing the worn craggy surface I knew when younger. The gate hasn't begun to lean yet, which is encouraging. I can only assume it brought me here. I want it in good shape so it can take me back. The closer I get, the more I feel a buzzing inside, and it's not just excitement. I place a hand on one of the pillars, my palm vibrating. It never did that when I was a kid! I'm ready to rush through it and return home. Only one concern stops me from doing so.

I turn around to face Daniel, who is still checking the ground every few feet.

"Do you see footprints from anyone else?" I ask. "My friend

wasn't wearing boots. Those must belong to the man I saw. Is there a third set of tracks?"

"Not so far."

"Keep looking. Please." I turn around and consider the gate. I feel as though it's beckoning to me, like it also wants me to return to my rightful place.

"I think that's it," Daniel says, standing upright and brushing himself off. "There were only two of you out here last night. Aside from a few deer."

"You're sure?" I ask while moving toward him. I stop after a few steps, noticing how the buzzing inside of me decreases the more I distance myself from the gate.

Daniel walks over to join me. "As sure as I can be, yeah. I don't see any luggage though. Where did you leave it?"

"At the base of a tree."

I make a half-hearted effort to find my backpack. Chances are everything got soaked and ruined anyway. The weirdo in the woods must have taken it. Hopefully he won't reverse engineer my phone and start a company called Skynet. If so, I'll willingly battle *Terminator* robots in the future. I'm done with the past. It's time to go home.

"This is where we part ways," I say to Daniel. "Thank your family for their hospitality. I appreciate your help and the clothes. I'd give them back, but I don't want to be naked when I get home."

He shakes his head in confusion. "You're going back to Alabama?"

"Not quite. Listen, you seem like a nice guy so uh… Let's see. Don't let them send you to Vietnam. No matter what. Practice safe sex in the early eighties, stay away from the Twin Towers in two-thousand one, and invest in Apple when that becomes a thing. Best of luck!"

His expression has shifted to concern. Soon it will turn to surprise. I approach the gate, the vibration building inside of me. This intensifies to a buzz as I walk through the center, the frequency reaching a crescendo… and then diminishing again as I pass through to the other side. I spin around, expecting to see crumbled ruins and a chain link fence. The scene hasn't changed. Daniel looks even more perplexed now. I would have preferred to disappear in style, but I'm not giving up yet. I was pushed through the gate from the opposite side, where he's standing now. You don't leave a building by walking through the door in the same direction you arrived in. That must be it! I walk through the gate again, slowly and deliberately, focusing on the humming inside of me while willing myself to return home. I even close my eyes when passing directly beneath the arch, where the sensation becomes the most intense. Just like before, the buzzing fades as I keep walking.

"Reggie," Daniel starts to say.

"Give me a second," I snap.

There must be some trick that I'm missing. Hannah pushed me, I fell back... Is that it? I walk backwards through the gate, and when that doesn't work, I try standing still beneath it. The vibration never ceases, but I also don't end up anywhere. How come? And for that matter, why did I travel through time at all? I've walked through this gate before when younger, sat beneath it, leaned against the pillars, and all manner of interaction without anything unexpected happening. So have countless others. None of my classmates went missing. The legends surrounding the gate have nothing to do with it being a doorway to the past. Only when it was falling apart did I—

The cold tingle of dread races up my spine. The gate is no longer complete in the present day. I saw the top of it break off and almost crush me, the pillars already listing dangerously. Whatever remains now must be in ruins, which means...

There isn't a gate in the future for me to return through.

"Reggie," Daniel says again, sounding more insistent.

I'd nearly forgotten he was there. "Yeah?"

"My dad is worried that you've been through some sort of trauma. Like what happens to soldiers when they come back from war."

"I'm not crazy," I say, tearing my eyes from the gate to look at him.

After a swallow, he continues, "A lot of the things you say don't make sense."

"They do to me."

"Then tell me again why you were out here last night. Or what you think you're doing now."

"I'm not crazy," I say through gritted teeth. "Come here."

He doesn't budge, so I step forward and grab his wrist. "I'm not going to hurt you. Put your hand here." I place it against one of the stone columns. I press my palm against it too and feel the stone vibrating. The sensation reminds me of a field trip to a farm that had an electric fence. I pressed myself against it when dared to and felt the hum of electricity through my clothes. My eyes are locked onto Daniel's as I search for any sign of recognition or surprise. Instead he looks even more concerned. "Nothing?" I ask in disbelief. "Here." I place his hand over mine, thinking the gate is reacting to me and that he'll be able to feel it that way. When his expression remains blank, I growl in frustration, take his hand, and pull him toward the center of the gate where the vibrations are the most intense. I place his hand over my chest, holding it there with my own, and plead with my expression. I need him to confirm what I'm experiencing. "Don't you feel that?"

The air is coming out his nostrils in bursts, his eyes wide, before he croaks out, "I feel your heart."

I stare into his pale green eyes and know that he's being honest. Then I let go of his hand, which drops to his side. I'm so frustrated that I'm on the verge of tears.

"I'm worried about you," Daniel says, no longer able to make eye contact.

"I get it," I say. "I know how nutty I must seem, how strange the things I say must sound, but you'd never believe the truth. I barely can and I'm standing right here." I need proof. "My backpack! We just need to find it. I'll show you my phone and… That sounds crazy, right? Why would someone have a phone in their backpack? Wait, do you even know what that is? Do you only use messenger bags or something? How do you carry books to school?"

"In a satchel," Daniel says.

I snap my fingers. "That's what I'm looking for. A satchel that goes over your shoulders."

"Like a rucksack?"

"Yes!"

I must seem like a raving lunatic, but good ol' Daniel leaps into action with me. We search behind every tree and even look higher up in case my memory is wrong and it's hanging from a branch instead. Nothing. I kick at piles of leaves, grope around inside of bushes, and even try standing still while pivoting to scan my surroundings, but I don't see my backpack anywhere. The creep in the woods must have run off with it.

"Where do the boot prints lead?" I ask Daniel. "Can you follow them?"

"Maybe."

I quickly decide that the merit badge was well deserved. Daniel tracks the footprints to another path, which leads us down to the riverbank and along it before disappearing entirely.

"What does that mean?" I ask. "That he walked into the water?"

"Possibly," Daniel says. "It's a good way to stop anyone from following you." He shields his eyes and considers the sky. "Or maybe his trail got washed away because we're no longer beneath the trees."

"Can you find it again? Farther down maybe?"

He humors me, but even I can see that it's hopeless. We walk all the way back to the bridge without finding another trace of booted footprints.

"There's something else you should know," Daniel says to me.

"What?"

"My dad says you can have a psychotic incident without realizing it. So you might think that you're making sense—"

"Don't try to gaslight me."

"Huh?"

"Everything I say makes sense where I come from. I promise. The only trauma I experienced was waking up here last night—"

"Which you still haven't explained," Daniel huffs. "You were out necking with a local girl?"

I shake my head. "No. Not exactly."

"Then what? Tell me!"

He sounds angry. Who could blame him? The honest truth won't make him think I'm any less crazy, but I try regardless, being selective with how much I reveal. "Yesterday afternoon, I was hanging out by the gate with my friend. I lost consciousness, and when I woke up, it was night and she was gone."

"Were you drinking?"

"Stone cold sober."

"Oh." He thinks about it, and it's a shame he's not dumb, because he comes up with a valid question. "Why did you say all those strange things before walking back and forth through the gate just now?"

"Because I was trying to figure out how I got into this mess."

His forehead crinkles again. "I think you should tell all of this to my dad. He can help you."

By doping me up in a mental institution, most likely. I can't think of a lie convoluted enough to explain my behavior to either of them. At this point, I'm better off trying to figure it out alone. Daniel will never let me stay out here on my own though. He'll return with his father in tow, or maybe some burley men from the local insane asylum. Time to do damage control. "I'll talk to your dad tonight," I say. "And I'll listen to what he has to say."

Daniel still looks concerned. "Can we please head back into town?"

"Of course."

I'll hang out with him for the day, and in the evening, tell Dr. Parker that I've decided to return home. Then I'll find a way of actually doing so. Alone.

Chapter 4

Back in my own time, the gate is broken. I think of this obsessively as Daniel and I walk down Main Street. When popping into the occasional store, I'm momentarily distracted by all the products I don't recognize, or the old-fashioned labels of the things I do, but it isn't long before my mind begins racing again. There must be a solution. If I could get someone in my time to rebuild the gate, then I should be able to return through it again. But how?

"I'm going to buy this for Gloria," Daniel says from next to me. "She loves Zagnut bars."

"I know," I murmur without thinking. "They're tough to find."

"Not in Illinois, they aren't," Daniel replies.

We're standing in the old bank building on Main Street, which is occupied by a handful of boutique shops in my day. Right now the space is dominated by a Walgreens pharmacy, although with features that I'm not used to. A counter lined with stools fills one wall, large letters above this advertising it as a soda fountain and dinette. I can't help but think of the Greensboro sit-ins, started by four brave black men who were denied service at a similar lunch counter. They refused to leave, inspiring others to do the same. And it worked! The racist company policies were dropped. Eventually. That won't happen for a few years yet. I remember the photos of peaceful protesters sitting on their stools while surrounded by an angry mob who poured sugar and ketchup over their heads, blew smoke in their faces, or burned them with cigarettes, and wonder if the same would happen to me if I tried eating here.

"You could always mail a few home," Daniel continues, a candy bar in each hand.

If only it were that easy. I'd send a message to my family telling them to rebuild the gate, so I could return. Hey, that's not such a bad idea! If I bury instructions in a time capsule now, and someone in the future digs it up… They'll think I'm crazy. Hannah might believe me, depending on what she saw when I vanished. How could I get a message to her specifically?

"Up to you," Daniel says, putting a candy bar back. "I'm buying this one for Gloria."

That's it! My grandma knows Hannah. All my friends love Granny Gloria. She could give Hannah a message for me. I'll make her promise not to deliver it until the day after my disappearance. Damn… I hadn't thought of it in those terms yet. Back in twenty-twenty-two, I'm a missing person. But not for long. I only need to convince my grandmother of today to hold onto a mysterious letter for the next sixty-odd years.

"How much longer until lunch?" I ask eagerly.

"We'll surprise her at work now," Daniel says. "I'm hungry too."

First we have to check out. The cash register is a huge mechanical beast covered in numbered buttons. The girl working the machine has to push down on them to manually enter the price instead of scanning a barcode. A single candy bar doesn't require much effort, but I'd hate to see someone check out an entire shopping cart of groceries that way.

We leave the car where Daniel parked it, walking a few blocks down to Henderson's Dry Cleaning. I once again use the time to think, but not of a cover story. That won't get me anywhere. Not if I want their help.

"Daniel!" the woman behind the counter says, already beaming at him. "Did you come here for clothes or company?"

"Company," he says sheepishly.

"I should have known. Gloria!"

My pulse picks up in anticipation. At the back of the shop, a woman my age stands up from a sewing machine and turns around. Her hair is short and curled, her body slender and covered in what looks like a lavender sleeveless jumpsuit with the legs cut off just below the knees. Her right eyebrow is arched higher than the other, giving the impression that she's amused by some inside joke that only she knows. Her dark sparkling eyes and wide smile are unmistakable as she notices Daniel. She's young, she's pretty…. And she's my grandma.

"Don't be too long," the woman behind the counter says.

"I won't, Mrs. Henderson," Gloria responds politely.

She practically pushes Daniel out the door, sparing only a puzzled glance for me. "You saved my life," Gloria says once we're on the sidewalk. "I was sweating up a storm in there!"

"Doesn't matter," I say. "All it does is make you glow. You're so beautiful!"

She looks me over before returning her attention to Daniel. "Who's this fool? And why is he wearing your clothes?"

Observant! My mom always said I got my smarts from her.

"He's your cousin," Daniel says before I can stop him. "Reggie."

"My what?" Gloria takes another look at me, focusing on my face, and it's almost like she recognizes me. Or not. "He's no cousin of mine!"

"She's right," I say before Daniel can protest. "But we are family." I hold out my hand to her. "You won't believe how excited I am to see you again."

"Again?"

"Yeah," I say with a dopey grin. I'm starting to enjoy myself. "Although it's been around six or seven decades." I nod at Daniel. "He thinks I'm crazy. Maybe I am, but I have a helluva story to tell you both anyway."

"I bet you do," Gloria says, taking Daniel's arm on the side farthest from me as she begins to lead him down the street. "I'm willing to listen to any ol' nonsense as long I get a bite to eat."

God I love my grandma!

"What's this all about?" I hear her ask Daniel.

"I don't even know any more," comes his weary response.

"I'll explain everything," I interject. "I promise."

We cross the street to a corner diner. I can tell Daniel isn't happy with me. When he looks in my direction, the normally earnest eyes are guarded instead. No wonder. I've just admitted that I've been lying to him. He's probably debating if he should call his dad or the police, but I can still make this right. I have to.

The inside of the restaurant is familiar to me, only because I've been to plenty of fifties-themed diners. The real deal is a bit more toned down. They too have the classic counter with stools and a jukebox, but the floor is covered in small tiles instead of black and white checks, and there aren't as many neon signs incorporated into the deco. The pink padded booths more than make up for this. We slide into one, the Greensboro protestors still on my mind, but Gloria seems comfortable here so I'm guessing we'll be fine.

I barely glance at the menu, hastily ordering a burger and fries so the waitress will go away. I want to clear the air. When I finally have the chance and two pairs of eyes are staring at me from across the table... well, it's not easy to get the words out, but I manage anyway.

"My name is Reggie Valentine. And I come from the future."

— — —

I've told them everything. The entire sequence of events that led me to a sticky-tabled diner in the nineteen fifties. I lean back and take a sip of cherry cola while assessing their reactions. Daniel's brow is knotted up, like he's still trying to put all the pieces together. Gloria has both eyebrows raised and is looking at me like I'm unhinged.

"I'm still waiting for the part that proves you aren't crazy," she says.

"I don't blame you. I can hardly believe it either."

"Because it's not possible," Daniel grumbles.

He almost seems angry at himself. Like he feels foolish for humoring me or for helping someone so deceptive. I'm not sure, but I do feel the need to make things right between us.

"If we can find my backpack, you'll have all the proof you need. Wait until you see my phone. It's more like a TV screen really. And a camera. It'll blow your mind."

"Right." Gloria sucks long and hard on a straw while scrutinizing me. I'm reminded of the time my brothers and I flooded the downstairs bathroom by stopping up all the drains. My grandma was the only adult at home and asked who was responsible. Yours truly, unfortunately. I wanted a swimming pool. My older brothers wanted to see me get in trouble. And she figured all of that out. I was grounded for being an idiot, and my brothers were punished for not being better role models. "You must have *something* from the future on you," she says. "Money?"

"No. Speaking of which, I um... can't afford to pay for my lunch."

Daniel glares at the table, like he's trying to burn a hole through the surface.

"What about your clothes?" Gloria asks. "Did you show up naked on Daniel's doorstep?"

"You're a seamstress!" I say in excitement. My grandmother is a skilled dressmaker. I even have a few custom shirts made by her hanging in my closet. It's no casual interest. She mastered her trade as an adult. I hope she knew her stuff when younger too. "The outfit I was wearing is at Daniel's place but..." I stick my legs out in the aisle, tearing at the laces of my right shoe before slipping it off and setting it on the table in front of her, chunks of dried mud scattering across the surface. She picks up the shoe without hesitation and brushes off even more dirt.

Daniel's face turns red as he sinks further down in his seat. We've attracted a few stares, but they barely register with me. I'm used to people watching my every move when I shop or do anything else. I'm sure Gloria is too. She's focused on examining the shoe. Despite the wear the last couple days have put on them, they still pop. The top of the shoe is a lightweight mesh fabric covered by ribs of shiny black plastic. The thick rubber soles have clear windows toward the bottom, showing off the orange and red springs inside. Plastic badges are fitted into the tongue, the bottom, and the back of the shoe, each asserting various trademarked terms intended to impress consumers.

"Very unusual," she admits. "Where did you buy these?"

"Check the label," I suggest.

"Made in Vietnam," she reads.

"I bought them down the street." After some hasty mental arithmetic, I add, "about sixty years from now."

"I don't even know where to begin with these," Gloria says. She passes the shoe to Daniel. "Have you ever seen anything like this before?"

He takes it, cheeks still red as he turns the shoe over in his hand. When he glances up again, he almost seems hopeful. "No. His outfit was kind of strange too. What are all these numbers and lines?" He's referring to the tag stitched onto the shoe's tongue.

After he hands it back to me, I do my best to explain. "The top row is what the shoe size would be in different countries. The lines at the bottom are a bar code, which is a sort of price sticker. I don't know what some of these other numbers mean but—" I can't help but grin, turning the label so they can see. "This right here? It's the date of manufacture." Not many shoe companies include that. Nike does.

"Three, sixteen, twenty-two," Daniel reads aloud.

He looks to Gloria in shock.

"That doesn't prove anything," she says, "but you've got my attention. If you're from the future, tell us something that's about to happen."

I think about it while putting my shoe back on. "I can come up with a major event, like the moon landing—"

"What?" Daniel says, sounding excited. "Really? We travel to the moon?"

"Yeah, but that's in the sixties. Toward the end. I can't wait a decade for you to believe me. I need your help now."

"What's going to happen this year?" Gloria presses.

I shake my head. "What happened sixty years ago today? Do you know? Because that's what you're asking me to do."

They look at each other and come up empty.

"Why do you live in my house in the future?" Daniel asks.

"I honestly don't know." My eyes move to Gloria. "But we both do. You live in the downstairs bedroom, just off the sunroom."

Daniel narrows his eyes. "We don't have a sunroom."

"Not yet," Gloria says. "What else?"

"I know that you two used to date."

Daniel turns bright red.

Gloria laughs. "We *never* talk about that to anyone!"

"You must still be close because you have a framed photo of him in your room."

This makes her cackle. Daniel covers his face and groans.

"This has been fun," Gloria says as she stands, "but I have to get back to work."

Daniel pays by leaving cash on the table, which seems careless, but nobody seems to mind as we go. I'm feeling increasingly desperate as we cross the street again, not having gotten myself any closer to a solution.

"Even if you don't believe me," I say, walking next to Gloria, "would you be willing to give someone a letter six decades from now? If they repair the gate, I might be able to go home."

"Sure, why not?" Gloria turns around to face me when we reach the sidewalk. "What are you going to do with yourself until then?"

I shake my head, not understanding.

"If I give your friend this note," she explains, "it'll take time to get the gate patched up. Or do you have robots who can build things lickety-split?"

"I wish." She's right. Even after Hannah reads the letter, she'll still need time to convince others to rebuild the gate. Until she succeeds, I'll be stranded here. "It might take a few weeks. I'm not sure."

Gloria turns to Daniel. "Think your family would be willing to take him in?"

"Maybe. I'm supposed to be dropping him off so he can live with your family."

"Oh yeah!" Gloria says, perking up. "You didn't explain that part. You said that we're family. We even live together."

I nod while biting my bottom lip. I intentionally avoided the subject because I felt it was too much to swallow.

"Sixty years from now," Gloria says musingly. "What's that make you, my grandfather?"

"You've uh… got it reversed," I say. "You'll be older than me by then, remember?"

"Oh right, so that means—" She clamps her mouth shut. Then her eyes narrow. "No."

"Happens to the best of us," I say.

"What?" Daniel asks, not having caught on.

"Oh nothing," I say casually. "Aside from the fact that you used to date my grandma."

She cackles again. Daniel seems disturbed by the thought.

"Mm-mm-mm," Gloria says, looking me over again. "You sure remind me of my Uncle Jack. I might just believe you."

"Really?" I hug her spontaneously, the sensation oddly familiar. For one of us anyway.

Gloria is grinning when I release her. "I said *might*. At least you've given me something to think about while I work. Any chance y'all can meet me afterwards?"

"I think so," Daniel says. "Especially when Dad finds out that he's still with me."

"Good. I'll see you both then."

She smiles demurely before returning to the dry cleaner.

"Wait," Daniel says, pulling a Zagnut bar from his pocket.

It's too late. She doesn't hear him. The candy bar is sagging noticeably anyway.

"It's totally melted," I say, swiping it from him. "And I'm still hungry. But don't worry. We can get a fresh one for your girlfriend before we pick her up."

"She's not my girlfriend," Daniel mumbles.

"How come? She's a stone cold fox. If she wasn't my granny…"

I nudge him playfully and get a reluctant smile.

"Hey man," I say as we walk down the street together. "I'm sorry for lying to you. Really. You've been so nice to me. I'll make it up to you somehow. How about a bite?"

I poke the partially unwrapped candy bar at his face, the chocolate dripping down my fingers.

"Stop!" he says, laughing as he dodges.

"This is how people apologize in the future. You have to eat it."

"But I paid for it!"

I take a bite. "And that makes it taste even sweeter. Try it."

I chase him down the sidewalk, the candy bar held out before me like a knife. By the time he slams into the Chevy Bel Air and leans against it, we're both panting, but I'm not done.

"Eat it," I insist. "Absolve me of my guilt."

He laughs again and finally complies. I feed him a bite, his pale-green eyes surprisingly vulnerable as they stare into mine. His delicate lips have melted chocolate on them as he chews. I try to imagine how good it would taste to kiss them. I break the tension by leaning against the car next to him and wonder what else the day will bring. So far, I've not only met my grandmother when she was my age, but I've also discovered that we share the same taste in men.

— — —

We return to Daniel's house to get refreshed, and to pick up my outfit from yesterday so Gloria can inspect it. Mrs. Parker looks distraught when meeting us in the entryway.

"I'm so sorry," she says when presenting me with a neatly folded pile. My shirt is fine, but the shorts have a dark triangular mark on them and smell like burnt plastic. "I didn't realize they were gym shorts," Mrs. Parker explains. "The material is so strange. The second I put the iron on them—" She shakes her head, as if unable to continue.

I'm trying not to laugh. Who irons shorts? Or a tank top? "It's totally fine," I say. "Nobody wears this style here, I've noticed, so I wasn't planning to either."

"You simply must let me replace them," Mrs. Parker insists while handing me a ten-dollar bill.

Lunch for the three of us had cost around half that much, so I figure it's more than enough. "Thank you, but I can't accept this. Especially after the hospitality you've shown me."

"I insist," she says, holding up a palm when I try to hand the money back. "And for goodness sake, please call me Melody."

"That's a beautiful name."

"It's poorly chosen," she replies with a titter. "I don't have a musical bone in my body."

Her appearance is surprisingly neat for someone burdened with housework and childcare all day. She shares the same delicate features as her son, including the pale green eyes and light brown hair. Judging from the narrow waist, she hasn't eaten a solid meal in ages.

"Everyone can sing," I reply. "It just takes a little practice."

"Oh, I'm hopeless." Mrs. Parker gestures for us to follow her. "What about you?"

"I play the piano," I explain. "I intend to make a career of it."

"Really? I keep reminding George that the girls need to learn an instrument before they get much older. Do you teach, by chance?"

"I do." Only for the past couple of years, at first because I wanted to add it to my credentials. As it turns out, I enjoy sharing my enthusiasm with younger students. Most of them have no love for the piano, forced to learn it by their parents, but a few have shown genuine interest and potential. "Back home, at least. I don't have a piano with me. I *knew* I forgot to pack something!"

"Oh darn," she says with a smile.

Mrs. Parker leads us to the kitchen and pours us each a glass of Kool-Aid from an ice-filled pitcher. I've only ever seen that done in commercials. She has the serving tray and everything.

"How did the visit with your family go?" she asks.

"We surprised Gloria for lunch," Daniel interjects. "She was… surprised."

"I bet! When do you get to see the rest of your family?"

"Tonight," I say, relieved that I don't need to lie to her. They really are my blood relatives.

"Won't that be nice?" Mrs. Parker says pleasantly. "I don't suppose you boys are in the mood to go swimming before then?"

"No," Daniel blurts out, before clearing his throat. "We just ate. It wouldn't be safe."

"It's just that your sisters want to continue swimming," his mother presses, "and I still have so much to do."

"We can watch them," I say, nudging Daniel. "Can't we?"

His mother's face lights up. "Oh, would you? That would be wonderful!"

Daniel glowers at me as soon as her back is turned, and I take pleasure in it, thinking of all the times my older brothers were roped into babysitting me. Before long we're in the park across the street, sitting on a bench while watching his sisters swim. I brought the freshly ironed clothes with me and pass them to Daniel so he can check them out. They don't make as big an impression as my shoes, which is probably why he asks to see those again instead. I decide to take them off, along with the scratchy socks he loaned me, so I can feel the cool grass beneath my feet.

Daniel takes one of the shoes to examine it, and when he thinks I'm not paying attention, scratches at the date on the label like I might have written it on. Fair enough. I'd nearly convinced myself that I was having my own *Truman Show* experience before I finally accepted the truth.

"Want to try them on?" I ask.

"Really?" Daniel glances over at me in excitement. "Think they'll fit?"

I place my bare foot next to his loafer. "We're about the same size. Go for it."

I witness a parade of cute expressions as he puts them on, ranging from surprise to puzzlement. When he has the shoes tied and stands up, he bounces on his heels a few times before laughing. "They're so squishy," he says.

"Comfortable," I correct. "Especially compared to yours, I bet. Can I try them actually?"

"Sure!" he says.

I do my own experimental stepping once I've slipped the loafers on. They're comfortable in their own way, but I can already tell they don't breathe as much, and I'm still not into the leather tassels hanging on each.

"Why are they so strange?" Daniel asks me while staring at his feet.

"I was having similar thoughts," I murmur. "The pair you have on are made for athletes. I don't fit the description, but my oldest brother does. He got me turned on to that brand, although lots of people wear them, even if they don't like sports. Hell, most of them don't even go for walks. Shoes are more like status symbols."

"That's ridiculous."

"I agree. As to your question, the reason they look so weird is because they're designed to make you run faster."

"So they work?"

"I don't know. Wanna find out?"

I grin at him and hunker down in the classic starting line pose. He's familiar with it. Daniel joins me at my side and matches my posture.

"When do we start?" he asks.

"Now!" I take off running without warning, already laughing, because his shoes are floppy by comparison. I still manage to maintain my lead until I reach a tree. "And back again!" I shout, launching myself off it.

The filthy cheater turns around when he sees me coming instead of continuing to the tree! I cry foul and pump my arms harder, but he's got this one. Daniel makes it back to the bench ahead of me, and I'm left jogging toward his victorious smile.

"Did you feel any faster?" I pant.

"Not really," he replies.

It's an honest answer. "I never felt faster in them either."

All the commotion has attracted the attention of the girls, who wade out of the water to join us.

"What are you doing?" asks Sarah, the oldest girl.

"Running from a ghost!" I exclaim theatrically.

"A ghost?" Lizzie asks, her tiny face worried.

"Yeah. He was dressed like a pirate captain. He kept talking about buried treasure and how to find it."

The girls look at each other with shining eyes. "Treasure?" they say in perfect unison.

"Yup! He left hints on where to find it in the water." I frown and shake my head. "I don't have a swimsuit though, so it's hopeless."

"We can help you look!" Lizzie says, trembling with excitement.

Soon we're walking along the shore. Daniel and I each grab broken-off branches that we can poke in the water while pretending to listen for the thud of a chest. We praise the girls when they fish out old cans and other trash, trying our hardest to interpret them as parts of the world's worst treasure map.

Eventually we all get tired enough to return home. Mrs. Parker is sitting on the front porch and seems pleased. She ushers the girls inside, telling them to take off their wet clothes in the downstairs bathroom, before turning to us.

"Did you have fun?" she asks.

"Yeah!" Daniel says, still smiling.

"Oh good." She looks back and forth between us before settling on her son. "It's so nice to see you playing with another boy again, Danny."

His face goes slack before turning bright red.

I slap him on the back while chuckling. "Don't worry. My mom still thinks I'm in diapers too."

He pulls away from the body contact and doesn't reply.

Mrs. Parker grimaces and shrugs. I smile at her reassuringly until we've gone inside. Then I glance over at Daniel, who looks downright ashamed, and wonder what I'm missing.

Chapter 5

We've already picked up Dr. Parker and dropped him off at home again. He seemed concerned to see me. Less so when his son explained that we're still planning to connect with my family, once Gloria is off work. Now I'm riding shotgun in the car with Daniel, feeling anxious about meeting everyone and if they'll take me in for the night, but the covered casserole dish resting on my lap provides warm reassurance. Mrs. Parker handed it to me just before we left. At least my great-grandparents won't have to worry about feeding an extra mouth tonight. I suppose that was the intent of her sending it along.

"Your mom is really nice," I say, mostly to get conversation going again. Daniel has been quiet ever since we returned home from hanging out by the lake.

"She's the best," Daniel says. "I love her."

"I feel bad that she had to cook dinner twice tonight."

"She just doubled the recipe. We're having the same thing." His mouth twitches in one corner. "Actually, she probably increased the recipe by seventy percent or whatever it would be to feed nine people instead of five. My mom is incredibly good with numbers."

"Uh oh," I say teasingly. "Someone's a mama's boy!"

He shoots me a look that I can only interpret as fearful, and I feel the need to ease his concern. "Most guys are, don't you think? I always have been."

"I love my dad," Daniel says, his voice strained. "He's my idol."

"That's cool too," I reply easily. "No reason it can't be both."

We're only a couple blocks away from the dry cleaner. Daniel has gone quiet again. I keep thinking about the comment his mother made, how it was nice to see him playing with other boys. It reminds me of grade school when an overly-concerned teacher contacted my parents because I spent most of my time with girls during recess. My parents tried to hide this from me, but the teacher made a comment about it to me on the same day she phoned my house, so I knew what the call was about. And I just happened to overhear my father's response.

"Good. Maybe he'll have more respect for women when he's older because of it."

I wonder if Daniel needs the same kind of reassurance, so I attempt to broach the subject.

"I take it you don't have a lot of guy friends?"

Daniel keeps his attention on the road. I barely notice when he shakes his head.

"Any reason?" I press.

He's so quiet that I'm not sure if he'll answer at all. Daniel brings the car to a stop in front of Henderson's Dry Cleaning and puts it in park. He's staring at the steering wheel when he says, "Dad felt it was for the best."

"Why, were you partying too much?"

Gloria comes bounding out of the dry cleaner and waves. Daniel gets out of the car to greet her. I watch as they hug and feel confused. When the teacher called my house, if my parents had been less enlightened, they would have urged me to spend *more* time with other boys. I'm not sure why Daniel's parents would want him to stay away from other guys but be okay with him hanging out with his ex-girlfriend… if they even know about that.

I climb into the backseat, carefully setting the casserole dish on the floorboard, so that Gloria can have the passenger seat. I'm not going to make my grandma ride in the back. She seems appreciative of that and perks up when I hand her the paper bag with yesterday's outfit inside.

She focuses on the tags first, and then the stitching itself, although not as long. "The labels are printed in a way I've never seen before," she informs Daniel. "The shirt has letters right on the fabric, and they aren't even sewn."

"Those tend to wash off eventually," I say. "It's annoying when you want to order the same thing but aren't sure what size it is."

They probably think I'm talking about a catalog instead of the internet, but that's fine. I care more about the verdict.

"I tried on his shoes," Daniel says. "They're from another planet!"

"Same one," I correct. "I'm not an alien."

Gloria turns around and scrutinizes me as if to confirm this. "You really do look like family," she says, shaking her head. "Here's what we're going to say to my parents. First of all—"

"Wait," I interrupt. "You believe me?"

"Enough that I'm going to convince my folks to take you in until we can get you home again. Now listen up: Uncle Jack is an alcoholic. The nice kind. I never felt afraid to be around him, but the man is a mess. He disappears for years at a time without us hearing from him. You should say that you're his illegitimate son."

"Gloria!" Daniel says in chastising tones.

"It's fine," I say with a chuckle. "There are plenty of single parents in my day. It's not frowned upon as much."

"Progress." Gloria says before continuing. "Uncle Jack probably has a few kids out of wedlock. I wouldn't say you're from Alabama though. He usually travels up and down the East Coast, so that would be more likely."

I shake my head. "I already told Daniel's parents that I'm from Alabama, and if your mom works for them, they must talk."

"Darn." Gloria leans her back against the passenger side door, so she can see us both. Then she snaps her fingers. "How about this? Let's say that your mother moved to Alabama, but that you weren't raised there your entire life. Does that work?"

"Yeah. I have some cousins in Savannah that I've visited a few times. I'll say we're from there originally."

She nods in approval. "That works. What I can't figure out is how we would've become pen pals. If you don't know Jack, so to speak, then how do you know me?"

We think about it in silence as the car heads west. That surprises me. I assumed that we'd be heading south to the impoverished neighborhoods that black families were shoved back into whenever they attempted to leave.

"Do you ever write your uncle?" Daniel asks his friend.

"On occasion. I do love him. But I never expect to hear back."

"If your uncle still comes around to see Reggie's mom on occasion, maybe he had one of your letters with him. Reggie could have found it and used the address to write you."

"Sounds like a stretch," I say.

"Stranger things have happened," Gloria counters.

"Where do you send the letters?" I ask. "Especially if your uncle moves around so much."

"To my great-aunt," she replies. "His mother."

"Jesus," I breathe. "I need a family tree to figure this out."

"No!" Gloria says, sounding excited. "That's perfect! Aunt Jeanie is ancient. And more than a little senile. So if your imaginary mother had her address, and you asked how to get in touch with your biological father..."

"You've lost me," I admit.

"Good. A confusing lie is harder to see through."

Damn! Who knew my grandma was such a schemer?

"I'll say that Aunt Jeanie forwarded your letter to me by mistake," Gloria clarifies, "and we started corresponding that way. I'll tell them I said you were welcome to stay with us, if ever in the area, not thinking you'd take me up on it—"

"—and surprise, here I am." I'm still not sure if it'll be enough, but it's hard to think of an alternative.

Gloria nods. "Have you ever met my Uncle Jack? In the future, I mean."

I shake my head. "I've heard my parents talk about him, but not often."

"Huh. That's weird. You've met my parents though. When they're older?"

"Only your mom. She was half-blind by then and mostly sat in a recliner while listening to the radio, but she was still around when I was little."

Gloria looks aghast at this news. "What about my dad?"

"Oh." I should have realized that I'm talking about people who are, in her mind, still relatively young and in good health. From my perspective they were always ancient. Or had already passed away. "We never met."

"He dies before Mama? How? When?"

"I really don't know. I'm sorry."

She stares at me before flopping around in her seat to face the front again. Daniel places his hand over hers and squeezes. It's a reminder that I need to be careful. What is history to me is still very much the present to them.

"We have a photo of your parents in the living room," I say. "They're both old in it, so I think they get to be together for a very long time."

I'm not sure if this news makes her feel better. I hear a few sniffs, but when she speaks again, it's all business. "You better say that you've never met your father so you don't get any of the details wrong. You should ask a lot of questions about him. I figure that's what would have brought you to Chicago."

"And a better life away from the South and all of its bullshit segregation policies."

"Amen to that," she replies. "Almost there now."

The neighborhood we pull into is only vaguely familiar to me. Many of the lots are still being developed, the houses in various stages of construction. All of them are small. The one Daniel parks in front of is no exception. I'm reminded of a child's drawing, since the house is a single-story cube with a pointed roof. I'm already worried there won't be enough room for me to stay. The front yard is just a patch of grass. Massive electricity pylons stand directly behind the building, but the vibe is tranquil when we get out of the car.

"How long have you lived here?" I ask.

"A couple years now," Gloria answers. "We were the first black family to buy a house in this neighborhood. Now there are three. We used to share a terrible apartment with another family, so no matter what you think, pretend to be impressed."

I feel genuine pride as we approach. This is the origin of my family! The privileged upbringing I had wouldn't have been possible without the hard work and sacrifices that my ancestors made. I already wish that I could tell my great-grandmother that the house she cleans for a living will one day belong to her descendants.

Gloria leads the way inside to a small living room, which is humble but tastefully decorated. I barely glance at it because a wiry woman has entered from the kitchen and is staring at me curiously. Her hair is shoulder length and has been straightened and curled again. She has the same alert eyes as her daughter, although she doesn't seem quite as energetic.

"What's this?" she asks with an uncertain smile.

"I've got a big surprise for you, Mama," Gloria says.

She launches into the story we came up with, but it isn't long before her mother holds up a hand to stop her. So she can address me.

"You're Jack's boy? Is that what I'm hearing?"

"I never really knew him," I say, skirting the truth, "but yeah. We're family." I hold out the casserole. "Surprise!"

She takes the dish from me as the front door opens. I turn and see a solidly built man dressed in dark blue coveralls. He pauses when taking off his brimmed hat and notices the four pairs of eyes staring back at him. When he sees me, he does a double-take. "What's going on?"

"I think you'd better sit down," his wife says, but she doesn't wait for him to. "This young man claims to be Jack's boy."

My great-grandfather tries to hang his hat on a nearby hook, but he's staring at me and misses, the hat tumbling to the floor. He doesn't notice, still eyeing me while the rest of the room holds its breath.

"Is Jack doin' okay?"

He seems worried about his brother, which makes me feel guilty. "I- I don't know," I stammer. "He wasn't around much. But I don't have any reason to think otherwise."

He looks me over again. I wish I was wearing normal clothes, or at least something that reflects my personal style. "What's your name?"

"Reggie," I say, moving toward him with a hand extended. "Reggie Valentine. My mother never married, so I have her name."

His hand envelops mine, strong and calloused. I'm worried if he squeezes too hard that my career as a pianist will be over. He doesn't though. Instead he releases me and nods toward the interior of the house. "Let's sit down and have us a talk," he suggests.

What happens next is a blur. Daniel excuses himself, saying he promised to be back in time for dinner, and leaves so quickly that we don't have a chance to say goodbye. I'm offered a beer (hell yeah!) and sit in the living room with my great-grandparents, who introduce themselves as Errol and Harriet. Mr. and Mrs. Parker also asked me to call them by their first names, but it didn't feel right, despite how nice they are. I don't have that problem now, and not because of the warm rush of alcohol in my blood. We really are family. They seem to sense it too, Errol especially. Gloria does most of the talking, but his attention remains on me.

"I see your father in you," he says at one point. "How he looked back when we were boys. I wish I could tell you where to find him, but he's sure to show up again. If you write another letter to Aunt Jeanie, he'll get it eventually."

"If he's sober enough to read it," Gloria says wryly.

Her mother pats her hand. "Why don't you go heat up the casserole that Melody was nice enough to send along?"

Gloria seems reluctant to go, and I don't want to be without her timely saves, but what can we do? She gives me a thumbs up before disappearing into the kitchen, leaving me on my own.

"Gloria didn't mention any of this to us," Harriet says with a sigh. "We weren't expecting you."

"She's a bit like her uncle," Errol grumps. "He always was a dreamer."

"Our daughter has a *much* better head on her shoulders!" Harriet says before seeming to remember me. "Sorry. Jack is a nice man, but he isn't the most responsible."

"I'm living proof of that," I say, and to my relief, they both laugh. The family sense of humor hasn't changed much, thank goodness. "Meeting you has already been great. I feel more in touch with my roots."

"And it's only been half an hour," Gloria says, making an early return from the kitchen. "Think how nice it would be if he stays with us for a few weeks!"

Harriet raises her eyebrows at this. "Did you set the table? If so, pour everyone a drink and then find something else to keep yourself occupied."

Gloria retreats, silent and sullen.

"What was your intention when making this trip?" Errol asks me. "You had to know that your father wasn't likely to be here."

"I'm not crazy about Alabama, and I thought Chicago might have more opportunities for me."

He grunts as if this makes sense. "What sort of work do you do?"

"I'm a musician."

"Next to useless, in other words," he says, exchanging a friendly smile with his wife.

"What do you play?" Harriet asks me.

"The piano."

"Oh, it's hard to go wrong with that," she says. "Are you any good?"

I sit up a little straighter. "Better than that. I'm great."

She whistles appreciatively. "The boy is confident. He's got that much down!"

Errol isn't as animated in his response. "Do you have any practical work experience? Not many people can make a living playing music."

A bunch of skills spring to mind, but most of them are computer-based and would be useless here. "I'm willing to do anything. I can help out around the house or um…"

"Could you get him work in the shop?" Harriet asks her husband.

Errol shakes his head. "I'm not sure. Do you know your way around an engine?"

I stare in response. "You mean like a car?"

He looks at his wife as if that answered the question.

"I can help you with your work," I suggest to her. "I'm great with a broom."

"He's a natural musician, all right," Harriet says, winking at me. "He claims to be the best there ever was and will tell everyone that while sweeping the streets."

"Whatever it takes to pay the bills," I say, not feeling discouraged. "I'm not here to freeload. I'll pull my weight one way or another. I just need a place to stay for a couple of weeks until I can get on my feet." By then, Hannah will have gotten my letter, the gate will be repaired, and I'll get to go home. They'll never see me again. Well, one of them won't.

"There's an awful lot to take into consideration," Errol says, not expounding further.

I get it. They need time to think. From their perspective, they've just met a nephew they've never heard of before. I don't push them for an answer. I assure them instead that I'll make other arrangements if they can't take me in, absolving them of any guilt or obligation. The weather is nice enough this time of year that I could camp out if need be. Daniel must have a tent, since he's a Boy Scout. I almost wish I'd thought of that option sooner. I could set myself up near the gate and test it regularly.

Then again, with the creepy man still out there, I'd rather not.

Wanting to prove how useful I can be, when Harriet says she'll get another round of drinks, I stand instead. I bring only two back. I don't want them to think I inherited Jack's bad habits. Then I return to the kitchen to help Gloria serve dinner. Soon we're all seated around a small table, eating tuna noodle casserole while carrying on a lively conversation. My hosts keep talking about Jack, wanting me to learn more about him, which is kind. I'm more curious about them, since they're my direct ancestors, and my questions reflect that. I learn that Errol grew up on a farm in the South, which is where he discovered a talent for repairing machinery. Harriet is the youngest of six siblings and left school early to begin working as a maid to help support her family. They met at a county fair and had shared dreams that brought them here. I'm hanging on every word, not having to fake my enthusiasm. By the end of the meal, the ice has been thoroughly broken. Gloria and I offer to clean up, which can't hurt how charitable her parents are feeling toward me.

"What do you think?" I ask as we stand at the sink together while washing dishes by hand.

"They don't buy it," she tells me. "They think you're nuts." Gloria waits until I look concerned before she bumps her hip against mine. "They love you! Are you kidding? They'll probably give you my room and make me sleep on the couch."

I wish I could share her confidence. When we reenter the living room, Errol stands and motions for me to follow him. We step out back where he lights up a cigarette. I shake my head when he offers me one.

"I wish my brother had been a better father to you," Errol says, "but you seem to have turned out fine without him. I keep thinking how, if the situation was reversed, I'd expect him to help Gloria if she ever needed him to. That's what family is for. So you're welcome to stay. I won't lie though. Making the house payments takes every cent we can muster. We've had a few close calls. If we miss even one, we lose the house and all the money we've put into it."

"That can't be right. Doesn't the bank charge late fees first? And give you warnings?"

"It's hard for black folks to get a loan," Errol grumbles. "Even up here. We had to buy it on contract."

"How does that work?"

"It means the little worm who sold us the place still holds the deed until we finish paying him off. He *wants* us to fail, so he can sell this house to someone else and keep the money we've given him. That's what happened to the first family who lived here."

"That's so fucked up!"

"Yeah." Errol spits on the ground. "The whole situation is a damn disgrace. And a common story for people like us, but we don't have any other choice. Anyway, I figure you staying here won't be much of a strain. It'll add to the grocery bill," he looks me over, "but not by much."

"I'll start searching for work right away," I promise. And I mean it. Even if I'm only here for a single week, I'd like to ease their burden instead of adding to it. For all I know, they might end up losing the house. My grandmother never said anything to make me think otherwise. I don't remember her talking about it. Maybe there's a reason for that. "Here," I say, remembering what I've got in my pocket. I try handing him the ten-dollar bill. He's already holding up a hand like he intends to refuse, but I insist. "Family takes care of each other," I say.

He accepts the money but doesn't pocket it yet. "We can't offer you a room of your own. We have a fold-out bed in the basement—"

"Perfect!"

Errol grunts. "I don't think you'll describe it that way once you've been down there. But it is dry. I've made sure of that. I'll ask around about potential work for you, and help you find a cheap place to stay if you decide to make Chicago your home."

"Thank you," I say. "I appreciate it. Really." My voice is strained with emotion. I feel proud to call these people family. They've clearly worked hard to give Gloria the best life possible, and their willingness to share some of that comfort with me is more than I could ever repay.

We talk a little longer before we go inside. Gloria is thrilled by the news. She gathers fresh sheets and the other things I'll need while Errol and I set up the fold-out bed. The basement is more like a cellar. The walls and floors are raw stone, the ceiling a jumble of wooden planks and pipes. They set me up in one corner next to a wooden shelf full of home-made preserves. I dread sharing a bed with spiders and other creepy crawlies, but

I won't utter a single word in complaint. Not to them and not to their daughter.

We return upstairs to the living room and talk while listening to jazz on a glowing radio the size of a toaster. The adults are clearly tired. Their bedroom is on the ground floor. Not wanting to disturb them, I return downstairs and stretch out on the bed while still dressed, adjusting to the unfamiliar surroundings while thinking about the day. Daniel in particular. He left so suddenly, almost as if he was glad to be rid of me. And we seemed to be getting along so well. Was that only the politeness of the era? The answer eludes me. I don't feel like I need to sleep yet either. When I hear the basement stairs creak, I raise my head and am happy to see Gloria gesturing for me to follow her, so I do.

— — —

The floors of the attic are wooden and strewn with old rugs. Large swaths of colorful cloth have been pinned to the angled walls that meet at a point, making the long narrow space feel like a tent, or maybe the interior of a stereotypical gypsy caravan. The entire vibe works for me. I ignore the small bed and gravitate toward the dresser where I see a portable record player next to a stack of vinyls. Listening to music downstairs while getting acquainted with my great-grandparents made me realize how much I've missed playing. My fingers practically twitch as I pick up an old James P. Johnson record.

"This isn't how I spend most Saturday nights," Gloria says from behind me.

"What do you usually do?" I ask, turning around to face her. She's wearing a pair of turquoise pajamas that make me think of the Chevy Bel Air.

"Sometimes we go to parties, when we can find them. Doesn't matter if anyone knows who we are. We'll crash any bash."

I'm going to have so much dirt on my grandma when I'm home again. I plan on teasing her mercilessly.

"When you say 'we,' you mean you and Daniel, right?"

She nods and pulls out the chair to a small writing desk. This is for me, as it turns out. She sits cross-legged on the bed. "We do everything together."

I'm not sure how much I want to challenge that statement. With anyone else, I'd ask for explicit details, but this is the woman who used to—or will eventually—give me baths with her gnarled old hands. I proceed with cautious curiosity. "You two used to be an item, huh?"

She smiles demurely. "Junior year. It didn't last long."

"How come?"

She's quiet before answering. "We decided that we make better friends, which is a shame, because he sure is a dreamboat."

I laugh. "He's a little hottie for sure."

Gloria seems confused. "That's a strange thing to say."

"You don't have that slang yet? When someone is attractive, we call them hot."

"So do we," she responds. "But you don't hear guys describe each other that way."

Oh. I know black history. I haven't studied gay rights nearly as much. I'm familiar with the Stonewall riots, but that doesn't happen until another decade from now. I'm not sure what people thought about gay people before then. I can't imagine that they were very accepting. Does that include Gloria? My grandma was incredibly supportive when I came out at fourteen. She simply hugged me and said, "That's wonderful news, sugar bean. I love you!"

Gloria still has a lot of living to do before she becomes the woman I remember. Attitudes will change drastically over the course of her lifetime. She might not be there yet, so I decide to test the waters.

"You can tell when a woman is attractive, can't you?" I ask.

"That's true."

"Guys can too. Most are just too hung up on being labeled gay to admit it."

"Gay?"

"Yeah, you know. Homosexual. Do you have that term?"

She nods while chewing her bottom lip. Even her brow is creased, so I decide to steer the conversation toward a more comfortable subject. I nod at the far end of the room, where a nook just past the stairs is cluttered with a sewing machine and garments stabbed full of pins. "How long have you been making clothes?"

"Since I was a little girl. I used to hand-sew outfits for my doll. Hey, in the future, do I have my own dressmaking shop?"

"Now I understand why I'm up here," I say with a chuckle. "You want me to play fortune teller."

"You have to tell me *something*," she says. "Anything!"

"Too risky. What if it changes the timeline?"

Gloria groans in frustration. "All I want to know is if I manage to open my own shop or not."

"Right, and let's say that you do. I tell you about it, and a few years from now when you find a potential retail space, you think 'This must be what Reggie was talking about.' You rent the place, it's the wrong location, it turns out to be a disaster, and you go broke before giving up on your dreams. But if I don't tell you anything, you might have doubts about the shop you nearly rented and wait for a better opportunity. Maybe that's where you meet your future husband, which I *really* need you to do, or I'll never exist. So if I steer you wrong now, I might be preventing my own birth."

"You worry too much," she says with a sigh. "Although I see what you mean. It's probably the same reason, when I'm older, that I never mentioned meeting you at this age."

"Holy crap! I didn't even think of that. Wow. Your older self never let on. If you don't play poker now, you should start."

"And for the record," Gloria says, getting up from the bed and moving toward me. "I brought you up here so you could write your letter. Now I'm wondering if there's any point. In the future, I'll know how and why you disappeared. I'll make sure the gate is rebuilt."

"Good point," I say after thinking it over, "but I'd still like to write the letter. I want Hannah to hear from me directly so she knows I'm okay, even if I don't make it home. And you'll need to get permission from whoever owns the land. That'll be the city, most likely, and they aren't going to do anything without a ton of signatures and outside money. Hannah can help you with that. Nothing stirs up social media like a middle-class white girl in distress. She'll probably go viral. The crowdfunding page will pull in millions."

"I understood about half of that," Gloria says, reaching past me to the desk. "This is my best stationary. Try to get it right on the first attempt."

I wasn't expecting to do this now, but that's okay. I've already thought about what I'd want to put into the letter. I explain what happened to me when I disappeared, and where I ended up, so Hannah will know. I promise to chisel her initials into the gate so she'll have proof. Then I plead with her to restore it so I can return home. The last part is the hardest. I write a message to my family and friends, in case I never make it back, telling them how much I love and miss them. I'm getting emotional and try to hide it. Gloria notices anyway, placing a square of cloth in front of me. I realize after a moment that it's for blowing my nose, which I do.

I place the letter in an envelope and write on it as much of Hannah's information as I can remember. After collecting myself, I rise and hand it to Gloria, who is flipping through a magazine on the bed.

"I'll put it in a hidden place," she tells me. When I continue to stare expectantly she adds, "If it wasn't a secret, it wouldn't be hidden!"

"Right, right. That makes sense."

"And now that I've done you a favor..." she says leadingly.

"Uh oh," I say when noticing the mischief in her eyes.

"I won't ask you about *my* future. But surely it wouldn't do any harm for you to tell me some general information."

"Like what?"

She shrugs. "Do things get better for people like us?"

"Yes," I say after hesitating. "But it's a long war with a lot of ugly battles. People still die because of the color of their skin. Scheming politicians still try to contain us to ghettos while depriving us of education, equal opportunity, and even the right to vote... But it's better than it used to be. Far from perfect, but we keep moving forward, no matter how hard others try to stop us."

I'm tempted to tell her that she'll live long enough to witness a black man take office as president, but I don't want to ruin the surprise. I still remember the way she cried when the election results came in, and how she hugged each of us gathered around the television. I also don't want her to expect that to be the end of it, especially considering the self-serving slimeball who slithered into the oval office eight years later.

"What about women's rights?"

"Way better! Nothing is perfect in the future, but in the next twenty years you'll see a lot of changes that you'll like." I try to imagine my grandmother in the flower-powered sixties and can't. Does she become a hippie? I have so many questions for her. How ironic that she wants to know the future, while I'm eager to get back to it so I can learn about her past.

"How about diseases?" Gloria presses. "Please tell me that cancer has bitten the dust."

"Still working on that one," I say.

"And other illnesses?"

I shrug. "Like what?"

"I don't know. You mentioned homosexuality. Is that an easy fix?"

It takes all of my willpower not to bristle at this. "Homosexuality isn't a disease."

Gloria seems confused. "But doctors already say that it can be avoided, if changes are made early enough."

"No it can't. There's nothing to avoid or fix. It occurs naturally. You might as well ask if there's a cure for blonde hair or brown eyes in the future."

"Those are physical traits," she counters. "Homosexuality is a psychological disorder."

I can't believe I'm having this discussion with my own grandmother! "Doctors might think that now, but I promise you, in my day it's proven to be biological. Only the truly deluded try to cure someone of it."

"You're sure?" she presses.

"Yes!"

"Oh." Her expression is pained, making me wonder if she has a secret that I was never aware of.

Then the pieces fall into place, and it's so damn obvious that I can't believe I missed it. Daniel. I almost speak his name aloud. Instead I clench my jaw and want more than ever to return home. Reading about the past can be difficult when confronted with all of humanity's stupidity, but to actually return there and witness it... I feel sorry for him. I'll try to help Daniel understand that he's not the problem before I go, but I want out of here. As soon as possible. I want return to a time when I can be annoyed by all the corporations who treat gay people like an exciting new sales demographic to exploit. That's such a small and trivial problem compared to having parents who try to cure you, or friends who think you have a psychological disorder.

"You'll give that letter to my friend?" I ask, needing a guarantee that I won't be stuck here forever.

Gloria nods, seeming confused by the change of subject.

"Good." I feel tired, emotionally more than anything. "It's been a busy couple of days. I'm going to turn in for the night."

"Okay."

I creep down two sets of stairs to the basement, strip off my clothes, and climb into bed, but sleep continues to elude me as my thoughts race. Most of them about Daniel. I revisit every interaction with him and see each from a new perspective. Then I think about his earnest eyes, the kindness in his voice, and how tragic it will be if those delicate lips are never kissed by someone that he truly loves.

Chapter 6

Sleep must have overtaken me, because the next thing I know, I'm being shaken awake.

"Get up or you'll miss breakfast!"

I open bleary eyes to find Gloria standing over me, wearing the same turquoise pajamas from the night before. Spry as can be, she races back up the stairs. I sit up and swing my legs over the edge of the bed, yawning a few times. Not wanting to put on the awkward outfit I wore the day before, I grab the clothes I arrived in and revel in their comfort after slipping on the muscle shirt and basketball shorts. Then I trudge upstairs.

I'm relieved to find the rest of the family wearing bathrobes while gathered in the kitchen. All the comforts of home. Errol is standing at the stove, moving scrambled eggs around with a spatula. Harriet is seated at the table. She nods and says good morning while Gloria darts back and forth between the refrigerator and the table to set things on it.

"Good morning everyone," I say around a yawn.

Errol looks me over and starts laughing. "Those are some real nice pajamas you've got there, Reggie."

The others laugh too, but I don't mind. If anything it sets me at ease, since it's the sort of good-natured ribbing I've come to expect from my family. "Pajamas?" I retort. "No no no. Back in Savannah, these are the *fanciest* duds that money can buy. I plan on wearing this to job interviews."

Errol chuckles appreciatively before focusing on his work again. When I offer my help, Harriet pats the table next to her and invites me to sit. "Pay attention," she says in a stage whisper. "This is how you treat a woman. I do nothing but cook and clean all week, so when Sunday rolls around, he makes sure I don't have to. He treats me like a queen."

"I'm going to barf," Gloria responds, but her eyes are sparkling.

"Is that really what people wear in Savannah?" Harriet asks, leaning back in her chair to take another look.

"You don't set trends by copying others," I respond. "I bet it'll be more popular in the future."

Gloria snorts while pouring me a cup of coffee. It's an acquired taste I've only recently begun to appreciate, so I'm glad when she leaves enough room in the mug for me to dilute it with milk.

"We should probably go shopping today," she says when taking a seat across from me. "You've now seen all the clothes that Reggie owns."

"I lost everything I had with me on the way up here," I explain.

"What happened?" Harriet asks, sounding concerned.

"I dozed off in a park, woke up in the rain, and ran for cover without my pack. When I went back later, someone had helped themselves to it."

"You're welcome to borrow some of my clothes," Errol says as he begins shoveling egg onto everyone's plates. "I can rip the sleeve off one of my shirts. That should about cover you from head to toe."

He's exaggerating, but not by much. I bet me and Daniel could both fit inside the coveralls he was wearing yesterday. It's a thought I wouldn't mind dwelling on longer.

"Can I borrow the car?" Gloria asks eagerly. "I wanted to make the rounds anyway."

"Don't you have enough clothes to experiment on upstairs?" her father chastises.

"Sure, but you've gotta grab those bargains before someone else does."

"I wouldn't mind staying home, Errol," Harriet says with a slight purr in her voice. "We can get cozy."

Gloria's eyes go wide and she starts shoving food into her mouth with desperate speed, like it will help her escape the conversation sooner. I focus on breakfast too, cutting open a steaming biscuit to spread butter and jam on it. I always like switching back and forth between sweet and savory.

"Did you ask Reggie if he wants to go to church?" Harriet

says to her daughter. "He might prefer that over shopping."

"It's okay," I say quickly. "My mom isn't very religious. She's more spiritual, if that makes sense."

"It certainly does," Harriet replies. "God sees how hard we work all week. When he said that Sunday was supposed to be a day of rest, I don't think he meant we should wake up just as early and rush out of the house like we always do."

"People after my own heart," I say appreciatively.

"Although we do have our own sort of church," Errol says with a smirk I find hard to interpret. "We can bring you with us next weekend."

"That's right!" Harriet says. "I think you'll like it there."

I look to Gloria for an explanation, but she shrugs with a subtle smile, clearly in on the conspiracy. I'll have to wait and see what they mean, if I'm still around then. If not, I'll ask her about it when we reunite in the future.

After breakfast, we take turns getting ready. I don't see any choice but to put on the clothes Daniel loaned me, including the socks, which I'm not feeling great about. Summer is still ramping up, but it's hot enough during the day that I've been sweating. Air conditioning doesn't seem to be common yet. Another day of running around in the heat, and I'm going to stink to high heaven. I've been helping myself to other people's deodorant after showering, and I've gotten creative about the way I brush my teeth. The less said about that the better. In other words, I miss my creature comforts.

I'm not sure there's a solution to my plight, as I tell Gloria while we're standing in the driveway next to a Ford Mainline. I've never heard of that model, but I dig the white-rimmed tires which stand out against the black body and its silver trim. While not nearly as stunning as the Bel Air, it has similar curves. I was never much into cars before, but I'll have a higher appreciation for the classics once I've returned home. *After* I've changed into fresh clothes. That'll be my number one priority.

"As much as I'd love some new threads," I tell her, "I don't have any money."

Gloria shrugs. "I figured."

"And I don't like the idea of anyone spending their money on me when I won't be around much longer."

"Don't be so stubborn," Gloria says, pinching my cheek. "Let your nice old granny buy you a present." She cackles and moves around to the driver-side door. "Besides, when you see the kind of places I shop, you won't be thanking me. Come on."

Soon we're cruising along the road with the windows down and the radio blaring. This is comfortable territory for me. I lean back in the seat, close my eyes against the wind, and tap my foot along with a jaunty Frank Sinatra tune I'm not familiar with. By the time we've rolled into town, a slower song comes on the radio, the DJ announcing it as "The Great Pretender" by The Platters. The lyrics make me think of Daniel again, and what it must mean to be closeted in this era. He can't go online to find out more about his sexual orientation, or fire up an app to meet someone like himself. I don't care if it changes history or creates an alternate timeline. I'm not leaving without making sure he knows that there's nothing wrong with him.

"Think we'll connect with Daniel today?" I ask when the song ends.

"Sure thing," Gloria replies. "He's at church with his family but we can meet up later."

Her forehead crinkles again, like there's some big concern that she needs to share with me. I think I get it. She might not have the right idea about what makes a person queer, but she stuck by her friend regardless, and in the future, she's always been good to me and my boyfriends. "I like him," I say, wanting to reassure her.

She looks relieved. "Me too."

"Even if he is kind of a nerd," I add.

"He's square all right," Gloria says with a laugh. "Why do you think he dresses like his dad?"

"You mean this isn't even in style?" I ask, yanking at the dopey shirt I'm wearing.

"Not for the cool kids," she answers. "We'll get you gussied up, don't worry."

She pulls into a church parking lot, which confuses me, because I thought that's what we wanted to avoid. The destination makes more sense when she leads me down the stairs of a side entrance to a basement filled with used clothing and housewares. A thrift store! One run as a charity, I realize as we begin to browse, which I feel guilty about until I remember that I literally don't have a penny to my name. I'm exactly the sort of person these stores are meant for. All of the fashions look out-of-date to me, so I choose what suits me and rely on Gloria to steer me away from anything that will make people think I'm a drip, as she puts it.

We visit two more churches, and by the end of our shopping spree I have button-up shirts both long- and short-sleeved, a cardigan jacket in black with grey stripes, more of the long shorts that I like despite the ultra-high waist, and a pair of classy slacks that Gloria promises to alter to fit me. We're walking down Main Street when I notice something odd.

"Why are so many shops closed?"

She looks at me like I'm not making sense. "Because of the Blue Laws. It's Sunday, remember? Stores aren't allowed to stay open. You're lucky we're in the suburbs. People downtown don't have as many options. *Everything* is closed there."

"And these laws prevent people from—"

"Having fun," Gloria says. "It's a religious thing. God hates grocery stores, apparently. Maybe that's where Eve really got the apple from."

"But we just went shopping at three different churches."

"Oh no no, it's okay when *they* do it." She rolls her eyes. "It was worse where we used to live. Here they let important businesses stay open, like the drugstore, so folks can still buy medicine or whatever."

That's our next destination. Woolworths is the only open store we see for the next few blocks. Thank goodness they sell more than just drugs. I wonder if that's how modern pharmacies became miniature supermarkets. They don't offer much in the way of clothes, but we pick up socks and tighty-whities—the sort of underwear I haven't worn since I was twelve. We also buy a toothbrush and other hygiene basics.

We've worked up an appetite by then, so we grab a quick sandwich from the lunch counter. Without incident, I'm happy to report, although I'll never get used to people smoking indoors, especially where food is involved. How did anyone put up with it?

"You've spent almost forty dollars on me," I say as we leave.

"Only so I don't have to look at you in those baggy clothes anymore."

"I'm still getting used to the price differences here. How much do you earn?"

"I do good work and Mrs. Henderson knows it, so I get a dollar twenty-five an hour.

"Which means you've blown a week's wages on me."

"You can pay me back when you get a paper route." My blank expression prompts her to add, "You know, the boys who ride around on bikes and deliver the newspaper?"

"Oh. I really will pay you back. I don't feel right about this."

"It's not so bad," Gloria says. "Mrs. Henderson lets me display the dresses I make in the shop window. Did you notice that yesterday?"

"I didn't."

"You'll see as we're passing by," she says while leading us to the car. "I sell them for fifteen apiece, sometimes more. There are a lot of rich folks around here."

"You're really serious about that dream, huh?"

"Yep! Although I feel like you would know that already if I was ever successful at it."

"You might have been," I admit sheepishly. "You know how it is with grandparents. They make you the center of attention. There are a lot of questions I never thought to ask. And to be fair, you weren't very chatty about your past. Even when I asked about Daniel. Maybe you did that on purpose so I couldn't give away too much while I'm here."

"My future self is so clever," Gloria says, winking over the top of the car before we get in.

"I at least want to know what your plans are," I tell her. "Is there some sort of school you're going to next?"

"No," she says firmly. "I plan on staying right where I am until the house is paid off."

"Errol mentioned the shady mortgage. That should be illegal. I think it is in my day. You can't always live with your parents though."

"True, but what am I going to do if they lose the house? They won't have a thing. And when are they supposed to retire? With the interest adding up, they're looking at another twenty years before the deed is in their name. They'll be in their sixties by then."

I never had to worry about my parents' finances when growing up. I'm embarrassed to admit that I don't even know if our house is paid off. Ten minutes later and we're parked in front of it. In the light of day, all I can see are the differences: The missing sun porch, the absent extension where my grandmother lives, the shutters painted blue instead of green… Home, just not quite yet.

Gloria must be having similar thoughts. "You're telling me this is where I end up living?"

"Uh… No. Forget I ever said that."

"I must marry a wealthy man. Or your mother does. What's her name?"

"Beyonce," I reply. "That was a joke! Please don't name her that. I'll never live it down."

Gloria tilts her head. "I think it's a nice name. Maybe I'll save it for one of her siblings. Does she have a sister? Or a brother?"

"I'm not telling you how many kids you're going to have. But I *am* your favorite grandson. Never forget that."

When we go to the front door, Mrs. Parker seems happy to see us. She hugs Gloria and tells me how nice I look. I changed clothes in the Woolworths restroom before we ate. I'm wearing a plain white button-up shirt and solid black shorts. No stripes, no checks, and no patterns that make me think of bowling alleys. I'm not sure what her son will think of my outfit, or how he'll feel about seeing me again. Mrs. Parker calls for him from the entryway.

Daniel appears at the top of the stairs, his eyes passing over everyone until they reach me. There they remain. He almost seems relieved to see me, the smile he flashes apologetic. Then he remembers his mother is present and tears his gaze away. That's fine. He just told me everything I need to know.

"Guess who's got the car?" Gloria singsongs when we're left alone. "C'mon, sweet stuff. Let's go for a ride!"

"You look sharp," Daniel says to me as we cross the front lawn.

"Thanks. I still have your old clothes. I'll wash them before giving them back."

"No! That's okay."

Gloria is skipping across the grass ahead of us and is almost out of earshot, so in a lower voice I murmur, "Are you sure? They probably smell like me."

His face grows a little red, his response strained. "Mom will launder them. It's no problem. Really."

Not only do I have his number. I've caught his eye. And if I'm honest, he caught mine long ago. That's good. I hope it'll make it easier to get through to him. When the time is right.

"Do you guys call shotgun?" I ask.

Daniel's confusion is short-lived. "You mean riding shotgun?"

"Yeah."

He grins and breaks into a run, shouting a single word over his shoulder. "Dibs!"

I lose the race, despite my two-hundred-dollar shoes. I have a nice view from the backseat anyway. Gloria is talking excitedly to Daniel as she begins driving, telling him how it went with her parents last night, and what we got up to today. Their dynamic is similar to what Hannah and I have together. It's clear that they love each other.

"You're the best," Daniel says to her after she tells him about my new wardrobe. He glances back at me with shining eyes. "Maybe I *should* let you pick out my clothes."

"I keep tellin' ya!" she responds.

"Hold up," I say in my defense. "I chose most of it myself."

"He wanted to buy a letterman sweater," Hannah says in disapproving tones.

"It had a big 'R' on it. My name is Reggie. I thought it would be cool."

They both laugh. I don't get why. Nor do I mind because I adore Daniel's grin.

"Where are we going?" I ask when noticing familiar landmarks outside the window.

"To the gate," Gloria replies. "We have work to do."

"You're leaving?" Daniel asks me, the joyous expression disappearing.

"I doubt that," Gloria says. "We only need to make some preparations. Besides, I'm eager to check it out again, now that we know what the gate can do."

Half a dozen cars are in the parking lot when we get to Churchill Woods. We can hear children playing after we pull into a spot and get out. Gloria walks around to the back of the Ford and pops the trunk. I'm surprised to see a hammer and chisel inside.

"I didn't tell you about that," I say with a glare. "You read the letter!"

"You didn't say not to," Gloria replies shamelessly.

"I shouldn't have to. It wasn't addressed to you."

"I'm just making sure my grandson keeps his promises." She shoves the tools into my arms and sticks out her tongue. "Let's go. I'm excited to try the gate. I'm hoping I'll end up in the Wild West."

"What's the chisel for?" Daniel asks as we progress down the path.

"I need to leave a message for my friend." I explain the plan during the rest of the walk, noticing how increasingly sullen he becomes.

"There she is," Gloria says as we approach the gate. "If I end up in the past, tell my parents to look for an old savings account in their name. They'll never need to worry about money again."

And with that, she takes off running toward the gate. Daniel gasps and I hold my breath as she passes beneath it, but like all the times I did the same thing when growing up, nothing happens. I almost question my sanity until I walk closer and feel the strange hum building within me.

"You've written the letter now," Daniel says. "Are you sure that won't be enough?"

"No," I admit.

"You've gotta try," Gloria says, returning to take my hand.

She pulls me toward the gate. I look back over my shoulder at Daniel's worried expression, not ready to leave him yet. Gloria is laughing like it's a game. I don't resist her much. That I ended up here seems so impossible. If there's any chance for me to return, no matter how small…

My entire body vibrates as we pass beneath the stone arch, but the world around me doesn't change. Gloria groans in disappointment when I fail to vanish. Then she lets go of me and grabs Daniel's hand instead, subjecting him to the same treatment. It's easier to relax and see it as harmless fun as she pulls him through the gate and pretends to cast a spell while speaking gibberish. Amusing as this is, it does make me wonder why the gate activated when it did. Because it fell apart? Did that spark some long-dormant power?

Gloria notices me standing there and staring. "Better get to work," she says, "before any ankle-biters show up to cramp our style."

"You mean rats?" I ask, glancing around in concern.

"No," she replies with a snort. "I mean children. You still have those in the future, don't you?"

I roll my eyes and walk around the gate, scanning the letters and numbers that have already been chiseled into its surface while searching for an appropriate spot. I linger on a square outline with the digits "65" hammered into the center, confused that anyone from nineteen-sixty-five could have left such a mark in the fifties. Then I realize it's probably from a century before. I choose the support pillar on the right, since it's the sturdiest in the future, and kneel in front of the side that people will see when approaching. I place my hand on the stone before beginning my work and feel it humming beneath my palm.

"Come check this out," I say to Gloria, explaining the sensation I get when nearing or interacting with the gate. She places her hand over mine before sliding it beneath to touch the stone. I watch her closely for any reaction... and she looks surprised!

"I have to pee," she says when pulling away.

"That's it?"

"Hey, it's serious business. I should have used the restrooms by the park entrance. Be right back."

I shake my head as I watch her leave. Then I look at Daniel, realizing that we're alone. "Want to try again?" I ask, pressing my palm against the stone.

He licks his lips nervously. Then he nods and moves toward me.

I stand as he nears. "The vibration is the most intense when I'm directly beneath the gate." I walk there and extend my arms, placing a hand flat against each column. "Especially in my chest. Put your hand there again."

He swallows and touches the back of his fingers to my sternum.

"Nothing?" I ask. When he shakes his head, I say, "Maybe it would help if you were touching my skin. Unbutton my shirt."

He hesitates, and I'm tempted to do it for him, but I know he's going to remember this moment. I wait him out. With trembling hands, he finally undoes the first button. And then another. He tries to use the back of his fingers again, but I shake my head.

"All the way. Full contact."

He searches my eyes. I nod encouragingly. He finally complies. I keep telling myself that I'm doing this for him, but there's a lot of comfort in being this close to another guy again. I'm tempted to pull him close and take everything I need. I know that would be too much for him, so instead I inhale deeply and focus on the warmth of his hand. My chest rises beneath it as I take another breath. When I do this a third time, he does the same, exhaling on the same beat as me. We're in unison.

I let my arms drop and wrap my fingers around the hand on my chest, gripping it gently. "What you feel inside… There's nothing wrong with it. You don't have a disease or a disorder. It's natural, I promise."

He stares into my eyes with a mad sort of hope. Then we hear a shriek and he pulls his hand away. A second later the sound is followed by a burbling giggle. Kids are playing somewhere nearby. We both realize this at the same time and laugh as the tension dissipates. I don't try to recapture the mood. Gloria will be back soon anyway. But I do want to continue this someplace where we won't be interrupted.

"Can we talk tonight?" I ask him. "Just me and you."

"In person, right?" he asks, looking fearful that I'll say otherwise.

"Yeah," I answer with a chuckle. "Definitely in person. When Gloria is ready to go home, tell her you'll give me a ride later on. Can you think of an excuse?"

"I'll try."

"Good." I watch him while buttoning up my shirt, smiling at the way he has his bottom lip trapped beneath a front tooth. Then I let him off the hook and move away to begin my work. I hunker down near the base of the pillar, use dirt to mark a rough outline of what I want to write, and start hammering. The shop class I took in junior high didn't prepare me for this. Daniel stays close to me, offering advice on how I should chisel thin lines first and work on widening them out from there. Once I've got the hang of it, he walks around the gate while examining the details, and when Gloria returns, he stands farther away with her, probably so they can still converse over the noise I'm making. A group of kids do interrupt us, but their attention spans send them darting off in another direction soon enough.

After my bones have been thoroughly jarred, I get up and

take a step back to consider my work. At the base of the pillar are now two large capital letters, HW, for Hannah Watts. There's no way she can miss it. That's what troubles me.

"I don't remember seeing this before," I tell the others as they rejoin me. "It's her initials. We would have noticed."

"Are you sure?" Gloria asks. "Maybe I filled it in with clay or something, so you wouldn't know what was going to happen."

"Why bother? We would have been excited to see her initials as kids but wouldn't have inferred anything as dramatic as time travel."

"Moss could have grown over it," Daniel suggests.

Or maybe dirt and spray paint had helped to obscure the letters. Even then… "I remember reading everything when we were little. Carefully. You know how obscene graffiti can be. Kids live for that."

Daniel nods. "There's some writing in Latin on this side that I always meant to translate."

"You're hopeless," Gloria tells him while shaking her head.

"Show me," I say, not remembering what he's referring to. He does, and I laugh, because I always thought it was random nonsense. "Omnia out nut-squash," I say, attempting to read the words aloud. "Any idea what that means?"

They both shrug.

"How old is this thing? People never spoke Latin in the United States."

"Maybe the stones were shipped over from Rome," Daniel suggests.

"There's a date over here," I say, leading them to where I saw the number earlier. "The gate must be from eighteen-sixty-five at least. Or maybe seventeen-sixty-five. It can't be from before that, since the Native Americans wouldn't have written numbers like these. Unless the stones were shipped from somewhere else as Daniel was saying."

"There's no apostrophe," Gloria points out. "Maybe it literally means the year sixty-five."

Daniel is muttering under his breath while counting on his fingers. Then he looks up sharply. "That's how far Reggie travelled back in time."

A shiver runs down my spine. "What?"

"Sixty-five years exactly," Daniel confirms.

That can't be a coincidence. I also don't know what it means.

"We should come back later with a pencil and paper to write everything down," Daniel says. "Even if it doesn't seem significant."

He's looking at me meaningfully, and it finally clicks that this is our excuse. "Good idea," I say.

"Don't you want to try the gate again?" Gloria asks. "Now that your friend has her proof, maybe she's able to raise enough of a stink that people volunteer to rebuild the gate. You never know."

It's worth a shot. And yet my feet refuse to move.

"Reggie?" she presses.

My eyes dart to Daniel long enough to see the unhappiness on his face. Then I shake my head. "I'll try again, but first I want to have a better idea of what we're dealing with. Let's get the Latin translated and everything else written down first. I don't want to walk through the gate and end up another sixty-five years in the past. When would that be?"

"The eighteen-nineties," Daniel answers.

"No thanks." The fifties are strange enough. I don't want to ride around in a stagecoach while trying to find cheap leather chaps with my great-great-*great*-grandmother.

I suggest we explore the park together, in case there is some other clue to help us, or any sign of what happened to my backpack and the man who stole it. We search but don't find anything. Gloria suggests we escape the afternoon heat by seeing a matinee. We drive downtown to the Glen Art Theater, which was a staple of my youth. The interior is different from what I remember, no longer divided into four separate screens. Our only option is *The Deadly Mantis*, which is basically a Godzilla rip-off but with a giant bug instead of a lizard. I'm braced for the worst special effects imaginable. Considering that they didn't have computers to rely on, the giant praying mantis puppet is remarkably impressive. The movie itself is subpar but made more fun by the people in the cinema jeering at the screen. I can't help noticing that Daniel chose to sit on the other side of Gloria, away from me. Did he have a change of heart? I'm still not sure afterwards when we go to White Castle for sliders. I wouldn't mind a little covert flirtation as reassurance. It isn't until we drive to his house that I finally get a signal from him.

"That was a fun day," Gloria says as we pull up, "but I have some alterations to finish before tomorrow. I *think* it should be safe to go home now."

"Your parents again?" Daniel asks.

"They sure love each other," Gloria replies, sounding exasperated. "Wanna meet up after work tomorrow?"

"That would be fun." Daniel shifts in the front seat so he can see me better. "Hey, Reggie. Why don't we go back to the gate with some paper? I want to make a record of everything written on it, in case that helps us learn more."

"You mean now?" I ask innocently. "That could work. If you give me a ride back to Gloria's house afterwards."

"What?" she says. "I can stay out longer."

Crap.

"Are you sure?" Daniel asks. "I was thinking of doing a charcoal rubbing. Remember when we went to the graveyard so I could get my merit badge? It'll be just as fun!"

"On second thought," Gloria says, "I also have a few letters to write. Promise you won't go through the gate, Reggie. I want to be there when you do."

"I'm staying away from it until we know more," I assure her.

After a round of hugs, she says goodbye, and we wave as she drives down the street. Then we face each other, blissfully alone.

"Let's go inside," Daniel suggests. "I'll grab some paper and—"

"We're not really going back to the gate, are we?" I try a lopsided smile. "I'd rather focus on each other."

"Oh." The sun is a crimson ball on the horizon. Maybe that's what makes his face appear a little pink, but I don't think so. "Should I ask to borrow the car?"

"Nah." I turn toward the park across the street. The lake is surrounded by trees, which will help shield us from the surrounding houses, and I know a spot that is especially private. "Let's go for a walk together."

He agrees. We're both silent until we've put distance between us and the house. Instead of asking him about his experiences, I decide to start by sharing some of my own.

"My band class took a school trip in middle school," I say. "Out of state, which was a big deal. We went to see the New York Philharmonic Orchestra, and while that was great... there was this guy. The hotel we were staying in had students from all over the country who had come for similar reasons. The first time I saw him, he was in the lobby and laying out his Pokémon cards. Those are sort of like baseball cards but with fantasy creatures instead of athletes. I was deep into collecting them at the time, even though most people my age were starting to notice girls. I hadn't though."

I glance over at Daniel, and he's nodding, like he knows what I mean. "So there was this adorable guy from the West Coast with a surfer vibe, laying out the same cards that I loved. I struck up a conversation with him, and he showed off his collection, but they didn't hold my attention. Not like he did. I could barely take my eyes off him. At first I told myself that I admired how he looked, as if I wanted to be more like him. What I really wanted was to know absolutely everything about him, including weird stuff like how his skin felt, or what his hair smelled like." I attempt to laugh away my embarrassment. "We only got to see each other before and after school-organized events, which is a shame, because we could have been good friends. Even if I wasn't attracted to him. He lived too far away though. Three days together. That's all we had. It tore me apart when we had to say goodbye. I was thirteen years old, had never been in a relationship, and somehow managed to get my heart broken anyway. That's when I realized who I am and what I want."

Daniel is staring at the path we're walking along, his brow furrowed. It's hard to tell what his thoughts are, so I press on.

"I wasn't able to accept the truth right away. I let myself miss him while trying to deny the reason why. I wanted to be like everyone else because that seemed easier. Safer. But it was too late. There were other guys at my school who soon caught my eye. And there were books and movies about gay men falling in love that I devoured in secrecy. That helped. The explicit stuff not so much, despite being hot. It was the emotional stories that resonated with me, since they matched what I was feeling inside. I saw what I could have with another man, and it gave me the courage to come out, first to myself and later to others."

"You didn't try to cure yourself?" Daniel asks incredulously, speaking up at last.

"People don't do that in the future," I respond after a moment's hesitation. "Only quacks believe it's possible."

Daniel sounds offended when responding. "My dad knows what he's talking about."

"I have no doubt that he's educated himself the best he can on the subject," I say diplomatically, "but new technologies allow for more comprehensive studies, and while there are still a lot of questions, the overwhelming majority of his peers in the future agree that there's nothing wrong with being gay."

I can tell this confuses him, so I try to clarify.

"That's the term most people use. Homosexual sounds too… I dunno. Clinical. Gay is a better fit, because we're a happy bunch of freaks, despite all the crap we've had to put up with over the decades. Public opinion shifts. It's a narrow majority, but most people are cool with it."

"With you being a homosexual?" he asks, seeming shocked.

"Yeah. Including my grandmother."

"Gloria knows?"

"She will. But she doesn't yet."

"Did she tell you about—" His jaw snaps shut.

"No. She didn't give anything anyway. I figured it out by reading between the lines. I'd rather hear you tell your story. If you're willing to talk about it."

He thinks in silence before nodding. I motion for Daniel to follow me and lead him to my favorite spot. I'm relieved to see that everything is just as I remember. We're on the far side of the lake now, where an alcove of trees shields a small circle of land from view. Water laps gently against the shore, a few fireflies drifting over the surface as frogs croak out a soothing rhythm. A bench is nestled against the trees, facing all of this. Being here always soothed me, no matter how upset I was when arriving. I'm hoping it'll do the same for Daniel. As we sit, I turn toward him on the bench, one leg pinned beneath me, so I can watch him as he speaks. Stars are beginning to twinkle in a sky that is fading from magenta to purple. I hope the dwindling light will last, because he sure is cute.

"Have you ever seen *Rebel Without a Cause*?" Daniel asks. He looks disappointed when I shake my head, but he presses on anyway. "Sal Mineo's character, Plato, the way he looks at James Dean, the little excuses he makes to touch him… It was like seeing myself on the big screen, but a better version who wasn't trying to smother everything he felt inside. I wanted to be like him. I wanted my own Jim Stark. And I almost got my wish. Everyone started dressing like James Dean after that movie came out, but there was this guy at my school who was always an outsider. He had a leather jacket, greased-back hair, and these jeans that were—" He swallows before continuing. "—*really* tight. We were never in the same class. I'd notice him in the hall on occasion, but after seeing the movie, I became obsessed. Sometimes I'd follow him to his next class. I didn't have a plan. I just wanted us to be close. In the same way that Plato wanted to be around Jim Stark. So I kept going back every day."

When I told my story, it brought back the raw emotion of a new crush, which always makes me feel high. Daniel sounds sad. His expression is glum too, especially when I ask, "Did you ever talk to him?"

Daniel's knuckles are white as he grips the seat of the bench. "Almost. I saw him in the school cafeteria once, which was unusual. I told my friends my stomach hurt and that I was going to see the nurse, when really, I just wanted to sit somewhere close-by so I could watch him. After a while, he noticed me looking. I froze, unsure what to do, and then he..." Daniel's chin starts to tremble. "He smiled at me. And it felt really nice."

He turns his face away to wipe at his eyes.

I give him a moment before asking, "What happened?"

Daniel takes a deep breath. "I smiled back. Some friends of his came up to him then, so he got distracted, but I held that smile in my mind. I felt so happy. I know how dumb that must sound."

"It doesn't," I assure him. "I totally get it."

Daniel sighs before continuing. "That same day, they played a film in sociology class, warning us not to hitchhike or get into cars with strangers because homosexuals were out preying on young boys. The same day! It felt like a sign from God to stop me from going down that path. When the narrator explained that homosexuality is a mental illness—"

"Daniel," I say, refusing to speak again until his vulnerable eyes meet mine. "What if the guy showing up in the cafeteria was a sign from God? Maybe he wanted you and him to be together."

"I was sure it was the opposite," Daniel says, shaking his head. "Like I was being given one last chance before I went too far. So I talked to my dad about it. I told him what I was struggling with and asked for help. He said it wasn't too late if we made some changes. I wasn't allowed to have guy friends spend the night anymore, in case I felt tempted. That was the pits on camping trips with my Boy Scout troop. Usually you share a tent with someone else and it's fun. You can stay up, talk, goof around... I mean, it's not like I have those same urges with *every* guy I see. Just a few. But my dad insisted. He told my Scout leader it was for medical reasons. This got around, and soon everyone was saying that I wet the bed at night. It reached a point where I invited the other scouts to check my sleeping bag in the morning. Some of them took me up on it. They didn't find anything, of course, but it was still humiliating. I was sixteen years old by then!"

"That's horrible," I say, wincing in sympathy.

"Yeah. Eventually I decided to stop hanging out with guys at all, figuring it was easier that way."

"Was it though?"

He shakes his head. "I lost friends. I couldn't explain why I wouldn't sleep over or go swimming. I guess they thought I didn't like them. If it wasn't for Gloria, I never would have gotten through high school."

"Just to summarize," I say. "So far, all your dad's advice has done is make you miserable. Right? Have the urges gone away? Or the fantasies?"

"No," Daniel says, his voice hoarse. "But what am I supposed to do?"

The question isn't rhetorical. He's searching my face, waiting for an answer. I can't remind him of Olympic medal-winning athletes who are out, or openly gay politicians, or even queer actors and musicians he can look up to as role models. He hasn't seen any of that and won't for decades. I also can't urge him to come out in an era when he might be beaten to death or subjected to inhumane procedures in a mental hospital.

"Be smart about it," I answer. "Live the life that makes you happiest while being cautious."

He shakes his head, like he's still uncertain.

"Does this feel wrong to you?" I ask, placing my hand over his. "When you touch me, does it feel dirty or sinful? Because for me, it's the only thing that feels right. If denying who you are makes you miserable, maybe you should start acting on your feelings instead."

My heart nearly breaks when he pulls his hand away. I almost grab him when he rises up, like he intends to leave. He doesn't stand fully though. He straightens, glances around while on high alert, and then sinks back down on the bench, his attention fully on me. His chest is rising and falling, his pale-green eyes open wide, like he's trying to decide if he should jump off a cliff or not. I think I know what he wants. I begin to reach a hand toward his cheek. It's all the invitation he needs. Daniel leans toward me. I slide my hand around to the back of his neck, but I don't pull him in. This needs to be his decision... but I sure as hell hope he makes the right one, because I really *really* want to kiss the boy.

"Reggie?" he asks.

"If I saw you looking at me from across a cafeteria," I tell him, "I'd smile too."

His chin begins to tremble again, but this time, he looks happy. Daniel closes his eyes and presses his lips against mine. I breathe in as he does so, having dreamt of this moment long before we ever met. Then I lean my forehead against his and say, "This is good. It's who we are."

Tears streak down his cheeks. I wipe one away with a thumb and release him, unsure where he's at emotionally. He grabs my hand to stop me from moving it away completely. After going rigid and looking around like a prairie dog searching for predators, he relaxes and intertwines his fingers with mine.

"This is crazy," he whispers.

"Which only makes it more exciting," I reply. "Forbidden love is the best kind. If it wasn't, people wouldn't still be talking about Romeo and Juliet. They would've been just another young couple who got hitched and had babies. What a bore."

"Is that what we're going to be?" he asks. "Another Romeo and Juliet?"

"With a happier ending, I hope." My stomach sinks when I think about returning to my own time. Maybe it's wrong of me to lead Daniel on like this, when I know I can't stick around, but I want him to have a positive experience with another guy — something he can cling to when doubt sets in late at night or when people try to change who he is.

"I don't want you to leave," Daniel says, perhaps having similar thoughts.

"I won't," I tell him. "Not yet."

"Good. Can we kiss again?"

I laugh. I can't help it, especially when I agree and he does another prairie dog search of our surroundings. When our lips touch, all I can think about is how good it would be to get him alone. I don't want to rush anything though, or play games with his heart, so I'll lead by example and be cautious. Although I do have something more important to teach him. Before I go home to my own time, I'll make sure he knows how beautiful love between two men can be.

— — —

"Being gay isn't a mental disorder." I'm stretched out on the front seat of the Bel Air as Daniel drives me home. My back is against the interior door, and I've slipped off my shoes so I can press my feet against his legs. I want to reinforce how good that sort of contact can feel. And I want to build him up with lessons I learned when coming to grips with my identity. "Biologists have documented homosexual behavior in animals, and I don't mean when a dog is so horny that he'll hump everything in sight. There's more to this than sex. It's emotional. They've seen that in animals too. Not only does same-sex courtship exist, but they'll also form families and even adopt."

"Get outta here!" Daniel says with an incredulous expression.

"I mean it. Such things might not get reported now, due to current attitudes, but in my day, gay penguins make headlines."

Daniel laughs, and I'm happy to join him, but I also want to make sure he understands the point.

"It's not limited to mammals. Bugs, fish, reptiles, birds... You name it. That's important. Nobody can claim that salmon turn gay because their fathers spent too much time at the bar, or because their mothers let them play dress-up in women's clothing. This is part of nature, not nurture."

"Gay fish?" Daniel repeats, looking concerned.

"Yup. It's enough to make a guy give up seafood. Almost."

He laughs again, and I've already decided that it'll never be enough. I want to hear that happy sound on repeat. Give me an extended house mix—a twenty-minute anthem that samples his voice, his laugh, and even his sigh, which is what I hear next.

"Growing up in the future must be nice."

"Yeah, it's easier, but people are people, including us. You still want to fit in during high school, even when you're trying not to. Sort of like all those 'rebels' who decide to dress like James Dean. They're only trading one kind of conformity for another. Maybe that's what it takes to figure out who you really want to be. I sure struggled with it, even with most of the country telling me that it's okay to be gay. And I had to put up with some of the same bullshit claims. Being gay doesn't make someone a child molester. That sort of behavior isn't exclusive to us. Straight guys do it too. And women. People aren't criminals because they're straight, but there *are* straight people who are criminals. You see what I mean?"

"By straight you mean heterosexual?"

"Exactly. Being one doesn't automatically make you the other. That's all I'm saying."

I let him dwell on this as he takes a right turn into Gloria's neighborhood and parks in front of her house.

"Uh oh!" Daniel says suddenly. "We told Gloria we were going back to the gate, but we didn't. I was supposed to write down the Latin words and everything else. What do we say to her?"

I consider this while slipping on my shoes. I think it's a bad idea for him to come out, but I also know how one lie can lead to another, each like a wedge that slowly pries a friendship apart. "We'll tell her the truth: We got distracted and ended up talking."

"And the rest? If she's supportive of you in the future, she might be the same for me now."

"That's not my decision to make," I say carefully, "but until you decide, it's better to be vague or ask for a subject to remain private, rather than be dishonest with someone you care about."

Daniel stares at me in awe. "You're so wise."

This makes me chuckle. "No, I'm actually a fool who makes a ton of mistakes. But as my grandma always says—"

"Learn from it," Daniel finishes for me.

We both laugh.

"I guess Gloria hasn't changed that much over the years," I say. "You told her about going to your dad for help?" He nods, so I continue. "Then you know how trustworthy she's been with that secret. Think about it. There's no rush."

"Okay. I'll see you tomorrow?" Daniel is biting his bottom lip, one of his knees bouncing up and down. When he adjusts the rearview mirror and checks the side mirrors, I realize what he's hoping for.

I lean over and kiss him, keeping it simple but long enough for him to savor. Then I pull back, smile, and say, "Yeah. See you tomorrow."

Chapter 7

The next morning begins like the day before, except that my hosts are in a rush. Gloria shakes me awake, I sit at the kitchen table, and they scarf down breakfast while I slowly consume my own. I offer to do the dishes and clean up, intending to pull my weight until I can offer help financially. They barely have time to express their gratitude before leaving in the same car. Once the kitchen is clean and I am too, I try to figure out how to find a job. I can't simply check my phone or boot up a laptop. I'm wondering if I should make my way downtown and look in windows for "help wanted" signs when I remember what I've seen in old movies. I grab the newspaper that Errol had been reading yesterday and flip through it.

I'm soon convinced that it's the fifties equivalent to the internet. Instead of websites or social media platforms, there are sections divided by theme, the articles squeezed and cluttered from all sides by advertisements. Some things never change. Although I do find these ads more engaging, since they reflect the current zeitgeist. Food is dirt cheap, I learn, often only costing a few dimes. Rent isn't so bad either. That's encouraging. I could get my own room for eight bucks a week, or my own apartment for a mere one hundred dollars a month. Furniture and clothing prices are oddly close to what I'm familiar with. Cheaper, sure, but not by a significant amount. I don't know how much a woman's girdle costs in my day, or if anyone still wears them, but ten dollars sounds like a lot when you can buy a pound of steak for seventy-five cents. Then it clicks. The pricier items are still manufactured in the United States. They're only cheap in the future because the labor is outsourced to other countries. That seems a shame. The people of my era often treat their possessions as if they are disposable. *When's the next version coming out so I can get rid of this one?* Somewhere between now and then we got our priorities mixed up. Essentials like housing and food should be the most affordable. If people have to save up longer for the rest, it would only make them appreciate those things more.

I realize that I'm waxing philosophical rather than getting to the task at hand, but that's something else a newspaper shares with the internet—it's an obstacle course of distractions. I'm amused by the TV listings that tell people the exact time and channel they'll need to tune in to (thank goodness for streaming), and if that's not archaic enough, radio shows are included too. I glance over at the weird cabinet with a fabric-covered front that occupies the living room. Daniel's family had one too. I should ask him what his favorite radio program is. I bet he has an answer. I force myself to start flipping through the pages faster until I reach a section full of little boxes filled with even smaller snippets of text. I'm reminded of Twitter, or at least what it used to be before social media platforms all became bland copies of each other.

As I begin browsing the classifieds, I realize they are more like Craigslist. Items are listed for sale, various types of relationships are sought, and employment opportunities are there too. Except there's an unexpected twist. At the top of each column is a bar that either says "Help Wanted – Male" or "Help Wanted – Female". That seems crazy to me. The right person for the job should be whomever is the most qualified, regardless of gender, but it gets worse. I'd been hoping to find office work, since I should be able to manage just as many words per minute on a typewriter as I do a computer keyboard. Such jobs are available... but only to women. They can be a secretary, a babysitter, a nurse, a maid, and other stereotypically "feminine" jobs. When I check the male columns, they ask for welders, salesmen, factory workers, mechanics, and accountants. That last one wouldn't be so bad if I was any good with numbers.

I emulate the movies I've seen by circling the few jobs I might qualify for. Then I lean back and wonder what I'm supposed to do next. There aren't any websites or email addresses listed. Some classifieds mention physical addresses where I could apply, although I'd rather call first to find out if the job is still available and what they require. That's the problem. I can't seem to find a single phone number until I notice an ad that specifically says, *call*

Mr. Foster at Palestine 504. Another ad above it simply ends with Palestine 1408. In fact, quite a few of the listings have a strange word followed by a few digits. I grab the phone number Daniel gave me before the drive home last night. I didn't bother looking at it then. I do now, unfolding the piece of paper to discover it says Vanderbilt 8861. What the hell am I supposed to do with that?

I walk through the house until I find an old phone sitting on a table next to the living room couch. The handset is attached by a springy rubber cord to the squat base, which has a plastic wheel in the center with finger holes. Next to each hole are letters and numbers. I try dialing just the numbers, having to pull on the plastic circle so it can spin back around, but this gives me a prerecorded message asking me to hang up and try again. Next I use the letters to spell out Vanderbilt, which takes forever. I'm only halfway through when I hear a tiny voice coming from the handset. I press it to my ear.

"Daniel?" I ask.

"Wrong number," someone says in a Brooklyn accent before hanging up.

Fun! I notice that the zero has the word operator next to it and try that, knowing that I'll get a woman, since I saw listings for that job too, although not for anyone with a penis. Sure enough…

"Operator. Who can I connect you to?"

"Vanderbilt 8861," I say, like it's a secret passcode.

"One moment, please."

It worked! The phone is ringing. A woman answers, confusing me again, until I remember that people used to share a phone line with the entire family.

"Mrs. Parker?" I ask.

"Yes. Who's this?"

"It's Reggie."

"Oh! How nice. You must want to speak with Daniel."

"That's right. Is he home?"

"I believe so. Just a moment."

I listen to some rustling. Then I wait. And wait. Eventually I hear Daniel tell his mom that he wants privacy, which makes me laugh. The past was so awkward!

"Reggie?" he says at last.

"Hey. Phones are crazy. Do you really have to dial the

operator each time you want to call someone? She can't still hear us, can she?"

The line is silent for a second. "I don't think so. Why didn't you dial me directly?"

I explain what happened and he ends up laughing.

"You don't spell out the entire word," he explains. "You only dial the first two letters."

"Then what are the rest for?"

"To make it easier to remember. So for Clearwater, you would dial C and then L before whatever numbers are after the word."

"Nice and simple," I grumble.

"How is it done where you come from?"

"I would literally just tap on your name."

"Huh?"

"I'll explain later. You said you have to work today, right?"

"Yeah," he replies. "I was just about to leave."

"Any chance you can give me a ride downtown? I want to do some job hunting."

"Just a sec. I usually walk, but I can see if Mom will loan me her car."

I hear a clunk, more rustling, and muffled snippets of a distant conversation. I guess the cords on these things don't stretch very far. Eventually he returns to tell me that he'll be right over. I feel bad about that, but it's not like I can call an Uber, and I can't afford a taxi. Ah, who am I kidding? I love that he's forced to see me again so soon. I try to be responsible by calling a few of the leads to confirm they're still hiring and open to seeing me. Once that's out of the way, I rush to check myself in the mirror. I'm wearing dark-gray slacks and a pink long-sleeve dress shirt. I practice introducing myself in the melodic but overly polite tones that everyone here seems to speak in, and when I get bored with that, I work on a seductive smile, having it ready for when Daniel arrives.

As soon as he knocks, I throw open the door and let him stare in wonder a few seconds before I drag him inside for a kiss. I don't let up until he starts laughing between gasping for air. "Reggie! I have to get to work!"

"Quit your job," I say, my arms still wrapped around him. I wonder if he's noticed how hard I'm getting. I'm about to pull his hips close so there isn't any doubt when I see that he's actually considering my suggestion. I should be a better influence. "Then again, that would mean we're both broke. I really do need to find work. Thanks for picking me up."

"I don't mind at all," Daniel says as he follows me out of the house.

Instead of the Chevy Bel Air, a seafoam-green hardtop is parked in the driveway.

"What's that?" I ask.

"My Mom's car," Daniel explains. "It's a fifty-three Plymouth Cranbrook."

"Your parents should give it to you," I tell him as we get inside. "It matches your eyes."

"That's what Dad said to Mom when buying it for her."

I wince, not liking that I'm using the same lines as his father. "Did he also put his head in your mom's lap while she drove him around?"

Daniel's face flushes with color. "I don't think so."

"Perfect." I stretch out on the bench seat and plop the back of my head in his lap, staring up at him.

Daniel looks all sorts of overwhelmed. He reaches down to rub a palm over my short-cropped hair. I grab his hand to kiss it. "What time do you have to be at work?" I ask innocently.

"Oh! Right!" Daniel reclaims his hand and uses it to start the car.

I let him focus on driving until we're on the main road.

"Where do you work?" I ask him.

"McChesney and Miller."

"The old grocery store?" I ask in excitement. "I remember that place! We used to go there when I was a kid." I don't mention that they closed down. My parents were devastated. "Are you a cashier?"

"Only when the girls take lunch," Daniel says. "I bag and stock mostly. Whatever they need me for."

"Do you ever carry groceries home for a customer?" I bat my eyelashes at him, even though he's watching the road. "If I go in there and buy some gay salmon, will you help me get it home?"

"I do that for Mrs. Gretchen ever since she lost her son. She's on her own now. But yeah, sometimes when customers buy more than they expected to and need help, I'll do what I can."

He missed the point completely, but I don't care. I love how earnest he can be. "You're a good guy, Daniel Parker," I tell him. I stare up his nose while he smiles, noticing that it's just as petite and perfectly formed as the rest of his features.

"Where should I drop you off?" he asks.

"The grocery store is fine. I'll walk from there."

He hits the turn signal. "Mrs. Edwards heard that I was on my way to pick you up and said that you can ride into town with her and the others every morning."

Gloria's mother. Of course! She's at Daniel's house right now, working as their housekeeper. "I'll do that."

"Although I've been thinking about getting my own car," Daniel says hurriedly. "When I do, I'll give you a ride anywhere you want. I just have to wait until graduation. Dad won't let me buy one until then."

I bet I can guess why. "I thought you were done with high school."

"I am. The ceremony is on Saturday. Do you want to go?"

"Sure," I say, reminded that I'll be missing my own.

"Really?" He sounds excited. "You'll stay that long?"

"Of course."

I'm treated to an ant's perspective of his goofy smile.

"You should probably sit up now," he says soon after, flicking the turn signal again.

I do so and watch him pull into a long narrow parking lot with only two lanes. The red brick building at the far end resembles an old schoolhouse more than a modern mega shopping mart.

"I guess it's not the best idea to kiss you here," I say after he parks. "We'll have to wait until later. After work?"

"We're supposed to meet Gloria again. Should we make another excuse?"

"Never ditch your friends just because you're dating someone," I say, bonking him gently on the nose. "We'll hang out with her and I'll find a way of kissing you when no one's looking. It'll be fun."

He's biting his bottom lip again. That must be his tell.

"You look really nice, Reggie," Daniel says breathily. "You'll make a good impression."

"Thanks, pretty boy. Let's hope my future employer thinks so too."

"Pretty boy?" Daniel scowls at me, which only makes his face more adorable. "I'm not pretty!"

I flip down the visor in front of him to reveal the mirror. "Take a look. You're crazy pretty. I can barely stand it."

He studies his reflection, seeming concerned. "Is that some sort of future slang?"

"Nope. You're pretty. You'll just have to live with it."

We say goodbye, settling for squeezing hands on the seat where no one can see. I walk to the end of the parking lot before turning around. Sure enough, Daniel is standing by the entrance, but he hasn't gone inside yet. I laugh and wave. Then I set out to try my luck, broke as can be, but feeling like a million dollars.

— — —

"I'm sorry, but we're no longer hiring for that position."

I turn around to make sure I'm at the correct store, but there's no mistaking it. The small space is arranged like a showroom. Vacuum cleaners are displayed in the window, and an area of the floor is filled with strips of various carpet and flooring, I guess so people can try them out. I'm facing a small reception desk, the young woman behind it watching me attentively.

"Did you just hire someone?" I ask. "I called half an hour ago and you said the job was still available. Door-to-door salesman, no experience necessary."

"We aren't hiring at this time," she repeats, her face growing red, but it's not the cute sort of blush I get out of Daniel. She seems indignant. Or maybe ashamed. "I'm really sorry. Truly I am."

Behind her is an office, a glass window and door allowing the occupant to see outside to the showroom. A burly hairy-knuckled man is writing something at his desk. He glances up at me, then away again. He doesn't know why I'm here. I could be a customer instead of someone looking for work, but I'm of no interest to him either way.

"Your boss wouldn't approve?" I ask.

I think I see her nod. The gesture is so minute that it's hard to be sure.

"Thanks anyway," I say through gritted teeth.

I'm tempted to smash something on the way out, but my parents raised me better than that. I would only be reaffirming whatever negative opinion the racist fuckwad has about people like me. I manage to keep my temper in check, but I do pound the pavement with a vengeance until I've blown off enough steam. One little setback. No big deal. A courier job is next on the list. I don't have a driver's license anymore, or a car, but maybe I can borrow a bike from Daniel. The receptionist doesn't seem to have any reservations about handing me an application, which gives me hope until I sit down with it. I didn't think to memorize Gloria's address, so I put down Daniel's instead. The same with his phone number. I don't have any experience, but the ad promised that wouldn't be an issue. I write Glenbard West under education, knowing that it existed long before the fifties. That just leaves references. Dr. Parker would be ideal, if I had his permission. Or his number. My great-grandparents spring to mind too, but I also don't have their info.

I'm not confident when bringing the application back to the receptionist. "Do you mind taking a look at this and telling me if I still have a chance?"

The receptionist humors me. She has a mom vibe that I like. She doesn't read far before her forehead creases. "Glenbard West?" she asks. "You mean the high school? Glenbard Township?"

"Yeah."

"We can change that. Don't you have any references? You could get one from a teacher. A letter of recommendation would be dandy. Or even a report card. Anything to show your work ethic."

"I'll try my best," I tell her when taking the application back. "Thank you."

I feel like an idiot as I leave. I'm not going to get a nice cozy office job. Not without any sort of provable reputation. I need to aim lower. I notice a newspaper that someone abandoned on a nearby bench and grab it after sitting. Turning to the classifieds, I find a cleanup job at a bakery. I can do that! Maybe they'll let me bring day-old donuts home, a prospect that has my stomach rumbling after I've entered the location and breathe in sugary-sweet air.

"I'm here to apply for the cleaning job," I say to the white-haired woman behind the counter.

"Just a moment."

She goes into the back and returns with an older man who might be her husband. He looks me up and down before grunting. "Any experience?"

"Not in a bakery, but I'm a hard worker and—"

"References?"

"Do you know Dr. Parker? The pediatrician? He can vouch for me." I'm not sure that he will, but it's all I've got. I have tremendous respect for Errol and Harriet, but they don't have the status of a doctor.

The man looks me over again. Then he shakes his head. "Sorry."

I don't know if it's the color of my skin this time, or my complete lack of credentials. My pride is injured regardless as I go outside. I graduated at the top of my class. I had my pick of scholarships and schools. I'm a damn fine musician, a decent tutor, and while I never hung with the popular kids, most people seem to like me. None of that matters anymore. Not here. To top it all off, I'm getting hungry and didn't think to bring a sandwich for lunch. I don't have any money. I'm nothing. Less than a week ago, I felt as though the opportunities of the world were laid out before me. Now I'm unwanted and completely useless. I consider walking to the grocery store where Daniel works to see if he can feed me, but that sounds so pathetic that I head north on Main Street instead, mentally mapping a route to Churchill Woods. I'll try the gate again, and if it works, I'll be free of this mess.

I don't make it far. I can't leave without saying goodbye to Gloria and her parents. I should thank them and come up with a story that explains my sudden disappearance. As for Daniel… I hesitate on a street corner, sigh, and turn around. I'll see if the pear tree I always passed on my way to school is already there, so I won't be as hungry. Then I'll figure out what to do with myself.

— — —

The afternoon is coming to an end, and I feel even worse than before. I had the inspired idea to stop by Gloria's workplace so she could write down the addresses and phone numbers I was missing. I made sure I had the details right about the school too, since the name must have changed between now and my time. Then I chased down more job listings that promised experience wasn't necessary. A few accepted my application, but I didn't get any interviews. None of the leads seemed even remotely hopeful, leaving me feeling dejected and unwanted.

I'm standing outside the dry cleaner when Gloria joins me.

She has a bag of clothes tucked under an arm. Homework, maybe. "How'd it go?" she asks.

I tell her, venting about the vacuum salesman job in particular, figuring she won't be surprised. And she isn't.

"I had a similar issue here," Gloria says, tilting her head toward the dry cleaner. "I could tell that Mrs. Henderson wasn't keen on the idea of a black girl working for her. I sized her up before leaving and brought her a dress the next day. It fit perfectly. I stayed up half the night working on that thing."

"Why?" I ask incredulously. "Why go to all that effort to work for a racist?"

"She's not so bad," Gloria says. "You have to keep in mind that, even if they don't have a problem with black folks, they might be thinking of the customers who do. Cashier jobs are for whites. Too front of house for the likes of us. We're supposed to be in back, doing the dirty work where no one can see us. Are you telling me that changes?"

"Yeah. I'm not sure it's for the better. A lot of the undesirable jobs are given to people of color. They *expect* to see you working behind the register or sweeping up."

"People of color?" she asks before grinning. "Ooh! I like that! It sounds like a union. I want to be President Purple. How about you?"

A pale-green car pulls into the spot before us, a pair of matching eyes staring at me from over the steering wheel. "Rainbow Reggie," I say. "What about him?"

"Little Boy Blue?" she suggests.

"No, I mean is he as cool as he seems. With us." The kind of day I've had can make it seem like the world is against you. My skin color is on display for anyone to see, but racism is like a curled-up serpent hidden inside of people. You never know it's there until it strikes.

"You really need to ask?" Gloria replies, walking to meet her friend.

She hugs him, Daniel smiling at me from over her shoulder, and I find myself wishing I could be next in line. I need the comfort and reassurance, but we don't touch each other.

They soon raise the subject I've been dreading. "Let's get a bite to eat," Gloria suggests.

"I'm fine," I say. My stomach isn't as humble. It growls.

Loudly. I had a few pears for lunch, but they were still hard and not very sweet.

"That lion in your belly disagrees," Gloria chastises. "We better take care of it before it starts gnawing." She turns to her friend. "Hey, I sold a blouse today! Remember the one with the tear that your mom was going to throw away?"

Damn... She's good. Gloria is making sure I know that she has extra money, so I don't feel guilty. I suppose my grandma has paid for my food plenty of times before. I never questioned it then. That's simply what family does. I feel better when we return to the same diner where we ate before, sliding into the booth next to Daniel, so that we're closer. Gloria doesn't seem to think anything of it. I wait until people stop looking in our direction. Once we've become part of the scenery and our order has been placed, I reach for Daniel's hand under the table. I only mean to hold it, but I end up gripping it instead, like he's my only anchor in a storm-ravaged sea. In other words, I need him more than I realized.

— — —

Being around Daniel makes me feel good, but the day continues to be frustrating. We don't find any time to be alone. Even when he drives me home, Gloria is with us. When we say goodbye, it's devoid of emotional intimacy or physical contact. I can't send Daniel cute texts during the evening, or secretly video call him from beneath the sheets. When he's gone, he's gone. Unless I want to sit in the living room and have a very public conversation. Gloria has a phone in her room, but I don't see that being much more private, nor can I think of a way of explaining why I'd need to talk to Daniel alone.

Everyone is worn out from the day, so after watching TV together, we each retire to our rooms. Although it isn't long before I hear the basement steps. I expect to see Gloria coming down them, but when a creak sounds more like a groan, I realize that it's Errol.

"How are you settling in down here?" he asks.

"Fine. It's nice and cool."

"That it is," he says, surveying the room. "We could move some of those boxes to make more space for you."

"That's okay. I wouldn't have anything to put there."

He turns around to face me, expression grim. "Gloria told

me what happened this morning. Fitzhugh's Home Appliance?"

"Yeah. That's the place."

"Harriet got enough lip from him once that she decided to buy elsewhere. I'm real sorry you had to experience that. You probably hoped you left such things behind."

"To be honest, I'd be willing to put up with just about anything if it meant finding work." I hate feeling like I'm a burden. Especially when the rest of my family is working hard each day. My parents never let me and my brothers lounge around for very long. We were expected to contribute. "Speaking of which, I don't suppose I can use you as a reference?"

He nods once, but not in answer to my question. "Is that the newspaper you were using?"

"Yeah."

"Uh huh. Come upstairs with me real quick."

I follow him back to the living room, which is unoccupied and quiet. He picks up a paper from the side table and hands it to me. *The Chicago Defender*. They're black-owned and have always been a force for racial justice. That's no secret. Anyone who advertises in this paper doesn't care what color you are."

I expect him to hand it over and wish me luck. Instead he sits down and opens the newspaper, asking what kind of work I was searching for. I sit next to him and explain what my intentions were.

"They'll only hire a black salesman if they want you selling in a black neighborhood," Errol tells me. "I don't know much about office work either, but there are some places that'll take you even if they don't know you from Adam." He taps one listing in particular and hands the paper to me.

Warehouse workers needed. Hard work, good pay. No experience required.

My eyes drift from the newspaper to the fine fingers holding it. If my hands get smashed between crates, or a box cutter slashes a tendon, my career as a pianist is over. I have nothing against manual labor. I only wish I could perform it with my feet.

"Might be worth a try," Errol presses.

"Okay," I say, thinking of all the work hazards he must expose himself to each day. "I'll go first thing tomorrow."

"Don't let small minds get in the way of big dreams," Errol says, clamping my shoulder and squeezing before he rises and retires to the master bedroom.

I browse more of the ads, becoming distracted when I notice one of the weird phone numbers. I fold the newspaper and look at the phone sitting on the table next to me. Then I check the clock on the mantle. It's nine thirty at night. Is that considered late? Not as late as ten. I listen to the house, hearing muffled music upstairs and nothing else. Then I pick up the phone and dial Vanderbilt 8861, praying I'll get lucky with who answers, but thinking ahead in case I'm not.

"Hello?" It's the same voice as the first time I called.

"Mrs. Parker? I'm sorry to disturb you. It's just that Daniel seemed confused when we were making plans, and I'm worried he thinks I need a ride tomorrow, even though I don't. Would it be possible to speak to him actually?"

"Of course! Just a moment."

I listen to a muted conversation, which sounds like Mrs. Parker assuring her husband that everything is fine. I should probably be more careful not to arouse suspicion. I wasn't in the closet for long. I'm not very good at it.

"Hello?" Daniel's voice sounds guarded.

"Hey, pretty boy."

I expect him to giggle bashfully or something adorable, so I'm shocked when he hisses, "Shut up!"

I hear a series of muffled sounds, then Daniel says much louder, "I've got it."

"Okay," his mother replies… through the phone!

The line clicks, like the call has been disconnected, before I hear a whispered. "Sorry. I was waiting for her to hang up in their room."

"Wait, your parents can pick up their phone and *listen to us*?"

"Yeah, of course."

My mom does things with databases that I've never understood and my dad is a tech fanatic. I don't think we've had a landline in the house since I was born, a fact I'm increasingly grateful for. "Can you tell when they're listening in?"

"You'll hear a click. Unless they are really careful."

I sigh. "Maybe we should talk some other time."

"No!" Daniel says. "I was hoping to hear from you."

"Oh yeah?" I lower my voice. "I was hoping for more of you. Anything I can get."

I wish I could see his reaction to this. Instead I listen to the quickening of his breath until he replies, "How?"

"You ever sneak out?"

"Yeah."

Not the answer I was expecting, but I like it. "Meet you halfway?"

He laughs, even though I wasn't kidding. "It's a long walk."

"True. Come pick me up then."

"They'll hear me open the garage."

"Hmm. How fast can you run?"

He laughs again. "What would we do anyway?"

"I'm sure we could think of something."

The line is silent as we both contemplate the possibilities. At least I hope he's thinking about it. That's all I've got on my mind. Although I'd settle for being close to him, even if we only end up talking.

"Start thinking of places where we can be alone," I tell him, "and I'll try to figure out how we'll get there."

"Okay. I better go. Just in case they check to see if I'm still on the phone."

"All right. See you tomorrow."

"I can't wait," he splutters. "Good night, Reggie."

"See you in my dreams, pretty boy."

I hang up the phone feeling optimistic about what tomorrow might bring. After going downstairs and getting in bed, I close my eyes and let a hand snake beneath the sheets. Then I imagine Daniel biting his bottom lip... until I begin to bite my own.

Chapter 8

As soon as Gloria shakes me awake the next morning, I join their frantic rush, hurrying to get ready so I can continue the job search.

"Better wear something practical," Errol advises me during breakfast. "If you dress too nice, they might think you don't have what it takes."

I can read between the lines, and I'm not offended. If I look soft, it's because I am. That doesn't mean I don't work hard or push myself to the brink of exhaustion in front of the piano. I've done so many times when learning a new arrangement, practicing technical exercises, or even writing a new composition. My hands and mind end up exhausted more than my entire body, but I've never shied away from rolling up my sleeves to get a job done.

Today will be no different, I promise myself. When I make it back to the present, and if I'm crazy enough to tell anyone about this, I don't want to explain that I ate unripe pears and mooched off my grandma to get by. I want a story I can be proud of.

I make sure to pack a lunch. Then I ride into town with the rest of the family. Gloria is dropped off first, Harriet soon after. While we're parked outside Daniel's house, I check his bedroom window, expecting to see him there. Had he been, I probably would have felt smug. Since he's not, I'm forced to accept that *I'm* the one who's hoping to catch a glimpse of *him*. So yeah… I have a serious crush on the boy and would rather spend the day together. I'll let him be my motivation instead.

Errol drives us south of Glen Ellyn to an industrial area that will one day be replaced by generic retail stores and chain restaurants. At the moment, I only see empty fields punctuated by railyards and warehouses.

"I don't work so far from here," he tells me. "If you manage to get the job, I'll be able to give you a ride each morning and evening. You'll have to find your own way home today."

"No problem," I tell him. "I'll wander around the area and slowly make my way downtown again while job-hunting. Someone has to be desperate enough to hire me. If not, I'll need you to be my getaway driver when I start robbing banks. How fast can this thing go?"

"Not that fast," Errol says with a grin. He stops the car outside the warehouse that advertised in the paper. "Stay quiet and respectful. They don't want to hire anyone who will be trouble."

"Got it."

I'm more nervous than I was yesterday, knowing that it'll be harder to bounce back from two consecutive days of rejection. There isn't a woman in sight when I enter the building. Rather than a receptionist, the hall I step into has a window set into it. The man stationed beyond has a security guard vibe.

"Yeah?" he says when I approach the window.

"I'm here about the job in the paper."

He doesn't say anything else until he hands me a clipboard and pen. Then he jerks his head to the right. "Sit over there and wait."

The form is basic. Personal info, previous jobs, and references. No mention of education. I'm better prepared this time. I use Errol as a reference, still unsure if Dr. Parker would be willing to vouch for me, or if a pediatrician's opinion would count for anything here. I wait for a good half hour before a door farther down the hall opens and a man appears, gesturing for me to follow him. He's white and in his fifties, his skin craggy and sunbaked. I'm led into an office lined with filing cabinets. The man sits at a small desk in the center of the room. I can't tell if he's the boss, but the collar of his short-sleeved dress-shirt sure isn't blue. He picks up a smoldering cigarette from the ashtray and nods at one of the chairs facing him, indicating I should sit, so I do.

"Let's see what you've got there," he says at last.

I hand him the clipboard. He studies it for a minute, exhaling smoke that drifts up to join the fog above our heads. Then he stubs out the cigarette and opens a desk drawer for a bottle of liquor and two shot glasses, which he sets on the surface.

"Care for a drink?" he asks.

"No, sir. Thank you."

He nods, making me wonder if it was a test. He pours himself a shot of something, knocks it back, and gasps. "You have any trouble with the law?"

"No, sir. Never." I'm tempted to launch into a speech about how I'm a hard worker and a quick learner, until I remember Errol's advice.

"You from around here?" the man asks.

"No, sir. I moved up from Alabama last week."

The man takes a cloth handkerchief from his pocket and wipes at the sweat on his forehead. "Who are you staying with?"

"My aunt and uncle."

"Is that who this is?" he asks, tapping my one and only reference.

"Yes, sir."

"Uh-huh. I can pay you sixty-five cents an hour, in cash, at the end of each day. If you're any good, I'll up it to seventy-five cents in a week or so."

"That would be great, sir! Is there any chance I can start today?"

He grunts in surprise but nods. "Wait out in the hall."

"Thank you."

I'm legitimately excited, which is ridiculous, because sixty-five cents would have meant nothing to me a week ago. Now it can buy me an entire meal, although it's not a good wage. Most job listings offer at least a dollar per hour, so I'm guessing that's the minimum. I bet they don't pay cash at the end of each day either. This is under-the-table work, a fact that's confirmed when I'm led to a locker room by an older black man with white hair crowning his otherwise bald head who introduces himself as Samuel.

"You'll see folks clocking in," he says, referring to a metal box on the wall, "but you don't need to worry about that. Just write your name here," he points to a clipboard hanging on a single nail, "and the time. At the end of the day, you'll sign out and get your pay."

Samuel shows me to a locker and leaves me there, returning with a gray coverall, similar to what Errol wears at work. This one has the name of the warehouse spray-painted on it in stenciled letters, making me think of prison uniforms. I put my sandwich in the locker and begin to step into the coveralls.

"During this time of year," Samuel tells me, "most people strip down to their skivvies. The second half of the day can get awfully hot."

I take his advice, wishing he'd give me more privacy. I'm soon grateful that he's staying close because my new workplace is a dark and confusing maze. The main area of the warehouse is lit only by dirty glass panels in the ceiling. Shelves made of metal girders hold dusty-looking bags and boxes that smell both chemical and earthy. The forklifts puttering around don't help the quality of air. I don't think they're electric.

"What's all this for?" I ask.

"Farm and construction," Samuel replies.

He gives a brief tour that mostly consists of him showing me the layout while announcing what I'll find in each section. That's it. No employee training videos to watch or safety protocol sheets to sign. I'm given a pair of goggles and gloves before being brought to a section where there's only one other guy. He looks relieved until he sees how I struggle with heavy lifting. Before long, I get a feel for the routine. A foreman strolls by, shouting what he needs. Our job is to pile it onto a four-wheeled dolly and push it out to a loading bay. We don't have to get it onto the trucks. That's someone else's responsibility, and it's a better gig, judging from how they get to be in the open air and aren't covered by a thin layer of powder. The bags I'm lugging are labeled *LIME*, but they sure don't smell like citrus. My eyes begin to burn as we work. The goggles I was given barely help. They're basically a pair of glasses with plastic shields to the left and right, but that doesn't stop the sweat from getting into my eyes.

The work isn't ceaseless. There are small breaks between fulfilling orders, thank goodness, because by lunch I'm already exhausted. The sandwich and apple I packed don't cut it. I'll bring twice as much food tomorrow, if I'm able to move at all.

Samuel notices me rubbing my eyes. "Are they burning?" he asks.

He walks away after I nod and returns with a floppy brimmed cap. "Pull it down nice and low," he says. "When the lime mixes with your sweat, it can sting something fierce. That'll help keep it out of your eyes."

I thank him. When I return to work, following his advice helps. I lose myself in my thoughts for the rest of the day, thinking about what I'll do when I get home to my own time. Trivial stuff, like which YouTube channels I'll check to see what I missed, or which restaurants I'll eat at. I plan to blow a day's worth of calories at the Cheesecake Factory, that's for sure. When I find myself wishing I could stream some music while working, I settle for humming the tunes under my breath. Thoughts of Daniel are never far away. I imagine him fretting over my broken and exhausted body while dabbing me clean with a sponge.

My coworker strikes up a conversation a few times, mostly about horse races and sports teams I know nothing about. He seems content to ramble on without much input from me, which is fine. He only says one thing that catches my attention.

"Quittin' time!"

I follow the flow of people back to the locker room. The few showers are occupied, so I use the trough-like sinks to rinse off, including my entire head. Some of the men next to me have soap with them to wash their armpits and such. Something else I'll be investing in, along with maximum-strength ibuprofen. After getting dressed, I ignore the guys who are clocking out and follow those who aren't down the hall to a different room. There, a man with a tight suit and pinched face is seated at a table, the sign-in clipboard in front of him. I wait in line, and when it's finally my turn, I tell him my name. He makes me sign next to where I wrote my name previously and I'm handed a plain white envelope.

Five dollars in single bills. I think of the tenner that Mrs. Parker gave me and have new appreciation for how generous she was being, considering I'll have to work another full day to earn that much. I check the clock on the way out. It's nearly five. I have no idea how I'll get back to town or to Gloria's house. I can't send my friends a text to see what they're up to or ask them for a ride. I'm outside and looking around for a bus stop when honking draws my attention. A black Ford Mainline cruises toward me. I'd run toward it if I had the energy. I manage a smile regardless.

"I didn't know where to find you," Errol says after rolling down the window, "but I thought I'd try here in case you got lucky."

"I'm not sure I'd call it luck," I say wearily when climbing in, "but I got the job."

I tell him about my day and he confirms what I suspected: I'm being paid off the books at a rate that's lower than minimum wage. If I was staying longer than a few weeks, I might be concerned. For now, the job meets my needs: I'll have money to spend while I'm here with enough left over to contribute to my great-grandparents' household.

We're driving home directly, which isn't what I hoped for, but I don't know how to meet up with Daniel and Gloria anyway. Once we've reached the house, I grab an apple from the kitchen and eat it while in the shower. Multi-tasking at its finest. Gloria is home by the time I get out. She's alone. I'm bummed until she hands me something.

"Here's the book Daniel promised to loan you," she says, making a snoring sound.

I turn the book over to read the title aloud. "*The New Collegiate Latin & English Dictionary*. Thrilling!"

"Don't stay up all night reading that," Gloria teases.

The truth is, I can hardly wait to get it downstairs. I didn't ask to borrow this book. I don't think Daniel has been back to the gate to write down the Latin phrase. There must be more to it, but I'll have to wait. Gloria wants to hear about my day. Dinner is ready soon after, and I'm so tired by the time we've eaten that I'm more than happy to sit motionless on the couch for an hour of *Kraft Television Theater*. I begin drifting off by the end and decide to retire when the credits roll.

I grab the Latin dictionary on the way and take it to bed with me. I flip through it until I find a single folded sheet of paper trapped between two pages. It's a handwritten letter. From Daniel.

Dearest Reggie,

I can't possibly express everything that I'm feeling, but I'll try. Before you came into my life, I thought I was alone in the world. I knew there were others out there, but I didn't think they would be anything like the handsome prince who showed up on my doorstep. You've roused me from sleep after a long cold winter, and now I'm burning inside. For you. I'm trying not to let myself think foolish thoughts. I know you won't be able to stay for much longer. So for now, I'll keep myself in check while savoring every moment we have together. I don't know what's going to happen. Only that nothing will ever be the same. And for that, I thank you.

Sincerely yours,

Daniel Parker

I press the paper to my nose, not at all surprised when I'm rewarded with a whiff of cologne. Classic. Although the only scent I associate with Daniel is soap. The paper smells an awful lot like his father. I imagine him sneaking into his parents' bathroom to spray the letter with cologne and it makes me smile. Mostly because I can picture his earnest expression, like he's on the most important mission in the world. I'm glad he took the time to write me. The day would have ended with disappointment despite its successes if he hadn't. I'm exhausted but unable to sleep, so I creep upstairs and knock on Gloria's door when I hear that she's still up.

I borrow stationary, saying that I'm planning to write a few more letters to people in the future. Then I go downstairs to the kitchen table to pen my response.

Hey pretty boy,

Your letter spoke of the fire you feel inside. I'm no stranger to it. I felt a spark each time I saw that framed photo of you in my grandmother's room. I wanted more, even then, without truly knowing why. I figured it out though: You helped me realize who I am. So if anything, I'm only repaying the favor. Now that we've met, the spark finally has the kindling it needs to burn. And it will burn, I promise. Both of us. The game we're playing comes at a price. Everyone pays it eventually. So please, don't hold back. We have to make the most of what we have, while we still can. A broken heart is better than one that is never used, so I'm willing to give it all to you. Anything you need. Everything you want.

Dreaming of you,

Reggie Valentine

I fold the paper, find the dictionary entry for *amor*, and tuck it against that page. Maybe it's too soon to describe what we have as love. Then again, a spark is technically fire, despite being so small and fleeting. I go downstairs to bed, thoughts of him like opium surging through my veins, the pain of the day forgotten as I lose myself in blissful visions filled with pale-green eyes and delicate kisses.

Chapter 9

The next day plays out like the previous except that I'm better prepared. I bring twice as much with me for lunch, along with the personal hygiene items I'll need to get clean after work. Before leaving the house, I give the Latin book to Harriet and ask her to please return it to Daniel. The grind resumes once I'm at the warehouse and I begin to question my sense of integrity, because it really is grueling work. What does it matter if I quit and walk out? My career isn't on the line. I'm basically working a summer job for extra pocket money. Then I think of explaining to my great-grandparents that I decided not to break my back every day, like they do, because it's too darn hard. Or worse, I imagine returning to the future to learn from Gloria that her parents ended up losing the house. The guilt and shame would last a lifetime. I can put up with stinging eyes and sore muscles for a few more weeks.

I was hoping that Daniel and Gloria would pick me up at the end of my shift, but they're either busy or unable. Errol is there to ferry me home instead, which I'm grateful for, despite not feeling very cheerful. The day has worn me down and more of the same is coming tomorrow. But I do get an unexpected treat that evening. We're sitting in the living room and about to watch TV when the phone rings.

"Reggie?" Harriet says after answering it. "Sure. Just a minute, hon."

She switches places with me so I'm close enough to use the phone.

"Hey," Daniel says breathily when I press the handset to my ear. "I got your notes."

Notes plural? I can hear voices in the background. His little sisters are chattering before being told to quiet down so that

Daniel can talk. He isn't alone. Neither am I. "Oh good," I say. "I hope they were uh… inspiring."

"Yes! Absolutely. Hey, I had an idea. My Boy Scout troop meets on Thursdays. You were so interested in the subject when it came up that I thought you might want to join me."

I do want to spend time with him but hanging out with a bunch of ankle-biters, as Gloria calls them, isn't my idea of fun. I'm picturing a church basement and a youth pastor with a poorly tuned guitar. Although that basement probably has unoccupied rooms or at least a coat closet we could sneak into for some snuggling. Assuming that Gloria doesn't tag along with us. I suppose she wouldn't be allowed to since… Oh! What a clever boy. "That sounds wonderful," I reply.

"Great! I'll pick you up at six. We can get something to eat along the way."

"I can't wait," I tell him. "In fact, I refuse to. Can you call the Boy Scouts and ask them to meet tonight instead?"

He laughs before an awkward silence stifles the conversation. We're both too monitored at the moment to say anything honest and open, so we confirm the details. Once we have, I take a risk and say, "It's a date!"

"Yeah," he replies with a nervous chuckle. "That's exactly what it is."

Nice. After hanging up, I give back Harriet's preferred seat and plop down next to Gloria.

"He's dragging you to one of his meetings?" she asks me, grimacing in sympathy.

"Yup. I don't mind. I'm ready for a night on the town."

Errol snorts. "We'll show you a real good time this weekend, I promise."

"But we hope you have fun anyway," Harriet chimes in.

I don't see how I can't. Even if I'm stuck learning to tie knots or something weird, at least we'll be in the same room.

The thought is enough to keep me going the next day. I pretend I took the new job not just for the money, but because I wanted the exercise. My arms certainly feel bigger, but they're probably only swollen. I hope Hannah gets the gate repaired soon. If not, I wonder what everyone will think when I return to the future as ripped as the Terminator himself. I just hope I won't arrive naked like he did when time traveling, although I always appreciated that part of the movie when I was younger.

After work, when Errol has driven me home again, I take a full shower. I don't have a lot of clothes to choose from, so I opt for the white short-sleeved dress shirt and black shorts combo again, figuring it covers both formal and casual. Then I make myself appear disinterested while waiting in the living room, when normally, I'd be pacing the entryway and looking through the windows.

I'm out the door as soon as the Chevy Bel Air pulls up. I get into the car so quick that I don't notice what Daniel is wearing until I'm right next to him. The seriousness of the military-green uniform is offset by the festive red neckerchief. I've never seen a soldier wear below-the-knee shorts either. When I notice the various patches sewn onto the shirt, it clicks. This is his Boy Scout uniform.

"Don't laugh," he says with a grumpy expression. "Gloria always teases me about it."

"I need you to pull down the street so I can kiss you," I tell him. "It's an emergency." Then I start counting down. "Ten, nine, eight—"

Daniel puts the car in drive and hits the gas, the tires squealing. I'm laughing so hard at the end of the block that I can barely manage to kiss him. But I do. He checks the rearview mirrors afterwards, worried about being seen, so I back off.

"What do you get up to at these meetings of yours?" I ask him as he resumes driving.

"Oh. Well, technically I'm too old to be a Boy Scout. Even if I wasn't, becoming an Eagle Scout means graduating from the program. With honors. But I liked the experience so much that I still volunteer as an instructor. I doubt I'll be able to once I start college, so it's just for the summer. And it's the only way I can really..." He glances over at me before realizing that he doesn't need to censor himself. "It's the only way I can see my guy friends without being scrutinized."

He doesn't mean that in a sexual way or anything romantic. I'm sure of it, and it breaks my heart. "In that case, I look forward to meeting everyone," I tell him.

"Really? Umm..."

"Out with it," I say, poking him in the ribs.

"The meeting was just an excuse. We *can* go, but I thought it would be more fun to see a movie."

"Yeah! Are you kidding? That's way better!" Although a cinema offers even less potential to find a private moment.

"Good," he says, sounding relieved. "Are you hungry? Where should we eat?"

"Panera or maybe Chipotle?" I'm deliberately messing with him. "You know what the current options are. Surprise me."

"How about A&W?" he asks.

"I love me some root beer," I say, not understanding what that has to do with eating.

"Great!"

We don't have far to go. He takes me to a place that resembles a Sonic in my day. The building itself is small and doesn't offer indoor seating. Two rows of covered parking spaces serve that function instead, each with a menu mounted on a pole. Daniel is enthusiastic about the Chubby Dinner, whatever that is, so I tell him I want the same. He gives his order to a waiter on roller skates. The other carhops are male too.

"I need a chart to figure out the gender divide you all have going," I say.

"What do you mean?"

"Men have one set of jobs and women have another."

Daniel nods as if he doesn't see an issue with this.

"If that's the case," I say, "then how come waitresses are women, but carhops are men?"

"They used to be women. Dad once told me that he liked this place better during the war, because the carhops were easier on the eyes. It was one of those dumb 'You know what I mean?' moments that I never know how to react to. I asked him why it changed and he said that men hung around to flirt with the female carhops instead of eating and leaving."

"Then we better contain ourselves when he brings our order or we'll never make it to the movie on time."

Daniel laughs. "They should let people pull up to the kitchen for their food. That way it doesn't get cold on the way to the car during the winter. Or wet when it rains."

"Now there's an idea worth investing in," I tell him. "They could call it a drive-thru."

"That doesn't make sense," he says, shaking his head. "You'd still have to stop to get your food. And to place your order."

"Back to the drawing board," I say, feigning exasperation. As much as I tease, I do find it charming that he's from a bygone era. Especially that uniform. I had classmates who were in the Scouts, which led to all the obvious fantasies. A few of which I wouldn't mind enacting.

"Do you want to see my merit badges?" Daniel asks me, misinterpreting my interest in his outfit.

"Yes," I reply. "More than anything."

He grins and reaches into the backseat to grab a sash. I notice a little cloth cap there, which he ignores. Daniel looks the sash over, his gaze insecure when offering it, like it won't be enough to impress me, so I try to show reverence when accepting it. I'm surprised by its weight. The sash itself isn't heavy, but he seems to have maxed out the available space with small round patches.

"You have to fill this up to become an Eagle Scout?" I ask.

He shakes his head. "Only twenty-one are required. Most of them have to be a specific kind."

"Like what?"

"Well, this one is for first aid," he says, leaning over and pointing at a yellow plus sign on a red background.

"I bet practicing CPR was awkward." His expression is blank, which stuns me. Drive-thrus are one thing, but… "Are you telling me that hasn't been invented yet? Mouth-to-mouth?"

His eyes dart down to my lips and he blushes.

"What about the Heimlich Maneuver?" I try.

He shrugs, like he's never heard of it.

"Remind me to swallow carefully while I'm here," I murmur, returning my attention to the sash. One of the patches is a red heart. "What's this one for?" I ask with half-lidded eyes. "Romantic prowess?"

"Personal fitness," he replies, laughing nervously. "The pull-ups were the hardest part. I practiced for months."

"Wow. That's really hot."

He looks surprised. "You think so?"

"Yeah. How many can you do? Grab hold of the roof we're parked under and show me what you've got."

The food arrives before that can happen. Our carhop hangs the loaded-up tray he's carrying on the Bel Air's door. Very clever. I'm careful when returning the sash to the safety of the backseat. I grab the army-style cap while I'm there and put it on. Daniel seems delighted when he turns around.

"Gee! That actually looks good on you!"

"Thanks," I say, tilting it for comedic effect. "I'm starting a new organization called the Man Scouts. We're recruiting former Boy Scouts if you're interested."

"Reggie!" he says in chastising tones, shaking his head.

Why does my name sound so much better when he says it?

I set amorous thoughts aside when he passes me a cardboard boat filled with battered chicken strips and fries. I douse this with ketchup from a glass bottle. Daniel turns on the radio while we eat. I finish my meal when he's only halfway through with his, I'm embarrassed to see. Especially when he asks if I want to order more.

"No. I usually don't eat like that. The new job really takes it out of me."

I tell him about it while he continues chewing, ending with the conclusion that I reached earlier in the day. "I keep thinking how I'd feel if this was it for me. If I had been born in this decade, working in a warehouse might be the only viable option, no matter what I wanted to do. At least back home I have college and a career to look forward to." Although much of that is due less to the era, and more to being born in a country and household that entitles me to such things. Daniel and I have that much in common. "Hey, what are your plans? I know you're off to college, but for what?"

"Medical school," he says, setting his trash on the window tray. "I'm going to be a doctor."

"Wow, that's great! We've both got it made then."

I expect him to agree with his trademark enthusiasm, so I'm confused when he remains silent.

"Dr. Daniel Parker has a nice ring to it," I prompt. "Although people might confuse you with your dad at times."

Now he's scowling at the dashboard.

I lean forward to catch his eye. "You know the nice thing about us sharing a secret? It means we can trust each other. With everything."

Daniel exhales. "I don't want to be a stupid doctor." He grimaces. "I shouldn't say that. My dad is the greatest. I admire the work he does, but I don't know if I can do it. I get squeamish at the sight of blood."

"Not the best trait for a medical professional to have. So what would you prefer?"

Daniel perks up as he turns toward me. "I know you don't want us to ask about the future," he says, "but you weren't kidding when you said we make it to the moon, were you?"

"It happens. I promise."

"How soon? Because if I can get an engineering degree fast enough, maybe I could be part of that."

"Dude! You should do it! There's plenty of time. You could work for NASA."

"Do you mean the NACA?" He pronounces each letter separately and one of them is off but…

"Maybe. Have you always wanted to be an engineer?"

"No. When I was a kid, I wanted to be a pilot. Then we took a family vacation to Hawaii, and while I'm not scared of flying exactly, I didn't enjoy it much. As for the plane itself…" His face lights up with a doofy grin. "It could have stayed on the ground the entire week. I would have explored every nook and cranny. *That* would have been the perfect vacation!"

"Then you've got to become an engineer, my man. There's no question."

Daniel's happy expression wilts. "I'm already enrolled at Pritzker. They've accepted me."

"That's part of the University of Chicago, right? Tell them you're interested in a different field. They must have an engineering program."

Daniel looks tempted before his shoulders slump. "My parents would kill me."

"Doesn't matter. Listen, I had the most amazing piano teacher. When he played, it was so beautiful that it literally brought me to tears. Multiple times. I asked him once why he was a teacher and not a performer, and he said that he didn't feel as passionate about it. I didn't understand. I kept comparing him to famous names, and in my mind, he was way better than many of them. He should have been a household name, so I went back and asked him about it again. I thought he might have some deep philosophical reason for not wanting to perform, but it was simple. He said, 'I was around your age and figured I had about forty years of work ahead of me, if not more, so I made sure to do what I like best.' That's it. I tried arguing with him, saying he could get rich as a recording artist and do whatever he wanted afterwards, but he kept pointing out that he wouldn't have been as happy."

Daniel nods, as if this makes sense, but his words don't line up. "My parents are paying my tuition. It's their money."

"Yeah, but it's your life." I hold up a hand to stop him from replying. "Hear me out. Let's say that you do what your parents want and become a doctor. Hell, you even marry a woman and have children, because that's what they want too. Then one day, your son or daughter approaches you, just before they start medical school, and admit that they'd rather be a park ranger. Are you going to force them to become a doctor anyway?"

"No!" Daniel says, as if that would be cruel.

"Your parents want the best for you, but that doesn't mean they know what it is."

Daniel is silent as he thinks. Then he turns to me. "Do we land on any other planets? And do we find life there?"

I laugh. "A lot happens between now and then. That's all I'll say. You could be part of history, Daniel. Your parents will be proud of you, believe me. I'll make sure you know where to apply. I can give you the right place and time. You'll do the rest."

I can tell he's tempted, but he doesn't commit. That's fine. I'm asking a lot of him between this and his sexuality. One small step for now. The giant leap will have to wait.

"What time does the movie start?" I ask after the carhop takes the tray and its trash away.

"Oh right," Daniel says. "We should probably get going."

Instead of starting the car, he begins to unbutton his uniform. Not that I mind but… "Should I take my shirt off too?" I ask.

He grins. "I only wore this so my parents would think I was going to the meeting. I'll get torn to pieces if I've got this on at the drive-in."

"A drive-in theater?" I ask, sitting upright. "For real?"

"Yeah. Ever been?"

"No. This is going to be—"

Daniel shrugs the shirt off his shoulders, and I can see now why he got that merit badge in personal fitness. He's not ripped by any means. He doesn't look like someone who chugs protein 'shakes on the way to the gym. His build is natural and sexy as fuck. His chest is just toned enough to give shape to his pecs, his shoulders and biceps rounded. His stomach is flat, at least the half that isn't covered by the high-waisted shorts. I'd like to get him out of those and whatever he has on underneath. Now that I know where we're going, that might be possible. The sun can't set quickly enough, because he sure looks…

"—amazing," I manage to squeak out.

He looks a little self-conscious, but I continue to stare, noticing the dark hair beneath his arms as he reaches in the back again, this time for a lemon-yellow shirt. It goes well with the olive-green shorts, which he keeps on, unfortunately for me.

"Ready to go?" he asks once dressed again.

"You have no idea," I growl, moving in for a kiss.

I stop when he glances around in fear. The reminder of our circumstances is welcome. I wasn't thinking clearly. I can wait.

But not much longer.

— — —

The drive-in theater is on the edge of the suburban sprawl, surrounded by wooded lots. We pull up to a small booth near the entrance. I insist on paying. Once I have, we slowly cruise toward a parking lot with a movie screen set up at the farthest end.

"Where should we park?" Daniel asks.

"I dunno. What's considered a good seat at a drive-in?"

"Somewhere around the center. Although people park on the edges when they're more interested in necking."

I can guess what that means. I'm picturing two giraffes with their necks intertwined—the visual image enough to imply some sort of intimacy. "Privacy is good," I say in neutral tones.

"I think so too." Daniel turns the wheel to the left but doesn't accelerate. "But if people see two guys parking there…"

"We'll be careful," I promise him. "And everyone around us will be distracted anyway."

That does the trick. He parks in the corner farthest from the screen. The concession stand is on the opposite side, so we'll be blanketed in darkness once the sun sets. It's already sinking behind a line of trees. Daniel rolls down his window and takes a metal box from a pole. Each parking space has them on both sides. They resemble old-style microphones, the kind enclosed in an aluminum casing with horizontal slits cut into the surface.

These are boxier and about the size of a super thick hardback book. A plastic red knob toward the bottom is labeled volume, which tips me off to its purpose. It's a speaker! Daniel rolls up his window most of the way, the speaker hanging from the glass. I'm surprised it can support the weight, but I copy him. Then I slide my hand across the seat, resting it on his thigh. He puts his hand over mine and smiles.

"What are movies like in the future?" he asks me.

"They're mostly indoors and used by incompetent parents as a babysitter," I tell him. When he doesn't seem impressed or amused by my answer, I add, "and the actors are all robots."

He squeezes my hand in excitement. "Really?"

"No." I feel bad for getting his hopes up, so I throw in some truth. "But we do have a way of creating animation that uses computers. Special effects too. That giant lizard movie we saw wouldn't have used still-frame animation or a physical model, although some of the charm is lost."

He's confused enough that I wonder if he knows what a computer is. I ask and he describes them as massive machines that fill an entire room, their purpose to perform complex mathematical equations. I get the impression they aren't attached to monitors yet, so it's hard to explain how they can replace an actor in a full-body leotard with a fantasy creature. I'm not sure I truly understand it myself.

The speakers crackle to life as a commercial is beamed onto the screen, animated hotdogs and popcorn singing a catchy jingle that urges us to visit the lobby. I'm out of the car the second the song ends, singing it along the way. Daniel has to rush to keep up with me. There's something magical about the concession stand. The building contains one long counter. We move along it like we're in a cafeteria, picking up ice cream, popcorn, and soda. I'm not worried. I'll burn the calories before lunch tomorrow.

"Are you in the army or something?" asks the girl working the register.

"No," I answer. "Why?"

Her eyes move to the top of my head. I'm still wearing the doofy Boy Scout cap! Daniel starts laughing. The little shit purposely didn't remind me!

"It's cute," he whispers as we leave the concession stand. "I didn't want you to take it off."

I leave it on until we reach the car. The movie is starting by the time we get there. Alfred Hitchcock himself appears on screen, telling us that we're about to witness a shocking true story. The monochrome presentation has me geared up for some classic film noir as the story begins. A man visits a bank of some sort. The tellers there are convinced he held them up previously, even though he didn't… and that's about as interesting as it gets. The police take the man around to other locations his doppelganger had robbed, most people identifying the innocent man as the culprit. The same scenario is repeated over and over enough that my attention wanders. I keep checking the sky, willing the night to come sooner. Or I look around at the throngs of teenagers who loiter in groups near their cars, their appearances reassuringly familiar. Many of them wear jeans with the cuffs rolled up or T-shirts without collars. An unusual number of the girls are in dresses with busy patterns and many of the boys have slicked-back hair, but there are plenty that I wouldn't have singled out as particularly unusual in my own time. They're a stark contrast to Daniel.

I turn my attention to him, concerned that he attempts to emulate his father so much. Not just the uncool clothes but his need to follow in his father's footsteps, despite them leading away from his dreams. I might be able to seduce him while I'm here and give him fond memories to cling to when I'm gone, but I'm worried that's all it will amount to. I want him to be happy and fulfilled, not nostalgic and regretful.

Daniel notices my stare and reaches over to take my hand. Once he does, I lift it to my lips and kiss the back, which makes him nervous, but the shadows outside the car have deepened. Enough for me to move closer. I lean against him, Daniel putting an arm around me after some hesitation. I can feel how tense this makes him, and not in a sexual way. He keeps glancing around, but it really is dark in our corner of the lot. I doubt anyone can see us. He must reach the same conclusion because I feel him relax.

Turning toward him, I reach around to the back of his head, pulling him in for a kiss. Then I shift as the intensity increases. His lips are buttery from the popcorn. I can't get enough of them. I'd like to swing a leg over his lap so we can really go somewhere. I bet I'd feel his hard cock rubbing against my butt. I glance down and see his shorts bulging. My own dick is straining against the tight underwear. We both need release. I slide my hand beneath his shirt, using my thumb to caress the pink nipples I saw earlier. Daniel gasps in appreciation, so I let my hand slide down to the buttons of his shorts. They're tricky to undo, so I lose patience and attempt to slip my fingers beneath the hem.

Daniel grabs my wrist and yanks it away.

"You okay?" I ask, sitting up to look him in the eye.

His expression is tough to read. "That's a little fast, don't you think?"

"We can move slower," I say, leaning toward him again. He pulls away. "Or not. Are you worried about being seen?"

"No, but this is our first date."

"That's true," I say carefully, "but it's not the first time we've hung out. I feel comfortable around you already. If you don't yet, that's totally okay. Consent is important. We can take our time. I'll let you lead."

"Thanks."

I'm not sure what to do with myself so I sit up again and offer my hand. He takes it. I turn my attention to the screen, hoping it will help deflate my boner. The falsely accused man is exonerated when the real criminal robs another store while he's in police custody. Now free, he visits his wife to tell her the good news, but her feeble mind can't handle the stress of the situation and she's institutionalized. So lame. I'm frustrated as the music swells and the movie comes to an end. Not because Daniel didn't want to go far enough, but because that's it for our date. One little taste of paradise before the drudgery of my daily life resumes.

I'm surprised then that he doesn't start the car. Only a handful drive away.

"It's a double matinee," Daniel explains when he sees my confusion.

"Really?" I almost ask the title of the next movie before realizing that I don't care. We get to be together for another hour or two. That's awesome! So why does Daniel look miserable?

"Are you mad at me?" he asks.

"No! Not at all. I just don't want to make the wrong move."

"I liked it," he says, chewing his bottom lip for a moment. "But I've never done anything like that before."

"With another guy," I tack on for him.

He shakes his head.

"For real? I figured you'd be popular with the girls. I mean, you're just so…"

He blinks pale-green eyes at me that make no assumptions.

"So cute," I finish with a sigh. He has me back on the emotional side of things. "You must have at least messed around. Some petting or uh, what did you call it, necking?"

"I've kissed a few girls," he says.

I wait for him to add to the list. He doesn't.

"Wow. Okay. Yeah, that helps put it into perspective."

"You've gone all the way?"

"With a girl?" I ask incredulously. "Ha! No. I'm gold star. I figured out I like boys early enough that all my experiences have been with them."

"*Them?*" he repeats, sounding concerned.

"I'm always safe, don't worry."

He doesn't look reassured, his forehead still crinkled up. "How many?"

Uh oh. "That depends on what you count. For me it's anything that involves messing around. More than just kissing obviously." I could spell out that sex doesn't have to involve penetration, in my opinion, but he already seems on edge. "So with that in mind, only about ten or so."

His eyes go wide. Then he turns toward the screen, even though it's blank, and I watch his jaw muscle clench.

"Not that there's anything wrong with it," I say tersely, starting to feel defensive. "Slut-shaming isn't cool. Everyone has their own standards."

"I wasn't calling you that," Daniel says, shaking his head.

But he's still not looking at me.

"How does it work here?" I ask through gritted teeth. "Everyone waits until they're married?"

"No," he grumbles. "Well… the women do."

"Of course. Double standards. How noble. So where does that leave us?"

"I don't know," Daniel says, sounding wounded. "I thought we'd figure it out together."

The fight goes out of me. He's inexperienced and confused. And he probably wishes I was too, so it would be less intimidating for him. "I want you to know that I was dating most of those guys. Sometimes you meet someone and you get caught up in the moment, but then you quickly figure out that they aren't a good match. So that's what most of them were. Failed relationships."

"And the rest?"

"I'm human. It's easier to meet other gay guys in my day. Imagine being a horny teenager and only needing to—" I quickly translate cruising apps into a term he'll understand better. "—call a phone number to find someone who feels the same way. I didn't do that often. I wouldn't be ashamed if I had. But I do want you to know that I'm an old romantic who prefers relationships."

He finally looks at me, his expression softening. "So which category do I fit into?"

Normally that would be a complicated question for me. A bad relationship can get in the way of dreams, put a strain on friendships, and sour everything else. After making too many mistakes, I decided to be more cautious before committing. I don't have those concerns with Daniel. I've seen enough to convince me that he's a genuinely caring person. There's only one issue.

"I can't stay much longer," I tell him. "But if I could, I'd want to be your boyfriend."

"Can't you be anyway?" he asks, his eyes full of need. "Even if only for a week?"

"I'm worried it'll hurt you when we say goodbye."

"It will no matter what," Daniel says, his chin trembling. "I hate the idea."

And I can't stand to see him unhappy. "Then we better make the most of it while we can. I won't rush anything that you're not comfortable with, but when it comes to what I feel for you... No matter what happens, at least I'll always know that you were my boyfriend."

Daniel's eyes are brimming with tears. "Really? You mean it?"

I barely start to nod before he throws himself into my arms. We fall back onto the seat together—with him on top of me—his kisses sweet rather than passionate, but they satisfy me more than sex ever could. I adore him. There's so much we don't know about each other, and our future holds very little potential, but somehow it doesn't matter. I want to be with him however he sees fit.

Daniel gets nervous when we hear honking. He pushes himself up on his arms to make sure the coast is clear. I take the opportunity to stroke the curve of his bicep, which makes him laugh, like it tickles. He sits upright again. I put my head in his lap so I can stare up at him. I don't plan on quitting either, no matter how much he starts to squirm under my gaze.

"You sure are a looker," I murmur, his cheeks turning as red as his lips. When he looks down at me, I reach up to feel their warmth, moving my hand up to the edge of his hair. I won't go higher, since it's swept back with styling product, as always. It must have some length to it though.

"You ever wear this down?" I ask.

"No. It gets in my eyes."

"I'd love to see it. Just once. It must be a real mess in the morning." God how I would love to wake up next to him and everything that implies.

"Do you ever grow yours out?" Daniel asks, rubbing his palm over my scalp.

"Yeah. You should have seen me sophomore year. Do you know what an afro is?"

"No."

"Just wait. You'll see plenty of them in the sixties. How come? Do you want me to grow out my hair?"

"I like you how you are," he says. "I was just thinking of a Frankie Lymon record I have. He's so adorable on the cover."

"The kid who sang *Why Do Fools Fall in Love*?" I ask, pretending to be jealous. "You show me this record and I'll beat whatever hairstyle he has. Ain't nobody stealing my boyfriend! Especially when I just got him."

He bites his bottom lip, looking positively thrilled, and I want nothing more than to lock ourselves away in his room for a weekend so we can continue goofing around without being interrupted.

The lights in the parking lot are turned off as the next movie begins, so I sit up. The screen explodes with color, which is a welcome change. Over the horizon of a windswept plain, three cowboys appear on horseback. I'm feeling hopeful until the cheesiest song begins to play, complete with lyrics that make sure to incorporate the title of the movie, which appears in giant glistening red letters more suited to a horror movie: *Gunfight at the O.K. Corral*

"This is what everyone is here to see," Daniel says, seeming interested himself. "The one before it came out ages ago."

I try my best to give the movie my full attention. Once past the intro, the tone is grittier, which certainly helps. I've just never cared much for Westerns. Or for movies with long action sequences. I turn down the speakers on my side, surprised when Daniel does the same.

"There was one experience I had," he blurts out. "With another guy. Sort of."

"I'm all ears," I say, welcoming the distraction.

"I was on a camping trip with my troop, and um, one of the scouts I didn't know so well, him and I were out foraging for mushrooms."

"As one does," I say with a straight face.

"Yeah. We didn't interact much normally, but he was trying to earn the same merit badge, so we teamed up. While we were out there, he asked me if I ever... By myself. You know?"

"Huh-uh," I say innocently. "Whatever do you mean?"

"You know," he insists, making a pumping motion with his fist.

"Oh! He asked if you ever choke the chicken, beat your meat, or spank the monkey?"

Daniel looks mortified before he starts laughing. "He called it shaking hands with the milkman. I had no idea what he meant even though I—" He clears his throat. "Have you ever done that?"

"Are you kidding? I'm a world champion. I run through a tissue box a week. My parents have to buy them in bulk."

"Me too," he admits. "Maybe not *that* much but a lot. So anyway, when I shook my head, he offered to teach me how."

I don't know how old he was at the time. I'm picturing him as he appears now, which suits my purposes. And since I'm using my imagination, this other guy might as well look like me. "So what happened?"

"He took it out without explaining."

"Took what out?" I ask, but this time I'm not joking around. "I want to hear you say it. That makes it hotter. Tell me the details."

"He took out his penis. It was already hard. I couldn't believe my luck. I'd been wanting to see that for years. Not his in particular, but any of the guys my age would have been exciting. He started rubbing it and told me it was okay to look. So I did."

"How was it?" I ask, resisting the urge to reach down to adjust myself.

"I kept thinking it wasn't as big as mine," Daniel said, "but I wanted to compare. He said I should join him."

"Did you?"

Daniel winces. "This is going to sound really stupid, but I wondered if it was a trap, like maybe my dad or one of the scout leaders asked him to test me."

"I don't think—"

"I know. It's obvious now, but the situation was intense. I got scared and walked away. So stupid!"

"There's nothing dumb about it," I reassure him. "Fear does strange things to us all, and when you're in the closet—especially in this decade—I don't blame you for freaking out."

"Thanks. I wish I hadn't though."

I choose my words carefully, not wanting to brute force my way into his comfort zone again. "If you ever want to give that scenario another spin, just let me know. We can shake the milkman's hand together."

I expect him to laugh. Instead he's staring at me. He opens his mouth, closes it again, and then looks around. When his eyes return to mine, they're filled with hunger. "Can we?"

"You mean right now?" I ask, not bothering to check our surroundings. Haul us off to jail, I don't care. I want this!

When he nods, I drop my hands to the hem of my shorts. Then I begin to unbutton them. "So this guy showed you his first, right?"

Daniel nods. Eagerly.

"Okay. Take a look at this." I make sure to pace myself, even though I'd rather rip my shorts open. Instead I slowly undo each button before folding back the flaps. The nice thing about tighty-whities is that they don't leave much to the imagination. Not when someone is fully hard, which I certainly am. I trace the outline of my cock, grabbing it through the fabric and pumping it a few times. Then I hook a thumb beneath the waistband and pull down, exposing myself to him. Daniel's eyes are locked onto my cock, his breathing heavy, so I decide to get him even more riled up by playing into the fantasy.

"This is my favorite technique," I say, sliding my hand across the dark skin. "Although this feels good too." I grab it tight and start pumping. "Wanna try?"

"Yeah," Daniel says, fumbling at his olive-green shorts. I'd almost forgotten that they're part of his uniform. Taking inspiration, I grab the cap from the dashboard and put it on again. He notices, and I can tell that he's into it. Especially when he finally gets his shorts open and pulls them down, revealing a wet spot on a pair of white cotton briefs. Precome! Nectar of the gods, as far as I'm concerned. Daniel doesn't bother with a strip tease. His attention is still on my cock when he pulls his out. Then his eyes move to mine to gauge my reaction. I'm not disappointed. Mine is a good inch longer, but his is fat and meaty. I wouldn't mind faceplanting into his lap, but I'll let him make that move if he's ready. For now, it's erotic not having permission to touch him.

"That's some Grade A thickness," I tell him. "Very impressive."

"Really?" he asks, his attention darting back to my own. "Have you ever measured yours?"

Of course. It's just under eight inches, unless I cheat with the ruler, but I like the idea of him figuring that on his own. "Nope. Maybe you can help me with that sometime."

His hand moves over the head of his cock, which grows increasingly slick.

"I like it wet too," I tell him, spitting into my palm.

On the screen, cowboys are growling at each other. They're in the middle of a knife fight, but that's never been my weapon of choice. Words are so much more satisfying.

"You said you wanted to compare," I say, sliding closer to him. I press a thumb to the base of my cock so it's vertical like a mast. He does the same, and for a moment we both just stare. Dicks are fun enough on their own, but when you've got two...

We both resume pumping, and I can tell from the way he's alternating between holding his breath and gasping that he won't last long. I know just the way to push him over the edge. I hastily unbutton my shirt, not because I expect him to fawn over my body, but because I don't want it to get messy. Then I pump faster, bringing myself to the brink.

"Wanna see me come?" I ask.

Daniel whimpers in response, and when two white ropes shoot across my stomach, he rips his shirt up and begins to moan. The fight on screen has gotten loud, thank goodness, because so is he. I keep pumping as he firehoses his stomach down, the load so big that I let go of myself to grab leftover napkins from the concession stand before any of it rolls off his hip and onto the seat.

"Damn!" I say. "How long have you been holding that in?"

"Since yesterday," he admits.

"That's it? Wow. We should open up a sperm bank. You could populate an entire state."

He laughs before seeming to remember where we are. Then he blushes and slides down on the seat. I hand him some of the napkins and get myself cleaned up, eager to move past this task to what needs to happen next. This is a first for him, of sorts, and I want it to be more than just sexual. Once we've pulled up our shorts, I angle myself on the corner of the seat with my back against the door and open my arms to him. Daniel scoots closer, resting his head against my chest.

"I'm glad I waited," he murmurs. "I wouldn't have liked it as much with that other guy. I didn't feel anything for him."

I kiss the top of his head as he clings to me. "You're so sweet. And yeah, you've got me feeling all kinds of things too."

"Does it scare you?" he asks.

The question is unexpected, but I don't need him to explain. We're already taking risks that might get us caught, and even if that doesn't happen, he's getting attached much too quickly. Normally I'd chalk that up to a lack of experience. I can't make the same excuse for myself. My sexual appetite has been satiated, but I still crave him. I could put Daniel inside my heart and let him curl up and sleep there forever. Even then, I'm not sure it would be enough. I want more.

Chapter 10

Two days have passed since our date at the drive-in. I didn't see Daniel again until Friday night, when he picked up Gloria and me after dinner so we could go out for a malt. They mostly talked in excitement about graduating the next day while I listened enviously. And now I've returned to my former high school, Daniel strolling alongside me in a graduation gown. The campus is smaller, since not as many of the extensions have been added yet, but the main building already exists. The interior hasn't changed much. I feel detached, which is odd. I expected to be overwhelmed by nostalgic memories when returning here, but I think I know why I'm not. When you strip a school down to its essence, it's the people walking the halls who make it special. Otherwise you're left with the same lockers and classrooms that can be found in any town.

The graduation ceremony is similar to what I've experienced previously, taking place outside on the football field. The gowns are black instead of green, but the rest plays out mostly the same as it did for my two older brothers. Tedious speeches are given, a band plays, everyone walks across the stage to collect their diploma when their name is called, and then it all comes to an emotional end. For the students anyway. This is my third time being in the audience, and it's always a tedious grind, but I can tell how much it means to those who are involved.

My own graduation ceremony isn't for another week... plus another sixty-five years. I'm not sure I'll make it back in time to participate. I can imagine how it would have gone: Hannah and I would roll our eyes during the speeches and whisper snarky comments to each other. Then we would clutch hands when our names drew near. I'm sure we'd be just as tearful as Daniel and Gloria are. Maybe I would exchange a longing glance with a former boyfriend, feeling that everything was water under the bridge now that high school was over. I'd almost certainly lose myself in nostalgia before the bright and shiny future distracted me again.

All of that seems so far away now. Unreachable. My mood is glum as we follow the crowd out of the stadium. When I see the classic cars in the parking lot—even the poorest of them a head-turner in my day—I'm reminded that I travelled back through freaking time and feel a little better, because who else has done that? Graduation ceremonies are a dime a dozen. I'd be crazy to pout over missing mine when I'm in the middle of an experience that most people would envy. With that in mind, I cease my brooding to focus on the present.

We don't have to worry about traffic. Daniel's parents made the sensible decision to walk to the graduation ceremony, since their house is so close. My great-grandparents left their car parked there too. The afternoon is blissfully cool as we escape the chaos, the puffed-up clouds drifting across the sky providing shade. The adults are ahead of us, along with the young girls. The rest of us trail them, Gloria and Daniel talking wistfully about the ceremony and everything they are leaving behind. I want to hug and kiss him in congratulations. Gloria is holding the flowers I bought, but I made sure to look at him when handing them to her. He seemed to understand why. I settle for putting my arms around them both as we walk, like anyone might with friends, but I give Daniel a squeeze before releasing them again.

Once we're back at the house, everyone gets refreshed and changed. I stay in the living room, despite wanting to be upstairs with Daniel in his bedroom. I'm not worried about what anyone would think. I simply don't trust myself. How could I not leap on even the smallest opportunity to express my feelings for him, no matter what form that might take? If one of his sisters should barge in, or if his mother overheard affectionate words, it could threaten Daniel's happiness. I won't take that risk. Not until the odds are more in our favor.

I answer the door out of habit when someone knocks, a young girl taking a step back to check the address before explaining that she's the babysitter. I usher her inside. Daniel's sisters won't be joining us for dinner, it seems. When leaving the house, we get into two separate cars. I stay with my family and Daniel goes with his. We're off to the Starlight Supper Club, whatever that is. The building doesn't offer many hints from the outside. It doesn't even have windows, making it resemble a bowling alley. When we enter, I'm pleasantly surprised. The decorations are elegant, favoring white cloth and gold accents. Tables line the dining hall, tended to by waiters in vests and bowties. The center of the room is countersunk, three steps leading to an area cleared for dancing and—at one end of this—the stage where a live band plays.

I'm wearing that same outfit that I had on during my job hunt; the pink button-up shirt and gray slacks. It's the best I've got, but I still worry that I'm underdressed. Even the band members are in full tuxedos. Daniel is wearing a light blue shirt and navy tie, along with a gray jacket. He chooses to sit between Gloria and me. I take the first opportunity to lean close and whisper. "Should I be wearing a suit?"

He studies my expression before he scoots back and stands, shrugging off his jacket. I'm concerned he'll try giving it to me, which would be a dead giveaway, but instead he hangs it on the back of his chair and sits again while loosening his tie.

"What?" he says when he notices his parents staring. "It's too hot in here."

He pockets the tie and undoes the first button of his shirt, matching my appearance. Then he resumes browsing the menu, like the issue had nothing to do with me, and I feel a surge of gratitude.

Dr. Parker requests a bottle of champagne when the waiter returns to take our orders, and it isn't long before we're each holding a bubbling glass flute. Nobody seems concerned that we're underage. Who am I to argue? It's practically doctor's orders!

"Here's to our new graduates," Mrs. Parker says when raising her glass.

"And to the next Dr. Parker," Daniel's father adds, nodding to his son. "I'm very proud of you."

I feel Daniel tense next to me, so I raise my glass, wanting to draw attention away from him before it becomes awkward. "And here's to future fashion icon, Gloria Edwards."

"You'll take the world by storm, baby girl," Errol says warmly.

Everyone sips champagne, except for Gloria, who leans close and whispers. "Is that a prediction? Or a fact?"

"Up to you," I say loud enough for Daniel to overhear. "We each make our own destiny."

"That's so true," Mrs. Parker interjects. Maybe I was a little too loud. "The world is your oyster, Danny. You can fulfill your heart's desire. That's such a gift! Don't take it for granted."

"You'll make a fine physician," Dr. Parker agrees, perhaps missing the point. "Even if you don't want to be a pediatrician."

"Thanks," Daniel manages before taking a swig.

"I can't believe how fast you've both grown up," Harriet chimes in. "Seems like only yesterday we watched you hunting Easter eggs together. Do either of you remember that?"

"I do," Gloria says. "It's the first time we met. He stole half my eggs."

"I had to," Daniel retorts. "You cleared the yard."

"Hey, nothing in the rules talks about leaving eggs behind."

"It's called good sportsmanship," Daniel shoots back.

"And sometimes you still seem like children, despite your age," Harriet says with an exasperated sign. "Maybe that's why I kept imagining you wearing diapers under those gowns."

"Mom!" Gloria complains.

"I was," Daniel says shamelessly. "The ceremony takes too long and they don't give you bathroom breaks."

Gloria looks mortified. "Please tell me you're kidding."

"It terrifies me that you even need to ask," I interject.

The appetizers arrive next. I'm not surprised to see a variety of shellfish, since that seems to be all the rage. I stick to the shrimp cocktail while avoiding the clams. Or are they oysters? I've never been brave enough to step into that culinary arena. Although watching Daniel slurp one down before licking his lips certainly helps increase my appetite.

"They're playing our song," Mrs. Parker announces.

Dr. Parker pushes back his chair and stands. "When she wants to dance," he explains to Gloria's family, "every song is 'our song.'"

"Oh, I like that." Harriet turns to her husband. "This just happens to be our song too, doesn't it?"

"Any excuse to get you into my arms is fine with me," Errol answers smoothly.

The adults are halfway to the dancefloor when Gloria turns an eager expression on Daniel. "Seems like it's ladies' choice."

She looks at me. "Nothing personal, but dancing with my 'cousin' would be strange."

"Not as strange as the truth," I murmur.

I watch as they join the other dancers, impressed just how smoothly Daniel and Gloria perform a waltz. When they spin, and he's facing in my direction, our eyes meet. Just like when I gave the flowers to Gloria, I can tell that—in his heart—he's really dancing with me.

When the song ends, Daniel's parents return to the table, but only Dr. Parker sits. Mrs. Parker holds out her hand. "We wouldn't want you to feel left out," she says.

"That's okay. This isn't really my style of—" She takes my hand, pulling me to my feet while ignoring my protests. Just because I can play a waltz doesn't mean I know how to dance to one. What's worse is the song that starts next has a completely different rhythm.

"Do you know how to do a foxtrot?" she asks when turning to face me.

"I appreciate this, Mrs. Parker, but I don't want to step on your nice shoes or—"

"I told you, call me Melody," she says, taking my right hand and moving it to her back. She places a palm on my arm while gripping my other hand, and I'm already lost. "It's easy. Just follow my lead. Left foot, and then right…" She moves backward, forcing me to step forward. "Now move to the left, and then bring your right foot along…"

I stumble but manage to recover without embarrassing myself too much. I hope Daniel isn't watching.

"You know what helps me?" Melody says. "Picturing it as geometry. Each step is a point, and when you move your feet, you're drawing a line to the next. So all we're doing now is creating a ninety-degree angle, like writing the letter L. Try to visualize it."

I do… and it helps! I worry less about each step being right and more about the shape we need to draw together. The only problem is that I'm quickly running out of dance floor. Melody sees me glance past her with concern, her expression reassuring.

"Now we just need to add a forty-five degree angle to the end of each L," she says, aiming our bodies toward the center of the dance floor. "Ninety-degrees, forty-five degrees. Now give me two ninety-degrees in a row."

Soon we're back in the middle of the floor. Daniel smiles at me when we breeze past. I'd return the gesture if I wasn't already grinning. My performance is far from perfect, but I'm having so much fun that I'm disappointed when the song ends and Melody points out that the main course has been served. On the way back to the table, I'm tempted to ask her if she ever worked as a dance instructor, until I remember something Daniel told me.

"You must really like math."

"Oh, it's just a hobby," Melody says dismissively. "Although a few years back, I sat down and drew the shapes that dancers make. Not the charts that show which foot goes where, but the pattern they create when moving across the floor. Some of them were exceedingly beautiful."

"A mathematician *and* an artist," I say in awe. "You're just full of surprises."

I can tell she thinks that I'm flattering her. I'm not. Daniel's mother has more depth than I realized. When we sit at the table and begin eating, I'm determined to learn more about her.

"Did you go to college as well?" I ask.

"Oh yes," she says while cutting into her steak. "I insisted. I didn't have any hope of finding the sort of work I wanted, but I thought I could at least be as educated as possible for the sake of my children. That's something we both feel strongly about, isn't it?"

She's addressing Harriet, who nods. "My education comes from a public library, and when I had my little girl, I made sure to bring her with me."

I don't realize how radical a notion this is until I notice how uncomfortable Dr. Parker seems, and how proud Errol looks while listening to his wife.

"Children are eager to learn when they see how much you enjoy it," Melody agrees. "I didn't have Daniel while I was still in school, of course, but during the war, when so many young men were called to duty, he seemed to enjoy being at work with me." She anticipates my next question. "I was an accountant at the Glen Ellyn State Bank, the same one my parents took me to as a little girl. Who would have thought?"

She has the same wistful tones that Daniel and Gloria did when waxing nostalgic about high school. I'm tempted to ask why she no longer works there, or as an accountant in general, but I don't want to stir up trouble on a special occasion. Although

I can't help feeling irritated that this issue continues to rear its ugly head in my day. Why don't we all have the same rights and opportunities? Is that such a big deal?

The topic of conversation moves on, so I let the matter drop for the time being. After gorging ourselves on our entrees, we're offered dessert. The other men choose chocolate cake. The women and I opt for cheesecake. At the end, we're all stuffed and nearly comatose. Dr. Parker insists on paying, despite Gloria's parents insisting that he shouldn't. I'm glad they give in. I bet this place isn't cheap.

"I always regret ordering so soon," Melody confides. "We should have danced more first."

"We have the solution to that," Harriet says, nudging her husband.

"We'd like to invite you to join us at the Silver Rattle," Errol says. "Our treat. It's a fantastic place to celebrate, and by the time we're all down there, I bet you'll find your toes tapping again, Melody."

"That's very kind of you," Dr. Parker says, "but we do have church in the morning."

"Come on, Dad!" Daniel pleads. "I've always wanted to go, and they're not going to let me in without you guys."

"It's not as though we have to stay until they close," Melody says, adding to the pressure. "The kids can drive us home if we're feeling tired. When's the last time we had a real night out?"

"Not recently enough, it would seem," Dr. Parker says with good humor. "Errol, you might have just saved my marriage with your idea. Thank you."

"Yes!" Gloria and Daniel exclaim in unison.

I don't have a chance to find out why they are excited until I'm in the car with my family again. For this trip, Errol is leading the way to downtown Chicago, the Parkers right behind us.

"What's the Silver Rattle?" I ask.

"The best place on Earth," Gloria answers.

"A night club," Errol clarifies.

"With a sense of community," Harriet adds.

"The best place on Earth," Gloria repeats. "I hope Mama is there tonight. That's the owner. And my idol."

"Mama is a black woman," Harriet explains.

She doesn't need to say more. I get the impression that a

woman-owned business is a rarity in this era, and when you add skin color to the equation, that makes it exceptional.

Downtown Chicago is positively jumping when we get there, the sidewalks teaming with people. I'm used to that around tourist spots like Navy Pier, but the nightlife in my day is more likely to be found in trendy neighborhoods such as Logan Square or Wicker Park. Here it still thrives, although the street we end up on is nearly devoid of life. The city proper is to the north, a residential neighborhood to the south. What surrounds us now are commercial businesses that have already closed. We park and rejoin Daniel's family before walking half a block to a long single-story brick building. Only a large man standing near the door indicates that it might be a club. A few men loiter further down the block, decked out in tailored suit jackets that hug their bodies tight and straight slacks that make their legs appear longer. I need to find out where they shop, because if I ever invest in formal attire while here, *that's* what I want to wear. I'm especially envious of the man in the purple jacket, who is leaning against the exterior while smoking, the bottom of one foot pressed against the brick. The very definition of cool.

Errol has a hushed conversation with the bouncer. They seem to know each other. I notice the door has a logo painted on it—a baby holding up a snake in one hand—before it swings open and music spills out onto the street. My legs start moving of their own accord, my feet matching the thudding rhythm, because *this* is what I've been missing. I've heard do-wop while here and listened to endless warbly ballads, but this is the music pumping through my veins. Every modern genre will spring from its roots; rock, pop, hip-hop… Jazz is the granddaddy of them all!

The club is dimly lit and smokey with a long bar to my left that I ignore. I'm more interested in reaching the main room, which isn't so different in layout than the Starlight Supper Club. The tables are much smaller and shoved against the walls, leaving more room for dancing. And boy are the people here shaking it! I may not know any formal dances, but my body always responds to the right kind of beat. I'm already shimmying my hips while staring at the stage. I see three guitars, a double bass, clarinet, trumpet, drums and—be still my heart—a concert grand piano! Right on cue, the heavy-set man sitting on the bench starts pounding the keys, his fingers a blur, and I feel like I'm about to blow a load while simultaneously breaking down into tears.

"Now *this* is a bash!" Gloria shouts from next to me.

I'd nearly forgotten that anyone was with me.

"Gee, it sure is nifty!" Daniel says in wonderment.

Gloria and I exchange a look before we both start laughing. We follow Errol to a table in the corner farthest from the stage. He leaves us there and goes with Dr. Parker to the bar. I'm only mildly disappointed when he returns with sodas for Daniel, Gloria, and me. I'm already buzzing. Who needs booze?

My attention remains locked on the stage, moving from player to player. Most of them are older and possess the understated confidence of someone who has mastered their craft. Their instruments are but mere extensions of themselves, their body movements minimal as they manifest little musical miracles. They make it look so easy.

Although a few are still learning. The lead guitar gets a few chords wrong. I doubt many people notice. The dancefloor is swinging. If I wasn't so taken by the musicians themselves, I might be out there too.

We're three songs in when a woman strolls on stage like she owns the place. She's short and heavy with buzzed hair, which is especially striking in this era. Most black women I've seen have straightened hair or wear styles that attempt to emulate what is currently fashionable for white women. She doesn't. Her sense of style is all her own, from the blood-red pants suit to the large orange shawl draped around her shoulders. She walks front and center, a spotlight reflecting off the bracelets, rings, and necklaces, surrounding her in a cluster of stars. And as it turns out, she *does* own the place.

"That's her!" Gloria says, grabbing my arm and shaking me in excitement. "That's Mama!"

"How y'all doin' tonight?" Mama smiles at the roaring response. "Good! That's what I like to hear. Now let's see if we can make the roof shimmy."

Without further ado, she begins belting into the microphone. The purr in her voice becomes a growl as she holds notes for so long that I'm convinced she has an extra set of lungs. Much like the men playing behind her, it all seems effortless. She points at people in the audience, winks at a few, and even walks over to the bass player to affectionately rub his bald head, all without missing a note. Toward the end of the song, she saunters off stage again, like it was all an amusing diversion from more important business.

"She's so amazing," Gloria breathes in between sets. "I've always wanted to design an outfit for her, but whenever I sit down to, I freeze up."

"Don't let yourself get intimidated," Daniel says from the other side of me. "You should work on it while pretending she'll never see the end result. Maybe that would take the pressure off."

Sounds like good advice, but I'm distracted by the man in the purple suit jacket I saw outside earlier, who is now climbing on stage. I watch as the lead guitarist stands, shakes the man's hand, and after a brief conversation, leaves to join a party at a nearby table. His friends pat him on the back while smiling, like he accomplished something. Meanwhile, the man in the purple jacket tunes a guitar. Not long after, another audience member approaches the stage and exchanges a few words with the drummer before taking his place.

"What's going on?" I ask.

"That's the community aspect we mentioned," Errol chimes in. "The audience gets to play with the house band while giving them a much-needed break."

I need a moment to digest this. "Anyone can play with them?" I ask.

"That's right."

"Do you need to sign up somewhere or—"

"Just go on up if you're feeling brave," Harriet says. "I tried singing once, and it was a gas, but I'm no Mama."

"That's okay," Errol says as he stands. "You'll always be my hot mama. Let's put some dents in that dance floor."

"I guess that's our cue," Dr. Parker says, getting up and offering a hand to his wife.

I rise with them, my chest tight as I approach the stage. I'm not nervous about performing. I'm only worried they won't let me. I make a bee-line for the piano like it's the hottest guy in the room. When I approach the man seated there, he's dabbing sweat off his forehead while looking at me with guarded hope.

"You know what you're doin'?" he grunts before I can get out a single word.

I nod, reach down, and play a simple blues scale in F.

"Good enough for me," he grumbles before standing and hobbling away toward the bar.

I sit on the bench, my breath short in anticipation. One of the other band members calls out the key we'll be playing in, and I miss it, but I'm not concerned. I lean back and let them establish a rhythm. The man in the purple jacket leaves his guitar in its stand and picks up a saxophone. The way he's keeping tabs on everyone makes me think he's the band leader. He starts blowing, and I start grinning, because I know the song. *St. Thomas*, made famous by Sonny Rollins. It's a jaunty little tune. My grandmother used to play it all the time. Half a minute later, the band leader turns to glance at me, and I realize that I haven't played a note.

No problem. I let my hands do their thing, laughing in sheer unadulterated joy, because this is my voice. Words have never been sufficient for me, too limited to express what I feel inside. I let the happiness pour out of me, my fingers bouncing from key to key in response. We're almost three minutes in when the man in the purple jacket turns to me again with a questioning expression. I nod in response. *St. Thomas* includes a solo for each instrument. The saxophone takes a break, meaning I'm the star of the next two minutes. People want to dance? I give them the jumpiest version of the melody I can manage, not holding anything back, because I know these guys have probably seen better than my best. Hell, they can probably manage it in their sleep, but I've got the extra energy to compensate. I'm on my feet for the last thirty seconds, really hammering the keys while looking to the double bass player to make sure he's ready. He's shaking his head, but more like he didn't expect so much soul from a kid like me. When I pass the song over to him, he puts me to shame. The dude must be pushing seventy, but he shows me what a lifetime of experience is worth. My eyes are glued on him until all the instruments come back briefly before the drum solo begins. He's easily the weakest of the quartet, but then he's not with the house band. Neither am I, so humility and focus are called for. I finish the song by supporting instead of trying to outshine. The saxophone carries us home, like a van full of optimism bouncing down the street, and the audience bursts into applause. It's a sound I love, but not nearly as much as the music itself. I'm relieved when the house pianist doesn't return to replace me yet.

The man in the purple jacket puts his saxophone in its stand and walks over. He's not much older than me. Mid to late twenties. He has a mischievous twinkle in his eye and a pencil-thin mustache. I don't know what he's wearing for cologne, but it's mixed with a hint of cigar and that, along with the cocky smile, makes me realize how good looking he is.

"Alonzo," he says, offering me his hand.

"Reggie," I reply while shaking it.

His grip is gentle before letting go. "You sticking around for a few more?" he asks.

"If you'll have me."

His response is a slow grin. Then he nods. "Let's see what else you can do."

I hold my own, but these guys have me on my toes the entire time. And I love it. I'm sweating up a storm three songs later and relieved when Alonzo addresses the audience. "We're gonna let you cool down for a hot minute," he says, "so get yourself somebody, or some*thing*, to hold. The bar is open folks!" Then he plays a riff, looking over at me with a raised eyebrow.

Round Midnight, another jazz staple, but not one that I'm as familiar with. I'll have to improvise. Alonzo begins crooning out lyrics about someone who is fine during the day but descends into heartache over an estranged lover as the night grows old. I search the audience for inspiration and find Daniel staring at me with rapt admiration that borders on infatuation. He's not the first to look at me like that. The stage has a certain magic, able to elevate the performers to a near-mythical status that—quite frankly—only creates unrealistic expectations. So I feel even more affection for him, knowing that this isn't why I caught his eye.

When the song comes to an end, so does my time on stage. The original pianist has returned and seems annoyed, like I overstayed my welcome. I don't know what the rules are, so I thank him. His response is inaudible over the applause. I can only smell the fumes of whatever he's been drinking. Worried he couldn't hear me either, I shake his hand, give an upward nod to Alonzo, and hop off the stage. I'm halfway to the table when Daniel and Gloria plow into me.

"That was amazing! Why do you ever stop playing? Are you famous in the future?"

They don't allow me to answer their questions before coming up with more, so I just laugh.

"Don't be too impressed," I say when they quiet down. "That's about the only thing I'm good at."

"We have *got* to start a band," Gloria says. "How hard are drums to learn? That'll be me. Daniel can sing. He was in choir, you know."

"Church choir," Daniel amends, already turning red.

Why do I find that so hot?

"Everyone at the table is impressed too," Gloria says. "I hope you're prepared to sign autographs. Come on."

"Actually," I say, looking pointedly at Daniel, "do you know where the restrooms are?"

"Yeah, they're…" He begins to point before it clicks. "I'll show you. I also have to go."

I turn to Gloria before we part, asking her to tell the others that I charge a dollar per autograph. Then I follow Daniel around the stage toward the back, nudging him when I notice an exit. After making sure we aren't being watched, we push through the door and end up in an alley that is blissfully deserted. Once the door squeaks shut, we're all alone.

"You're really talented," Daniel says. "I've never seen anything like it."

"You have," I reply as I move close. "It just feels a little different when it's someone you know."

"I had no idea," he says, shaking his head. "You said you could play, but so can one of the guys in my troop, and honestly, listening to him is painful. You made me feel…"

"What?" I ask, pressing myself against him.

He grabs my hand and places it over his chest. His heart is racing, and it moves me, because mine beats just as hard for him. I slide a hand around to the back of his neck as we kiss. He responds by wrapping his arms around me, pulling us together as his back hits the exterior wall. We're deep into it when the door squeaks again, but we're not quick enough. By the time we manage to put a respectful distance between us, we've already been seen.

By the owner of the club.

Mama looks us over, her expression difficult to read. "Love makes fools of us all," she says, "but then, I suppose that's half the fun. Go on back inside, gentlemen. Mama needs a moment to herself."

"We weren't—" Daniel begins.

"—going to leave without telling you how much we love your establishment." I finish for him. "Thank you for having us."

"And for making my graduation extra special," Daniel adds.

She seems mildly amused by this. "Tell the bartender that Mama said you could have one on her. That was one helluva performance in there. And out here."

I grab Daniel's hand before he tries to deny anything again and pull him inside.

"Do you think she saw?" he asks.

"Yes. And she didn't care."

He looks to the closed door. "Really?"

"She offered to buy us a drink, didn't she?"

Daniel blinks. Then he smiles. So do I. His worst fear just came true. We were caught, and it wasn't the end of the world. Seeming emboldened by this, after glancing around, he steps forward and gives me a quick peck on the lips. "Reggie?"

"Yeah?"

Daniel swallows, seeming overcome with emotion. Then he shakes his head. "We better rejoin the others."

"Okay. Let's go."

He doesn't move, choosing instead to stand there and stare at me, so I laugh and give him a gentle push in the right direction. Then I follow along behind, buzzing with the same emotion that I'm certain he very nearly put into words.

Chapter II

I spend the next morning alternating between yawning and smiling. We were at the Silver Rattle until past midnight. I would have happily remained in the club until they kicked us out, but the older folks insisted that we had to go. I replay the music in my mind, remembering how good it felt to play a piano again, and can't stop smiling. In other words, I'm still caught up in the afterglow.

Gloria and I are sitting in the living room when we hear honking. We were expecting Daniel, but he usually comes to the door and knocks. Consulting each other, we shrug and go outside to see what the commotion is. We catch Daniel standing next to his mother's car while wearing a pair of shades and trying out different poses. Then he notices us, crosses his arms over his chest, and juts out his hip to make contact with the car.

"He's hopelessly uncool," Gloria murmurs as we approach.

"Yeah," I say, feeling a surge of affection for him. "He is." A little louder I add, "What's all the commotion, young man? You're disturbing the prayers of your good Christian neighbors."

Daniel glances around in concern. "Really?"

"No, not really," I say, stealing his shades and putting them on. "Are you in a hurry or something?"

"Huh-uh," he says, taking a step back and gesturing at the car. "Look at what my parents gave me!"

Gloria groans. "I was hoping they'd give you the Bel Air. Or maybe a brand-new Thunderbird."

"This is a great car!" Daniel says defensively.

"And it matches those pretty eyes of his," I add, watching him turn pink.

"I don't know what to do with either of you," Gloria says in mock exasperation. "I really don't." She takes a step back and grins before addressing her best friend. "Hey, we finally have our own set of wheels!"

"I know!" Daniel responds with equal enthusiasm. "We can go anywhere we want!"

We take advantage of the newfound freedom, Daniel driving us up north for lunch. Afterwards we visit a swap meet, which takes place in a stadium parking lot so people can sell or trade directly from their cars. We browse the usual second-hand items you'd find at garage sales, Gloria gravitating toward clothes she can repurpose. I pick up a few more shirts and accessories so I'll have more options.

We cruise the Eisenhower Expressway in the late afternoon, which Daniel and Gloria seem weirdly in awe of. They keep saying how much faster everything is now, and where they want other highways to be built. That's when I realize that the interstate system is new. Obviously it wasn't around when settlers were hauling wagons across the country, but when growing up, I took it for granted as a permanent feature of the landscape. I have a better appreciation for it now, especially since the lanes aren't congested with traffic yet, allowing us to zip around the area. We stop for pizza in the evening and joyride some more before Daniel drops us off at home. We're all dreading work the next day.

"Let's re-enroll in high school," Gloria suggests with a sigh. "We couldn't have learned *everything*. Just a few more years, then we'll be responsible."

I share her sentiment when getting ready for bed that night. I'm about to strip off the T-shirt I'm wearing when I hear knocking. I turn and see a shadow moving beyond the basement window. I can only imagine one possibility. I'm not disappointed when I stealthily creep outside and see a green Plymouth Cranbrook parked outside. The interior light turns on and off again.

I hurry across the yard and hop inside. Daniel is behind the wheel and biting his bottom lip.

"You snuck out?" I ask him.

He nods. "I wanted to see you again. I thought we could… Would you like to go parking with me?"

"Parking?" I can guess what that means. "Are you in the mood for some necking?"

Daniel nods again. Then he drives us to a dark corner of the neighborhood and pulls over next to an undeveloped lot. He stretches an arm along the seat back, his fingertips touching my shoulder, and stares at me. I stare back, shaken by the intensity of what I feel for him. Much like the gate, every time we get close, my insides start to buzz. I slide across the seat, tilt my head so we can kiss, and realize just how much better things will be now that Daniel has a car. We'll still have to steal each moment together while hidden in the shadows, but at least there, we'll have some privacy to call our own.

— — —

The next week wears me down, the work no easier than when I started. I thought I'd get used to it, and in some ways I have, but my body still aches at night. Even with the precautions I take, my eyes often end up red and watering. Enough that I wonder if I'm doing permanent damage to them. It's not all bad. At the end of each day, Daniel is there to pick me up. Gloria is with him, of course, but I don't mind now that we have another option when we need to see each other. Daniel doesn't sneak out every night, but he picked me up for lunch on Tuesday, and stopped by for a repeat of what we did at the drive-in movies on Wednesday night. He still hasn't touched me in any way more intimate than a kiss, but I'm letting him take things at his own pace. The anticipation is kind of hot. I just hope there's payoff eventually. I'm thinking the moment has finally arrived when I get into his car Friday afternoon.

"You have to come home with me," he says. "Right away."

I start to get hard just hearing those words. "Is there something you want to show me?" I ask innocently.

"Yes," he says, eyes narrowing in suspicion. "Did Gloria tell you already?"

He isn't referring to sex then. I'm clueless as to what awaits me as we enter the house.

"In the dining room," Daniel says, leading the way. "Quick!"

He sure is excited. When I follow him and see what he means, I feel as though I've traveled forward through time. The unfamiliar table and chairs have been moved aside, making room for a Steinway Model B Grand Piano. I know the exact make because it's been part of my life for as long as I can remember. My hands are shaking as I sit on the bench. I only manage to play a single chord before emotion overwhelms me and I start to cry.

"Are you okay?" Daniel asks, sitting next to me.

"Yeah," I croak, running my hands across the polished black wood affectionately. "This is the piano I learned to play on."

"You mean—" Daniel looks at the instrument with wide eyes. "—the exact same one?"

"Yup. It being here, in this room, is the reason I fell in love with playing. My parents were always shooing me away from it because I'd make too much noise, but I couldn't get enough. I even lost interest in my toys. All I wanted was to sit here and make music."

I let my fingers move across the keys, playing a swelling melody that reflects the affection I feel for the instrument. To be reunited with my piano now, when I'm separated from everything familiar, is almost as reassuring as my parents showing up to tell me that everything will be okay.

Daniel's sisters rush into the room. I wipe away my tears and play them a lighthearted tune, the girls dancing around while holding onto each other's hands. Melody joins us soon after, eyes lighting up as she watches me play. Everyone claps when I've finished, which is sweet of them.

"What do you think?" Melody asks me. "Danny came up with the idea but... Is it a good piano?"

"The absolute best," I rave.

"Wonderful! I'm so pleased. The delivery men had a terrible time. I'm not sure we'll ever get it out again."

"You won't," I say, remembering how my parents told me that the piano came with the house.

"Do you think it's appropriate for children?" she asks, still seeming uncertain. "To take lessons on, I mean."

I guffaw, thinking of the endless hours I spent here resisting my first teacher before finally giving into form and structure. "Oh yeah! It's perfect for that."

"What a relief!" she says, beaming at me. "Now all we need is you."

My mouth drops open.

"Do we start today?" Sarah asks me.

"He hasn't agreed to teach you yet," Melody chastises. Her expression is sympathetic when she addresses me again. "You aren't obliged to, of course. But when I heard the way you played the other night... Danny already has so many talents. I worry the girls haven't found anything they are passionate about yet. We'll pay you of course."

The sentiment is nice, but I won't be around long enough to teach them much. I feel oddly guilty about that. "This must have cost you a fortune."

Melody waves a hand dismissively. "The store I bought it from had a clearance sale. I didn't want a new car anyway. Where do I ever go? Besides, George usually walks to work during nice weather, so his car is often in the garage if I need it."

"That's why you should have given it to me," Daniel says, laughing when his mother swats him.

I shove my reservations aside for the moment and turn to the girls. "I'm afraid I have some bad news," I say theatrically. "Not everyone is cut out to play piano. You have to pass a test first." They look appropriately concerned. I shove Daniel off the bench, which delights them, and pat the empty spaces to either side of me. "Come on up here. Let's see what you can do."

Once they are clustered close to me, I crack my knuckles, wiggle my fingers like I'm about to cast a spell, and say, "Let's rock!" Then I use a single index finger to poke one of the black keys, and then another and another. It's the same silly song that most kids start out learning. Sarah already knows the lyrics and begins singing along.

"Hot cross buns! Hot cross buns! One a penny, two a penny, hot cross buns!"

"I think we have a real natural here," I say, "but can you play it? Look, I'll show you one more time."

Before long, the girls are taking turns, stopping to bicker with each other or to push the wrong keys while the other is playing. That's perfect. All I want is for them to engage with the instrument and recognize it as a source of fun.

Melody seems pleased, offering to get us all a glass of Kool-Aid. I stand when she leaves for the kitchen and turn on Daniel.

"You talked your mom into this?" I whisper, gesturing at the piano behind me. "What are you doing? You know I can't stay."

He straightens up and juts out his chin defiantly. "Why not?"

I check to make sure we're being ignored by his sisters before I reply. "Well, for starters, my family must think I'm missing or dead."

"Not if they get a letter from you explaining everything. We'll include evidence. I've been thinking about that actually. If we can get your photo into one of the newspapers, they'll have to believe. I'll pay for the advertising space and everything. We can make it say whatever it needs to."

"And then what?"

Daniel's brow furrows up, like it's obvious. "We'll make sure to save a copy for your parents. Gloria can give it to them. Don't you think they'll listen to her anyway?"

"No, I mean, what am I supposed to do with myself? Work in that warehouse the rest of my life instead of pursuing my dreams?"

"You could teach piano. I'm sure my mother would let you have other students over."

"And that's it? I never go home again?"

"You could." Daniel swallows. "Just… not yet."

He turns away when his mother reenters the room, probably to hide the emotion on his face. If she's anything like my mom, she'll be able to read him like a book. I accept a glass of Kool-Aid and sip from it before returning to the bench to teach the girls other easy tunes. I figure the more they can show their father when he gets home, the happier everyone will be about the new piano. It is, after all, one of the greatest gifts I ever received. I simply never realized who gave it to me until now, or his reason for doing so. Daniel wants me to stay. I catch his eye, my heart fluttering when he offers an apologetic smile, and wonder if I can put off returning home until the end of summer.

— — —

"Don't you think it's time to try again?"

I pretend not to hear Gloria when she says this. We're in the rumpus room of someone's house, a term that makes me chuckle each time I hear it. As far as I can tell, it's just a finished basement with a small wet bar and a few diversions like a dartboard and radio cabinet. Music is playing from a small record player on a shelf. People our age are standing around or lounging on the couches and chairs. Technically it's a party, but for a Saturday night, it sure is tame. The punch is spiked, so there's that, but all anyone wants to talk about is how they already miss high school or what their plans are. Daniel and Gloria introduced me to a few of their friends, and while they seemed nice, I'm happier squeezed between my people on a loveseat, like we are now.

"It's been three weeks," Gloria presses. "That's how long you said it would take to repair the gate."

"Yeah, but that was just an estimate," Daniel counters, leaning forward to see her better. "Who knows how long they'll really need."

"Which is why I thought he'd want to try again," Gloria retorts, raising an eyebrow at her best friend. Then she looks at me. "When's the last time you were out there?"

"Not since we—"

"—wrote down the Latin," Daniel says hurriedly.

Oh right! I'd forgotten we used that as an excuse.

"Did you translate it?" she asks.

"Yes." Daniel's nodding becomes more emphatic when he sees my questioning expression.

"What's it say?" I ask.

"Everywhere and nowhere." Daniel shrugs. "Total nonsense."

"Does that mean anything to you?" Gloria asks me.

I shake my head. "Sounds like someone trying to be profound. Maybe an ancient Roman teenager wanted to impress his girlfriend."

Gloria finds this funny. I'm hoping it's enough to distract her from the subject, but she's got her teeth sunk in it like a piranha. "I was thinking we could go out there tomorrow. We'll have a picnic first, as a going-away party, just in case it works."

"What's the rush?" Daniel grumbles.

"Well, for starters," Gloria replies, "my future daughter probably hasn't slept since her son disappeared. Considering the nurturing and attentive parent I inevitably become, I must be exhausted from staying up all night to comfort her. Does that sound about right? I'm a saint in the future, aren't I? Tell him."

I pantomime zipping my lips shut.

Gloria rolls her eyes and addresses her best friend. "I'll miss him too, but we really can't keep him here. Reggie has his own life to return to. Just imagine how it would feel if *you* got lost in the past."

Daniel crosses his arms over his chest and takes a single-minded interest in the dartboard, refusing to look her way again.

"There's no harm in going out there tomorrow," I tell him while appearing to address her. "I doubt it'll work anyway."

"I'll ask my mom to make her deviled eggs," Gloria says. Her eyes move away from mine and go wide. Then she grabs my arm and starts talking through clenched teeth, like a ventriloquist. "See the dreamboat who just sailed into the room?"

I glance toward the basement stairs and watch a handsome black guy with an athletic build stroll over to the punch bowl. "Yeah. What about him?"

"Does he look familiar to you?"

Of course not, but I make a show of scrutinizing him, even though I'm mostly just checking out his butt. "Nope. Never seen him before."

"You're sure?" she asks when he turns around, notices her, and waves. "He doesn't look like your grandpa by chance?"

"He does actually," I say, sitting upright. "That's him!"

Gloria's grip on my arm tightens. "Really?"

I laugh. "No. Sorry." The truth is, I've only seen photos of my grandfather. He died in a car accident before I was born. I wonder if I should tell her that, so she can try to prevent it. That would surely change my life and who knows what else. My grandmother never seemed unhappy or lonely, but then, I'm not sure if she would have shown those emotions to me, even if she was.

"Then why does he keep looking at me without coming over?" Gloria hisses in frustration.

"Maybe he thinks we're an item."

Gloria sticks out her tongue in revulsion. "Blech!"

"I agree, so Daniel and I are going to make ourselves scarce while you try your luck. I need some fresh air anyway."

"Is my hair okay?"

"Are you kidding? Why do you think he keeps looking over here? You're stunning!"

She smiles in appreciation before releasing me. "Thank you. Now get out of here."

"Yes, ma'am," I say.

Daniel stands with me, still not speaking a word to his friend. I wait until we're outside and beneath a tree on a sleepy residential street before attempting to reason with him.

"Gloria is only trying to help. She doesn't know what we have together."

"You do though," Daniel says. "So why did you agree?"

"Because she's right. People are worried about me."

His jaw clenches. "I don't care."

I'm tempted to say the same, but I wouldn't truly mean it, and I know he doesn't either, because his shoulders slump soon after.

"My mom would cry herself to sleep every night," Daniel mumbles, "even if someone showed her a dumb newspaper clipping that proved I was safe."

"Yeah. I'm sorry. It sucks."

His brow crinkles, probably because of the slang, and I want nothing more than to kiss away his confusion. I can't. Not here. It's frustrating. If the gate takes me home tomorrow, then we have less than a day together. I don't want to spend it resisting my impulses and stifling any affection I feel for him.

"Don't go to church tomorrow," I say. "Please. Come get me instead."

His eyes search mine, and I see reflected in them the same raw emotion that hounds me.

"Is that okay?" I ask. "We can tell Gloria that you invited me, like the Boy Scout meeting. Do you think she'll want to go?"

"To church?" Daniel sputters. "No. Not in a million years."

"Then we'll have the house to ourselves. You don't have to do anything with me. I just want to be alone with you."

"I want that too," Daniel squeaks. When he says my name, it sounds pained. "Reggie..."

"I know. But I'm here now, right? We can be sad about it later. This is still the good part. Let's enjoy it." I tilt my head toward the party, but he shakes his.

"Can we go for a walk instead?" he asks.

I consider our surroundings, noticing how much darker the sidewalks are, since streetlamps aren't as frequent or nearly as bright yet. Plenty of opportunity to be close without being seen. When I nod, he takes my hand, and together we venture out into a night that might be our last.

Chapter 12

I wake up early on Sunday and eat a quick breakfast alone before taking a shower. When dressing, I opt for a simple T-shirt and shorts, so I won't stand out if I make it back to my own time. I'm trying not to dwell on that half of the day, but it's a rumbling cloud on the horizon that can't be ignored. I write a quick note to my great-grandparents, claiming there was an emergency with my mom that I needed to rush back to Alabama for. I thank them for their hospitality and put all the cash I have in the same envelope. This is placed beneath my pillow. I plan on telling Gloria about it before passing through the gate.

With my preparations out of the way, I quietly slip outside and wait at the end of the driveway until Daniel's car arrives. When it does, I climb inside and stare, because his appearance has changed. The hair that is usually swept back and to the side is now hanging loose, the bangs long enough to touch the top of his cheekbones while framing those gorgeous eyes of his.

"You always wanted to see it down," Daniel says. "I figured this might be your last chance."

I lean close, intending to kiss him and run my fingers through his hair, until I remember that we can be seen. I don't want to put him at risk. Especially if I won't be here to protect him. Fuck. This is going to be rough.

"Take me home," I say, leaning back. "You look so damn beautiful that I don't trust myself here."

I reach for his hand, needing some sort of contact, and when this isn't enough, I rest my head in his lap again. Daniel strokes my head during the ride. I take his hand to press it to my lips. Of all the thoughts running through my mind, few are sexual. That's not a good sign. All I can think about is what our life together might have been like if I could stay.

"Nobody is home, right?" I say as we walk inside the house.

When he nods and shuts the door behind him, I don't waste any time. I kiss him, sure, but I also hold him tight, not wanting to let go again. When I pull back, I notice his glum expression.

"Don't be sad," I plead. "Not yet. Come on. I know what will cheer you up." I take his hand and lead him to the dining room. "I'll play you a song. Anything you want. What'll it be?"

Daniel smiles at the offer, which is flattering in itself. "Oh umm... I don't know. What sort of music do you like? Is it much different in the future?"

"A little." I sit at the bench, Daniel walking around to lean against the piano's body so he can watch me. "You want a preview?"

"Yeah!" he says, perking up.

"Okay. Man, where to begin? The sixties are coming up and that means... The Beatles!" I treat him to a medley of their upbeat hits like *Ticket to Ride* and *Penny Lane*, avoiding sad songs like *Yesterday*. I don't have the lyrics memorized so I make up half of them, figuring he won't know the difference anyway.

"Gee, that's really swell!" he says when I finish with a portion of *Here Comes the Sun*.

"The artists of the sixties are some of the most legendary. There are so many you need to see in concert, while you still have the chance. I'll make a list actually."

"What about the seventies?" he asks. "Are they any good?"

"Uh, yeah! I'll let my good friend Elton John tell you about Buh-buh-buh Bennie and the Jets." I could spend all day playing EJ tunes. Daniel seems unsure what to make of the current song, so I segue into *Rocket Man*. "Maybe you'll like this one more, space boy." This time I know the proper lyrics and sing them gleefully. I consider myself a competent vocalist. Enough to get by on my own, but I prefer to have someone else perform that role when possible. Daniel hasn't really heard me sing until today. He's got that starstruck expression again, but I can't take the credit. I'm only channeling the greats like Stevie Wonder, Kate Bush, Billy Joel... I take him on a breakneck trip through pop music history, although the closer we get to the present, the more he struggles.

"What was that?" he asks with a sour face.

"*Teen Spirit* by Nirvana. It's not really a piano song. We can skip the nineties for now, although I'm always up for some Tori Amos. Let's get closer to my time."

My eyes are half-lidded as I play a sample of Alicia Key's *Fallin'*, and I can tell that he most certainly has. When he checks his watch, I don't think it's because he's getting bored. "One more," I tell him, patting the bench. "Come on over here."

As soon as he's sitting next to me, I kiss his neck, making him laugh. Then I focus on my final offering, John Legend's *All of Me*, grateful that he hasn't heard it overplayed to the point of apathy, because it's a beautiful song filled with raw emotion. The kind that should be treasured, not piped through store speakers to sell more clothes. I know the complete lyrics and sing them, despite the risk of him mistaking the words as my own. Aren't they close enough though? If not each and every line, then the sentiment at least?

I'm so into the song that my eyes are closed, and when I open them at the end, I see the wet trails of tears on his cheeks. I wipe them away with my thumbs before kissing him.

"Can we go upstairs?" I ask.

He nods and stands. I watch as he checks the doors to make sure they're locked. He does the same when we're in his room. Daniel turns around, pressing his back to the door while staring at me.

"What counts for people like us?" he asks. "For a first time, I mean."

"Whatever we decide," I tell him, shaking my head. "Don't get hung up on things like that."

"I want it to be with you though," he says, expression vulnerable.

I move forward to take his hands and pull him away from the door. "There's no rush."

"Isn't there? We're out of time."

"Yeah. I guess so, but I don't want to do anything that you're not ready for."

"I am," he insists. "Don't make me imagine what we could have done. I'm ready. For everything."

That's a very long list, but I think I know what he means. Ideally we would build up to it, and have important conversations beforehand, but he's right. This might be the first and last time that we get to be together. I don't know what dynamic he expects, but I can meet his needs either way. I'm versatile. And selective about who I do that with. Trust is required. For me, an emotional connection is needed. I have that with Daniel. In spades.

"How do we begin?" he asks.

"Follow your instincts," I suggest.

He kisses me, his hands moving beneath my shirt. I lean back and take it off. He does the same, and when we kiss again, our bare torsos press together. His heart pounds against my chest, like a drum stirring up insatiable need inside of me. I'm done denying how I feel about him.

"Daniel..." I pull back to say.

"I love you, Reggie," he blurts out. "I love you so much!"

I smile, surprised that someone so innocent could steal my thoughts with such skill. I kiss him on his lips, his forehead, and his nose before I respond with the truth. "I love you too, Daniel."

We need a moment to wipe at our eyes while guffawing self-consciously. Then I reach for him, bringing our bodies close again. When I feel him tugging on the flap of my shorts, I step back to make it easier. He's already seen what I have to offer, on a few occasions, but I have a feeling this time will be different. Once my shorts and underwear hit the floor, he looks up at me.

"Can I?"

"I'm all yours," I tell him. "Anything you want. No need to ask."

He gingerly takes my cock in his hand, letting it rest in his palm, like he's measuring the heft, before he finally wraps his fingers around it. He pumps while making impressed sounds under his breath, even saying "wow" at one point, which I find more endearing than flattering. When he drops to his knees and takes me into his mouth, I remember my own first time and pull back, not wanting him to gag. Considering that he's probably never seen gay porn, he does fairly well.

"You don't have to suck that hard," I say patiently. "The softness of your mouth feels good enough."

Those green eyes look up at me, questioning as he tries again, and I just about lose it. He's so damn pretty. "Do you want to see what it feels like?"

Daniel seems reluctant to stop, but once he stands again, he positively rips at his shorts to get them open. I move him to the bed so he can sit. I love it when a guy has his legs spread with his balls hanging over the edge. I'm not disappointed. I take a moment to commit the scene to memory, especially the expression that is both nervous and hungry. Then I get down and show him what I can do, starting slowly by tickling the head of his cock with my tongue. He leans back, resting on his elbows, like he plans to enjoy himself. That suits me just fine. I take him in my mouth inch by inch, savoring the sweet taste of his excitement. He's gasping and moaning by the time I work my way down to the base, his balls high and tight like he might be getting close.

"Want me to keep going?" I ask.

He shakes his head. "No! I don't want it to be over."

"Me neither," I say, crawling into bed.

I lower myself on top of his body, resting my head against his neck, and we hold each other. His chest rises as mine falls. Our cocks are flexing and demanding attention but we ignore them. I kiss Daniel and then move down to lick his pink nipples, delighting in his laughter. When I notice him straining to check me out, I get out of bed, acting up for him while showing off. I flex what meager muscles I have—although the warehouse has certainly made them rounder—and stretch myself out in alluring postures. I'm also enjoying the view. Seeing him sprawled out in bed with everything on offer… I'm thinking we should finish up and go for round two. Daniel slides out of bed and onto the floor, crawling forward on his hands and knees to take me in his mouth again. I let him bring me to the brink before making him stand so I can return the favor. Before long, I'm ready to seal the deal, if he wants. I can tell he's on the verge.

Daniel stumbles back. "Wait," he gasps. "Not yet."

"Okay," I say, "but maybe we should put down some towels. This is a lot of buildup."

He laughs. "How do we... You know. Do the rest?"

I breathe out. The boy is crazy. No matter which position we end up in, I won't last seconds. I'm too turned on. "We need lube," I tell him.

He only seems momentarily confused, going to his dresser drawer and digging around in the very back until he finds a tube of something. Maybe it's what he uses when alone. I don't recognize the brand name, but it's goopy, clear, and smells neutral, so it'll get the job done. I'm about to point out that we need protection, but it's been long enough since I was with someone, and recent enough that I was tested, that I'm confident we'll be fine.

Daniel takes my hand, pulling me into bed with him with his back against the mattress. I guess that answers the question about our dynamic. I sit next to him, get some of the goo on my fingers, and lean over to kiss him. When I slide my hand between his legs, he flinches before relaxing again. I stay on the outside, wanting him to experience how incredible that alone can feel.

"Have you ever done anything like this by yourself?" I ask him.

He grimaces. "Would that be weird?"

"No! Not at all. In fact, it's great. You've done this too?" I slide a finger inside.

Daniel gasps and nods. "It feels so intense. Especially when you do it."

He might be in the closet, but thank goodness he didn't limit his self-exploration, because that'll help make this easier. I engulf him in my mouth again, and when he hisses in warning, I give him mine to suck on like a pacifier as we slowly work our way up to three fingers. Soon he's writhing in pleasure, his expression pleading with me.

"It'll be easier if I'm on my back and you lower yourself on top of me," I tell him.

Daniel seems reluctant, but not for the reason I fear. "Do we have to? I want you on top."

I'm guessing that's what he always imagined in his fantasies. I'll make it work. I position myself above him, rubbing my palm along his muscled thighs. All that tromping around in the woods while camping with the Boy Scouts gave him some gorgeous legs. He spreads them like a butterfly's wings, and I press against him, intending to take it slow, but he grabs my waist and starts pulling me in. He stops soon after.

Daniel's mouth is open and he's holding his breath. I'm worried that I've hurt him when he lets out a long breathy moan. Then he reaches for my neck and drags me down for a kiss. I move my hips back and forth, rocking him gently while slowly working my way deeper inside. Each time he winces, I ease off, but it's never long before he's pulling at me again, wanting more. We've reached a steady rhythm when he stops playing with himself and pounds the mattress with a fist.

"Ungh. I can't keep doing this."

I freeze. "Does it hurt?"

"No! It feels too good. I can't hold out any longer."

"You don't have to," I tell him, picking up the pace. "Just tell me when you're ready."

Daniel bites his bottom lip. "I want you to go first."

"You've got it." I start pumping faster, his eyes pleading with me not to stop, so I don't until I'm growling with each thrust, overwhelmed by the pleasure as I explode inside of him.

I reach down to knock his hand away so I can do it for him, loving how sweetly he says my name. "Reggie… Oh my gosh… Reggie!"

I feel Daniel throb in my hand and lean over to kiss him as he comes. My hips slow to a gentle sway as he gasps for breath and pounds the mattress again. I hope he always does that. Even if I'm not around to see it, which I already hate the idea of. I don't know if he's having similar thoughts, but he wraps his arms around me with sudden urgency. I relax my weight on him, still inside as he squeezes me close.

"I love you so much," he whimpers.

"I love you too, Daniel. Nothing can ever change that. No amount of time or distance. I'll love you just the same."

His arms tighten their hold. He doesn't want to let go, and I'm glad, because…

I don't want to either.

— — —

"How can anyone think that's wrong?"

We're at my favorite spot again, in the park across the street from the house I grew up in. After cuddling in bed we took a shower, unwilling even there to separate for long. We kept clinging to each other, as if it could stave off the inevitable. Once dressed, we stood at the kitchen counter while preparing food for our picnic. Then we left the house to sit on the bench, not wanting Daniel's parents to discover us together. He told them he wasn't feeling well as an excuse to skip church—mild nausea that he'll claim has passed.

"Sometimes, when I did things by myself," Daniel continues, "I'd feel guilty and pray for forgiveness. Not this. No one will ever convince me that we did something wrong, Reggie. It was beautiful."

"With you it was," I say. "But you have to be careful.

163

Especially from the late seventies on. There's a new disease that is sexually transmitted and—"

Daniel grabs my hand. "I'm not doing that with anyone else. Ever again."

"I want you to. When you find someone worthy of your love. Just be careful. Don't let anyone hurt you or be cruel..." My voice falters. "I wish I could take you with me."

"I thought about it," Daniel says. "Do you think it would work?"

"Doesn't matter," I say, shaking my head. "Your family would be just as devastated to lose you, and I don't think you'd see most of them again. Sixty-five years is a long time. How old are your parents now?"

I can see how much the thought wounds him, so I don't press the point. He checks his watch and stands up with an apologetic expression. The plan is for him to go home again, tell his parents that he's feeling better, and pick me up on his way to get Gloria. I give him a reassuring smile as he leaves. Then I sit alone on the bench and struggle with conflicting desires. Can I stay? If there was a way to make it work without hurting the people I love, I would, but I can't seem to find the solution. I wish I understood the gate better. It only works when falling apart? How does that make sense? If I could travel back and forth between the two eras, I'd have it all.

I say as much to Daniel when he comes to collect me. "Ever read anything in your science fiction magazines about time gates?"

"No," he says. "Usually it's a machine you get into or a little gizmo that makes it possible."

"A plot device."

"Yeah. They never make much sense."

I almost promise to figure out the gate so I can return, but then I imagine him waiting for me year after year, always disappointed and never moving on. I'd rather he find someone he can be with, despite the thought making my heart want to break. We're both lost in thought until we reach our destination.

Gloria is in a chipper mood when she climbs into the back seat with Tupperware containers. "How was church?" she asks.

"We didn't go," Daniel says, surprising me with his honesty. Especially when he adds, "I wasn't feeling well so Reggie and I hung out in my room."

"Oh. How are you doing now?"

"Great," Daniel says with a swallow. Then he manages a smile before turning around to face her. "It was a beautiful morning."

"Yeah," I say. "It really was."

"Well I enjoyed sleeping in. Guess who I dreamed about?"

"Leroy?" Daniel and I say in unison.

Since getting his number at the party last night, Leroy has been Gloria's favorite subject. "I'm a little disappointed he didn't call me first thing this morning," she says. "Not that I would have answered. You don't win a race by lying down at the starting line, if you know what I mean."

I hold up a hand in protest. "Hearing my grandmother discuss her boy-bating techniques could result in lifelong trauma. Can we all agree on that?"

Gloria is shameless. "You wouldn't *exist* without those techniques, so you better give me enough details to recognize the right man when I see him. I bet it *is* Leroy. You just don't want me to know."

Her antics are a welcome distraction. By the time we've spread out a blanket at Churchill Woods, a cheerful sun is shining in an optimistic sky. Daniel and I set aside our sorrow while we eat. Gloria attempts to squeeze me for future spoilers. So I tell her a story about the turn of the century when robot servants began kidnapping human babies, directly from the crib, and replacing them with shiny silver robot copies, not understanding that we could tell the difference.

"They were trying to keep the human population down while infiltrating our ranks, but one of those robot babies, Mark Zuckerberg, grew up to become the savior of the entire human race when he invented a powerful weapon called social media."

"How can a robot grow at all?" Gloria asks, her eyes narrowing in suspicion. "Aren't they made of metal?"

"Yeah. Alien metal. I mentioned that part, didn't I? The invaders from Planet Disco who visit Earth in the seventies? Better hide your sequins. That's what they come here for."

She tosses a deviled egg at me, which I feel graze my ear as I dodge. Close one!

Our mood grows somber as we pack up everything and head into the woods. Gloria sighs heavily. "I wish there was a way you could send a letter back to us, so we know that you made it okay.

Although I guess I'll find out when I'm super old."

"Oh right. I'll see you when I get home."

"What about me?" Daniel asks. "Am I still alive?"

I look to my grandmother, almost expecting her to have the answer. Instead she asks another question.

"We're still friends," Gloria says from the other side of me. "Aren't we?"

"I don't know," I admit. "You never mention him."

Gloria stops in her tracks. "That can't be right. Even if he avoids you because of paradoxes or whatever, you must hear me say that I'm going to visit my friend Daniel. He must call at the very least."

"Phones are private in the future. I wouldn't know if he did."

"Do you think I'm already dead?" Daniel asks.

"I don't know. I'm sorry."

We stand there awkwardly before I take the lead. They aren't making this easier on me. I think of my parents as motivation and remind myself that I still don't know what happened to Hannah. What if I return to the present and discover that she disappeared at the same time as me? I'm the only one who might be capable of helping her.

As kids, whenever the gate came into view, we'd usually race to it and run right through the middle. Now I approach cautiously, like it's a dangerous animal.

"I guess this is goodbye," Gloria says to me.

"We'll see." I turn to Daniel. "Can I talk to you alone for a second?"

He nods.

"Future stuff?" Gloria asks, her tone serious for once.

"Sort of. There are things I need to tell him that you can't hear yet."

"Okay. Should I go somewhere else or…"

"No, it's fine." I set down the picnic basket next to her. Daniel does the same with the bag he's carrying. "We won't be long."

We backtrack down the path before turning right to pick our way through the trees, ducking behind the largest one I can find. He attempts to kiss me, tears already in his eyes, but I put a hand on his chest to hold him at arm's length.

"Listen, I need you to promise that you'll try this again with someone else."

"I don't want—" he starts to protest.

"I know. I don't either. But that's only how we feel right now. You have your entire life ahead of you. So do I. We've gotta think long term. What happens in our twenties? Or our thirties, forties, or fifties? Do you want me to go through life without someone to love, just because I can't be with you?"

"No," he responds hoarsely. "I don't want you to be lonely."

"That's how I feel about you. There are other guys like us out there. You just have to be brave and go find them."

He shakes his head, his expression imploring me to stop, but I can't. This is too important.

"Promise. Give me that reassurance so I won't worry about you as much, and I'll do the same. Right now." I take his hands in mine, like we're at the altar and about to exchange vows. "When we're separated, it's going to devastate me. I'll let myself ache for you. I'll mourn everything that we could have had. You'll be a scar on my heart that I carry with me for the rest of my life. But I will find someone else. And when I do, I'll tell him about you, because you're amazing, Daniel. You're sweet and smart and everything that I've been looking for." I swallow and make myself focus on what needs to be done. "But I promise to move on anyway. You'll be less sad knowing that I have, even though the thought hurts us now. Okay. Your turn. Please. Say that you will."

"I promise," Daniel squeaks out, "but there's no way I'll ever love him like I do you."

He throws himself into my arms. I hold him there until the crying stops and his breathing is no longer ragged. Then I wipe away his tears for the second time that day and take a step back. His eyes are pink from crying, but hopefully Gloria won't notice. Or if she does, she'll probably assume he's sad about losing a friend. I take his hand as we walk back to the path.

When we reach it, I have to let go of him, and it feels terrible. Neither one of us says much for the remainder of the way. I'm struggling to keep it together.

"This is the moment of truth," I say after hugging Gloria.

I already told her about the note and money for her parents. All that's left is to leave. I start walking toward the gate. Then I stop and turn around.

"Could you guys wait on the other side?" I ask them. "That way I can still see you."

"Yeah," Daniel says, tromping forward with determination.

Gloria cries out in alarm when he walks *through* the gate. He doesn't disappear. Instead he stands on the opposite side while glowering.

"You scared the life out of me!" she says, marching toward him. "You could have ended up anywhere!"

"Then why is it okay for him to go through?" Daniel growls, gesturing at me.

"Guys!" I say loud enough to get their attention.

They turn to face me with questioning expressions.

"Here goes," I say, walking toward the gate.

I feel the vibrations build inside the closer I get. And I'm scared. I don't know why. Maybe I'll travel even further back in time, but I don't think that's the issue. Part of me can't help feeling like I'm making a mistake, because I really *really* like him. I've never felt this way about anyone before. I keep my eyes on Daniel as I take the last few steps, wanting him to be the final thing I see. The stones are close enough for me to touch, the archway directly above me now.

Pale green eyes fill with tears. So do my own. And then...

Daniel's expression changes to surprise. I take another step. And another. When I turn around, the gate is six feet behind me, the vibrations lessening. It didn't work!

"What happened?" Gloria asks.

"Nothing," I splutter. "Ha ha ha!"

"You don't sound very broken up about it," she retorts.

Of course not! I glance at Daniel, but he has his back to us. Probably to collect himself.

"I guess they haven't managed to repair the gate yet," I say.

Gloria shakes her head. "I don't understand how it could possibly take so long. I'll have known about this for most of my life. There's no way I won't plan for it. Unless I *do* make sure the gate is repaired, and it's still not enough to get you home."

"I have no idea," I say dismissively. "Delays happen. We'll try again some other day."

"I guess we could make this a weekly thing," Gloria says. "Just don't expect me to get so emotional next time. You know what? While we're here, I want to take another look at those markings. There has to be a clue that we're missing."

She walks closer to the gate to inspect it. I join her, and when I hear Daniel approaching, I stand up straight and catch his eye, flashing a tentative smile. The expression on his face is pure relief before he smiles back. I have no idea what's going to happen next. I only know that it's not over between us yet.

Chapter 13

Another work week has come to an end, my happiness increasing along with my frustration. Daniel makes every excuse to see me, bringing lunch for us to share in the warehouse parking lot and picking me up at the end of each shift. Our entire relationship seems to take place in his car. Most nights he'll drive to Gloria's house once it's late enough so we can park somewhere for a rare moment of privacy. That's where we are now. Daniel is buttoning his shorts. I finished twenty minutes ago. We took turns blowing each other so one of us could keep a constant lookout, and while that was hot, I want more for us.

"I miss holding you," I murmur as I slide close to him. Even this action has him checking the mirrors, and rightly so. Interracial couples face tremendous backlash in this era, and when it's two dudes... The consequences could be as dire as us losing our lives. I take his hand in mine regardless, unable to resist the comfort of his closeness. "I want to sleep in your arms, wake up together in the morning, and have breakfast without having to hide who we are. I'd never stop kissing you."

Daniel smiles and pecks me on the lips. "Nothing is stopping you now."

It's easy to prove him wrong. I begin kissing him on the lips, not letting up until he pulls away to check our surroundings. Then he recognizes the point I'm making and sighs. "What can we do?"

"Well," I say, lifting my butt in the air so I can slide a hand into my front pocket easier. "I put together an Excel spreadsheet on my fancy new iPhone." I pull out a folded piece of notebook paper. Daniel doesn't ask me to explain the joke. Unless it's something important or that he's curious about, he just assumes I'm referencing weird future stuff. "After doing some budgeting, the situation is looking hopeful."

I hand the paper to him before I explain the hastily scribbled numbers.

"I'm going to insist I get the seventy-five cents an hour my boss promised me."

Daniel grunts. "It's criminal how little they pay you."

"Sure, but at least it's tax-free. I can do a lot with six dollars a day. That combined with what your parents pay me for piano lessons…" I visit his house twice a week, each girl receiving an hour of private tutoring, which pulls in an additional ten dollars a week.

"One hundred and sixty a month," Daniel says with a nod of approval.

"Is that good? How much do you make?"

"About the same."

He works six hours a day and doesn't have to tutor in addition to his normal job. That doesn't seem fair, but I'm not surprised.

"Now check this out," I say, reaching into my other front pocket for a folded-up strip of newspaper.

Daniel laughs. "I wondered why your shorts kept crinkling."

"Drives the guys wild," I say with a wink while handing the clipping to him. It's from the classified section of the paper that advertises apartments for rent. "See the listings I circled?"

Most of them are described as furnished rooms and only cost around ten dollars a week. I worry about there being enough privacy, like the old movies with nosey landladies who keep tabs on everyone who comes and goes. One ad promises a private entrance. That could work.

"How come all of them are furnished?" Daniel asks. "Those are usually more expensive."

"Because there's no sense in me having my own place if there's not a bed. Or a couch or even a kitchen chair. I don't have anything but clothes really. Look." I point at my favorite listing, which is for a one-bedroom apartment near the university. "One hundred a month isn't bad."

"You still have to pay for utilities and food."

"I know a guy who works at a grocery store. He can probably get me a discount."

"And this one is so far away," he says, tapping the apartment I like most. "How would you get to work?"

"Public transportation. I'd have to wake up even earlier, but just think of everything we could do there. Not just sex. We could have a candlelit dinner or take a bubble bath together. I want to experience all that romantic stuff with you. Imagine having somewhere to go where we can finally be ourselves. Most of the time we can't even talk openly."

Daniel fights down a smile. "What would you say to me?"

"Only one way to find out," I reply. "What do you think of my plan?"

He nods, slowly at first before it picks up speed. "Let's take a look in person. How about tomorrow?"

Which is Saturday, thank goodness. "You'll drive me around?"

"Of course," Daniel says. "I'll do anything for you."

I smooch him on the nose. "You might live to regret those words when I have my own place."

"Try me," he says, his attempt at bravado ruined when he covers his mouth and titters.

I shake my head, crazier about the boy with each passing day. "You better get me home then. I need to crash. Besides, we don't want your parents to realize that you've been sneaking out." That remains on my mind as he begins to drive. "How hard will it be to stay the night at my place?"

"I'm an adult now," Daniel says assertively. "So I shouldn't have to ask permission."

"I agree, but if you're living under their roof, they get to call the shots."

"True. I wish I'd started school already. I'll have my own dorm room then."

"With a roommate?" I ask.

"Yeah."

"Too bad. And even more reason to get the apartment near the university. That way you're nice and close. Just a short walk to my bed every night."

"Will you still be here in the fall?" he asks after a pause.

That's a very big question. Staying would mean missing out on my own education, but at the moment, the choice isn't mine to make. The real question is when I'll attempt walking through the gate again. It sure as hell won't be this week or the next. Not after the emotional wringer we were put through last time. Maybe when August rolls around, I'll feel more motivated to try.

"Who knows," I say. "I'm not in any rush."

Daniel pats my leg as we near Gloria's house. It's less a sign of affection and more a reminder that we're sitting too close together. Likewise, when it's time to say goodbye, there's an awkward moment when we want to kiss but can't. Too many residential windows surround us. Sure it's the middle of the night, but that's even more reason for someone to peer outside at the car idling there.

"I'll stay with you," Daniel says. "When you get a place. I won't let anyone stop me."

"Good," I say, reaching for the door handle. I stop to watch his face before speaking again. "I love you, Daniel."

His eyes always get watery when I say that to him. He swallows before responding. "I love you too, Reggie."

"See you tomorrow," I say.

"I'll be there."

Neither one of us moves. "I could sneak into the house with you," I suggest. "Sleep beneath your bed. You'd have to slide some fried eggs underneath there in the morning, but I wouldn't mind."

"Me neither," Daniel says with a guffaw. "I'd be under the bed with you."

"Then let's hope we find a place before it gets pathetic. Good night, pretty boy."

"Good night, Reggie."

I still don't budge, but this time it's on purpose. Daniel starts laughing while pushing at me, and after resisting him a little longer, I decide the fleeting physical contact is enough to tide me over until tomorrow, when I'll no doubt want even more.

— — —

We begin apartment hunting the next morning. Gloria doesn't want to accompany us. She's stressing about the date she has with Leroy tonight. At least I think it's a date. She's insisting that Daniel and I tag along in case he's a creep, so technically we're only going to hang out as a group. But it's clearly more to her, judging from the way Gloria has worked tirelessly to alter the dress she wants to wear. She's getting her hair done professionally too, which I gather doesn't happen often. We'll meet her later.

The day belongs to Daniel and me. I'm buzzing as we drive down the highway toward Chicago. I rest my head on his lap as I so often do, grateful that seatbelts haven't been invented yet, and hang my feet out the passenger-side window. Occasionally I'll reach over to mess with the radio. When I can't find anything but commercials, I flip around to mess with my boyfriend.

"What's the big idea?" he complains when I shove my tongue into his belly button. "I'm trying to drive! And you're making me worry that it's not clean."

I don't share his concern. Daniel always tastes like he just scrubbed himself down with a bar of soap. I wouldn't be surprised to learn that he bathes twice a day. Maybe I'll find out when he's staying at my new place.

"That's even worse!" Daniel cries when I worm a finger down the front of his shorts to tickle his pubic hair. "We're almost there. Don't you want to see the neighborhood?"

That gets my attention. I sit up and imagine myself walking down the street, visiting the shops we pass, or interacting with the people I see. I'm not blown away, but I also wouldn't mind living in the area. We're just in time for our first appointment. An older woman with an Eastern European accent gives us a tour of the room she has for rent and the common area that I would have access to. I went into the day prepared for racism. I would do the same even in my era, so I'm not surprised when she only addresses Daniel and loses enthusiasm when it becomes clear that I would be her tenant. The room didn't offer enough privacy anyway. The next place is friendlier, but with the same issue of not having a dedicated entrance. I'm tired of sneaking around, so no deal.

We're at our fifth appointment when even Daniel notices a pattern.

"What do you expect in terms of references?" I asked a middle-aged man.

"That won't be necessary," he says, turning to Daniel. "You seem like a fine young man."

Daniel's brow furrows up as he points to me. "*He's* the one who is interested."

"Oh." The man looks me over. "What sort of references do you have?"

"I can get you one from Eartha Kitt," I say with a straight face.

"I used to play in her band. Oh, and my father is the ambassador to Canada, but I suppose that doesn't count since he's family. I can ask the Prime Minister though. He was at our place for dinner a few months back."

The man isn't sure what to think when he shows us out. I chuckle to myself once we're on the sidewalk again. Daniel doesn't seem nearly as amused.

"I'm sorry," he grumbles.

"It's fine. I didn't like the place anyway."

"Doesn't it make you angry?" Daniel asks with a scowl.

"When it catches me off guard, then yeah. Otherwise I try not to give small-minded people the satisfaction."

We take a break to have lunch, and I pick up the latest edition of the *Chicago Defender*, remembering that whoever advertises in their classified section cares more about money than race. I find three more promising leads. Daniel shows me how to use a payphone at the train station so I can call them. That's amusing, mostly because I make him squeeze into the booth with me, pretending to be too confused to work the phone until he does. A couple of the apartments we view afterwards have potential but end up being more expensive than advertised.

"Supply and demand," one man tells us. "I've had four other people come look today. Two of them made me offers. If you want it, you've got to be willing to top their price."

I didn't realize that bidding wars would be part of the process. I'm not discouraged. The one-bedroom apartment near the university is the final appointment of the day, and the one I'm most excited about. Enough that I'm willing to rent it sight unseen. When we arrive at an old stone building on a tree-lined street, my infatuation increases. The unit I'm interested in is on the ground floor and has a door that opens directly to the back. No hallway to pass through where prying eyes can cast judgement. Only direct access to a tiny apartment that has everything I need. We're standing out back with the woman who showed us the place, and I'm imagining myself out there soaking up the sun, when she asks a question.

"Which of you is interested in the apartment? It isn't both of you... is it?"

"Just me," I clarify.

She looks relieved. "Oh good. I don't rent to homosexuals."

"That's fine," I say without missing a beat. "We don't rent from bigots."

I put my arm around Daniel and guide him away, ignoring the way his face contorts and the little disgruntled noises he's making. We're halfway to the car when he turns around, like he intends to march back to the apartment and give the landlord a piece of his mind. "She can't talk to us that way!"

"I don't agree."

Daniel stops, his anger now directed at me. "How can you say that?"

"Because in my day, there's always a baker who refuses to make a cake for a gay wedding, or a venue that refuses to host the reception. People get up in arms when it happens and insist the baker or whoever can't refuse service to anyone. I can only speak for myself, but I'd rather see their true colors so I can decide if I want to support them or not. Do you really want some homophobic bastard silently seething in resentment while he makes a cake that is supposed to be imbued with love? The landlord back there doesn't deserve my money. I'd rather give it to someone who does."

Daniel frowns in disapproval. "So you think it's okay to refuse service to someone based on color or creed?"

"Public spaces and services should be available to everyone. Opportunity should always be equal. But when it comes to private businesses, I want enough transparency for me to identify the dregs of society so I can avoid them. I should be allowed to ask if they have a problem with me, and they should have the freedom to admit it if they do. At least then an informed decision can be made. Let the court of public opinion decide if those businesses survive or not."

"I still don't like what happened."

"Me neither, but you can't stop a hurricane by banning the rain. Some things are inevitable. You can forbid people from having certain beliefs, but that only makes them cling to them more. I don't know the solution, Daniel, but we'll never find it if we're muzzling each other—or worse—banishing anyone from our social circle who disagrees with us. I've had more than one person admit they were unsure about gay or black people before getting to know me. There's a lot of power in finding common ground and building from there. That's why I love music so much. It's a universal language."

Daniel is silent as we resume walking to the car. I figure I've given him plenty to chew on, but he sure digests it fast. "On one hand, you're saying that you want to know upfront if someone is racist or homophobic, so you can avoid them. But you're also saying that racist and homophobic people have changed their mind when they got to know you. So which is it?"

I think about it and laugh in exasperation. "A little of both. Business owners are one thing. When it comes to personal connections, I wish everyone would be a little more tolerant and patient with each other. Segregation is wrong. Anti-discrimination laws are important, but they aren't a solution. If they were, I wouldn't be dealing with the same crap sixty-five years from now."

"I hate that people are cruel to you, just because of your skin color."

"I don't like it either. But thanks."

When we get into the car, Daniel sits pensively behind the wheel without putting the keys in the ignition. "One question," he says. "What's a gay wedding?"

"The same as any other wedding."

"Yeah, but… It can't be *exactly* the same. Not legally. Right? Is it a symbolic union?"

"Aren't they all?" I tease. "I get what you're asking. They're exactly the same. You're in for a long wait, but eventually, people like us can get married. Legally."

His eyes are wide, like his wildest dreams just came true. "Really?"

"I'm not proposing," I say quickly, "but yes. After a drawn-out battle, we get the right to make it official. Does that help restore your faith in humanity?"

He nods while swallowing against emotion. "I wish you could tell my parents that. Or better yet, show them."

"I know," I say gently. "Love is a powerful catalyst for change. You'd be surprised how many parents claim they don't want a gay child but end up changing their minds when theirs turns out to be."

"How do you do it?" Daniel asks, staring at me in wonder.

"Put up with crap like that? I've been practicing my entire life."

"No. How do you always make me see hope? It's like you recognize the good inside of everyone."

"I wouldn't go *that* far. I've met some truly reprehensible people. But generally, I find when you separate most folks from their politics, that they are decent and willing to get along." Unless they are posting online, but there's no sense in traumatizing him with that particular horror story. "The few exceptions aren't worth the emotional energy, in my experience. Forget about the dumb landlord and her ignorant views. Give all that attention to me instead."

Determination galvanizes his features as he leans close to kiss me. He doesn't even check the mirrors. Be still my heart!

"Do you want to keep looking?" he asks when pulling away.

I take his wrist and tilt it to check his watch. We have plans to meet Gloria in a couple of hours. "Let's head back and recharge before we go out tonight."

"Okay."

I pay attention to how long it takes us to drive back to his house, knowing that public transportation will be slower, and begin to have doubts. As much as I'd like to live downtown, the logistics would be a headache. I'll search closer to home.

"We're kind of going on a double date tonight," Daniel says, glancing over at me with sparkling eyes. "Have you thought of that?"

"No, but I sure hope Leroy is a good kisser."

He shoves me and laughs. "I'm *not* dating Gloria again. Or any other girl. Not after what I've experienced with you. There's no competition."

"Music to my ears," I say. Then I turn up the radio, plop my head into his lap, and let myself enjoy the rest of the ride, happy that the night—much like the day—will be spent with him.

— — —

We're absolutely on a double date. Even if the other diners at the steakhouse assume Daniel and I are chaperones. Gloria is wearing an electric blue dress with dark spots that form a daisy pattern. She looks lovely. Her hair is styled to one side with a fabric flower tucked into it. As for her date, Leroy is sporting a green letter-jacket and jeans—a look that works well for him. He has a brawny build and thick kissable lips that hide flawless teeth. His features are broad and even, and I like his deep rumbling voice.

I'm less fond of being seated next to him, worried that Daniel will compare us. We have a similar skin tone and hair style, one of us lanky, the other taking up more than his half of the table. He doesn't have my honey-golden eyes though, which I fix flirtatiously on Daniel any chance I get. My boyfriend looks delicious in a peach dress-shirt and brown slacks. Tired of wearing the same clothes, I borrowed a lavender button-up shirt from him. While it wouldn't necessarily be my go-to style for a date, at least the dress shirts of this era don't always have busy patterns.

Dinner is entertaining, I suppose. Leroy enjoys talking about sports. After checking the table, I decide the rest of us enjoy looking at him, no matter what he has to say. He seems nice enough. On occasion he's considerate enough to ask Gloria about her life. She seems completely taken by him, but it won't last. I don't mean that in a judgmental way. The man simply isn't my grandpa, who by all accounts, was incredibly charming.

Once we've finished eating, Leroy insists on paying for Gloria's meal. Feeling competitive, I do the same for Daniel, although I have to disguise my chivalry. "I'll cover yours so the waitress doesn't have to split the check three ways. You can pay me back later."

"Thanks." Daniel smiles, understanding my true intent.

I love how he gets me. I usually only click with friends like that.

"Where should we go next?" Leroy asks.

"The drive-in?" Gloria suggests.

We're using Daniel's car tonight. I do *not* want to be trapped inside it while my grandma makes out with some (admittedly hot) jock in the backseat. So I'm relieved when Leroy shoots down this idea.

"I've already seen everything they're showing," he says.

"With who?" Gloria asks pointedly.

"My pals," Leroy says innocently. "Who else?"

"Hmm," Gloria says. "Let me ask around and find out."

"We could go bowling, I suppose," Daniel suggests.

"Yawnsville," Leroy replies. "I don't want to hang around a bunch of high school kids."

"Me neither," Gloria says, shooting me a glare when I snort. "We'll go somewhere that's really buzzing."

"Oh yeah?" Leroy says. "Like where?"

She looks to us in desperation. Daniel shrugs helplessly. I'm no use either.

"The Silver Rattle," Gloria blurts out.

"Isn't that some sort of club?" Leroy asks, sounding interested. "Can you get us in?"

"Yes," Gloria says. "Well... Probably. I've been there so often with my parents, I'm sure they'll recognize me."

As being underage, but I don't say this aloud. Leroy is hyped about the idea, so we pile into Daniel's car and drive downtown. Once there, I look around for alternatives, but the great thing about Chicago in the summer is that you don't need to go indoors at all. The lakefront is gorgeous to walk along and offers an impressive view of the city's skyline. The architecture always inspires me, although I'm not sure that Leroy will appreciate it as much.

"Is there live music?" he asks as we walk toward the club.

"Yes!" Gloria says, almost manic at this point. She has to know that we're heading toward disaster. "Do you like to dance?"

"You betcha!"

Leroy is a big guy, but the bouncer at the door still dwarfs him. The man takes one look at our group and shakes his head. "No kids."

"Don't worry," Daniel says, his voice sounding artificially deep. "We're adults."

"You've seen me here before," Gloria says. "Remember?"

"Jog my memory," the bouncer says, holding out his hand. "Let's see your identification."

Nobody moves.

The bouncer grunts. "That's what I thought. Come back in a few years. We'll still be here. Now put an egg in your shoe and beat it."

We trudge to the end of the block and stop there to decide on a new destination. I suggest strolling along the lakefront, and Daniel backs me up, but Leroy isn't having it. "If I wanted to go for a walk, I would've stayed home with my dog."

"You have a dog?" Gloria asks while fanning herself. "What's his name?"

"Bruiser. Even though he's more of a scaredy cat. Last week I watched a squirrel chase him around the yard."

"That's so cute!" Gloria enthuses. "Maybe he needs a confidence boost. I can make him a football jersey to match yours."

"Hey! Really? That would be swell!"

Ugh. I tune them out while trying to think of an alternative plan. I'm worried we're going to end up stuck in the car after all. I turn and look longingly at the Silver Rattle and notice a couple of guys standing outside, the streetlight reflecting off a purple jacket.

"Be right back," I say before walking in their direction.

I'm halfway there when Alonzo raises a hand in greeting.

"Hey, Cupid!" he shouts. "Where have you been?"

"It's Valentine," I say when closer. "As in Reggie Valentine."

"Whatever you say, my man. Are you back here to tickle the ivories? We sure could use you tonight."

The two men he's with nod in agreement.

"What's up?"

"Jerome had an early dinner," Alonzo explains, pantomiming like he's drinking from a bottle. He must mean the piano player I replaced last time. "We're doing our best without him but still sound flat. Come on in and get the crowd jumping."

"Uhh…" I tilt my head away from the club. "Can we talk real quick?"

He smirks before pushing himself away from the wall. "No sweat."

Once he's out of earshot from the others, I explain the situation.

"I see," he says, squinting down the street at my friends. "Tell you what. If your crew happened to be in the alley out back, I bet they wouldn't find anyone watching the door. You know the place I mean, right?" He smiles in a way that makes my ears burn.

"I think so, yeah. We'll be okay once we're inside the club?"

"Once you're on stage, I doubt even the pigs would have the indecency to drag you off again. Not when they hear you play. See you soon, little cupid."

And with that he saunters away. I return to my friends to tell them the good news. Leroy claps me on the back, nearly knocking me over, and we're all in a jovial mood when creeping down the alleyway. I make sure to wink at Daniel when passing the spot where we kissed. As I open the door, the alluring sound of

181

nightlife beckons us to enter. Soon we're in the thick of it. Alonzo was right. People are talking and drinking, but the music doesn't capture their attention. I don't blame them. What I hear sounds more like rehearsals.

"You kids better have your parents' permission to be here," says a voice from behind us.

We all jump, but it's only Alonzo. He looks us over, lingering on Leroy in particular, but not for the reason I initially suspect. "Lose the jacket or you'll be the first person the cops target. As for you, baby face," he says, addressing Daniel, "don't go anywhere near the bar. Or a drink." Gloria is the last to receive his attention. "Girl, you look fabulous. Just keep being you."

"Oh!" she says, straightening up. "Thank you. I will!"

Leroy steps in front of her protectively, but Alonzo is done with them. He grabs me by the arm and starts pulling me toward the stage, shouting over his shoulder, "You can have your friend back at the end of the night. We'll go easy on him, I promise."

Daniel and I lock eyes as I'm whisked away, but he's soon lost in the crowd. A couple of the guys on stage seem to recognize me, the double bass player nodding his approval as I take my seat.

"Okay," Alonzo says to us. "Let's freak these cats out with *Brilliant Corners*, get them moving with *Shake, Rattle, and Roll*, and make them sweat with *Saturday Night Fish Fry*. Then we'll quench their thirst with a little *Pink Champagne*. You dig that?"

This last sentence is directed at me. I know how to play one of the songs and have at least heard two of the others. That's not much to go on, but I nod anyway. We start with *Brilliant Corners* and I'm forced to improvise. The saxophone does most of the heavy lifting, Alonzo's eyes half-lidded as he stands near me. We play well off each other, the drums providing a backbone rhythm. I have no idea how close we get to the original composition, but by the end, Alonzo seems satisfied and takes us into a classic that is comfortable territory, despite not being a favorite of mine. The dance floor fills up during this song and goes completely wild by the next.

I don't think to look for my friends until after Alonzo calls out the next set and I'm already playing. Gloria and Leroy are easy to find. They're front and center. I already knew my grandma can dance, having witnessed it plenty of times during family get-togethers. It's Leroy who surprises me. If his moves on the football field are anything like what I'm witnessing now, he earned the scholarship he bragged about during dinner.

It takes two more songs until I find Daniel. He's standing off to the side, between the dancers and the rows of tables. Shadow makes it impossible for me to see his expression, but he must notice how often I keep looking, because he walks closer to the stage after the next set ends. Someone comes to ask us what we'd like to drink. After ordering a water, I return my attention to him and pat the bench next to me, like I often do when at his house. I only mean it as a joke, or maybe as a way of telling him that I wish he was near me. The last thing I expect is for him to climb on stage, which he does.

I scoot to the right, toward the audience, so he can sit on the far side of me. He does indeed have a baby face, and I don't want to get the Silver Rattle in trouble. Despite the caution, it takes all my willpower not to kiss him.

"I'll leave as soon as you start playing again," he says. "I just wanted to say how amazing you are."

"Thanks, but why not stick around?"

"I couldn't—" Daniel sputters. "I don't know how to play *any* instrument."

"They don't know that," I murmur.

"Ready?" Alonzo asks.

I nod when he looks at me. He notices Daniel, of course, but seems more amused than anything.

"What do I do?" Daniel hisses in panic.

"Move your hands above the keys on your side, but leave some room for me to do my stuff."

That's all the advice I can offer. Daniel pretends to play. I slip my hands beneath his, when needed, grinning nonstop, because I love that he's next to me. I even lean over and sing to him during one of the songs, *Ain't That a Shame*, by the legendary Fats Domino. The stage is dimly lit. I doubt anyone can tell what we're doing or see him clearly. Aside from my bandmates, but they seem chill.

When we play a slow song, Daniel moves closer to me so our shoulders are touching. Not far away, I can see my grandmother dancing with her date. Warm contentment fills me. Everything seems right with the world. But it doesn't last. A form hobbles over while I'm still playing. It's the pianist from last time. I guess he decided to finally show up. Daniel scoots away when noticing him and stands when Jerome gestures for him to get out of the way. Then he plops down next to me, like he intends to take over in the middle of the song. I look to Alonzo for guidance and see him scowling.

"Go on now," Jerome slurs from next to me, his breath making my nostrils flare. Someone has been hitting the sauce extra hard tonight. "This ain't a toy."

"You can't wait—" I begin before Jerome knocks my hands away.

I resist the urge to elbow him in the face. I do *not* like being interrupted mid-song, especially in such a rude manner. To his credit, even drunk off his ass he's a good enough player to take over seamlessly. I slide off the bench and collect Daniel, who is equally outraged.

"Was that rude?" he begins to rant. "It seemed rude! Or is it normal for musicians to—no, it can't be. The way he barged in like that... Where's the owner?"

"We're underage," I remind him before clenching my jaw. "And yeah, that was a dick move." I force myself to take a deep breath. "But it was a few seconds of an otherwise incredible night, so forget it."

Daniel's expression is determined when he nods, like he doesn't want to let me down, and that makes it easier to let go of my own anger.

"Maybe we should step out back a moment," I suggest.

"Okay."

We're halfway to the door when a couple of girls cut us off and ask if we'd like to dance. I'm searching for an excuse when Leroy comes to the rescue, whether he intends to or not.

"I thought you were a wet blanket during dinner," he says, barging between the two girls to grab my hand and pump it. "Turns out you're real swell, daddy-o!"

"Golly," I deadpan. "Thanks."

"I'm so sorry!" Gloria says, catching up with him. "He's umm... had a few."

"What? You know we're not supposed to—" I stop myself, since the two girls are still there, and address them instead. "It'll have to be a rain check for now, ladies. Next time?"

They nod, giggle, and hurry back to the dancefloor as another song begins.

"We should probably be best friends," Leroy is slurring into my ear. He has an arm around my shoulders and is leaning his weight on me. I'm not sure how much longer I can support him.

"Let's get you outside for some fresh air," I say, attempting to walk in that direction, but he's too heavy.

"You seem lost," a new voice says.

We all turn to find Mama standing there, her expression difficult to read.

"I trust y'all had a good time tonight?" she asks, an eyebrow raised in Leroy's direction.

"Yes," I say. "Sorry about that. Won't happen again. We'll get him out of here before it causes any trouble."

"Oh right," Gloria says, snapping to attention and ducking under Leroy's other arm. "Thank you for having us, Mama. I'm such a big fan!"

"That's sweet of you honey," Mama purrs. "I love your dress."

"Thank you!" Gloria says. "I actually—"

"She's so pretty," Leroy interrupts. "Like a filly." His head lolls in Gloria's direction. "You're my pretty filly."

"Have a nice night now," Mama says tersely. "Just a moment," she adds as we're lugging Leroy away.

When I glance over my shoulder, she's looking at me. Daniel takes my place under Leroy's arm, and I promise to rejoin them outside.

"You sure know your way around the piano," Mama says, attention on my friends until they disappear out the back door. "How long have you been playing?"

"My entire life."

She doesn't gasp or ask if I'm serious. I suppose she's met plenty of people like me.

"I'm sorry it had to end so disrespectfully," she continues. "Jerome's sister was like an aunt to me. Otherwise I would have sent him packing long ago, no matter how good he plays. I wanted to thank you for stepping in tonight."

She reaches into the bodice of her dress to pull out some folded bills and peels off a twenty. I'm protesting as she hands it to me, but I don't resist very much, since it's nearly a week's pay.

"You come see us again," she says, "whenever you like. Just ask for Alonzo."

"I will. Thank you."

"My pleasure. Do you have a number, honey?"

She doesn't seem interested in me romantically, so I don't think she wants to go on a date. "Vanderbuilt 8861," I reply, "although you'll probably have to leave a message. But if you ever need me again—"

"After the talking-to Jerome will get tonight," Mama drawls, "I better *not* have need of you any time soon."

"Fair enough." I thank her again, but before I leave, another idea occurs to me. "You know that dress my friend is wearing? She made it herself. And I know for a fact that she'd be thrilled to make something for you."

"Oh yeah?" Mama says, already sounding open to the idea. "My mother was a seamstress. She could look at anyone from across the room and size them up. If your friend is that good, she already has everything she needs from me. Including my permission."

"I'll let her know," I say, fighting down a grin.

I hurry outside to rejoin my friends, eager to tell Gloria the good news, but I decide to wait until we're home. Just in case her date barfs in the car and she needs cheering up.

Chapter 14

Two more weeks pass before I finally get my own place. I didn't have much luck finding one until I was on my lunch break with Samuel, the older guy who showed me the ropes on my first day at the warehouse. When I mentioned the ongoing search, he studied me and said, "You look like you keep your nose clean."

I figured he didn't mean a coke habit, so I confirmed that I wanted to live somewhere quiet, and he told me about a long-stay motel. Gloria drove me there later and the office confirmed they had a vacant furnished room. I paid a month in advance after viewing it. Daniel doesn't know about it yet. I decided to wait until the weekend to surprise him. Now that Saturday has finally rolled around, I'm ready for the big reveal. He doesn't know where we're going as I feed him directions that take us northeast toward O'Hare.

"Turn here. And park."

Daniel complies, his expression confused as he leans forward to look through the windshield at the motel, which is a beige two-story brick building. "What are we doing here?"

"Judging from that blush, not what you're thinking. Although you're not exactly wrong. Come on. I'll show you."

I lead Daniel up a set of external stairs to the landing above, only needing to pass one other unit before reaching my own. I unlock the door and let it swing open so he can enter first. I know he won't be blown away. The room is wide and shallow with a single window near the door to let in natural light. A kitchenette is next to a bathroom that includes a full tub. I have a bed, a small table, and a couple of cushioned chairs with wooden frames.

"Home, sweet home," I say after closing the door behind us.

Daniel spins around to face me. "Really? You live here now?"

"Yup! I moved in yesterday." Which mostly meant bringing

my clothes here, although my great-grandparents were nice enough to provide me with sheets, blankets, and towels, since those aren't included in the price. But hey, for ten bucks a week, what can you really expect? Not air conditioning, unfortunately. Daniel is already pulling at the collar of his shirt.

"It *is* a little warm," I say, moving to the window. I open it and pull shut the lighter layer of gauzy curtains that allow air through while still providing privacy. "And we'll have to be quiet during certain activities, but otherwise it's a little slice of paradise, just for us."

"When can I move in?" Daniel jokes.

"Immediately," I say without hesitation. And I mean it, whether he realizes it or not. I'd never make that offer to someone I'd only been with for a couple months, but our time is so limited that I don't hold back with him. Not anymore. "I thought you'd be more interested in the bed than the kitchen."

Daniel is standing in front of the small range, like it's the most exciting feature. "I can cook for you!" he says, opening a mostly bare cabinet to check inside. "We'll need to go shopping first, but this is fun. We can do whatever we want without anyone asking questions."

"That's what I had in mind," I say, moving toward him.

Daniel begins fanning himself with a take-out menu, but I don't think my words are the reason.

"It helps if you aren't wearing as much," I say, stripping off my T-shirt in demonstration.

Daniel stares before doing the same. Then he starts working on his shorts, which makes me laugh.

"Hold up," I say. "There's something in particular that I've been looking forward to, ever since we did it last."

I take his hand and walk with him to the bed, getting in first and stretching out on my back. Then I open my arms to him.

Daniel crawls in, looking uncertain. "You want me to be on top instead?" he asks.

"That's not what I meant," I say, grabbing him once he's above me so that our bare chests are pressed together. "I just want to hold you."

Our sex life has mostly taken place in the car, or in a rush at his house when the risks were minimal enough. And once or twice in the woods. That's been fun, but it hasn't allowed us to indulge in the tender side of love. I tighten my arms around him and breathe in the scent of his skin. When I kiss him, his eyes are vulnerable as they search mine. I know he wants reassurance, and I'm happy to give it to him.

"I love you, Daniel."

"I love you too," he says, still seeming hesitant. "Does this mean you're staying?"

He obsesses over that. I guess I do too, but without verbalizing it as much. "I'm here, aren't I?"

This makes him happy. Daniel pecks me on the lips before relaxing his weight. We're content to murmur to each other while growing increasingly sweaty, but it doesn't feel bad. Especially as the realization sinks in for us both that we could lay there for hours and not be disturbed. With the right excuses, we'll steal entire days and nights for ourselves. We're finally free to do whatever our hearts desire. For instance...

"What if I wanted to be on top?" Daniel asks at one point.

"Do you mean as the starting position," I ask, wanting to be sure, "or *really* on top?"

Daniel's brow furrows in confusion before he puts it in terms that can't be misinterpreted. "I want to be inside you."

"We can try that," I say, already getting my hopes up, because I've only dated guys who had a firm preference either way. If he likes it both... well, no sense in getting ahead of myself. "Do you mean right now?"

"Yeah," Daniel says, pressing his hips against me. "I want to be with you."

We separate long enough to undress each other completely. I intend for us to start slowly by going through our usual routine, but Daniel doesn't seem to have any patience for this. He keeps positioning himself between my legs, like he wants to get straight to it, which only makes me hornier. I get up to grab cooking oil from the kitchen and duck into the restroom to make sure it's a good time. The stars have aligned. When I return to the main room, I close the window and pull the heavy curtains shut, leaving only a sliver of light that cuts across the bed. Daniel is on his back, propped up on his elbows, his expression emotional. This is another first for him. He begins to rise when I rejoin him, but I push on his chest so he's flat on his back.

"We're starting this way," I say as I climb on top of him, "because it's been a while, and you're really thick."

"Too thick?" Daniel asks, sounding concerned.

"We're about to find out." I lower myself onto him, my eyes on his as I talk him through the process. "Nice and slow. Little motions only. Let me lead, okay?" He looks surprised when the head of his cock pops inside, enough that I manage to grin instead of wince. He's so damn cute. And big. I wish we had better lube, but I'm determined not to let him down. After easing down in tiny increments, my butt finally makes contact with his hips.

"That's it," I gasp, moving gently back and forth to make sure I'm ready. "You can take over from here."

He pulls out too far and slides back in quicker than I would prefer. I'm struggling to find pleasure through the pain when his hands move up to touch my face. I lean over so he can kiss me, and after he does, I feel his breath on my lips. "We're part of each other now," Daniel says, his voice hoarse. "I never knew it was possible to feel this way about someone."

"Me neither," I admit. This isn't my first rodeo, but I've never experienced this sort of intensity. It lives up to the impossibly romantic fantasies I had when younger. This is more than just sex. I feel like we're connected in a way that transcends the physical. Although that aspect feels good too, now that I've relaxed enough to enjoy myself.

Daniel starts pumping his hips, his gaze locked onto mine. When he asks if he can be on top for real, I nearly somersault onto my back. Before long, I have my legs wrapped around his hips and am doing everything in my power not to cry out with each thrust. Seeing that pretty face above me, his eyes wet with emotion, does it for me in every way imaginable. He doesn't last much longer. I'm right behind him, stifling our moans by pressing my lips against his. Then he collapses onto me, both of us content to hold each other while whispering sentimental declarations of love. Eventually the heat gets to us, so we retreat to the cool waters of the shower.

"What did you think?" I ask him while there. "Which way do you prefer?"

"Tough to say," Daniel replies. "I like both for different reasons. Can we do it again?"

I glance down and notice that he's standing at full attention. "You mean the same thing?"

He bites his bottom lip. When I nod, he slides behind me,

and I decide the ten bucks a week is money well spent. I just hope that the medical bills won't be too expensive, because the boy is going to put me in the hospital. But how could I possibly say no? My heart is too crazy about him, and so is the rest of me, judging from the way my body rises to the challenge as he wraps his arms around me.

— — —

"Reggie! Your mother called."

Daniel and I look at each other, equally perplexed. We've just arrived at the house for another tutoring session, Mrs. Parker meeting us in the living room.

"My mother?" I repeat.

"Yes." Melody hands me a piece of paper. "This is the message she left. I hope everything is okay. Would you boys like something to drink? It's terribly hot outside."

"That would be nice," I say. "Thank you."

I wait until we're alone before I read the message aloud. "Call your mama when you get a chance. Jerome is in the hospital." I look up at Daniel and laugh. "That's the piano player at The Silver Rattle. She probably wants me to fill in for him."

"Should we tell my mama that your mama is actually *the* Mama?" he asks with a straight face.

God I love him. "No, this is good. Your parents probably wonder why I never hear from mine. I'll call her back later."

Melody returns with a tray of lemonade, which Daniel serves to his sisters when they show up for their lessons. He leaves the room soon after to collect fresh clothes and other essentials to leave at my place. Over the past couple of weeks, he's spent quite a few nights with me, our appetite for each other insatiable. I've experienced that before. My first boyfriend and I were so relieved to finally have someone else to get off with that most of our relationship was spent between the sheets. But with Daniel, emotion is never far behind, no matter how riled up we are.

I focus on teaching his sisters, seeing extensions of him in their faces, which only makes me want to try harder. Sarah is showing real promise. She doesn't have the same level of enthusiasm that I did at her age, but she's on her way to becoming a competent player. At the end of both lessons, Daniel still hasn't returned to the room, so I let myself freestyle on the piano, playing songs that I miss or simply letting spontaneity guide my hands. I'm so into this that—until I stop playing—I don't realize Melody is leaning against the doorway while listening.

"Reggie Valentine," she says, walking closer, "I think you're simply wonderful."

"Thanks, but it's nothing you couldn't do." I scoot over on the bench. "Sit down. I'll teach you something."

"Oh, I couldn't," Melody says, but she joins me regardless. "I'd rather listen to you play."

I'm happy to oblige, treating her to a piano version of James Taylor's *Fire and Rain*, which everyone else will have to wait another decade to hear.

She shakes her head halfway through the song. "How did you get so good?"

I choose my words carefully, recognizing an opportunity. "I was lucky to have parents who supported what I wanted to do."

"And it was always this?" she asks.

I nod. "Love at first sight. That's the only way I can describe it. Nothing else grabbed my attention like the piano did. I'm sure it's the same for many people. Daniel was probably diagnosing his friends and putting Band-aids on their knees as soon as he could walk."

"Not exactly," Melody says with a strained expression. "He was always a squeamish boy. It took him longer than usual to get his merit badge in first aid."

"My mom wanted me to be a lawyer," I confide.

"They do make good money."

"True, but she mostly liked the idea of having a son who could sue anyone that messed with her."

Melody laughs. "I suppose that would be useful."

"The same with having a doctor in the family." I bring the song to an end and turn to face her. "What did you think Daniel would grow up to be?"

Melody exhales. "Science was always his best subject, and I know that for quite a long time, he wanted to become an engineer."

"That's right. He's mentioned it a few times."

"Still?" She looks shocked by this news. And maybe a little pale. I think I know why.

"He gets really enthusiastic whenever the subject comes up," I say. "But I also know that he wants to make his dad proud." I idly play the opening to *Year of the Cat* before pulling my hands away. "What about you? When the nest is empty, where do you plan to fly?"

She laughs, but without much humor. "It's more of a gilded cage than a nest."

"What do you mean?"

Melody checks the doors to make sure we're alone, reminding me of her son. "Only that I have a luxurious life, and that the children will always need me, no matter how old they get."

"Sure, but they won't rely on you as much. Once the girls get a little older, I imagine you'll have more time to do whatever you want. Another bank job maybe?"

"I'm not sure they'd have me."

"Then don't take 'no' for an answer. People are always telling me what I can't do because of the color of my skin. I enjoy proving them wrong."

She seems to reassess me. "That's very brave."

I shrug. "I find it easier than going against my own nature. That's a battle with no end. Do you know what I mean?"

She nods. "If only I were still your age."

"If only I was yours," I counter. "I have to take any job I can get to pay the bills. You have choices. Don't let anyone else make them for you." I play the melody from David Bowie's *Changes* before remembering something. "Could I use your phone? I'd like to return that call now."

"Of course! If you want privacy, you could use the phone in Daniel's room."

"Okay. Thanks."

"Thank *you*," Melody says as we both get up. "You've been a good influence on Daniel. I'm glad you've become so close."

"Me too." If only I could tell her how much her son means to me. I settle for, "He's a good kid."

"And my favorite." She covers her mouth. "Oh, please pretend I didn't say that!"

"My lips are sealed," I promise.

When I go upstairs to Daniel's room, I find him napping on his bed. We've had some late nights recently. I'm perpetually behind on my sleep, but that's how it was in my own time. There's always too much I want to accomplish each day. I sit at his desk and dial the number Mama left for me. Daniel stirs, sitting up with slightly mussed hair to watch in curiosity. The phone rings six, maybe seven times, and I'm about to give up when the line clicks and I recognize Mama's voice.

"Jerome took a spill down some stairs," she says once I've identified myself. "He'll be laid up for a few weeks. Maybe longer, considering how much he's drinking."

"I'm happy to step in for him," I say.

"The gig is five days a week, with Mondays and Tuesdays off. You'll get five dollars each night plus your share of tips."

"Oh. I'd be working nights?" I say this for Daniel's benefit. He nods encouragingly.

"When else, honey? Make it six dollars then, but you better bring the same enthusiasm I saw before."

"You've got it."

"Good. I'll see you tonight. Be here by eight."

The line clicks and goes dead. I hang up the phone and grin. "Mama wants me to—

"I heard!" Daniel says. "This is great news!"

"Yeah. I need to borrow a calculator though."

"A what?"

I shake my head in exasperation. "You live in the dark ages, you know that? Help me crunch these numbers." I speak the equations aloud like I do with my phone and Daniel tallies the numbers up for me. "So basically, I'll be making the same amount of money that I do now, but by doing work I actually like."

"Plus tips," Daniel says. "Even if that's only a dollar a night—and I bet it's more—you'll almost be making an additional week's pay."

"And you'd be okay with me working so late?"

He looks less than certain but nods regardless. "I want you to be happy."

"I'll make sure that you can always get in to see me. That'll be a stipulation, or I won't play."

"You will either way," Daniel says. "I don't want you working at that warehouse anymore."

"Tired of massaging my sore muscles?" I ask in hushed tones.

"I'll still do that," Daniel murmurs in response. "All you want. But I'll be glad that you're doing what you're truly meant to."

I sit next to him on the bed. "I was just talking to your mother about that. About your future specifically. I think she can relate to what you're going through."

"What do you mean?"

I'm silent before answering, listening for footsteps in the hall. "Do you really think she feels fulfilled?"

"She loves being a mother," Daniel says defensively. "She loves us!"

"Yeah. I love you too, but I still have dreams and aspirations beyond our relationship. So do you. Why would she be any different? Doesn't it seem weird to you that she's home all day, especially when you and your siblings are at school and someone else cleans the house?"

"My dad takes good care of her," Daniel says, scowling at me.

"That's fine. I don't get the impression that she minds. But everyone likes to feel useful. Did you hear the way she talked about working at the bank?"

"I was there. Everyone at the bank loved her. I was so proud. I still am but..." Daniel frowns. "I remember on her last day, when she had to leave, how she sat in the car and cried. She would usually try to hide that from me, but it's like she couldn't. Not then."

"Your mom understands how you feel," I say gently. "She'll support whatever decision you make. Don't spend your life doing what others want you to. That's the entire point of coming out. You learn to be strong enough to embrace who you truly are. The people who love you will come to respect that, I promise."

His brow is crinkled as he gnaws on a fingernail, so I don't press the issue further. Instead I get up and go to his closet. "Tonight's my big debut. Help me find something to wear."

Soon he's holding up different shirts to see how they look on me, his worries forgotten. But not completely, I hope. I want him to be happy too.

Chapter 15

August arrives much too quickly, forcing me to make a decision. I'm sitting in my motel room, the morning cool enough to leave the curtains open. The sun spills across the table in front of me, the pad of notebook paper I've been writing my thoughts on glowing with golden light. Pros and cons. I've weighed so many options by listing those out, but this is one of the toughest choices, because on both sides, I have a good life.

In the year twenty-twenty-two, I'm about to start college and launch my career. I have friends and a supportive family. I come from an era that is increasingly accepting and progressive, despite a few setbacks. I'm happy there.

In the present, as I've come to think of it, I've already begun that career. I quit my job at the warehouse. Every night that I get to perform at The Silver Rattle leaves me feeling both inspired and satisfied. My education continues too, although I'm learning from passionate veterans instead of well-informed teachers. As for friends and family, I have those here. I think of the Fourth of July, when we barbequed in the backyard of my great-grandparents' house and later drove down to Lake Michigan to sit by the water and watch fireworks illuminate the night sky. So I'm happy in the past as well.

Daniel is the tie-breaker. I don't have someone to love in the future. Maybe I would have found a suitable guy, but there aren't any guarantees. I've had boyfriends before, some that I loved, but I've never felt anything like this. I adore Daniel so much that my heart aches with yearning, even when we're together. And when we're not, he fills my thoughts, appearing in my daydreams, featuring in my fantasies, and making me smile and sigh in equal measure. There's only one place I can find him, and it's not in the future.

I stew over the possibilities, always reaching the same

conclusion before starting over again, just to be certain. By the time I'm finished, the sun is warming a nearby wall instead of the table. I grab my wallet and shake out a dime. Then I leave my room and go to the payphone outside the motel office. I call Gloria and ask her to pick me up, alone, so we can go to the gate.

"Did you bring everything?" I ask when she pulls up.

"Yes," she says, looking concerned. "Shouldn't Daniel be here for this? He'll want to say goodbye."

I shake my head, unwilling to reveal my plan. She's been pressuring me to try again. Daniel told me that she spoke to him privately. She's concerned that I no longer show any interest in going home. I pat the small square in one of my pockets and take reassurance from it. Then I change the subject.

"Did I tell you what Mama was wearing last night?"

Gloria latches on to this topic. She's been struggling with the outfit she intends to design for her, wanting to get it exactly right, so she always appreciates hearing any hint of Mama's preferences. This keeps her sidetracked until we're walking through the woods toward the gate, a heavy cloth bag in my hand.

"Why *isn't* Daniel here?" she asks.

"There's no point," I say. "You and I need to talk. But not yet."

She's uncharacteristically silent during the final stretch. I stop a safe distance from the gate and turn to her. "Do you have the letter?"

She nods at the bag I'm carrying. "It's in there with the chisel and hammer. If you have a different plan in mind, shouldn't you try walking through first, just in case it works?"

I shake my head before dropping the bag and squatting next to it. I find the letter I wrote to Hannah that explains what happened to me. Then I slide my hand inside my pocket and take out the matchbook I brought along. I use the bag to obscure my actions and shield the flame from wind as I set the letter on fire. I'm soon forced to hold it at arm's length so I won't get burnt.

"What are you doing?" Gloria cries, moving as if to stop me.

The flames begin to singe my fingers. I drop the letter and stand over it, making sure it burns completely.

"Why would you do that?" Gloria demands. "Don't you want to go home?"

I answer her by taking out the hammer and chisel. I kneel next to the gate where I carved Hannah's initials and aim the chisel, intending to destroy my previous work, but Gloria grabs my shoulder to pull me away.

"Stop it!" she cries, prying the tools from my hands and tossing them away. "Are you crazy? You'll ruin everything!"

"That's the point," I growl, shrugging her off. "I'm not going home. Ever. Do you hear me?"

She shakes her head in disbelief. "Why would you say that?"

"Because I love him." I stand to face her, fists clenched and shaking at my sides. "I'm in love with Daniel, and he's worth staying for."

Her face is a mask of shock. "I knew how he felt about you but..."

"But not me?"

Gloria takes a deep breath. "I wondered. You haven't shown interest in anyone since you got here. And you two spend so much time together. Even when you think I don't realize."

I take her hands, my anger replaced with concern. "You can't tell anyone. Please! I don't want him to get hurt. You have to be his friend still. You have to keep loving him. That's crucial. Otherwise—"

She yanks her hands free. "Of course I love him! He's my best friend. Who he loves doesn't change a thing."

"What about me?" I say, my throat growing tight, because she might have accepted me in the future, but it would devastate me if she didn't now.

"I think you're an idiot," Gloria mutters, kicking away the chisel, "but I still love you."

"Thanks. I love you too."

She takes a deep breath. "So... You're together?"

"Yeah," I say, brushing away my tears. "He means everything to me."

"Obviously," Gloria says, looking toward the gate. Then she sighs. "This isn't good."

"Why not?"

"Because you don't belong here. What about your parents?"

"We'll figure that out together. You must have known all of this when I was growing up. I don't remember you dropping any cryptic hints that I shouldn't stay. 'Never stray too far from home' or anything like that. I've thought about it. You didn't talk to me about your teen years or try to prepare me for what was to come. If what I'm doing now is wrong, you would have told me, or tried to stop me from coming here. But you didn't. I saw you—the *older* you—the morning I disappeared. You acted like it was any other day."

Gloria has that look on her face. The one that says she's done with nonsense. I saw it plenty of times as a child. "What about your mother?" she presses, sidestepping my justifications.

"I'll hold her as a baby. She'll know me still. When she's old enough to understand, we'll tell her the truth. And when I disappear, I'll still be there as an old man. One she's known her entire life."

"If you live that long."

"If I died prematurely, you would have had the gate torn down before I could get near it."

"I might still."

"You don't," I say. "For whatever reason, you leave it alone and let me come here. This is your decision as much as it is mine."

She stares at me. Then she growls in frustration and stomps to the edge of the clearing. I watch her for a moment. Then I collect the tools, kneel, and begin my work. I add an extra line to the top and bottom of the H, creating two squares. They look familiar. When I add a line to the top of the W and another at the bottom, forming three triangles, goosebumps chase down my arms. I recognize the shapes I've made. I probably touched them as a child, pretending they were buttons or mystical symbols instead of what they really are: a change of heart.

"These exact shapes were already there when I was young," I tell Gloria when she approaches again. "All of this was meant to happen. I'm doing the right thing."

"It doesn't matter what you carve," she responds, "or how many letters you burn. I still know what happens. I can make sure the gate is repaired."

"I know," I say, raising the hammer. "That's why I have to kill you."

She looks momentarily concerned before rolling her eyes. "I'm not worried. You've already told me that I live to a ripe old age. In fact, I might go play in traffic, since I'm basically invincible. Does that sound crazy? Because it's what you're doing.

Letting what you *think* you know dictate your actions."

"No," I say, tapping my chest. "All my decisions come from inside here. The only thing I know for sure is that I want to be with him."

I expect her to snort at this cloying declaration. Instead she looks impressed. "Wow. You really love each other, don't you?"

"Yes. And I know that might seem strange, but believe me, it's no different than the love you and everyone else feels."

"I'm not sure about that," she murmurs. "I wouldn't even move out of state for Leroy."

I laugh, out of relief more than anything. "You'll keep our secret?"

"Of course," she says. "It's just…"

I hold my breath.

"I have so many questions."

"Ask them," I say. "Don't hold back. I'll be completely open with you. I want you to understand him, because there will be plenty of people in his future who don't. Daniel will need you. So will I. Both then and now."

She helps me gather everything up. Then we walk from the gate, leaving it behind, and sit elsewhere in the park, talking until the sun is high in the sky and our problems seem just as far away.

— — —

"I've got another song for you," I tell Daniel.

I'm sitting at the piano, having just finished tutoring his sisters. Now they've gone out to play. Melody is at the grocery store. The house is empty.

"It's not that wrapping paper music again, is it?" Daniel says as he sits next to me.

"Rap music, and congratulations, because you're the first white guy in history who doesn't get it."

"I'm willing to try again."

"Some other time. I have news for you. You keep asking me to stay so…"

My skin tingles as I begin to play one of my favorite Carpenter's songs. I could happily lose myself in the music alone, but the lyrics are too important not to sing. "We've only just begun…" Daniel stares at me, and when that line comes around again, I nod to show him that I mean it. He smiles during the upbeat refrain, and I'm only halfway through it when he throws his arms around my neck. A classic is a classic though, so I don't stop playing, even when I miss a few notes. I make him listen to the entire song, and by the end, he's crying. I am too.

"You mean it?" he croaks.

"Yeah," I say. "I'm staying here. With you."

His sisters burst into the room, chasing each other while one of them screams something about a frog. They barely notice us as we wipe at our eyes, laughing nervously when we're alone again. A few seconds later we hear Sarah shouting for Daniel. Whatever they need him for, I'm okay with it. We have all the time in the world now. His mother returns home soon after, and I promise him that we'll talk later that evening. That's when I had originally intended to tell him. We help his mother unload groceries, shooting shy smiles at each other when we can get away with it.

We socialize just long enough to put in an appearance. Then we leave, my work the perfect excuse, because I need Daniel to drive me there. We still have plenty of time, but I mention needing to get ready. We're both eager to reach the safety of the car.

"What's this mean?" Daniel asks as he begins to drive.

"That we're about to find out if you're still into me," I reply, "now that I'm no longer a limited-time offer."

"I'm super into you," he replies, grinning while shaking his head. "So over-the-top in love with you that it's not even funny." The happy expression falters. "What about everything else though? Like your family?"

I swallow before answering. "I'll see them again. Eventually. For now, I still have family here. I won't be alone."

"I can guarantee that," Daniel says, reaching over to take my hand.

We talk about the implications during the rest of the drive. The truth is, I don't have all the answers. I think of a distant cousin who moved to South Korea to be with her fiancé. I didn't see her much before. Now she's never around. The same could have happened to me. If I'd fallen in love with a hot French guy and decided to move to Paris, I would also be leaving my family behind in the name of love. The only difference is how impossible it'll be to visit them or even call.

Daniel and I end up in bed as soon as we're through the door to my place. Also not planned, but sometimes we can't help ourselves. I still want the evening to be special, so while he's catching his breath afterwards, I fill the bathtub and add plenty of soap flakes to create bubbles, just how he likes it. Then I light candles and place them around the room, get into the tub, and call for him to join me. He wears a goofy grin as he slides into the water, and for the next few minutes, we experiment with putting our legs in different positions so we can face each other, his smile never fading.

"I also have something to tell you," he says at last. "I talked to my parents the other night. About my future."

"You mean college?" I sit up in excitement, water sloshing over the edge.

"Yeah. I told them what I really wanted to do. My mom was the best. She was on my side for the entire conversation."

"And your dad?"

"He's less certain," Daniel says, his smile faltering. "But he agreed that there's no harm in me taking slightly different classes, since I'll need many of the same credits anyway. I'm done pretending though. I'll keep an open mind, like I promised him, but from now on, when someone asks what I'm going to school for, I'll tell them it's to become an engineer. Even if he's around to hear it."

"That's great! I'm proud of you."

We lean forward and kiss. I put a pile of bubbles on his head while we're doing so. Daniel doesn't seem to notice when he leans back again, the pyramid of suds wobbling with every movement.

"I want to help put a man on the moon," he says. "That'll make my dad see that this is the right decision. You'll tell me when and where I need to be?"

"Yeah. I'll be there watching you make it happen."

His smile returns. "I love the sound of that. Say it again."

"I'm staying."

Daniel grabs the side of the tub and starts sliding his legs around, like he's trying to get at me. After laughing, I solve the issue by turning around and stretching out. His arms drape around my neck as I lean against him.

"This is the best day of my life," Daniel whimpers, as if he's about to cry from sheer happiness.

"It's not over yet. In a little bit, we're going to get dressed and go to dinner. My treat. Then you're going to drive me to The Silver Rattle, and while I'm up there on stage playing, you'll be all I'm thinking about. We'll come home again afterwards so I can hold you the entire night. All the way until morning."

"And then what?" Daniel murmurs.

"I don't know that part of the future," I tell him. "But I'm looking forward to discovering it with you."

He squeezes me tight, whispering that he loves me. Then he starts to nibble my ear until I laugh. I end up sliding farther down in the tub, but that's okay, since it allows me to rest my head on his chest. I could spend the rest of my life this way. I suppose that's what I'm committing to. The thought doesn't fill me with trepidation. I don't experience any pangs of doubt. We belong together, and with any luck, that's how it will always be.

Chapter 16

"This is our last song of the evening," Alonzo says into the mic, turning to me with a twinkle in his eye. "And we want to dedicate it to the newest member of our ragtag bunch. We will all miss Jerome, who has moved on to the pampered pastures of Philadelphia with his daughter and her family. Lucky for us heartbroken fools, a cupid came along to keep the love flowing. This song is for you, Reggie Valentine, but I'm gonna need some help singing it."

Mama strolls onto stage and shoots me a wink before grabbing a standing mic and belting out a song, *Cupid's Boogie*, a cute duet that she shares with Alonzo. He showed me the sheet music earlier. The song is about two people who intend to get married, but before they do, the woman wants to make sure her man knows that she'll be in charge. The back and forth between them is playful and has me laughing. I hammer the piano as they sing, moved that they chose to dedicate a song to me.

I've been playing full-time at The Silver Rattle for more than a month now, and it's been an education. During the day I often go thrift shopping for records and bring them back to my motel room. I splurged on a portable record player so I can learn the popular music of the era. When I'm done tutoring Daniel's sisters, I use the time to practice playing what I've been listening to, which the entire Parker family has been extremely supportive of. The littlest girl, Lizzie, loves to dance and has some serious moves. I wish we could get her on stage, just for one night, because I'm sure people would adore the way she swings her arms and bobs her head.

When the song ends, I clap along with the audience, grinning at my boss and her cousin. Then I get off stage and retreat to a dark corner of the club where Daniel meets me at the end of each show. I kiss him, listen to his words of praise, and promise I won't be long as I go to collect my money. This has become our nightly routine, although that will likely change soon, since school has officially begun for him. So far he's managed to keep up with the late hours.

I hurry to the backroom that is used for an office, surprised when I open the door and a familiar smell fills my nostrils. Mama waves her hand through the thick cloud of smoke to clear it.

"I usually wait until I'm done counting," she says from behind a desk, holding a joint out to me, "but I've got the fiercest cramps that don't know when to quit. Do you smoke?"

"Only when I'm on fire," I say before taking a drag.

Her laugh is husky as she resumes putting bills into stacks. The wide room is divided into two areas that bleed into each other. Mama's office is off to one side, and a lounge area is on the other with couches and a coffee table. I've hung out here plenty of times before. The rest of the band won't be far behind. They usually go to the bar for a drink first. I sit across from Mama and help her sort coins as we take turns hitting the joint. I haven't been high since ending up here, and it has me feeling good.

"You sure have a dedicated fan out there," she says. "You can bring him along with you next time. I don't mind."

"You mean in here? Really? I'll do that. Thanks."

She's quiet as she begins doling out everyone's pay, but her eyes keep returning to me. "Must not be easy, that kind of love."

We've never talked about it before. Even when I asked if Daniel could be put on the list so he could always get into the club. Mama simply said, *Make sure he doesn't bring any trouble with him.* I think she was referring to Leroy or anyone else who might want to indulge in underage drinking. Considering that she caught me and Daniel kissing before and didn't seem to have an issue with it, I don't see the harm in opening up to her.

"Being with him is easy. It's only hard when other people make it that way."

She slides a small stack of bills across the desk to me. "You know, there's a place where you can dance together and nobody will mind. Wilson's Watering Hole over on Halstead and Webster. It's a private club, but if you tell them Mama sent you, that should get you through the door."

"Thanks," I say, pocketing the money before I resume sorting.

She shakes her head. "I don't know how it works with men, but I do know you should never keep a lady waiting."

I laugh, resist the urge to kiss the woman, and leave to go find Daniel. He's resting his head on a table not far from where I left him, which must mean he's really tired, considering how sticky they can get.

"It's past your bedtime young man," I say, mussing his hair. "C'mon. I'll get you tucked in."

Daniel raises his head, manages a sleepy smile, and gets up. He wobbles like a drunk as we meander toward the exit. The late nights are definitely coming to an end for him soon. He keeps looking at me funny on the way out, especially once we're on the sidewalk and I start singing the theme song to *Good Times*. He can judge all he wants, but his best friend watches the reruns religiously when she's older.

"You smell strange," Daniel says once we're in the car.

"Oh! I got stoned with Mama."

"Really? What did you drink?"

"No, I got high," I say, pinching the air by my lips and pretending to smoke. "Weed. Cannabis. Marijuana."

"Reefer?" he asks, staring at me instead of starting the engine.

"That's the one. We should write our own word conversion book, so we understand each other better. Man… there's gotta be a shorter term for that. Oh! Ha ha! A foreign language dictionary. Duh. Although that's still three words."

"You're on drugs?" Daniel says, sounding panicked.

"Yeah. I smoked up a little. I'm not super-baked or anything. Just a little fried. Speaking of which, I'm hungry. Do you guys have Dunkin' Donuts yet?"

Daniel's mouth becomes a flat line. "I don't understand you sometimes."

"That's why we need the dictionary thing."

"No, I don't understand how you could do this to yourself. Were you forced?"

I laugh, tickled by the seriousness of his tone. "I was told the first one was free, and since all my friends were doing it, I basically had to."

"Really?"

I snort. "No! I was offered and accepted. That's all."

Daniel's scowls. Then he finally puts the key in the ignition. "I'm driving you to the hospital."

"Oh my god," I say, spluttering laughter. "I'm fine! I've done this a million times."

"You *what?!*"

"Okay, maybe not *that* often, but I know what I'm doing. We're good. Let's go home."

He's so adorable when he looks worried. I can't resist reaching out to pinch one of his cheeks, and once I do, I pull upward on it to try and make him smile. This only works for half of his face, which sends me into another fit of laughter.

"I'll take you to my dad," Daniel says, swatting my hand away. "He'll know what to do."

"About what?"

He looks at me like I've lost my mind. "Reggie, you're addicted to drugs!"

"No, I'm not. I love you, but you're overreacting. Reefer is legal in the future."

Daniel is aghast. "You can't be serious."

"Maybe not in every state, but it's going to happen. Especially considering that all of Mexico and Canada have legalized it. The United States is trapped in a weed sandwich, and Illinois is the cannabis infused mayo. *Something* has to be open still. I just want a burger."

He has his back to the driver side door now, as if I'm the Ghost of Christmas Yet to Come and I've just shown him a dystopian vision of the future. "It's legal?"

"Yeah. Just like alcohol. You have to be a certain age to partake, but that's it."

"That's terrible."

"It's fun," I say, grabbing him and trying to shake the seriousness out. "We need to loosen that tie."

"I'm not wearing one."

"Then stop acting like you are."

"Are you saying you *want* me to do drugs?"

"I'm saying you should try everything in life at least once. Except maybe crack or heroin. Too addictive. Oh, and fisting. I'm not judging anyone, but that can't be healthy, right? Especially when they go all the way up to the elbow. Aren't they displacing like… internal organs or something?"

He doesn't answer me. Instead he starts driving, occasionally shooting a concerned glance in my direction. I try to be quiet, so he'll have less to worry about, but the strain must have been a sativa, because I'm bouncing with energy. I turn on the radio, gasp in wonder at the gorgeous city lights, and make up silly lyrics until he starts fighting off a smile. I keep working at him all the way home, and by the time we exit the highway, the crinkles have left his forehead.

Daniel turns to me after parking in front of the motel. "You aren't a beatnik, are you?"

I laugh. I can't help it.

He soon joins me and adds, "Never let me catch you playing the bongos or reciting bad poetry. I couldn't stand it."

"I can't promise anything," I say, letting myself topple over to his side of the seat.

Daniel pushes me away. "And I *do* like to have fun, you know."

"Oh yeah? How would you like to go dancing with me?" When he looks to the upper landing where my room is, I shake my head. "Not there. In public. I heard of a place where we'll be safe."

"Really?" he says with guarded hope.

"Yup. What do you think?"

Daniel's smile is all the answer I need, but I make him promise anyway, just for fun.

"Do you think I should smoke reefer?" he asks, looking uncertain.

"No, but only because you don't seem like you need anything to take the edge off or to have a good time. If you ever feel like you do, then yeah. Give it a try. I think it's a better option than drinking. Until then, try not to judge too harshly. Everyone has a vice."

"What's mine?" he asks.

"I dunno. What gives you the most kicks?"

He looks up to the landing again—at my room—but for a different reason than before.

"I guess you're not so tired after all," I say, sliding my hand over to his and squeezing it.

"It helps me sleep," Daniel says innocently. "Can we?"

I answer him by leaping out of the car and racing him up the stairs.

— — —

Some days are harder than others. No matter how happy Daniel makes me, and regardless of how much I enjoy playing at the club and tutoring, I still question my decision to stay. I've had a few pathetic nights where I sing songs to myself out of nostalgia, usually while crying and thinking about my parents and everyone I miss. I even find myself wishing my dumb brothers were around to barge into my room and tease me, like they always used to.

I worry about Hannah, remembering how happy she was when I invited her to prom. I hope she's not sad. I am, on occasion, but I think that's normal. My oldest brother participated in a foreign exchange student program and spent six months in Switzerland. He said the first month was like a vacation, but after that, he really started to miss home. So I figure this is long overdue for me.

The guilt is the worst. My grandmother, the one I know in the future, couldn't have warned me about what would happen *after* I disappeared. Even she wouldn't have known how my parents would react. My mother was always so affectionate and caring. What if this breaks her heart? I keep telling myself that I might be there with her now as an old man, but I don't know if she'll be okay with missing out on so much of my life, especially since she won't be born for another thirteen years and won't remember much until the early eighties. That's a long time for a mother to go without her son. And what about my dad? He always made time for me, no matter how demanding his day was. Does he feel helpless to do anything about my absence? Does he blame himself, even though he shouldn't?

I wonder too about missed opportunities. Like everyone, I've searched for my own name on the internet, and I never read about some other Reggie Valentine who was an R&B legend back in the fifties. I always felt like I could make it big. Or at least go viral on social media. I'd eagerly take that flash in the pan, since it's more than most people get. I don't need fame and fortune to be happy—my piano teacher convinced me of that—but I do want to share my music with the world. Dozens of people crammed into a club is nothing compared to millions and millions of views.

Considering how many misgivings I have, it's a testament to my love for Daniel—or perhaps his love for me—that I can be so carefree around him. As if the fifties are where I've always been. I only feel that way when we're together, so I allow myself some self-indulgent grieving when we're not and pray that my decision doesn't hurt too many people. When the doubt and sorrow become too much to bear, I only need to seek out Daniel so his kisses can chase away the pain. And it works. Every single time.

— — —

I'm sitting in the living room where I grew up, surrounded by a family that isn't my own. I'm usually not so cognizant of that fact, but the footage on the screen has me yearning for my parents. They might be able to offer comforting words or an explanation as to why the world has stopped making sense. After a tutoring session with the girls, Melody invited me to stay for dinner. Daniel and I had plans to go out before the evening news sidetracked us. Now we're all gathered around the television and staring at a small monochrome screen. On it, swarms of angry white people are gathered outside a school. The disgust on their faces reveals the hatred in their hearts. The reason for all the outrage? Nine black students, under the protection of federal troops, entered Little Rock Central High School today, but the story began three years ago when the Supreme Court ruled that segregated education was unconstitutional.

The Little Rock Nine, as they'll be remembered, were the first black students chosen in Alabama to attend a desegregated school. They were supposed to start in early September instead of now, at the end of the month, but that didn't go so well: The students had been called before the first day of school and told to meet at the back of the building where it would be safer to enter. Elizabeth Eckford, whose family didn't have a phone, never got this message. She arrived the next morning unaware that an angry mob was waiting for her outside the school. The news program reruns clips from that day, showing a teenage girl in a freshly ironed dress. Angry white people stalk alongside her, their sneering expressions devoid of sympathy. Members of the Arkansas National Guard are there too, but they don't defend the girl. Instead, following the bigoted governor's orders, they form a blockade to stop Elizabeth from entering the building. She retreated to a nearby bus bench, the angry crowd following her. Elizabeth would describe in interviews how she was spit on by the people surrounding her. She suffered a barrage of slurs, including someone who suggested they hang her from a tree. They wanted to lynch a fifteen-year-old girl who had only shown up for class. That was her supposed crime. Elizabeth kept her composure, which is admirable if not downright heroic, but it's all too easy to imagine Gloria in her place. This really gets my blood boiling.

The news program cuts to interviews of white men, chuckling and nudging each other as they explain that such people don't belong here—that they have their own schools. They fail to mention how underfunded and delipidated those schools are. When the newsreel cuts to a stuffed dummy hanging from a tree, children striking it gleefully, it's more than I can take. I'm on my feet and out the door before anyone can stop me.

Nine black students. Out of hundreds, if not thousands, who are white. That's all it took to make people feel justified in abusing and harassing a teenage girl, who was unaccompanied by anyone who could offer protection or guidance. The abuse, both physical and verbal, will continue during the rest of the year for all nine students. Some of the white kids will try to burn Melba Pattillo in a bathroom stall. They fail but will be more successful later when throwing acid in her eyes. Elizabeth will be pushed down a flight of stairs. The three boys will get beaten up while being forbidden to defend themselves, lest they be suspended like Minnijean Brown is after dumping a bowl of chili on some racist asshole's head. Each and every one of the Little Rock Nine will face death threats, and when Ernest Green becomes the first black student to graduate, he'll be told by the principal that he doesn't need to show up at the ceremony to collect his diploma. Ernest does anyway, making history through his fortitude.

None of that has happened yet. The story of the Little Rock Nine has always upset me, but it's different without decades of progress separating me from past horrors. These events are unfolding *right now*, a mere six hundred miles away. Each of the black students will go to bed tonight with anxiety filling their guts, and if they're anything like me, what little sleep they get will be filled with feverish nightmares of what might befall them the next day. They were chosen because of their good grades. All they want is a decent education. The only difference between them and the other students is the color of their skin. And the legacy of slavery that was forced upon their ancestors. Instead of an apology or any form of reparation, they'll suffer small-minded cruelty for the rest of the school year and for decades to come. How can anyone justify that in their mind? How can people witness such rancid hatred and continue thinking that *nine young students* are the problem? It's sickening. And maddening. I can't stand it anymore.

I want to go home.

I become aware of my surroundings and realize that I've reached Saint Charles Road, which will take me the rest of the way to Churchill Woods. Without even thinking about it, I was heading for the gate. I pick up the pace while feeding into my anger, so I'll have the courage to press on. When a pale green car pulls over in front of me, I turn around and walk the other way, because this isn't about him. Staying here feels too much like condoning the era and its travesties. My sacrifice will be miniscule compared to what most people of color go through here.

"Reggie! Please!"

My throat grows tight at the sound of his voice, and when I feel his hand on my shoulder, I spin around, having found a target for my frustration.

"Leave me the fuck alone!" I snarl. "I'm done with all of you!"

His expression is wounded, but not confused. "I know," he croaks. "I'm ashamed of being white sometimes. I really am. All the terrible things that we've done, and that we continue to do... A few years back, when Emmett Till died, I would have gladly shed my skin. I was the same age—fourteen years old—when they murdered him. I couldn't believe that anyone would be so cruel."

Emmett Till was a Chicago native who went down to Mississippi to visit his uncle. While there, he visited a small grocery store to buy gum and purportedly whistled flirtatiously at the cashier. Or so they say. He also whistled as a trick to overcome his stutter, and he often clowned around to make his friends laugh. No matter his intentions, a few days later, Emmett Till was taken from his bed at gunpoint while his relatives watched helplessly. Emmett was tied up and thrown in the back of a truck. His captors brought him to a barn where they beat, tortured, and shot Emmett before throwing him in the Tallahatchie River. When his body was found, Emmett's mother insisted that it be sent back to Chicago for an open-casket funeral, so everyone could see how mutilated and disfigured he was. The public was invited, including the press. Photos were published in newspapers across the nation. No longer could people turn a blind eye to the lynching that continued to claim hundreds of black lives in the South and elsewhere.

"When I saw those photos—" Daniel whimpers and struggles to continue. "How could people be so heartless? How could anyone stand there and watch another person suffer, or even worse, actually *hurt* them like that? He didn't look human anymore. It's like his face was reflecting our own ghastly image back at us. We're the monsters! And when you showed up in my life…" He grabs my arms. "I'm so scared, Reggie. I don't want anything like that to happen to you. I worry so much, especially when we're apart. I'd die to protect you. I swear I would! I'd do anything, so if you need to go home, I won't stand in your way. Not if that's what keeps you safe. I love you enough to let go."

He hugs me and starts to sob. I'm aware that cars are driving past us. He must be too, but he still clings to me while weeping. My arms remain at my sides as my own tears begin to flow, the injustices of the world too vile to stomach. The men who killed Emmett Till were acquitted by an all-white jury, even though they admitted to abducting him. Months later, once they could no longer be tried for their crimes, those same men shamelessly admitted in an interview that they had indeed killed Emmett. They faced no consequence for this confession. Instead they were paid thousands of dollars for the interview. Decades later, the woman who Emmett supposedly harassed confirmed that her testimony had been false. She couldn't even remember if he actually whistled at her.

The details of the case are truly horrific. I rarely let myself think about them in depth. They make me question my faith in humanity. When that happens, I try to see past the ugliness to acts of compassion and kindness, bravery and resilience. Rosa Parks was thinking of Emmett Till when she was asked to move to the back of the bus. He was with her during one of the greatest moments of history. I hope that brought his mother comfort. I know that she'll continue to speak publicly about her son for the rest of her life, so that he won't be forgotten. As for me, I finally raise my arms and pull Daniel close, trying to let love guide my actions instead of fear.

Chapter 17

Leaves skitter across the sidewalk, a hint of smoke in the chilly air, as Daniel and I walk down Glen Ellyn's main street. He's been wonderfully patient about driving me everywhere, although I try to take the train or bus when he's busy with his classes. Currently we're on the way to his house so I can teach his sisters. Seeing the paper jack-o-lanterns and witches hanging in store windows along the way reminds me how exciting this time of year was during my childhood.

"Is Halloween popular in the fifties?" I ask.

"Oh yes," Daniel says. "Don't make any plans for us. My parents always ask me to take Sarah and Lizzie trick-or-treating."

"Can I tag along?"

"Of course! They'd love it. So would I." He shoots me a bashful grin. "Gosh, should we dress up? I know we're too old, but I still enjoy it."

"Sure," I say distractedly. On the street corner ahead of us is someone vaguely familiar, but I can't quite place who he is. The man has thin white hair and a bulbous nose. The Hawaiian shirt and white trousers don't offer any hints. He seems to recognize me too, although with the same amount of uncertainty. This changes when his attention turns to who I'm with.

"Daniel Parker," the man says as we approach. "How are you doing, son?"

"Just fine, Officer O'Brien."

It all comes back to me with a jolt, that first confusing night here when I ran from the woods and got into his antiquated police cruiser.

"And your family?" O'Brien asks. "My granddaughter was at your father's office just the other day."

"We're all doing well," Daniel replies. "I hope it wasn't anything serious."

"Nothing to worry about. She only needed her polio vaccine." O'Brien is openly staring at me now. "Wait, is this the boy I picked up in the park that night? The one I brought to your house?"

"Yeah," I respond. "Long time, no see."

"I always wondered what happened to him," O'Brien says to Daniel. "I figured he was a drifter. Or nuttier than a fruitcake."

"Thanks!" I say, irritated that I don't seem to be invited to the conversation.

"Has he been much trouble?" O'Brien asks.

"Ask him yourself," Daniel spits. "He's not my dog."

My anger is deluged by a wave of affection for him. Daniel clenches his fists while glaring openly at the police officer.

O'Brien's mouth falls open. Then his head swivels and he finally addresses me. "I can see that you haven't been a good influence."

I raise my hands helplessly. "Hey, I just run and fetch the ball when he asks. Oh, and I try not to potty on the carpet or else I get the newspaper."

O'Brien looks between us, shaking his head in disapproval. "I wonder what your father would think of this behavior."

"We can go ask him," Daniel says, still fuming. "His office is just a few blocks away."

"Maybe I *will* have a word with him," O'Brien grumbles.

"That won't be necessary," I interject, preferring to defuse the situation, because I don't think anything we can say will change his views. That, and there's something I've always wanted to ask him. "We were just arguing about sports, and you caught us in a heated moment. Sorry."

This seems to appease him somewhat. "Oh. I take it you heard the game yesterday. I don't think the Lions stand a chance this year. My money is on Cleveland. They started the year strong and will end it that way."

"I bet you're right," I say, not having a clue as to what sport we're discussing. "Hey, speaking of the night you picked me up, do you remember how I was running from some guy in the woods?"

O'Brien waves at a woman who is passing by before shaking his head. "No."

"You seemed to know him. Or at least why he was out there."

He looks blank for a moment. "This was Churchill Woods? Was it raining?"

"Yes," I confirm.

"You must have run into Pete Babbage."

"Who?" Daniel asks.

"Pete Babbage. I bring him food when the weather is bad and he can't make it into town."

"Is he homeless?" I ask.

"No," O'Brien says, standing up straighter. "He's a veteran. Like me."

"But he lives in the woods?" I inquire as delicately as possible.

"He built himself a campsite out there," O'Brien snaps. "You boys leave him alone, do you hear me? He isn't bothering anyone. He's just a bit troubled by what he went through, that's all. He deserves peace and quiet, so don't go poking around."

"I was only curious," I reply.

"Well if I hear about him having any trouble, guess who I'm going to haul in for questioning?"

"We'll be on our best behavior," I assure him.

"You do that." O'Brien turns his attention to Daniel. "Tell your father I said hello." He jerks a thumb in my direction. "And don't let this one get you into trouble."

"I'll try to keep him on a tight leash," Daniel grumbles.

"Such a charming person!" I say once we've walked away.

Daniel rolls his eyes. "I'm sorry that he—"

"You've got nothing to apologize for. We just found out who scared me that night. I bet he heard me yelling for Hannah and went to see what the commotion was about."

Daniel is quiet for a few paces. "Do you want to go back to your own time? Is that why you asked?"

"No," I say instantly. "Sheer curiosity. Nothing else." Although I am tempted to find Pete Babbage and ask if he took my things. Especially if I could get my phone back. Then again, it's been nearly half a year. The battery is probably dead, I honestly don't know if I had a charger with me, and there's no signal anyway. It would be fun to show Daniel a piece of tech from the future, but I can't imagine a useless brick impressing him much.

"That's a relief," he says as we turn down a residential street. "There's something I wanted to talk to you about. Do you like the motel where you're staying?"

"I'm not attached to it or anything. Why?"

"Because I can't stand my roommate. He snores the entire night. And farts. That dorm is so small that there's no escaping the smell."

"So that's why you've been staying with me so much."

"Among other reasons," Daniel says with a blush. "But we practically live together anyway. So I thought…" He looks over at me to gage my reaction.

"You want to get our own place?"

"I won't be upset if you don't want to," Daniel says, studying his feet. "It's just that we spend an awful lot of time downtown lately. We only come back here for your piano lessons, or to see Gloria. So it would make the most sense if we both lived in the city."

I can't help smiling. "And I'd really *really* like it."

His head whips up. "You would?"

"Absolutely! I hate sleeping without you. And it would mean that you don't have to drive me around as much. I could get home and to the club without your help. Instead of you having to stay up late, you could keep the bed warm for me."

"That sounds so nice," Daniel says with a guffaw.

"Yeah. One question though. What will your parents think?"

"We'd have to get a two-bedroom apartment," he says with an apologetic grimace. "And have separate rooms. But it would only be for show."

"Can't we get two twin beds in the same room, like all the married couples on TV?"

"My grandparents *still* do that," Daniel says, shaking his head. "So old fashioned!"

"Totally. I don't mind the need to pretend. If we were in my time, I'd be begging you to come out. Here, finding a way to live with another guy is progressive enough for me."

"Any ol' guy?" he asks, clearly fishing for a compliment.

"Yeah. As long as he's hot and healthy, I'm not picky. Why? Is your current roommate good-looking? I'm a heavy sleeper. And I can crack a window."

Daniel shakes his head, not taking the bait. "Why do I put up with you?"

"I'll remind you later. When should we start looking for a new place?"

"This weekend, I thought."

"Uh-huh. And when are you going to let me take you out dancing? We've been talking about it for ages now."

"I know," Daniel says. "School is harder than I thought it would be."

He literally fell asleep during dinner once. Like, in the middle of it, when we were still at the table. So I've been giving him the time he needs to rest up and adjust to his new schedule.

"How about tonight?" Daniel asks. "You aren't playing at the club, and if we're out late, I can skip my morning classes. I wouldn't mind."

"I bet you wouldn't. Let's do it!"

I'm more animated than usual when teaching his sisters, and as soon as we're done, I forgo my self-indulgent playing time to join Daniel in his room so I can watch him pick out an outfit. Most of his possessions are still there, since his dorm room can't accommodate them all. I let him choose based on his own tastes and the style of the era and don't make snarky comments when he opts for what looks like a tweed suit jacket. I even shrug when he holds up a maroon tie. I'm kind of into his retro look now. It's cute. Although he could combine a cowboy hat with a kimono and I'd probably still find him hot.

"What are you going to wear?" he asks.

"You'll see."

I found a great deal on a jacket the last time I went thrifting with Gloria, but I haven't let him see it yet. Tonight will be ideal for the grand unveiling.

"Don't you look sharp!" Melody says when we come back downstairs. She's sitting in the living room with her husband.

"Going somewhere special tonight?" Dr. Parker asks, rustling his newspaper before folding it.

"Out to a bar," I say. "We're going to catch ourselves some fillies."

"You aren't really going to a bar, are you?" Melody asks, appearing worried.

"Nope," I reply. "It's just as well. Neither one of us knows how to ride a horse."

"I do, actually," Daniel says from next to me. "I have a—"

"Merit badge?" I finish for him. "Then it's not hopeless. Do you have one for sneaking into bars undetected?"

Dr. Parker laughs, not seeming concerned. Melody stands to fuss over her son, straightening his tie and making him promise that we won't get into trouble. Then we drive to my place, where I grab some clothes before shutting myself in the bathroom. Daniel knocks at one point and says something flirtatious, but I don't let him in. Only when I'm completely dressed do I take a step back to consider myself. I have a black leather jacket on over a white T-shirt. The jeans are tight—cupping my bulge nicely— and cuffed at the ankles. I slicked back my hair with pomade, resulting in a series of glistening waves. I only wish I'd thought to buy a pack of smokes to complete the look.

I strut out of the bathroom with attitude while wearing a permanent scowl. Daniel sees me and slowly stands up from the kitchen table, like he's picking up a girl for prom. He looks me over, focusing on different details of the outfit before he licks his lips and swallows. "Wow," he manages at last.

"Do you like it?" I ask, feeling self-conscious before remembering the role I'm supposed to be playing. I cross my arms over my chest and lean against the wall. "Not that I give a damn. This town is the pits. Where can a fellah go for a good time, huh?"

"So you're new in town?" Daniel springs over to me with a grin. "I'll show you around. How many tattoos do you have? Can I see your knife?"

"What's the big idea, asking me so many questions? Get outta here, ya twerp!"

He laughs, running his palms over the lapels of my jacket. "This is so hot! Is it your Halloween costume?"

"No," I respond, moving his hand to my T-shirt and placing it over my heart. "I thought you'd want to finally go on a date with that greaser who caught your eye."

"Like make-believe?" he asks, looking thrilled. "Okay! But only once we're back here again. I like the real you. I don't want to hear about your old man not understanding you or whatever."

"Well he doesn't!" I growl. "Nobody in this godforsaken town does!"

"I do," Daniel says, turning and pressing his back to me theatrically. He even drapes an arm across his forehead. "All the other girls say I'm too bad—too *wild*—to be their friend. I'd do anything for a guy who would take me away from here. Where's your bike?"

"Parked out front. Are you ready to go?"

He turns around with a naughty expression. "We could just pretend to go and stay here all night."

"Nope. I'm not putting out again until I get that dance you've been promising me."

He laughs. "Let's go then."

We stop for a burger on the way downtown. Then we drive north, to where Wilson's Watering Hole is supposed to be, except we walk up and down the street twice without finding it. We're more meticulous on our third attempt, finally locating a nondescript door between two businesses with thin faded letters that spell out the name. The door is locked when I pull on it, so I try knocking instead. A small square set into the surface swings open, a stern face filling it while sizing us up.

"Yeah?" the woman grunts.

"We're here for the bar?" I say, not meaning for it to come out as a question. "Mama sent us."

The woman continues to stare.

"Mama from The Silver Rattle," I explain. "She said we'd be safe here."

The little window slams shut before the door opens just enough to let us in. I'm less than impressed as we walk inside. The place is small, with a bar on the left wall and a dozen or so square tables taking up the rest of the space. Everyone is seated except around the bar itself, where they stand. I can hear light music, but I don't see any dancing.

"First time here?" asks the woman who let us in. She's heavy-set and middle-aged. I nod as she settles down on a barstool next to the door. "No loitering out front," she barks. "When you leave here, you keep walking. Only sit in pairs. When you hear the bell, switch partners."

"Okay," I say, only understanding half of it.

Daniel looks uncomfortable as we walk deeper into the place. We're being watched by just about everyone, and I'm not sure what to do with myself, so I lead him to the bar. The bartender has slicked-back salt-and-pepper hair and a giant mustache that curls at the ends. He looks like he stepped out of a Western saloon. His eyes sparkle like the glass he's polishing.

"What can I get you boys?" he asks.

"Two sodas," I say. Desperate to dispel the tension, I add, "Make them extra fizzy."

The bartender smiles and sets down the glass he was working on. "Is this the first time you've experienced my watering hole?"

The way he says this makes it sound dirty, and I decide I like him already. "It is indeed. Are you Wilson?"

"I am." He takes two bottles from a refrigerator and uncaps them. "How did you find out about us?"

"Mama, the owner of The Silver Rattle."

"Oh, that's a fine club!" Wilson enthuses. "I'd love to have live music here someday. Are you boys together?"

"Yes," Daniel confirms firmly. Probably because he's getting the most stares.

"Alas," Wilson sighs. "I can hear hearts breaking across the bar. Are you starting a tab?"

"Sure," I answer.

"Great! We ask all our patrons to pay their tabs in advance. Cash will do nicely."

I laugh and slide a bill across the bar to him, insisting that he keep the change.

"Put it in the piggy bank, sweetheart," Wilson replies.

On the bar next to us is an empty pickle jar with a handwritten sign taped to it, which reads *The Fund*.

"What are you saving up for?" I ask him.

"A little starlight between dark nights," he says with a wink. "Why don't you make yourselves at home?"

I guess that means finding a table. I'm a bit confused about who is with who, since there seems to be an even mix of men and women at each. We choose one that is unoccupied and sit, but we don't even manage to set down our drinks before someone clears their throat. At the table next to ours, a woman catches my eye and shakes her head.

"Is someone sitting here already?" I ask.

"No," she says. "That's the problem."

"What do you mean?"

She stares a moment before the man seated across from her murmurs something. Then he gets up along with another guy and they leave together.

"Come sit with us," the woman says.

She's ramrod thin and older than us. A fur stole is around her neck and a brimmed hat sits on her head like a bowl. The woman next to her is beefy with slicked-back hair. She's wearing a suit. I assume they're together.

"That's very nice of you," I say, "but we just got here and—"

"It's the rules," her partner grunts. "We won't bother you."

When we still don't move, the thinner of the two leans closer and whispers. "Men have to sit with women. In case the police show up."

"Got it! Umm... Thanks." We quickly move to their table. The woman who first addressed us smiles and resumes talking to her partner. "Sorry," I say a second later. "This is our first time."

"Oh!" The woman extends a hand and introduces herself as Betty. Her partner is Chris. When I ask which pronouns they prefer, they stare at me blankly.

"I'm from out of town," I offer as an explanation before introducing myself.

Daniel does the same, his anxiety revealed in what he asks them: "How often do the police show up?"

"They usually aren't trouble," Chris replies. "That's what the fund is for."

"The tip jar?" I ask.

She nods. "Wilson pays off the police, but you never know who will walk in that door. Could be someone on patrol who doesn't know the arrangement, or someone looking to make trouble. A reporter for instance. They like to put our names in the paper, and there have been some blackmailers recently."

"What?" Daniel asks, sounding panicked. "Does that happen a lot?"

"Hardly ever," Betty says, shaking her head at her partner. "Don't scare them off. They're so young!"

"Even more reason to be cautious," Chris retorts. "We've seen what can go wrong. The sooner they learn, the better."

"We're all ears," I say, taking Daniel's hand beneath the table.

This isn't what I wanted for him. I thought we'd be entering a sanctuary—a place where we could finally be ourselves without fear of persecution. I'm not sure that exists yet. Talking to Betty and Chris is informative though. They tell us how they've been together for over a decade, and that they consider themselves married ever since a private ceremony they held. Now they live in the same building, although in separate apartments to avoid suspicion.

"You can't be careful enough," Chris warns. "You never know who is watching."

"And yet," Betty says, "you still have to take *some* risks. Otherwise we wouldn't be together at all."

"That's true," her partner admits. "And it's worth it. But boy do I wish we could walk down the street while holding hands."

"We do sometimes," Daniel says. "Late at night. And only between streetlights."

"That's so sweet," Betty enthuses.

"It's sad," Chris counters. "Do you think straight people ever worry about being caught holding hands with anyone? I wish they knew what that feels like."

Daniel looks at me, and I wonder if he wants me to reassure him that it's possible in my day too, and it is… but not without risks. I'm glad he's hearing all of this. He needs to learn these lessons, and now that I'm staying, I do too.

"At least we have places like this one," Betty says, "where we can have fun and dance. Oh! That's another rule. If you're dancing and you hear a bell ring, you need to get away from each other and choose someone of the opposite sex to partner with. Doesn't matter who. It's almost fun, like musical chairs."

"Where does that take place?" I ask. "Do they move the tables out of the way or something?"

"You haven't seen the back room yet?" Betty asks. "The front is where you come if you want to talk."

When they see us glancing around, Chris points to a door in one corner, painted the same dark color as the wall. Daniel and I look to each other in excitement.

"Have fun, you two," Chris says with a dry chuckle.

"Thanks! It was nice meeting you."

"You too!" Betty says. "You're always welcome to sit with us."

"We'll do that."

I take Daniel's hand and we walk to the back. When I open the door there, the light music becomes louder. The volume is lower than most clubs would keep it, maybe so we'll be able to hear the bell, but it's enough to get my body moving. I wish house music had been invented already. I've already heard an interesting mix of old cabaret songs, French chansons, and of course the do-wop and R&B that's so prevalent now. A swing number is playing at the moment. Guys are spinning each other around and girls are swaying in each other's arms. I see lips locked together, hands gripping buns, and plenty of other shameless displays of homosexuality.

"I love it here!" Daniel cries.

I take his hand again and lead him out onto the dance floor. I don't really know how to move to a beat like this and don't care. I let my body shake, twirl, lurch, and stumble. It's all good. That's what I love about being around other queer people. None of us fit in by definition. We're all freaks, which is the best thing you can be, because it's so liberating. A slow song begins to play, so I take Daniel in my arms, and when I kiss him right there where everyone can see, I can tell that it's just as electric for him as it is for me.

"You've done it again, Reggie," he murmurs against my neck.

"What's that?" I ask.

"Shown me how beautiful the world can be."

I lean back, just enough to see his face, and recognize that he's done the same for me. I don't know if I'd look on the fifties as kindly if not for him. He's the most beautiful thing I've found here, or anywhere for that matter, and I feel incredibly lucky that he's mine.

Chapter 18

Daniel and I are at the Museum of Science and Industry, visiting its annual Christmas Around the World display. A giant tree fills one of the main halls, stretching into the open second floor. Smaller trees form a half-moon around it, each decorated with a different country's traditions. We've already seen the display from the ground floor. Now we're upstairs and leaning over the railing to view it from above. That was the plan, but I can't help noticing that Daniel's head is pointed in the wrong direction. I follow his gaze to a man in an all-white suit. His hair is pitch black and wavy. I don't need to get closer to know that his russet skin is unblemished and practically glows with vitality. I've seen him before at Wilson's Watering Hole.

"Funny looking tree," I murmur. "Isn't he?"

Daniel stands upright, his face red. "Sorry. I thought I recognized him."

"You did. I caught you staring at him the last time we went dancing. He's incredibly hot."

"That's not why I was looking at him," Daniel splutters.

I frown and shake my head. "I'd rather hear big truths than small lies. I've stared at him too for the same reason. What's wrong with that? We've pointed out guys who catch our eye before."

"Yeah, but..." Daniel shrugs.

I think I get it. "Those other guys weren't an option. Because as far as we knew, they were straight."

He nods. "Don't worry, I don't want to be with him."

I turn and lean against the rail. "Are you sure? Because I've noticed him checking us out before."

"I would never cheat on you!"

"I'm glad. I won't do that to you either. But we could bring him home with us one night."

Daniel does his best imitation of a fish out of water. "How could you even say that?"

I'm confused. Maybe he is too. "You get what I mean, right? We would *both* sleep with him. That's not cheating."

"It's infidelity!" Daniel cries. "Just because we both do it, doesn't make it okay!"

I stare at him and laugh, certain this is all a misunderstanding. "No no no, we won't take turns with him. We'll all be together. You know what a threesome is, right?"

Daniel glares at me. Then he stomps away. Once I get over my bewilderment, I chase after him. "Talk to me," I say. "I don't get what you're so upset about."

"We're supposed to be together," Daniel says, pivoting on me. He glances around self-consciously before leading me toward a Wright Brothers display that is unattended. "We're in a relationship," he hisses. "Why would we sleep with other people?"

"Don't you want to?" I ask. "I shouldn't be the only guy you've ever had sex with."

He pulls back from me. "You're cruel."

"No," I say, starting to feel defensive. "I'm being respectful by inviting you to discuss the dynamics of our relationship. I'm not going to do the old-fashioned thing where the man calls the shots. Which of us would that even be?"

"Don't act like my morals are outdated," Daniel growls. "You always do that! This isn't me 'being silly' because drugs aren't legal yet. You want to invite other people into our bedroom. It's sinful!"

"I'm totally fine being monogamous," I say in exasperation. "If that's what you want."

"I'm more concerned about what *you* want," Daniel grumbles, moving to the next display.

I follow him, but we aren't alone. There are too many people around to talk openly. He gravitates from crowd to crowd, which is frustrating, because I want to get this resolved. Daniel is trying to glare a hole into a model of the solar system when I grab his wrist and pull him off to the side.

"Things are different where I come from," I begin.

"I knew you were going to say that," he says, shaking his head. "Let me guess: Your parents were always bringing people home with them. You probably set an extra place at the dinner table, not knowing who would come through the door."

"Don't be ridiculous," I grumble. "My parents don't sleep around."

"But most people do?"

"Yes!" I say, my voice rising. "They do that even now, behind each other's backs, because some baseless morality forbids them from even discussing it. All I want to do is talk about our options!"

"There aren't any," Daniel mutters. "Not in my mind. If I'm in a relationship with you, nobody else is invited. Even for a sleepover."

"That's fine. You wear me out, usually in a good way, so I don't really care."

He resumes walking through the museum but seems too lost in thought to notice any of it. "I don't want you to cheat on me," he says eventually. He sounds sad, like it's inevitable. "I'd rather let you do whatever you want."

"That's the conclusion a lot of guys have reached." I reply. "Historically, we're not the best at keeping our dicks in our pants. So instead of letting that ruin a good thing, there are couples who decide to make allowances. And why not? Some things are only considered bad because we've been told they are. Our love, for instance. We both know there's nothing sinful about that, right?"

"Which only makes me want to protect it more," Daniel shoots back. "What if we meet someone you like better than me?"

"What if you do?" I say gently. "I've been with other guys before. I know how you compare to them and that makes me want to stay. It feels like a choice. I want you to have the same benefit of experience. There's also a part of me that wants to *prevent* you from being with anyone else, so I don't have to worry about how I stack up. But standing in the way of your growth and limiting your experiences is my version of immoral. Way more so than allowing a little sexual exploration. I wouldn't have offered if I didn't think our love was strong enough to survive that."

"It sounds nicer when you put it that way," Daniel murmurs.

I watch his jaw clench as he continues to think. "I'm happy, Reggie. I don't want to be with anyone else. I like the fantasy, or when we role-play, but you're all I need."

"Great!" I say. "Now that we've talked about it, I'm happy."

"Really?" He searches my face. "You don't want to sleep with anyone else?"

"The biological urge will always be there. I wonder if the museum has a display about that. But no, to answer your question, I don't feel the need to mess around. You satisfy me. In all sorts of ways."

He exhales in relief. "The future sounds really confusing."

"Yeah well, I find the past just as baffling. We come from two very different worlds, but that only makes what we have more interesting."

And occasionally frustrating, because we should at least hold hands now, even if we can't kiss and make up. Instead we continue walking through the museum, Daniel checking his watch on occasion. We have an appointment he's excited to keep. That's why I'm dressed in the best outfit I have—a pinstripe suit that he bought me as an early Christmas gift. I've stood in front of the mirror while wearing it more often than I care to admit. Especially after Gloria altered it so that it would fit tighter. Alonzo was so impressed when I showed up at the club wearing it that he's pushing for the entire band to get matching suits. Best of all, he wants Gloria to design them. She's sold a few dresses to Mama now, each one sparkling more than the previous. It's a theme. I'm not sure if sequins are my thing, but hey, I'm willing to try.

Once we've left the museum and have driven deeper into the city, we park again and hustle through snow flurries to a department store I've never heard of called The Fair. The massive twelve-story building no longer exists in my day. I'm craning my neck as we walk through various departments, looking for gift ideas and a hat to go along with my suit. After riding an escalator up a couple of floors, we walk to a corner of the building where a photo studio has been set up.

"How do I look?" Daniel asks, turning toward me.

"Handsome." I coax some stray hairs back into place and resist the urge to kiss him. "Your mother is going to be thrilled."

She wanted Daniel to have his portrait taken as her Christmas gift. Cut from the same cloth, Daniel asked the same thing of me. Photos are much less common than in my era. Personal cameras exist, but you have to buy film for them, use the entire roll, and then bring it somewhere to be developed. That's a far cry from seeing a digital reflection of yourself and tapping the screen as much as you want until satisfied. I let Daniel go first, since he seems excited by the prospect. I stand next to the camera and watch him, my heart thudding as I'm hit by a sense of déjà vu. The suit he's wearing, the exact way his hair is styled, the angle of his body, even the subtle smile... I've seen it all before except in black and white. His eyes lock onto mine, filled with kindness and love, just as the flash explodes.

Another moment in history, this one a crucial part of my past. When staring at his photo as a child in my grandmother's room, I never once dreamt that I would be there during the moment it was taken.

When it's my turn, I put all of my feelings for him into my expression. This manifests as a grin. He makes me so incredibly happy. I hope that shows in the final photo. We'll have to wait to find out. We're given a card so we can collect them on another day. When browsing the store afterwards, I'm not at all surprised when he picks up a gold frame lined with mother of pearl. "This one is nice," he says, turning to me. "What do you think?"

"I think I love you," I say, knowing that he'll buy it regardless. Otherwise I wouldn't be here.

"What do you mean 'you think'?" Daniel says demurely. "I want you to be certain."

"Hmm. Well, that depends on how your photo turns out. If it's good, I'll know for sure. If you blinked, we're finished."

Daniel laughs. Then he notices a different frame with sculpted roses and grabs it instead, setting the other down. "Never mind! Mom will love this one."

I check the back of my hand to make sure it's not disappearing. So far, so good. I tell Daniel that I'll catch up with him when he takes his choice to the register. I wait until he's gone before I grab the mother of pearl frame and rush to a different checkout counter. I'm going to need one for his gift anyway, and it seemed to catch his eye. Although I don't understand how the frame will end up in my grandmother's possession. Why would he give it to her? And replace my photo with his? So that

I would see it as a child and events would play out how they were meant to?

Another possibility occurs to me then, one so grim that it makes my stomach sink. What if Gloria has the framed photo in her room because she wanted something to remember Daniel by? It's not unrealistic to think that he might not be alive by then, but now I'm wondering how much longer we have together. Does he die of old age? Or does something happen to Daniel much sooner than that?

— — —

My legs wobble and my back muscles clench in agony as I carry the final cardboard box up the stairs. I haven't felt this worn out physically since working the warehouse job last year. I'm smiling regardless, because after months of anticipation, we're finally moving in together. Daniel's parents insisted that he stay in his dorm for the remainder of the semester, which was paid in advance. We started searching for a new place shortly after the holidays, settling on a little two-bedroom apartment above a liquor store. The only other unit up here belongs to a nice older woman who is nearly deaf. I'm not sure she can see that well either, since she calls both of us Daniel, despite some very obvious differences in our appearance. I doubt she'll have any suspicions about the nature of our relationship. His parents are another matter.

"Last one?" Melody asks as I enter.

"Yup. That's it."

"Thank god!" Gloria says with a groan. She's spread out on the living room floor. "I'm not budging from this spot until tomorrow. Or ever."

"We'll stack books around you to make a coffee table," I say, setting the box down with a thud. "Why does he have so many?"

"Most of what's in there is probably magazines," Dr. Parker chimes in while shaking his head. "He never could get enough of those science-fiction stories."

He's who I'm worried most about. Daniel's mother seems excited that we'll be living together. She keeps making suggestions about where we could put things before arranging them that way for us. I don't mind. Dr. Parker was much less enthusiastic until he saw my room. It's the smallest of the two, and the one we won't be using. I found a used mattress and frame listed in the classifieds. The rest of the furniture was sourced from thrift shops. I'm glad I went to the effort, especially when seeing the relief on Dr. Parker's face. He must have at least suspected. Now there is room for doubt. An entire bedroom, in fact.

My suspicions are confirmed when I'm moving some of the clutter into my room and he joins me there.

"This is a big step for Danny," Dr. Parker says. "I'd worry less if he was still living on campus, but I suppose he's well on his way to becoming a responsible adult. He attends classes all on his own, maintains his grades, and seems to be taking good care of himself."

"I'll watch out for him, if that's what you're worried about," I say, hopping up on a dresser to take the weight off my legs. "You shouldn't be. He's a smart kid."

Dr. Parker nods his agreement before sitting tentatively on the mattress across from me. "I keep thinking of his future, which should be prosperous, no matter the career path he chooses. Although I am concerned that he doesn't seem to have much luck with women. What about you?"

"Something about being up on stage makes people see you differently. And when you work at a club like The Silver Rattle..." I wink conspiringly. "Yeah. I get offers almost every night." That's the truth. I always tell women that we're not allowed to get involved with the customers, even though Alonzo is doing his best to prove otherwise.

"Could you take Danny under your wing?" Dr. Parker asks. "I like the idea of him bringing someone home to meet us."

"I'll do my best to teach him everything I know." There are still a few positions we haven't tried yet, for instance. "Although he seems happy to me. What else matters?"

"True," Dr. Parker says before looking toward the door. "Although I wouldn't have been as successful without Melody. She encouraged me whenever I doubted myself and supported me whenever I felt weak. I know how hokey that must sound at your age, but as you get older, you'll want someone you can rely on."

"Daniel will find that," I assure him. "And he'll do the same for that person in return. I figure it works both ways. You push each other to do whatever is necessary to feel fulfilled, right?"

"I suppose so," Dr. Parker says, as if the thought hadn't

occurred to him. "You're a surprisingly mature young man, Reggie. I'm glad that you and Danny became such close friends."

I feel guilty about deceiving him. He seems like a decent man who tries to be forward-thinking, even if he doesn't always get it right. We rejoin the others in the living room, and it isn't long before Daniel's parents leave to return the truck they borrowed. Once we've said goodbye, I lower myself down into a dining room chair that's still in the living room. Mostly because the narrow kitchen doesn't have room for it, and there isn't a dining room to speak of.

"How much longer are you going to lay there?" Daniel asks Gloria.

She attempts to raise her head before it falls back down again. "Forever. Or until you make me something to eat."

"I'm too tired to cook," Daniel says, plopping down on the couch.

"Don't look at me," I say when two pairs of eyes swivel in my direction. "I don't have the energy. Has pizza delivery been invented yet?"

"We don't have a phone," Daniel says. "It won't be installed until next week."

"We can survive until then," Gloria murmurs. "We just have to ration whatever food there is."

"Fine with me," Daniel says with a sigh.

"So I can stay here?" Gloria asks, sitting up. "It's not like you'll be using Reggie's room."

"You can stay overnight on occasion," Daniel says cautiously.

"Let me live with you," Gloria pleads. "C'mon! I've never had my own place before."

"You'd blow our cover," I point out.

"We'll tell everyone that me and Daniel got back together," she says. "It'll *double* your cover!"

Daniel looks at me, as if the decision is mine, but I pass it back to him. "That could work," I say. "Although we'd have less privacy."

He knows exactly what I mean. "Maybe it's not such a good idea," Daniel says quickly. "Besides, what would Leroy think?"

"He'll be in on it," she says, before shaking her head. "No, that won't work. He can't keep a secret. I like him, but he's not too bright."

"Oh darn," I say unconvincingly. "I guess poor ol' Daniel and me will have the place all to ourselves then."

"I'm so jealous of you both," Gloria moans. Then she gets to her feet. "Okay. Come on, you two. Let's venture out and find some food."

I watch, motionless, as she pulls Daniel to his feet. It takes both of them pushing and prodding me before I'm willing to stand. Daniel smiles at me when he locks the door behind us. Then we tromp down the stairs and outside. We have a separate entrance next to the liquor store. I only wish it locked too because we've already seen confused customers come inside the entryway before leaving again.

"Can I at least stay over tonight?" Gloria asks.

Daniel and I glance at each other, our expressions weary, but not because of her. There's no way we're doing anything romantic tonight. We're too worn out. "Sure," he says. "It'll be fun. We can play cards."

Gloria is surprisingly muted in her response. I don't find out why until half a block later. "Did you see those creeps?" she asks. "They were giving me the evil eye."

I glance over my shoulder and see a pair of men loitering outside the liquor store. I noticed them earlier. Their faces are sunken and hard, probably from a lifetime of drinking. They were standing there at the beginning of the move, and that was hours ago. Then again, the weather is unusually mild today, especially for January.

"Choose whichever one you think is cutest," I say. "That way you have a partner when we play cards tonight."

"We could play bridge!" Daniel says excitedly.

Gloria grimaces. "I'd rather invite Leroy over if we're going to do that." She perks up at the idea. "Would you mind?"

Daniel looks over at me with a hopeful expression. "Bridge!" he repeats.

"Fine with me," I say, "but if anyone from my future shows up unexpectedly, I don't know either of you, understand?"

"What the heck?" Gloria says in protest. "I'm cool!"

"Are you saying I'm not?" Daniel looks to me for reassurance. "I'm super cool. Aren't I, Reggie?"

"No. But I love you both. Now be quiet and find me something to eat. Otherwise I'll resort to cannibalism."

"He means you," Gloria says. "Reggie can't eat me or he'll never be born."

I start looking Daniel over, like I'm trying to decide which part of him I'll eat first. That's enough for him to take the lead. But for the record, I think I'd start with his lips, considering how sweet they always taste.

Chapter 19

Daniel and I visit Wilson's Watering Hole every couple of weeks, preferring to end our dates there. What better way to top off the night than by going where we can be ourselves? I love watching him dance. Daniel does this funny thing where he makes two fists, which he holds at shoulder height while jerking his elbows toward his hips. Sort of like someone flexing their biceps. He turns his head from left to right while doing so, stepping in the same direction. I have no idea where he picked that up, but it's the cutest thing I've ever seen.

Even better are the slow songs. Sometimes he'll wrap his arms around me. Or he'll take one of my hands and put the other on my back, so we can see each other and talk. That's what we're doing now while discussing vacation options. Spring break is still a few months away, but we both like the idea of getting away from the city.

"Florida is where everyone goes," Daniel argues. "It's traditional."

"Which is why we should avoid it. I don't know how gay San Francisco is yet, but we should ask around and find out. If it's anything like I remember, you'll love it."

"You've been there before?" he asks.

"No. But I've watched plenty of... Err, I've seen documentary films about it."

"You've watched videos on the internet," Daniel says, laughing when I look surprised. "You've been talking nonsense since the day I met you. I've picked up on some of it. From what you've described, the internet must be a new version of television, right?"

"Even better. Imagine having access to all the art in the world. Paintings, music, movies, books, and yeah, TV shows too.

Everything. We're also able to connect instantly with anyone, no matter how far they are, and talk face to face. Best of all, it gives people like us a safe haven to express ourselves. You still have to put up with the opinions of others, but at least you can find like-minded friends. An older guy came to our gay youth group and talked about how lonely it was to grow up without that." I snort. "What am I saying? You know better than I do."

Daniel's face is scrunched up. "What's a gay youth group?"

"Honestly? It's like filling a jar with drama and then kicking it down the stairs."

I'm about to explain what I mean when a bell begins to ring. We both look confused before remembering what it means.

"Switch partners! Switch partners!"

These words echo around the room. Daniel clings tighter to me, but that's not what we're supposed to do. I glance around and see Chris and Betty not far away. They've noticed us too. I drag Daniel over and pass him off to Betty, barely having time to reassure him.

"We'll be okay," I say. "Just keep dancing. Don't even look at me."

I step aside and take Chris's hand, assuming the same position I was in with Daniel. Although I have to move her hand to my shoulder when she attempts to take the lead.

"What usually happens?" I ask her, keeping my eyes trained on the door.

"They stick their head in and leave, as long as they don't see anything too wild." Chris swallows. "Last time they went after the crossdressers but left the rest of us alone. Why'd I have to wear this stupid suit tonight?"

Because it's what feels right to her. And now she faces persecution because of it.

"Why don't we slip out the exit?" I ask, referring to the door that leads out to the alley.

Chris shakes her head. "If they're looking to arrest anyone, they'll have cops waiting out there. It also looks suspicious, like rats fleeing a sinking ship."

"And they're cats, waiting for us in the lifeboat."

Before she can reply, we hear the crashing sound of breaking glass, followed by shouts. Chris's hand clutches mine painfully tight.

"I take it that doesn't normally happen?"

The blood draining from her face is all the answer I need. We both look over at Betty, who nods her head toward the exit and begins dancing with Daniel in that direction. We start to follow, moving deeper into the crowd, when the door to the dance floor is kicked open. Police officers swarm through it, clubs raised above their heads, which is enough to send the room into a panic.

"Run!" Chris says, still clutching my hand instinctively.

She pulls me toward where we last saw Betty and Daniel, but people are swarming in all directions now. Someone slams into me, hard enough to make Chris lose her grip on my hand. I manage to stay on my feet, but I can't find her again. I spin around, trying to locate Daniel, and catch Betty's eye. Her expression is questioning. So is mine. We both shake our heads before resuming our search.

"Daniel!"

I call his name over and over. Others are doing the same, the emotion in their voices an unmistakable mixture of concern and fear. Like me, they make no attempt to leave, unable to do so without knowing if the person they care about is safe. Not everyone shares this problem. The room begins to clear out, but plenty of police are arriving to take their place. I see a baton smack an old queen across the face and feel warm drops of blood splatter my cheek. I don't even slow down to wipe it off. I keep searching for Daniel. I finally catch a glimpse of him getting pushed further into the room by the crowd. A cop attempts to grab me, and while I manage to dodge him, I slip and fall. I have to roll to the side to avoid being trampled. While trying to get to my feet, I scurry across the floor in the direction I last saw Daniel. He's not far away once I'm standing again, his expression filled with transparent relief when he spots me too.

"Reggie!" he says, reaching for me.

A police officer tackles Daniel from the side, pinning him to the ground. I stare in disbelief before marching forward, intending to pull the bastard off him.

"Hey, Johnson! Get that nigger!"

The words barely register before something hard hits me over the head and I topple to the ground. I try to push myself up again until a foot comes down between my shoulder blades and pins me in place. When my vision clears, I see Daniel with his cheek pressed to the floor. His pale green eyes are wide with terror, like his worst nightmare has come true.

"Stop it!" he cries. "Don't hurt him. Please!"

It's the last thing I hear before someone grabs my hair, pulls my head off the floor, and slams it back down again. Then the world goes black.

— — —

"Quit yer moanin'! You're fine. Get in the goddamn truck!"

When I return to consciousness, two sets of hands have me by the arms, my feet dragging across the pavement until I'm shoved into the back of a paddy wagon. My thighs collide painfully with the bumper as the police push from behind, causing me to topple onto the truck bed. They roll me the rest of the way inside, where more police officers grab me by the shoulders and toss me onto a bench. My head is throbbing. I squint against the pain, searching the dark interior for any sign of Daniel. I try to say his name but the sound comes out as a croak. Soon the doors are shut, and I can't see much of anything at all.

"Jeffrey?" someone calls out.

"Liz? Are in you here?"

"Michael? Honey? Are you okay? Wake up, baby. Please."

I add my voice to the others, but I don't hear the response I need. Please let him be okay. If Daniel tried anything heroic, there's no telling what they might do to him. I feel someone next to me and instinctively seek out their hand, which is bony and unfamiliar, but I need the comfort. They must too, judging by the way they squeeze back. I repeat this on my left side, telling myself that we're stronger when united, even though all we do is cry while listening to muffled shouting from outside the truck. The engine rumbles and the paddy wagon lurches, taking us away from anyone who cares about our fates. I grapple with panic and despair until someone with a vicious lisp begins ranting about the police and the injustice of it all, their anger helping to embolden me.

"Has anyone been through this before?" I ask.

"This is my third time," says a weary voice to my left.

"What happens?"

"They'll lock us up until our court appearance. Depending on who you are, you might do time."

That's exactly what comes next. We're unloaded at the

police station, looking like we've barely survived a war. I don't remember anyone fighting back, so why are we so bloody and beaten? That's a rhetorical question, of course. I know why. Fear. Ignorance. Hatred. Bigotry. All the usual culprits.

We're shoved into cells that are little more than cages. It's standing room only in mine. The benches are full of drunks. Someone already puked in the toilet before we got there. I stand at the bars, pressing my face between them to see into the other cells. I'm about to call Daniel's name when a police officer walks down the row, hitting the bars with his baton to force everyone to stand back. I turn away and ask the people around me if they know what happened to Daniel and describe him while trying not to sob. They don't have answers, only questions of their own.

The police come to remove us from the cells, one by one. I guess so they can book us officially. The process takes hours. I'm one of the last to go. The only people remaining in the cell with me are black, brown, or transparently queer. I'm relieved to escape the stench and misery, but I don't feel safe, unsure if I'm about to suffer more abuse. An officer asks for identification. I tell him the truth: My wallet is in my coat, and my coat is at the bar. He doesn't seem concerned. It's not like they could run it through a computer anyway. He writes down my information, all of which I invent, except for my name. I want people to be able to find me if they come looking. I keep asking to make a call, but the process is all that seems to matter to them. My fingerprints are taken, as is a mugshot. Considering how bad the police roughed us up, we probably do look like criminals. My clothes are confiscated and replaced by a jumpsuit. When I'm given a dime and brought to a payphone—an officer keeping a death grip on my arm the entire time—I dial Gloria's number. I hate to wake my great-grandparents, but I have no choice.

The line starts beeping. Gloria must be talking to Leroy or one of her other friends.

"It's busy," I say to the man guarding me.

"Tough luck." He grabs the phone and hangs it up.

"I don't get to try again?"

"That was your call," he says, yanking me toward the cells.

We turn down a different hallway than before. The cells here aren't as densely packed and have bunk beds instead of benches. I peer into each one we pass, hoping for some sign of Daniel. Or even Betty or Chris. I hope they got away. There were so many cops though. I don't see how they could have.

I'm put into a cell with three other men. I don't recognize anyone from the bar.

"He's not one of the queers, is he?" asks a man on the top bunk.

"Shut the fuck up," the police officer replies as he shoves me inside.

I move to the only free bed, which is a lower bunk, and sit there.

"Are you?" a voice says from above me.

"Hey man," I say, making my voice deeper than it normally is. "I just play in a band."

"Where at?"

"The Silver Rattle. The cops came in and busted everyone up."

"Fucking pigs," the voice above swears. "I love that joint."

I'm dealing in half-truths, but I'm too damn scared for my convictions to matter right now. I curl up in bed, which barely feels more comfortable than a hard floor, and pull a thin sheet over me. Then I spend the rest of the night trembling, braced to be attacked again at any second.

— — —

I thought it would all be over the next day. I was sure we'd be set loose with fees to accompany our new bruises. Instead I sat in my cell until forced to leave for a meal, which I skipped, preferring to stand off to one side of the dingy cafeteria with my back pressed against the wall. I did the same for lunch, forcing down a soggy roll so I'd have something in my stomach. A court-appointed lawyer saw me in the late afternoon. I expected him to be a lifeline to the outside world, or at the very least a much-needed ally, but he wasn't interested in hearing my side of the story. Instead he cut me off, saying I should plead guilty and accept the punishment. Then he left without another word. I didn't see him again until I was brought before a judge, who asked how I pleaded.

"Not guilty. I didn't commit a crime."

I imagined the judge would question this statement, allowing me to finally tell my side of things. Instead he denied bail and told me that I'd be informed of the date of my trial.

That was a week ago.

I've been rotting away in the same cell ever since. The men I'm trapped with seem more bored than dangerous. I don't intend to become a diversion for them to focus on, so I mostly stay quiet, although the man in the bunk above mine sometimes asks if I know a certain song. I keep telling him that I only play piano. No way in hell am I going to sing for him. The idea creeps me out. They don't seem to mind me sitting next to them at lunch. Especially when I give them most of my food. I don't have much of an appetite anyway. I decline to use the showers when offered. I'm too terrified of being raped. I often jolt awake during the night, frightened by every noise I hear, even a simple squeak, because anything could happen here. On my fifth day, the two guys on the upper bunks got into an argument that turned into a fist fight. I pressed myself into the corner of my bed in terror, especially when the guards came to beat them into submission.

I feel abandoned. I don't understand why my family hasn't made contact. Maybe there's nothing they can do until the trial. I can't stop worrying about Daniel. What if they hurt him? Or worse? I'm a mess by the time they bring me in front of a judge again. I finally see someone I recognize from the bar. I don't know him well. We've never spoken, but I recognize his lispy voice from the paddy wagon. He's called in front of the judge before it's my turn.

"What do you have to say for yourself?" the judge asks.

"I was dancing in a bar when the police came in and beat the hell out of me and my friends," the man responds. "How is that a crime? Who did I hurt?"

"Yourself," the judge responds. "I recommend you find friends of a higher moral caliber, and that you spend time in a church instead of frequenting seedy establishments."

"The church won't have me," he spits in return. "Neither will this miserable city. I'd leave if I could."

"You'll be free to do so after you've served a month in jail," the judge replies. "Now is there something else you'd like to say? Because I'm more than happy to hold you in contempt."

"Go fuck yourself!" the man screams. "I'm not free either way!"

I watch as the bailiff drags him from the room. As much as I admire his audacity, any brave speeches I had planned go out the window. I can't take an entire month of this. I need out, no matter how much pride I have to swallow.

"Reginald Valentine," the judge says when switching to my file.

I'm brought before him, shaking as he stares at me from over his glasses. "And what about you?" he asks. "Also out for a night of depravity?"

"No, sir," I reply.

"You'll address me as 'your honor.'"

"Sorry, your honor."

He doesn't seem to hear me. A clerk has approached him and is whispering in his ear. The judge looks at me again, eyebrows raised. "You'll be released into the custody of your physician," he says, banging the gavel. He moves on to the next case without giving me a second glance.

I'm not sure what happened, but I'm hopeful, even when they leave me in another holding cell. Half an hour passes before I'm taken to a counter to collect my possessions and allowed to change into my own clothes. Wearing them makes me feel human again, which at the moment isn't worth much to me, considering the blood that stains my shirt and how it got there. A police officer escorts me to a reception area. Dr. Parker is waiting for me there. I figured he might be the physician the judge was talking about, but I'm disappointed to see that he's alone.

"Can you handle him on your own," the police officer asks him, "or would you like me to stick around?"

"That won't be necessary," Dr. Parker says. He waits until we're alone before addressing me. "Are you all right?"

"Where's Daniel?" I reply.

"At home."

"Is he okay?"

Dr. Parker seems taken aback by this. Then he motions for me to follow him.

"I need to know," I say, refusing to budge.

"He's shaken," Dr. Parker replies, his attention darting down to my clothes. "But he'll be okay. Where did that blood come from?"

"My head. And someone else's face."

Dr. Parker frowns. "Come outside. Please."

I follow him out to the street. The day is cold but bright. I'm tempted to lose myself in the crowd, leave the city, and never return. If it wasn't for Daniel, I would.

"Let me take a closer look," Dr. Parker says.

I let him examine my head, wincing when he touches the lump that still hasn't subsided completely. "You must have put up a fight," he concludes.

"No, actually I had just watched your son being assaulted by a police officer for no reason, but before I could help him, they hit me over the head from behind. But hey, anything to keep the populace safe from two guys who wanted to dance, right?"

"I think we both know that wasn't the issue," Dr. Parker says. "Where's your coat?"

"At the bar."

"I see. The car isn't far from here. We better get you inside where it's warm."

I follow him down the street, unsure what to say, because I don't know how much Daniel told him. Maybe he got scared and claimed he didn't know it was a gay bar. He could have pinned it all on me. I honestly don't care. I only want to avoid saying anything that will make his life more difficult. I do have one question though.

"How did you get me out?"

"You'd be surprised whose children I've treated," Dr. Parker responds.

"Including judges? He said I was being released into your care. What's the condition I suffer from?"

"Homosexuality." Dr. Parker looks over at me, as if waiting to see if I'll deny it.

I won't. We're way past that now. I'm quiet as we continue walking until I think of a way to make him see sense. "Let's say you have a patient with a hairline fracture in their wrist. You notice it while doing an X-ray. When you mention the fracture to the patient, they insist that they've never had any trouble with their wrist. What would you recommend?"

Dr. Parker looks puzzled before answering. "I'd tell them to be cautious when picking up heavy items or engaging in sports, but that they should otherwise go about their business."

"Sounds like good advice to me. I'll be more cautious in the future."

"I see your point," he says, "but there's a big difference

between a physical injury and a psychological disorder."

"Only if the disorder is real," I retort. "Remember when they used to diagnose women as having hysteria? That's where the term hysterectomy comes from, isn't it?"

"The wandering womb," Dr. Parker says with a nod. "Ancient Egyptians used to think it moved around the body, causing blockages and all manner of ailments."

"My best friend did a report on it in high school. *The History of Hysteria*. How long ago did they finally stop accusing women of having this fictitious disease?"

"About five years ago," Dr. Parker admits after clearing his throat. "That doesn't automatically invalidate other mental disorders."

"Fair enough. People have all kinds of ticks, but if they're relatively harmless, why does it matter?"

We've finally reached the Chevy Bel Air. I'm already shivering. I climb inside and rub my hands together to warm them. Dr. Parker starts the car to get the heater running, but he leaves it in park.

"What you and Daniel are doing *is* harmful. Look at what has happened already."

"No, that's what other people did to us. You don't blame a rape victim for having a hole."

He looks over at me sharply. "That's not a nice way to talk about women."

"I wasn't being gender specific. I have an honest question, so please give me an honest answer. What are you so scared of?"

"That this will continue happening," Dr. Parker says. "That next time Daniel might not be as lucky. What you describe as harmless could get you both killed. Why would I allow my son to continue practicing homosexuality when it clearly does him harm?"

"What happened?" I ask in concern, abandoning the point I was trying to make. "Did they hurt him?"

"He's fine," Dr. Parker says before exhaling. "Although he seems determined to get into trouble. Daniel kept coming down here to the police station each day to raise a fuss. I was worried he was going to be arrested again."

"And here I thought you rescued me out of the kindness of your heart."

"That too, because I really do like you, Reggie. But I wouldn't be a good father if I didn't put my son's needs first."

"That's all I'm asking you to do. There are risks, it's true. We'll be more careful. Or move somewhere safer."

"And? What happens when Daniel applies for a job and they ask about his family? Do you really think they'll hire someone who is in that sort of relationship?"

"He can lie."

"He shouldn't have to."

"I agree, but that's what you're asking him to do by marrying a woman. Or do you really think you can cure him?"

"I've been assured by my colleagues that it's possible."

"Okay." I lean back with a sigh. "Let's get to the bottom of his condition, starting with where you went wrong. What part of Daniel's upbringing caused his homosexuality? Were you an absent father? Because he sure has a lot of happy memories of you. Maybe he spent too much time around his mother and sisters, but oh wait, he was always running around with the Boy Scouts, so he actually had plenty of male influence. Not enough vegetables? Could that be it? I'd be surprised, considering the meals I've had at your house. How about church? Although you went every single week, didn't you?"

"Stop," Dr. Parker says, shaking his head.

I won't. "Daniel has had an incredibly good life. His father is a pediatrician! You've done absolutely everything right up to this point. Except maybe when you told him to spend less time with his guy friends. He couldn't even have sleepovers. Did that help? Is he cured? You can try blaming me, but we both know he didn't show any interest in girls before I was around. So what is it then? What caused this and what's the magic cure?"

"There are treatment options we still haven't tried."

"Including aversion therapy. Have you looked into that yet? They'll show homoerotic images to your son and zap him with electricity each time until the negative association gets so bad that he can't stand to look at men at all. How will that go down in job interviews? Do you imagine he'll be happy then, wincing each time he meets someone he genuinely finds attractive?"

"You're surprisingly well-informed," Dr. Parker says.

"Thanks, but you must know the history of medicine better than me. How often did humanity try to change what they didn't understand, only to make the situation worse? There's nothing wrong with him, Dr. Parker. You can psychoanalyze Daniel for the rest of his life or put him under a microscope. You won't find a grinning demon inside, or a chemical imbalance, or an unchecked virus. Daniel was born this way. So was I. The only issue is how other people choose to treat us. You can torture your son for the rest of his life in the name of trying to find a solution. Daniel will go along with that for you, I have no doubt. You're his hero. Or you can be the forward-thinking man you've always been and support him instead."

Dr. Parker is deep in thought. I wait with bated breath. And I'm disappointed.

"You're an intelligent young man," he says. "But you don't have a proper understanding of the world. You will one day. For now, I think it's best if you and Daniel no longer see each other."

He puts the car in reverse and backs out, as if the discussion has ended, but I'm not giving up yet.

"Setting aside the issue of homosexuality," I tell him, "think how many parents have tried to forbid their child from seeing the person they love. Does that end well? Ever?"

"It can if you go peacefully."

I laugh without humor. "Do you really imagine that if I leave, it won't break Daniel's heart? This is *love*, Dr. Parker, and I'm afraid there isn't a cure for that either. Although I bet some quack in the past tried his best."

"Is that what you see me as? A quack?"

"No. I think you're a good father who is making a bad mistake. Talk to Daniel. Really listen to him. He's still the same boy that you've always known. You only have to adjust your expectations slightly. He can be happy, but that won't be possible if you force him to deny who he truly is. Daniel needs you now more than ever. Don't turn away from him."

"I don't intend to," Dr. Parker replies.

I've said enough. Let him think it over. We're not far from my apartment anyway.

"Are you coming inside?" I ask when the car pulls over in front of the liquor store.

"No. Thank you."

"If you have any questions, please don't hesitate to call. I'm willing to talk about any of it with you."

He nods his appreciation. "If your head bothers you, let me know. For now, you should probably get cleaned up."

I must smell horrible and look even worse. I get out of the car, not surprised that the two idiots are standing there leering at me. The men Gloria noticed often loiter outside the liquor store while sipping from flasks. Ignoring them, I rush upstairs and unlock the door, relieved that the key was in my pants and not in my jacket. When I call his name, the apartment answers me with silence. That's when I realize what Dr. Parker meant when he said that Daniel is at home. He didn't mean here.

They took him from me.

Chapter 20

"Are you okay, son?"

Errol asks this as soon as Gloria ushers me into the living room. Harriet stands to give me a hug. A sob escapes my lips when she does. I'm too reminded of my mother, who I want to see more than anyone else right now. Almost. I'm not sure if Daniel knows that I'm out of jail. Gloria was surprised when I called her. She came to get me immediately. Then she spent most of the car ride back to her place ranting angrily about the police. I'm reminded of when, in the future, she saw Black Lives Matter protestors being teargassed on TV. It was the only time I heard my grandmother drop the F-bomb. Repeatedly.

"Are you hungry?" Harriet asks when releasing me.

"Starving," I admit.

"You look skinnier than ever," she says, guiding me toward the kitchen.

"Hold on," I say, turning to her daughter. "Are you going to call Daniel now?"

That was the plan so we could meet here, away from his parents.

"No," Gloria says. "I'm going to drive over there and pick him up so they can't make any excuses."

"Thanks," I say, hugging her before she leaves.

"They really think you're a bad influence?" Errol asks incredulously as we sit at the table together.

I grimace. "They're trying to protect him, I guess."

Gloria's parents don't know the full truth. They were only told that Daniel and I were at a bar when a police raid happened. If they have any suspicion as to the nature of the club, they don't voice it. In between bites of the chicken salad on toast that Harriet sets in front of me, I describe how the night unfolded. They shake their heads in disgust but don't seem surprised.

"We certainly saw our share of injustice in the South," Harriet says, eyes darting to her husband.

Errol nods. "I've done some time behind bars myself."

"Really? What for?"

"Nothing more than speaking my mind. The story isn't worth repeating. I'll tell you one that is. I was just a little boy when my father said he had something important to show me. I still remember how huge the sun was on the horizon as we walked toward it. He stopped us on the outskirts of town in front of a tree. An old black man was hanging from one of the branches. He was about your size. I doubt he could have done much harm to anyone. I thought for sure that he would give me a scare, but he didn't move. I'm not sure if I understood what death was until that moment. I broke down into tears, but my father wiped them from my eyes and told me to look again. He said, 'That's what'll happen to you, if you're not careful. Just do what they say, at least until you can get away. Or better yet, steer clear of white folks completely, because you don't want no part of their world.'" Errol's brow furrows up as he struggles with emotion.

Harriet puts her hand over his. "We tried to teach Gloria the same thing," she says, "without showing her just how ugly it could get. We always told her to be careful, and to come across as polite while being smart."

My throat is tight, because "the talk" is a lecture that black parents still give their children in my day. *Don't argue. Keep your hands where they can be seen. Don't make any sudden movements.* White people tell their children to seek out the police when they need help. In black culture, parents teach their children to fear for their lives, and for good reason. "There has to be a better way," I say in frustration.

"That's what we thought," Harriet says. "It's the reason we came to Chicago, hoping it would be a safer place to raise a family."

"And then the neighbors moved out," Errol grumbles.

Harriet swats his hand. "Shush!" She looks at me and sighs. "Gloria doesn't know. She was so excited when we finally got this house. We don't want that happy memory to be tarnished by what happened, so please don't tell her."

"Two days," Errol says. "That's how long we'd lived here before the neighbors put up a 'for sale' sign. We thought maybe they already had plans to move anyway, but we asked around, and they'd only been in that house for a year." He exhales. "Things are better here regardless."

"There's still plenty wrong," Harriet says. "A good many things need to change. But we're getting there."

"Not quick enough for my liking," Errol mutters.

I nod my head in agreement, because no matter how much progress has been made, all anyone has to do is pull back the mottled rug of the United States to reveal the writhing racist maggots beneath.

We talk a little longer before Errol goes out to shovel snow. I stay inside and help Harriet in the kitchen, but my attention is always on the clock as the minutes slowly tick by. I don't know if Daniel is willing to see me anymore. Or if he'll be allowed.

Then again, I don't envy anyone who stands in Gloria's way. I hear a noise from the front room and turn just in time to see her enter the kitchen. She greets her mother and then tilts her head toward the living room, so I'll follow. I'm so nervous about what she might say that blood is hammering in my ears.

"He's here," she assures me. "Upstairs. In my room. He didn't want to reunite with you in front of anyone."

"Thank you," I say before taking the stairs two at a time.

Daniel is standing at the top of them while holding open the door for me, his chin already trembling. I grab his hand as I pass by, pulling him into Gloria's bedroom and shutting the door behind us. A desperate noise escapes my throat as I take him in my arms. We clutch at each other, pulling back only long enough to check for injuries or other signs of harm.

"I love you, Reggie," Daniel squeaks. "They can't keep us apart. I won't abandon you, no matter what."

I'm too emotional to speak. I can only lead him to the bed, where we take turns spooning each other, whispering promises that this will never end.

— — —

Daniel didn't spend a single night in jail. Like me, he was hauled in and kept in a holding cell, but only for an hour. He was able to reach his parents after being processed. Dr. Parker contacted the judge responsible for setting bail, which was paid immediately. Daniel was released, and the charges were expunged from his record. He tells me all of this while squirming with guilt, but I don't blame him. The system is stacked against people like me. I wouldn't have felt any better to learn that he'd suffered as much as I did.

"I tried to reach you," Daniel says over a bowl of oatmeal when we're home again. *Our* home. The apartment. They can't take that away from us. I'll pay both halves of the rent if his parents cut him off. "I kept calling the police station over and over again, but they wouldn't let me talk to you or tell me what was happening, so I went down there and—"

"You told me this yesterday," I gently interrupt.

"I don't care," he says. "I want you to know that you weren't forgotten. Gloria's parents tried too. Errol went to the police station in person."

"I didn't know that!"

Daniel nods. "They said he wasn't family because his last name is different. That's so wrong. I even went to The Silver Rattle. Everyone tried to help."

How ironic then that only Dr. Parker was capable of releasing me, the very person who is most against us. I have him in mind when insisting that Daniel go to his usual classes, even though he doesn't want to leave my side. He agrees with my reasoning though. We don't want to give his parents further ammunition. I'd rather they see how we support and care for each other.

The phone rings a couple of hours after he has gone.

"Reggie?" Melody breathes when I answer. "How are you? I'm terribly sorry about what you went through."

"Thanks," I say, "but Daniel isn't home right now."

"That's fine. I wanted to speak with you actually. The girls would normally have their lessons with you this afternoon."

I already have a lump in my throat. She's going to fire me. I just know it. "Yeah."

"Well, I wanted to ask if you'll still be there."

I wait for her to say that she'd prefer if I didn't come at all. She doesn't. "Do you still want me to teach them?"

"Yes, of course! You are *always* welcome in my home, Reggie. I'm very fond of you. So are the girls. Please say that you'll be here."

I'm sick to death of crying but tears well up anyway. "Thank you, Melody," I manage to get out. "I'll see you later today."

"Wonderful! I look forward to it."

Daniel gives me a ride over after class. We enter the house

together while on guard. Melody hugs her son and kisses him on both cheeks, like she's always done, except this time I get the same treatment. She even adds an extra kiss on my forehead.

"Keep him safe," she whispers. "Okay?"

I nod, barely able to hold it together. His sisters act like nothing has happened. I doubt they were truly aware, aside from missing two lessons. I envy how simple their lives still are, but I wouldn't go back, even if I had a choice. We make sure to leave the house before Dr. Parker gets home from work. I'm not angry with him. I very easily could be. I'd rather find a solution though, because no matter how much Daniel loves me, I know his heart will continue to break until he has his father's approval again.

— — —

I'm confused, two days later, when sitting in Mama's office. We haven't started playing for the night, and she's already slid a stack of cash across the desk toward me.

"What's this?" I ask.

"Last week's pay."

"But I wasn't here."

"That's no fault of yours," she says with a glare, but her disapproval isn't directed at me. "I wanted to help you. Believe me, baby, if I could make the cops do what I want, they'd never set foot in this club again. Or this town, for that matter. I would've made your stay more comfortable once they moved you to county. I do have influence there. Remember that if you ever find yourself in the same situation. God forbid."

"Thank you," I say. "Are you sure about the money?"

"I am. Your cut of the tips is in there too. The band insisted."

I swallow. "Do they know why I was in jail?"

"Yeah," a male voice says from behind me. I turn to see Alonzo waltzing through the doorway. "Lots of people do."

He puts a newspaper in front of me and taps one of the columns. A brief article describes the raid on Wilson's Watering Hole, followed by a list of names of who was arrested.

"They put it in the papers?" I snarl in disgust.

"The press are cockroaches," Alonzo spits. "As if you haven't suffered enough. People lose their jobs over these articles."

Or get outed to family members in the worst way possible.

"Ain't gonna happen," Mama says. "Not under my roof."

"Do you plan on keeping it a secret?" Alonzo asks.

"You mean what happened to me?"

"No. Who you are."

I look at the paper again, my eyes running down the list. Daniel's name isn't on it. "No," I say. "I'm not ashamed."

"Good," Alonzo replies, putting his hand on my shoulder. "You shouldn't be."

We're in the middle of playing a set that night when, at the end of the song, he waves the crowd into silence. "You may have noticed that Reggie Valentine has joined us on stage again. After a stint in jail."

The crowd jeers playfully, like I was caught stealing from a cookie jar.

"That's right," Alonzo continues. "He even made the papers. Seems he was out chasing pretty boys at the kind of bar that the police don't like. Do you know what I mean?"

The crowd is more muted in their response.

"I see that you do," Alonzo growls into the mic. "Let me tell you now, if you also have a problem with him, you can get the fuck out of this club and never come back. Do you hear me?"

The crowd roars in response. I meet the eyes a few people and they nod in support.

"Excellent," Alonzo says. "Now let's set this cat loose and see what he can do."

I'm filled to the brim with emotion, but I don't cry this time. Not with a piano in front of me. I put everything I've been feeling into my performance, especially the love, because hate isn't worth dwelling on. I won't let it bring me down. I won't lose my faith. There are good people in the world. That's who deserves my attention. And my devotion.

— — —

I always enjoy watching Daniel play the role of older brother. He's usually very patient, catering to his sisters' needs or bringing them back in line when they wear on his parents' nerves. That's the best part actually, seeing him be strict, his serene face trying its best to appear stern.

"Go outside and play," Daniel is saying to his oldest sister. "Take Lizzie with you. Reggie has an important performance he needs to practice for."

"It's cold out!" Sarah complains.

"Then bundle up. We only need half an hour. Build a snowman or something."

After some grumping and feet stomping, the girls finally leave, the front door slamming shut. Daniel rejoins me in a dining room dominated by a piano and checks the clock. We wouldn't usually be here on a Friday. I'll have to leave for work before long. It's going to be a busy night at the club, but we've tried making the most out of Valentine's Day regardless. Daniel even skipped class. Despite the need to appear responsible, I was fully behind the decision. We spent the morning in bed, in the shower, at the breakfast table, and cuddled up on the sofa. I would have been happy to remain there the entire day, but I know he's excited to surprise me with something. I have a good idea of what it will be. I sure hope I'm right.

"Did you learn how to play it?" Daniel asks, setting the sheet music on the piano stand.

"Yup!"

I memorized the song, in fact, despite not knowing the title or the lyrics. Daniel blacked those out with a marker. I watch as he sits on the bench, seems to think again, and goes to stand next to the piano while facing me. Then he swallows nervously and nods for me to begin, already blushing, before he opens his mouth to sing.

"My funny valentine…"

The opening line already has me smiling. I won't pretend that he's the first person to draw attention to my name on this holiday, or try to make it into something special, but nobody has ever sung to me like this. His voice is low and soulful, expression apologetic as he sings playful lines about someone who isn't the best looking, or the most ripped, but is somehow more beautiful than anyone else in the word. From the perspective of the singer anyway. That's the message I get as he croons the final verse, asking me to never change. Asking me to always stay.

"Those are just the lyrics," Daniel starts to splutter when he's finished. "I think you're *very* handsome and—"

I don't let him get any further. I go to him and kiss his delicate lips. "Promise me you'll do that again."

"Sing?" he says with a pink face. "It's so intimidating. I'm used to singing in choir, where nobody can really hear you."

"You have a great voice." He shouldn't pursue a career in music or anything, but it sounded nice enough. The sentiment made it all the more special.

"Not compared to Chet Baker," Daniel murmurs. "His voice is so alluring. Some people mistake him for a woman when they first hear him sing, but I like that because it feels… I don't know. Softer."

Which guys are raised not to be. I can understand how subversive that must seem to him, especially in this era.

"And he's really cute," Daniel adds.

"Hey, who was this present for," I ask, pretending to be insulted, "me or him?"

"For you," Daniel says with a shy smile.

"Then let's hear it again."

"Really?"

"Yeah!" I get behind the piano. "Let's make music together."

Daniel grins sheepishly, but this time when I play the song, he sings with more confidence. I'm stunned by his beauty. That's nothing new. Not a day goes by that he doesn't do something small that surprises me or makes me realize just how much I adore him. There's no question of me staying anymore. As far as my heart is concerned, I'm already home.

Chapter 21

The piles of snow have finally melted. The biting winds have slowed. The sun lingers a little longer in the evenings before departing. The cold weather will likely return for another week or two, since Chicago winters always overstay their welcome. For now, I'm able to walk home from The Silver Rattle instead of taking a bus or catching a ride. It's nearly two in the morning when I reach our apartment, the liquor store dark and quiet. Even the creepy men who have been standing outside more and more as the weather warms up have crawled back into whatever hole they crawled out of. I wish they would stay there. They've been making snide comments lately and paying more attention to us than I would prefer. So far I've managed not to engage. I'm hoping they'll get bored and leave us alone.

I'm surprised when unlocking our front door to discover so many lights still on. The apartment is usually dark except for the lamp next to the couch, which is enough for me to slip inside, get undressed, and join Daniel in bed. I start turning off the lamps when I glance toward the bedroom door and notice my boyfriend peeking around it.

"Don't get upset," he says, his voice shaking. "Promise me."

"What's wrong?" I ask while moving toward him.

Daniel pulls back. "It's nothing. I don't want the police to get involved. Not after what they did to you."

I keep following him until we're both standing in the bedroom. When I speak his name, he finally turns toward me, and I can see a dark crooked line as thick as my thumb under one eye. "What happened? Did somebody punch you?"

"It was only an argument. I'm fine."

"Who did this?" I ask, cradling his cheeks in my hands to examine the injury.

"You have to promise not to go after them," Daniel says.

"Them?" I clench my jaw and shake my head. I can't make that promise. What twisted pieces of shit could do this to someone so nice? I already want to kill them!

"What happened?" I growl beneath my breath. "Tell me."

"I had just come home from school—" Daniel begins.

Those assholes in front of the liquor store! I turn around and march back to the living room, intending to leave, so I can find the bastards and make them pay.

"Stop!" Daniel says, grabbing my arm. "Please. I feel safer when you're with me."

He moves around me to the front door, making sure that it's locked. Then he presses his back to it with a concerned expression. For me. He's the one with a black eye, but he's worried about me getting hurt instead. That's enough to make me sit on the couch, if only to alleviate his concern. I'm going to kill them though, no matter what the story is. My mind is already filling with violent fantasies.

"Okay," I say through gritted teeth. "Tell me."

Daniel moves away from the door and sits next to me. "I had just come home and walked up the stairs. One of those guys who are always hanging around outside, he was up here, which shocked me. I asked what he was doing. He said he'd just finished helping Mrs. Henderson carry in her groceries. Then he got real close to me—god, his breath was terrible—and he said, 'Why are you always hanging around that...' I won't repeat the word he used."

"Does it begin with an N?"

Daniel licks his lips and nods. "Yeah."

Not the first time someone has called me that. It won't be the last either. What infuriates me is that someone hurt the man I love. "Then what?"

"I said he couldn't talk about you like that. I told him to leave the building and never to come inside again or I would call the police. He just laughed and said 'Go ahead. I'll tell them that a couple of pansies are screwing each other upstairs.'" Daniel's jaw moves, but all he gets out at first is a strangled sound. "I think they know about us."

"They might not think it's actually true," I reply. "To them it's just an insult."

Daniel shakes his head. "Remember last week? When we left the apartment together? They asked if we were going on a date."

"Wait, when did he actually hit you?"

"Oh." Daniel swallows. "When I tried pushing him down the stairs."

"You *what?!*"

Daniel scowls. "I was angry about what he called you. And I wasn't trying to push him *down* the stairs exactly. Just toward them. Although I wouldn't have minded if he fell."

I lean forward and kiss him on the nose. "I love you. But you should have gone inside where you'd be safe."

"I wish I would have," Daniel says, looking vulnerable. "He got mad and said not to touch him. That's when he decked me. I didn't see it coming. I was knocked to the floor and... What are we going to do, Reggie? I'm scared. At least his friend wasn't around. What if he is next time? And one of us is alone? I don't know how to fight even one person. Maybe we should move."

"We shouldn't have to," I say. This conviction is rendered meaningless by the bruise beneath one of his pale green eyes. Nothing is more important to me than keeping him safe. "Where will we go?"

"I don't know." Daniel's voice is strained. "Back to Glen Ellyn?"

"I know you think it'll be safer there," I say carefully. "But we'll stand out even more than we do in the city. It'll be harder to hide who we are."

"We did okay at the motel."

I shake my head. "That's nowhere near your school. Or the club." I think people were starting to notice us at the motel anyway. One of the neighbors asked me who Daniel was. Twice. We need to find somewhere safe for gay people, which is a tall order in the fifties. "Can you switch schools? If we can make it to the end of the semester, we could move somewhere else. San Francisco. Or maybe New York. It's worth a try."

Daniel's face is lined with concern. "What would I tell my parents?"

"The truth?"

"Yeah, but don't you think that'll prove my dad right? He keeps telling my mom that I'm in danger because of us. I'm scared that he's wearing her down."

"Or maybe it'll make them realize how difficult it is to be gay, so your father will figure out that it isn't a choice. Why the hell would anyone wish this on themselves?"

This seems to wound him, and it takes me a moment to figure out why. "Your love makes it worth it," I assure him. "I didn't mean to imply otherwise. I'm just frustrated, because if we were in my time, this wouldn't be as much of an issue. The police can't raid a gay bar or do anything else sketchy without there being consequences." Thank goodness for cell phone cameras. "We'd be safer there. Hell, we could move to Boys Town. It's an entire neighborhood, right here in Chicago, that's full of gay people."

"I wish we could," Daniel says. He staring off into the distance and chewing his bottom lip when his eyes go wide. "Maybe we can."

"Huh?"

He grabs my hand. "Don't be mad."

"Now what?"

"I lied to you." Daniel's voice is laced with guilt. "I know it was wrong, and that I shouldn't have, but I was caught up in my feelings for you and—"

"Daniel!"

"Sorry." He takes a deep breath. "Remember the Latin phrase we found on the gate? The one I translated? Do you remember what it said?"

"Something corny about being everywhere and nowhere, right?"

He shakes his head. "That's only what I told you. I didn't want you to know what it really said in case it helped you get home."

"Wow. I'm... flattered, I guess? I honestly don't mind. I wanted to stay anyway."

Daniel looks relieved. "Really? Even back then?"

"Yeah. I was looking for excuses. What's it really say?"

"Every*thing* or nowhere," Daniel says, leaning back dramatically.

I nearly laugh. "Hate to break it to you, but you could've been honest and it wouldn't have made a difference, because I don't know what that means."

"I wasn't sure either. I'm still not, but I've had plenty of time to think about it. My theory is that you have to take everything you brought with you through the gate when leaving. That's why it hasn't worked so far."

I mull this over. "More bad news: I don't have everything anymore. I lost my backpack and all the contents, so even if you're right—"

"I know where to find it," Daniel says. "I think."

Okay, *that* gives me pause. "Since when?"

"Recently," he says with an apologetic grimace. "It just happened to come up recently when I was mentoring at a Scout meeting. We were talking about building semi-permanent shelters in the woods when a boy mentioned one he saw in Churchill Woods. I wasn't sure what he meant, but when I asked him later, he talked about running into a strange man while hiking out there. I think it's the same person you encountered. What was his name? Pete something?"

"Babbage," I say. "Did this kid tell you enough for us to find him?"

"The general vicinity. How hard could it be to locate a campsite?"

All of it sounds like a longshot to me. We'd have to find a homeless veteran in the woods, hope he still has my things, and then bring those to the gate without knowing if that would make it work again. And there's a bigger issue that needs to be addressed first.

"Are you sure you'd want to come with me? You know what that would mean. And who you would have to say goodbye to."

"Gloria would still be there," Daniel says. "My sisters too. Probably. Maybe we could use the gate to come back here on occasion to visit. If we can figure it out."

"There aren't any guarantees, Daniel. You have to treat it like a one-way trip. You can't make this decision based on the potential to return here again."

"I know," he says glumly. He wraps an arm around mine, sliding down on the couch to rest his cheek against my shoulder. "You said it was possible for us to get married there. I know it's too soon for that kind of talk. But I also know that I would want to. When we're ready."

Jesus, that's about as close as you can come to proposing to someone without actually doing it. The crazy thing is, I agree with him. I don't even need to think about it. We're still three months shy of our one-year anniversary, but what we have together is so good that I can't see our future playing out in any other way. I want to marry him too.

We stay up the rest of the night talking about what life in the future would mean for him. His career, for instance. From his perspective, NASA hasn't been founded yet. In my day, it's still reinventing itself after grounding the space shuttle while the private sector takes up the slack. I can't promise that he can help put the first woman on the moon, because technology will have evolved well beyond his current understanding. He would need to catch up on so much. Those who share his aspirations won't have that disadvantage.

I'm also concerned that fear might be clouding his judgement. We're both tired and anxious. I bring him to bed so we can nap through the morning. When we're awake again, I suggest a course of action. Daniel listens and agrees. Instead of going somewhere for spring break, he'll move back in with his parents. I'll stay with Gloria and her family. We'll tell them that our apartment is being fumigated, which is only a half-truth, because we are indeed attempting to avoid some disgusting roaches. He'll be safe. And if it turns out that we still want to leave, at least we'll have spent extra time with the people we're going to miss most.

— — —

We're three days into spring break by the time we visit Churchill Woods. Not to go anywhere. Daniel only wants to test his theory. We bring the outfit I was wearing when I first arrived in the past. I haven't worn the shoes lately, preferring boots so I can tromp through the snow with impunity. Winter feels increasingly distant now. Fresh buds that have yet to blossom can be seen on the trees, perennial flowers bursting through the undergrowth with colorful cheer as sunlight shimmers through the naked branches above. I feel high, either from the optimistic weather, or because it feels good to be around him again. Spending less time together hasn't been fun—the nights especially—but it was the right thing to do. I've been back to the apartment. The drunks outside the liquor store try to provoke me each time, unleashing the most banal of slurs. I haven't told Daniel about that yet. I don't want it to influence his decision.

I let our problems recede to the back of my mind and focus on him. We take turns attempting to juggle pinecones. I push him up against a tree where we kiss. I do a terrible imitation of a squirrel just to make him laugh. We challenge each other to a race and spend most of it trying to cheat instead of actually running. He even pretends to sprain his ankle. I'm walking over to help him when I do the same and fall to the ground, calling his bluff. Of course he rushes over to help me, his own fake injury forgotten. Every moment spent together is pure bliss. Maybe that's why we both get so quiet when the gate comes into view.

"I don't think you should get any closer," Daniel whispers, as if it might awaken and swallow me whole.

Not that I'm feeling any braver. "Agreed. How should we do this?"

"I'll go," he says, reaching for the bag that I'm holding. Inside it are clothes from another century.

"What if you disappear?" I ask when handing the bag to him.

"If I end up in the past, I'll mail the clothes to you or put them in a safe deposit box. I'll get them to you somehow so you can follow."

"And if you end up in the future?"

"I don't think that will happen. The Latin implies that it has to be everything, and that includes you. Then again, when you came here to the past, that wasn't a requirement. Maybe it only matters on the return trip?"

"Your guess is as good as mine. Best of luck."

He doesn't move. Not until I offer to try it myself. That gives him the courage. Daniel takes the folded shirt, basketball shorts, and Nike shoes from the bag and carries them as a stack in his arms, my socks and underwear balanced on top. Classy! Daniel walks through the gate and nothing happens, although when he turns to face me again, he looks surprised.

"What's up?" I ask.

He shushes me into silence and squeezes the bundle of clothes to himself. Then he blurts out laughter. "It feels almost like... like they're purring!"

"Yes!" I say in excitement. "It's the same deep rumble. You can feel that coming from my clothes?"

He shakes his head. "I'm not sure. Maybe we should try something else. Give me the shirt you have on."

"And my jeans and underwear too?"

"If you don't mind," he says demurely.

I take off the light jacket and shirt I'm wearing and toss them to him. And yeah, maybe I puff out my chest a little too, because we really do miss sharing a bed. While standing beneath the archway, he sets the future clothes aside and clutches this era's garments to his chest instead. He sets one bundle down and picks up the other a few times before he's finally satisfied.

"There's a difference. It's not only in my head."

"Or in mine," I say. "Give me back my clothes. I'm getting cold."

He walks over to me and tries to hand me my shirt. I take and toss it aside before kissing him, not letting up until he pulls away to look around.

"Can we really do that here?"

"No," I say. "Buy maybe over *there* we could."

We wander off the path, venturing deep enough in the woods that we're unlikely to be seen. No matter how heated it gets, I still look around on occasion while hoping to see a strange man wandering by, because it seems as though Daniel was right. Everything that came through the gate still resonates with it, and out here somewhere are my stolen things. If we can get them back, Daniel and I might just be able to run away together.

— — —

"This is the worst spring break ever."

I'm hanging out with Gloria in her attic bedroom as she sorts through fabric samples. She'll hold one up to me before grunting if she doesn't like it or tilt her head side to side if she does. Then she'll write down notes next to her sketch of the new suits the band and I are planning to wear. Mostly just on special occasions when we want to really dazzle the audience. Now I'm wondering if I'll ever see those suits in person.

"Do you sometimes wish you were still in school?" she continues.

"College? Yeah, I guess so. Right now especially."

"*Everyone* should get spring break off," Gloria says. "Why do we have to keep working?"

"There aren't any snow days either when you have a job. What a rip-off."

"Forget the snow." She holds a plaid square to my chest and

grimaces before setting it aside. "We should be partying on a beach somewhere."

"At least we have each other," I try.

"Exactly," she says, turning to face me. "I thought you were going to spend the week here?"

"That was the plan." It's easier after work, at two in the morning, to simply return to the apartment. Even the creeps aren't outside at that hour. And it allows me to make certain preparations.

"So where are you staying?" Gloria asks. "Are they done fumigating? Because you only spent the first few nights here, but Daniel has been at his house the entire week. What's going on? Are you two having trouble?"

"No. But…"

She raises her eyebrows. "Uh oh."

"If anything strange happens, I want you to have this." I reach into my pocket and take out an extra key to the apartment. I've been searching for an excuse to give it to her. "Check the dresser drawer in our bedroom, beneath the T-shirts at the very bottom. You'll find letters there that I'd like you to give everyone."

"You're trying to go home."

She's good, but I can't let her know that she's right. I'm too concerned she'll try to stop us. "I'm being cautious. I almost went home last year, when I got upset about the Little Rock Nine, so I figured it's a good idea to be prepared in case I disappear suddenly. That way you won't have to explain where we went."

"*We?*" Gloria repeats, fabric samples falling to the floor. "You're trying to take him with you!"

Shit. "I didn't say that."

"You also didn't deny it." She crosses her arms over her chest and waits.

I don't care how young she is. I can't lie to my own grandmother, so I tell her everything that happened, finishing with, "Please please *please* don't tell Daniel that you know. I want him to decide on his own."

"You're worried that I'll talk sense into him."

"No. I'm worried he's going to get hurt. Again."

She swears under her breath. "I knew that story didn't add up. He was walking across campus when a random football hit him in the eye? Then again, if it was going to happen to anyone, it would be him." She shakes her head to clear it. "You can't do this."

"It's the only way I can think to keep him safe."

"I know but..." Gloria takes a deep breath. "If you go, Reggie, it's not a big deal, because I'll get to meet you again someday. I'll get to watch you grow up and all that good stuff. If you take Daniel away from me, who will I have left?"

"Leroy?" I suggest.

"You mean the chump who's down in Florida right now, instead of spending spring break with me? I sent him a Dear John postcard."

"What? You didn't!"

"You bet your ass I did. Remember on Valentine's Day when I found *two* receipts for flowers in his room? I only got one bouquet. Get this: The other day I saw Darcy Sullivan walking down the street, and as soon as she saw me, she turned around and practically started running."

"You think he's cheating on you?"

"I'm done either way. Stop distracting me. I don't want to lose my best friend."

"I don't want to lose him either. Tell me something: Why do you think you have that framed photo in your room?"

"When I'm older?" Gloria shrugs. "Because we're friends."

"But it's the frame *I* gave him. It's supposed to have a photo of me inside. What happens between then and now? Because when I saw the police tackle Daniel, and when he got that black eye, I felt a jolt each time like..." I shake my head. "Dr. Parker isn't completely wrong. People die for being gay. That's how it is for us black folks too, and usually I can deal with that, but not when it comes to Daniel. All I care about is making sure he's happy and safe. We have a better chance of that where I come from."

Gloria sighs and sits on the mattress. "Can't we just buy a cabin somewhere and live together, far away from all the jerks and bigots?"

I plop down next to her. "Don't worry. Our plan probably won't work."

"And if it does?"

"Just make sure you bring your father with you when going to our apartment."

She shakes her head. "That's not what I mean."

"I know. And I'm sorry."

Gloria sighs. "Will you at least tell me before you try again?"

I'm quiet before answering and decide to be honest. "I don't want to, because you'll want to be there, he'll see how sad you are, and if that's not enough to make him stay, he'll think about how his parents will be even sadder."

"Then trust me not to get in the way. I'd still like to know."

"Okay. I'll tell you. Daniel and I are going to search the woods for Pete Babbage tomorrow. I'll call if we find anything. Even if we do, we won't try the gate yet. I want to make sure he knows what he's agreeing to."

"I hope you don't find what you're looking for," Gloria says, leaning against me. "And I also hope that you do. If that makes sense."

"It does." I put my arm around her and squeeze. "That's how I've felt since I got here."

I miss the future, but I also know that I'll miss the past. It's comforting then, that no matter where I end up, Gloria will be there. Thank goodness too. She might be my grandmother, but since arriving here, she's also become my best friend.

— — —

We're quiet when picking our way through the underbrush of Churchill Woods. I don't even make a snarky comment when Daniel occasionally squats to check the mud for tracks. I want him to be successful. The thought of returning to my own time has begun to haunt me day and night. I could have it all there. I'll resume my education. I'll be surrounded by my family and friends again. Best of all, Daniel will be with me. I'll show him the wonders of the future and be there to console him when he inevitably begins to miss his own time. I know what that feels like and can help him get through it. Once we've both graduated and settled into our careers… Who knows? Maybe we'll take it one step further.

"Another boot print," Daniel says, standing again.

"Just one?" I ask.

Daniel shrugs. "He must make sure to step on leaves. Or the roots of trees. If you aim for the trunks, that can help hide your tracks."

"In other words, he's paranoid."

"Or really *really* tall. The last print was half a mile back." He shields his eyes and stares in that direction. "Maybe he's in the woods on the north side of the road."

"Officer O'Brien meets him in the parking lot on this side. He was waiting for him in the rain."

"Probably because it's closest to the park shelters, which is where I would go if my tent was leaking. The restrooms would be useful too. I'd make sure my campsite wasn't too far from there, although the Boy Scout I talked to said he found it while heading east. I guess we have to go even deeper."

"If you still want to."

Daniel nods. I keep giving him little opportunities to bow out, or to offer alternative solutions, but he seems intent on learning more about the future, as if prepping for a trip. As we continue walking, for instance, he asks if college is different and if I think he'll have trouble adjusting. I ask him if he can type, and to my surprise he can, so I assure him that the rest is easy. He'll catch on quickly. Even my great-grandmother had her own email address before she passed away.

"Whoa!" Daniel says.

We've just crossed a creek by walking across a fallen tree, and I can see what he's referring to. Boot prints. All over the place. They look the same as the others we've found. Daniel soon confirms this, addressing me in a whisper.

"He spends a lot of time here. We must be close!"

I barely hear him. Peering at a tree, I notice strips of cloth tied to the branches. I nod toward this, Daniel following my gaze to a distant clearing.

"What's the plan?" he asks in hushed tones.

"We hope that nobody is home."

"And if he is?"

"I'm not sure. Any ideas?

We look at each other helplessly and shrug at the same time. This makes us laugh, but we quickly grow somber again. We stand there listening, unable to hear any sort of movement or activity. Just the usual sounds of the woods.

"Let's go," I suggest.

We creep toward the cloth-draped tree and soon see more unnatural objects: a stripped-down bicycle frame, a lidless cooler, and a cardboard box filled with mismatched shoes. We pause next to these things to listen again, but there's never any sign of another person. Only what they left behind. The clearing, when we reach it, is an absolute mess. The branches of the surrounding trees are draped with old clothes, shopping bags, bleached newspapers, and tattered rope. In the center of this is a tent ringed by junk that includes a toppled stack of rubber tires, broken wooden crates, barrels with rusty metal strips sticking out the top, and trash. Lots and lots of trash.

"The scout said it was a mess," Daniel whispers, shaking his head, "but I never imagined this."

I nudge him and nod toward the tent. What if someone is inside, listening to us? I can't imagine sneaking up to it and peeking inside. That seems like a good way to get knifed in the eye by a crazy hobo. So instead I indicate that we should be prepared to run before I call out, "Hello? Is anyone home?"

We both become statues, not even breathing, while waiting for a response. We don't hear so much as a rustle from inside the tent. I call out a second time with the same result.

"I think we're good," I say, leading the way forward.

"Why does he drag so much junk back here?" Daniel asks, poking around in the nearest pile. "This old sign is from the gas station that burned down when I was a kid. That's on the opposite side of town!"

"Ever seen the show *Hoarders*?" I ask, knowing that he couldn't have. I've watched it a few times as a guilty pleasure. At first anyway. Who doesn't like seeing a house messier than their own? Once the reality sets in and it becomes clear that most hoarders suffered a psychological trauma in the past, or are mentally ill, that's when it stops being funny. "The poor guy is probably messed up from what he saw during the war."

"I guess so. Hey, look! There's a lock on this! Whatever is inside must be important."

I join him. The wooden box is wide and short with no frivolous decorations. The flat lid is secured with a heavy padlock.

"Do you think your backpack is inside?" Daniel asks. "We could break it open and see."

I'm glancing around for a crowbar or something similar when my stomach sinks. "Look over there."

He does and notices the same thing; a wooden trunk with

another padlock hanging from the latch. We walk toward it, noticing other containers along the way. A rusty metal box, a rotting chest, even a small refrigerator tied shut with rope. There's a definite theme here.

"Where do we even begin?" Daniel asks.

"With whatever is easiest." Many of the containers have junk piled on top of them to hold the lids shut. I start tugging on the refrigerator rope, trying to loosen the knot. Progress is slow until Daniel brings over a shard of metal with a jagged edge. He uses this to saw through the rope. When it falls away and we open the refrigerator door, all we find inside is more junk. Glass jars filled with mold, a rotted-out radio, dented pots, a broken lantern...

"Do you think your stuff could be in there somewhere?" Daniel asks with revulsion.

"I'm not eager to find out."

"Me neither. Most of it seems like it's been there longer than a year." He picks up a Redbook magazine. "This is from fifty-two and it was on top."

I'm more than willing to accept that assessment at face value. I shut the refrigerator door and we move on to the next box. Daniel jiggles the lock and tries to pry off the latch. He isn't having much luck. I keep looking at the tent, still worried that someone is inside. With my things. I *really* don't want to check in there. It seems inevitable though as Daniel gives up and tries his luck on a trunk riddled with holes. I watch him for a moment before creeping toward the tent. I reach for the fabric of the door flap with a trembling hand...

"Oh look!" Daniel cries, causing me to pull my hand back with a yelp. "Just like we had at school."

I press a hand over my pounding heart before walking over to join him. He's standing next to another barebones wooden box, except this one is secured with a combination lock. The kind with a plastic spinning dial.

"I've never seen one with a green face before," Daniel says.

"I have," I say, my throat tight. "That's exactly what I had on my locker."

"Really?" Daniel sounds disappointed. "I thought everything would be electronic in the future. Like you would have to insert a special computer chip to unlock it or whistle a certain song."

I ignore him, my fingers spinning the dial back and forth

in the same way they did during four years of institutional education. When I finish and yank on the body of the lock, it pulls away from the metal loop.

"It worked!" Daniel says, staring at me in wonder. "Wait, that doesn't make sense. Why would Mr. Babbage use a lock he didn't know the combination for? Unless..." Daniel grabs my forearm in excitement. "Unless it's really you!"

"Uh... What?"

"The man in the woods! He must be you from another time! Don't you see? It's just like the time travel stories I read. They usually have a mysterious character who turns out to be someone we've already met except—"

"Daniel."

"Yes?"

"Pete Babbage is white."

"Oh." He scratches the back of his head sheepishly. "Then why would he use a lock on something that he couldn't open again?"

"I don't think he cares if he can get inside." There's junk piled on this box too, but not nearly as much. I shove it off with little effort. "He only wants to keep other people out."

I pocket the lock, since I brought it here with me, and flip open the lid. The box is stuffed full of more junk. A naked doll missing an arm, old phone books, a musty pillow... and a backpack laying right on top of it all. I recognize it instantly. We finally found my missing stuff!

"HEY!"

We both turn, the lid of the wooden box slamming shut with my backpack still inside. An apparition is rushing toward us. He looks like a caveman wearing multiple layers of filthy clothes. His hair is long and matted, the unkempt beard bristling in all directions. I recognize the wild eyes from my first night here. They're trained on me, the man continuing to shout as he bears down on us.

"You kids get out of here! These are my things. This is my home. Go on! I'll beat you senseless!"

"We don't mean any harm!" Daniel says, scurrying out of the way.

I'm not as quick. I still have to stand and turn around, and by the time I do, he grabs the front of my shirt in two clenched fists. "What did you take? Give it back to me!"

His rancid breath makes my nostrils flare. The rest of him doesn't smell so great either.

"You took *my* things!" I shout back. "They're mine!"

The fists gripping my shirt begin to shake. "You little thief. Give it back. All of it!"

He releases a hand so he can start patting me down. I struggle against this, but I'm not fighting him off exactly. Part of me wants to punch, kick, and headbutt him to get away, but I restrain myself. I'm not entirely sure why until I see Daniel creeping up behind the man. He has a bent metal pole gripped in his hands, wielding it like a baseball bat. His expression is conflicted, as if he doesn't really want to hit him, even to save me. I don't want him to either. It reminds me too much of the police who rushed into Wilson's Watering Hole with batons raised above their heads.

"Wait!" I shout, mostly at Daniel. "Let's talk. Please. I can explain."

The man tenses. Then he resumes his search. I don't resist him this time. I watch him instead, thinking again of those hoarders and how damaged they were inside.

"Your name is Pete, right? Pete Babbage?"

He feels the lock through the fabric of my jeans and reaches inside the pocket to take it back. Then he releases me while clutching it, peering at me in suspicion. "Who are you?"

"Reggie Valentine. My friend behind you is Daniel Parker."

He spins around to see who I'm referring to.

Daniel drops the metal bar he's carrying. "Hello, Mr. Babbage. We only came here for some missing property."

"What's he talking about?" Pete says, backing away from us both.

"You found something of mine," I say, pointing at the lock in his hand. "Otherwise, how would I have known the combination?"

This gets his attention. He checks the lock, maddened eyes darting back to us repeatedly, like he suspects a ruse. He must be somewhat reasonable though. Otherwise it would be impossible for Officer O'Brien to bring him food or meet him in the parking lot.

"Can I see it again?" I ask. "Let me show you."

He shakes his head. "Tell me the numbers."

I do. There's some trial and error as I remind him in which direction he needs to spin the dial, but he manages to get it unlocked again.

"We didn't come here to steal from you," I explain. "I lost something important—a backpack—and needed to find it again. That's all."

"What took you so long?" Pete demands. "You don't care. People always abandon their things."

"And you keep them safe?" I ask.

He nods. "They become mine and I take care of them, like their owners should have."

That's some twisted logic considering how most of what he "rescued" is exposed to the elements and rotting, but I can't expect him to think in my terms. "Thank you for doing that, because I didn't mean to abandon my things. Do you remember seeing me in the woods at night? I got scared and ran off, but I did come back the next morning. By then, my stuff was gone."

He doesn't seem moved by my speech. I try to think of what the therapists say on the hoarder show, but they mostly just stir up shit to keep the audience engaged. "I can tell that this is a private place. Your sanctuary, right? We don't want to trouble you more than necessary."

He doesn't react, but at least he's still listening.

"Can I at least show you what I came for?"

I walk to the wooden box and place my hand on the lid, seeking permission. When he nods, I open it and am sorely tempted to grab my backpack and run. I don't even touch it though. "I only need my backpack and the lock you're holding."

His eyes flick between the objects and myself. "What for?"

"Because I'm lost too, and as strange as it sounds, this backpack is my key to getting home again. I can't leave without it. Please. I just want to go home."

For whatever reason, this seems to move him. His eyes tremble with moisture. Then he nods. I very carefully lift the backpack from the chest, noticing it has some heft, like it hasn't been emptied. I just hope the contents match what used to be in there. I'm tempted to check, but I don't want to parade it all in front of him when he clearly has trouble letting go.

"Thank you," I say, putting one of the straps over my shoulder. "I need the lock too."

I hold out my hand.

He doesn't budge.

I try a different tactic. "What do you like to eat most? I'll have Officer O'Brien bring whatever you want, the next time he comes out here."

"You know Trevor?" Pete asks.

"Since I was a little boy," Daniel chimes in. "My mom makes amazing oatmeal cookies. Do you like raisins? I know she would be willing to make some for you."

Pete looks between us and seems to reach a decision. He hands me the lock. "Go away. I don't need any cookies. I want to be alone. Just go."

I thank him again and move toward Daniel. Turning our back on him is the worst part, each step tense as we're braced for another outburst or a sudden attack. We make it back to the creek without any trouble. Once there, I can't resist stopping to check my backpack. I unzip it and peer inside. Everything is accounted for. He must have searched it or he wouldn't have found the lock, but I guess the phone didn't mean anything to him. I feel its reassuring weight in my hand.

"Reggie," Daniel says from next to me. "We better go."

I glance at him and then over my shoulder. Pete Babbage is standing at the edge of his home, watching us with suspicion. I leave the phone in my backpack, shoulder it again, and together with Daniel, put as much distance as we can between us and the strange man in the woods.

— — —

I wait until we've returned to the parking lot before taking off the backpack again. I've been dying to go through it, but I keep worrying that Pete will have a change of heart like the hoarders who agree to a solution until it comes time to actually part with their things. We stand next to Daniel's car with the backpack balanced on the truck as I open it and start sifting through the contents. There's plenty of junk that I cleared out of my locker, and as far as I can remember, it's all still in there. What I really want is my phone, which I pull out. Tapping the screen doesn't do anything. Pressing the button on the side doesn't wake it either.

"I guess the battery is dead," I say, handing it to Daniel.

He takes it, turning it over to examine both sides. "Is this glass? Like a TV screen?"

"Yeah."

"And the rubbery stuff?"

"That's just a case to protect it."

"Oh. I thought it was a camera too. Where's the lens?"

"See those circles on the back?"

He looks at me like I'm crazy. "They're too small."

"You'd think. The dot there on the front is a camera too."

"What? It's even smaller! So you just plug this into someone's phone jack when you want to make a call?"

"Not exactly. Those are the volume buttons you're pushing, and if you squeeze both at the top simultaneously, it turns the phone on and off."

"Like this?"

"Yeah, but—"

A fruit-shaped icon appears on the screen. Daniel nearly drops the phone in his surprise. When it continues booting up and a lock screen appears that shows me and Hannah making silly faces, he looks at me in wonder. "It's not even plugged in!"

"Battery powered," I say, sharing his surprise, albeit for another reason. "I must have turned it off before putting it away. Let me see it real quick."

He passes the phone to me. The battery has thirty-eight percent remaining. Not bad! Facial recognition gets me past the lock screen. There isn't a signal, of course, but there is plenty I can show him. He moves closer to see, making sounds of amazement as he watches me navigate to my photos. Then he gasps as I start flipping through them. "That's my best friend, the one who was with me when the gate nearly fell on our heads. Oh, and here's *your* best friend, sixty-five years from now."

I push play on a video. In it, an old woman has a carrot held to my throat. "This is what I do to people who interrupt my stories," Gloria says, pretending to dispatch me by slashing the vegetable across my neck. We made the video for an aunt who always calls during her favorite show.

Daniel guffaws and then covers his mouth with a hand while shaking his head. "She looks so old!"

"Your Gloria would be mortified to see this."

"She shouldn't be. She's still pretty."

"The hottest," I say fondly. "Do you want to see the rest of my family?" I navigate to a group photo and try introducing them, one by one, but I'm too emotional to get their names out.

"I guess you haven't seen them in a long time," Daniel says in sympathy. "Even in a photo."

"Yeah. I miss them. Hey, here's another one. Do you recognize the place?"

On the screen I chase my brother down hallways and through rooms, trying to steal back the bag of fast food that was supposed to be my lunch.

"My house!" Daniel says.

"No," I correct. "That's *my* house."

The video starts to replay, Daniel still just as fascinated. "This is sorcery," he says. "I feel like my head is going to explode."

"That's nothing. Come here. We'll make a video together."

I hop up on the trunk of his car and ask him to do the same. I scoot closer, hold the camera out at arm's length like millions of people will do in the future, and hit the button to record a video.

"I can see myself!" Daniel says with a laugh.

"That's right. How long did we wait for those photos of ours to get developed?"

"A week," he says. "How long will this take?"

"It's recording."

"Right now?"

I laugh. "Yeah. What do you want to say to everyone in the future?"

"Oh! Umm. I've heard so many good things about you all and uhh… I'm really fond of this guy here, so thank you for sending him. I can't wait to meet each of you in person!"

I push the stop button. "Do you mean that?"

"What?"

"You really want to come back with me?"

"More than ever," he says, still transfixed by the screen.

I try to imagine him wandering down the street with his head down—like everyone in my day—so he can stare endlessly at his phone, and hope the future won't change him too much.

"How do you develop the film?" he asks.

"You don't."

I tap a thumbnail and push play. A small version of me and Daniel appears on the screen and runs through the same conversation we just had.

"Do I really sound like that?" Daniel asks, looking aghast.

"Yes, and don't worry, everyone has that reaction. Come here. Let's try a photo instead."

I lead him toward the edge of the trees. The parking lot is mostly empty, so I feel safe holding him from behind, our heads close together as I take the photo. The image fills the screen once I have. I've only seen us together like that when we're both standing in front of a mirror. We make a beautiful couple.

"I wish I could leave that photo for my parents to find," Daniel says, "so they would understand why I had to go with you."

"Are you sure you want to?" I ask, lowering the phone. "Once the excitement wears off, you'll miss the world you knew."

"You stayed for me," Daniel says. "I'll do the same for you." He slips out of my arms and turns around. "Let's go now."

"What, you mean *right now*?"

He nods. "Yeah. Before anyone can stop us. Remember how O'Brien said he'd come after us if we bothered Mr. Babbage? What if you get locked up again?"

"I doubt that will happen. We didn't do anything wrong."

"How is that any different than last time?" Daniel points out.

"Touché."

"Spring break is almost over too," he continues. "We'll need to decide if we're going back to our apartment or not. I don't want to keep living with my parents. I want to be with you."

"But what if you—"

"Who knows, Reggie," he says, taking my hand in his. "So much could go wrong. I'll never be one-hundred percent certain about this, but I'm willing to risk it anyway. For you."

"Okay," I say, the breath tight in my chest. "Let's go home."

Chapter 22

We stuff everything in my backpack before setting off for the gate, discussing along the way how we'll proceed. If this works, I want to make sure he returns with me, so I come up with a ridiculous plan.

"You should wear the backpack," I tell him. "And the clothes I arrived in."

"Even the dirty underwear?" he asks with a snort.

"*Especially* the dirty underwear. Over your pants preferably. That's how we do it in the future."

We're almost manic at this point, intoxicated by a mixture of excitement and nervousness.

"Do you plan on sending me through first?" Daniel asks. "We should have gotten some rope from Mr. Babbage. You could have tied it around my waist. That way you could pull me back if I end up in the past."

"If that happens, we're becoming gay cowboys together. Promise me."

"Only if we can be outlaws who rob banks."

"Hell yeah! We'll use the money to open the first-ever gay saloon."

Our banter comes to a strangled halt when the gate appears ahead of us. I swear I can feel it pulling on me more than ever, as if it can sense that I've finally brought all it demands.

"I think it's going to work this time," I tell him. Setting the backpack down, I pull out my old clothes except for the socks and underwear. I'm not that cruel. "Put them on over what you're wearing. No kidding. Let's do the shoes too. We'll put yours in the backpack." We considered going to his place first, so he could bring more with him, until deciding his outdated clothes wouldn't be any more useful in the future than mine were here.

Keepsakes, like photos of his family, might make it too difficult to go through with this. We're talking about that openly now. I don't want Daniel to change his mind. He doesn't either.

I watch as he switches shoes and pulls the shorts up over his pants. The muscle shirt will be too tight, so I wrap it around his neck like a scarf. Then I stand back. He looks ridiculous.

"Is any of this truly necessary?" Daniel asks.

"Probably not. Hold on. I'm going to take another photo."

"Don't you dare!" He looks at the gate again and swallows. "Want me to try first?"

"No," I say. "We'll go in together."

He shoulders the backpack. Everything else from my time is stuffed inside. I take his hand and lead him forward. I can feel my skin begin to tingle as we near. I stop us both just in front of the old worn stones.

"Last chance to turn back," I say.

Daniel's smile is full of wild abandon. "No way. I love you too much, Reggie."

"I love you too," I say, leaning close.

He shakes his head. "Kiss me on the other side. Where it's safe."

I can't help but laugh, imagining him trying to make out with me everywhere we go. We'll turn a few heads in the future, that's for sure. "Okay. Are you ready?"

Daniel nods and takes the first step. Then the next. He spins around, pulling me along by the hands. I follow him, entranced by his pale green eyes. My entire body is humming. The hair stands up on the back of my neck, goosebumps racing down my arms. Daniel is directly beneath the gate now, his expression pure adoration. I step forward and wrap my arms around him, the vibrations building to a single high-pitched note that fills my head and shakes my bones.

"Sorry," I say, bringing my lips close to his. "I just can't wait."

Before we can kiss, his forehead crinkles with worry. That's when I notice that I can see straight through him to the trees beyond. Daniel is fading. I must be too. It's working! I attempt to tighten my grip on him, my arms passing through air. My feet are next. I fall straight down, plummeting through darkness while scrabbling to grab hold of him again. I open my mouth to call his name but not a sound comes out. I'm lightheaded, the air forced from my lungs, my mind squeezed by an invisible pressure until I have no thoughts left to think.

— — —

My feet collide painfully with the ground at the same moment I return to consciousness. I lose my balance and fall onto my knees. My first impression is darkness, followed by cold. The world around me has changed. Night has fallen. My bare legs are wet and freezing. I look down to see them submerged in snow. That's when I realize I'm naked. A pair of basketball shorts rests on the snow near me, and not far away, the toe of a Nike shoe is sticking out.

"Daniel?"

I scurry over to the shoe and grab it, but it isn't attached to anything. I move my hands through the snow, only making contact with the ground beneath.

"Daniel?"

I glance around while listening for a response, unable to see far through the white flurries. I'm still in the woods. I can smell as much from the air.

"DANIEL!"

I shout this at the top of my lungs. The silence I get in return sends me into a panic. I stand and lurch around, searching for any sign of him. I find the backpack, tearing into it and pulling out my phone to activate the flashlight. I swing this around in trembling hands. I can see the fallen stones of the gate and the solitary pillar that remains upright. I'm back in my own time, but where is Daniel? He should be nearby. Unless…

"No!" I cry, unwilling to entertain the thought. He must be here somewhere! I fall to my knees again and swipe at the snow with both arms, hoping to reveal him. He hasn't woken up yet, that's all. I'm going to hear him sleepily calling my name, any second now. Jesus, why am I naked? Another item of clothing is nearby, the muscle shirt still curved into a circle like it fell through him rather than off. Where is he? I remember the concerned expression on Daniel's face just before my hands passed through him. Why would that happen when we were both leaving?

Unless he didn't make it.

"No. No no no!"

I scurry toward the gate, reach the same spot where we last stood together, and crawl through on hands and knees. Nothing happens. I get to my feet and walk back and forth, crying his name over and over again, hoping it will bring me back to him. I push on the one remaining pillar, wanting to topple it and activate whatever magic whisked me away. I beat the butt of my fists against the stones while begging for the universe to be merciful.

"Please, please, please. Give him back to me. I'll do anything. I'll stay this time. Please!"

I crumple onto the ground, my skin stinging from the cold. I should at least put some shoes on. The pair Daniel placed in the backpack are gone. I use the flashlight to be sure. Then I swing it around to find the missing Nike shoe. The light reflects off metal. A fence has been erected around the gate, but not the half-assed version that Hannah and I passed through so easily. This fence is sturdy, forming a box all around me, like the kind you see protecting dangerous electrical equipment. Nobody is getting in. Or out. I find an area of fence that's designed to swing open, a padlock hanging from the handle. In the middle of the door, a handwritten sign has been posted.

"Beneath her initials. Call me. -GG"

Granny Gloria. She always signed birthday cards with those two letters. I don't understand the message until I remember Hannah's initials. I rush back to the pillar, digging in the snow beneath the squares and triangles. My fingers make contact with a plastic bag. I pull it free. Inside are my clothes. Not what I'd been wearing earlier in the day, but a coat, jeans, and more than I haven't seen for nearly a year. I put these on, my limbs already stiff from the cold. Once I'm dressed and shrug on the jacket, I shove my hands into the pockets and feel something metal and jagged. I pull out a key, staring at it dumbly before rushing to the fence and using it on the padlock. It works. I shove the fence door open, but I don't leave. Instead I turn around and gather up my things, stopping only to sob before forcing myself to press on. Once I have everything shoved into my backpack, I stand before the gate and think of him. I picture his serene face in my mind, remembering the shape of his smile and the sound of his laughter. Then I step forward, willing myself to return to the past.

Nothing happens.

"I'll come back for you," I croak. "I'll figure this out and come back. I promise."

I return to the fence defeated and heartbroken. That's when I notice the sign again. *Call me.*

I take out my phone, and a few taps later, press it shaking to my cheek.

"Reggie? Is that you?"

Another sob wracks my body. "Granny?"

"Oh thank god! I'm coming to get you. Did you find—"

"Yeah. What happened to Daniel?"

"He's fine. I'll meet you in the parking lot."

The line beeps and goes dead. Hope explodes in my heart. Daniel is fine! What does that mean? Is he here? Did he arrive earlier than me or show up somewhere else? I trudge through the snow until I find the path. Then I start running, slipping on occasion but unwilling to slow. I need to know what happened. I need to see him again. I break free of the woods, slowing when I see the bridge Daniel and I crossed not half an hour ago that is now covered in snow and lined with icicles. Another late winter, it would seem.

My lungs are burning by the time the parking lot comes into view. I see my grandmother's Mercedes idling there, warm clouds billowing from the exhaust. The driver-side door opens as I near and a thin woman with poofy gray hair steps out. I watch her teeter across the slick pavement. Gloria latches on to me as soon as I'm close enough, her lined face crinkling with concern.

"Are you okay?" she asks, pulling back to look at me.

"Fine," I pant. "Just cold."

"Let's get you inside."

"Where's—"

"Get inside," she says in a firmer tone.

A lifetime of conditioning compels me to obey. The heater is running full blast when I sink into the passenger seat. I hold my hands near the vents to thaw them. Jogging here got my blood pumping and my torso warmed up, but the rest of me is still numb.

Gloria settles into the driver seat, her attention on me the entire time. She looks relieved. "I wasn't sure if you would make it back. I only knew that you disappeared back in fifty-eight. You could have ended up anywhere, for all we knew."

"Please," I say. "I need to know."

Her sigh is enough to make my stomach sink. "Daniel is still in the past."

"You said he was fine!"

"He is. Or will be. He had a good life."

"No," I say, not wanting to hear it. "This isn't over. Tell me how to get back to him!"

"Do you have the key I put in your coat?"

"Yes."

"Let me see it."

I dig it out and hand it to her. She takes it and puts it in her own coat pocket, the one farthest away from me. "I'm sorry," she says.

If she was anyone other than my grandmother, I'd have some very unkind words for her. "Do you really think that's going to stop me? I'll tear down that fence with my bare hands."

"And then what?" she asks calmly.

"I'll go back!"

"Did you try already?" She sounds genuinely curious.

"Of course!"

"What happened?"

I study her for a moment. "You don't know?"

She shakes her head. "I've spent a lifetime trying to figure it out. I did plenty else, but every few years, I'd look into it again. At first in books and at libraries, and later on the internet. I even talked to some old timers about it, after you disappeared. As far as I can tell, the stones aren't a gate at all."

"What are they then?"

"A stitch in time."

I clench my jaw. I don't have the patience for this. "How do I make it work?"

"That was never its purpose."

"Then how do I get back to him?" I snarl.

Gloria raises her eyebrows at my tone before her expression softens. "I keep forgetting how fresh all this is to you."

"I just left him," I say, my voice warbling. "He's probably still standing there, waiting for me to come back."

She nods, her expression sad. "Until after the sun went down. Nobody could find him. I didn't think to look there until late at night. Even then I had to drag him away from the gate. He didn't want to leave."

"Please," I say as tears begin to stream down my face. "Help me. I just want to get back to him."

"Why do you think I did so much research?" she says, dabbing at her eyes with a tissue. "He was heartbroken. I didn't know how to bring you back, but I thought I might be able to send him to you somehow. I tried my best, sugar bean. I really did."

My body is wracked with sobs but I force myself to calm down. There has to be a way. I just need to think. If it was possible once, it can happen again. "We'll rebuild the gate. And we'll tear it down with me beneath it, like last time."

Gloria hesitates before responding. "I don't think that's a good idea."

"Why?"

"Daniel will have to explain why."

I stare at her. "He's still alive?"

"Yes."

"Take me to him," I say. "Right now. Please."

She nods and puts the car in reverse. "You'll want to brace yourself. He won't be as young—"

"I know." I wrap my coat tighter around me and lean against the door, sinking down as I continue to cry. I want to get it all out before I see him.

"Your mother will be excited that you're back," Gloria is saying. "I kept promising her that you'd be okay. I tried to explain what really happened. They nearly put me in the looney bin."

"Don't tell them I'm here," I grumble. "I'm not staying."

She's quiet while continuing to drive. The car is making all the familiar turns, bringing us closer to home, like she intends for me to see my family anyway. Except she turns three blocks too soon, pulling up in front of a small ornate house with a manicured lawn. The clock on the car radio says it's nearly midnight, but the house is still lit from inside by a warm glow.

"He's expecting you," Gloria says, sending a quick text on her phone. "I'm guessing you'll be awhile, so I'm going home, but call if you need me. Or wake me up when you get back. I don't mind."

I have so many questions, but none are as important as seeing him again. I get out of the car, noticing the different bushes and plants, each carefully trimmed. Did he choose them? What about the birdfeeder on the front lawn, already filled with seed for the next morning? Is that a passion of his now?

I reach the front door and raise my fist to knock, but it feels wrong. We live together. He's my boyfriend. So I open the door instead and am greeted by warmth. The air smells like Daniel's house used to. A little different, but similar. Lights are on in the living room. I can hear music playing, the voice sorrowful and hard to pin down. Chet Baker. I have a knot in my throat as I walk toward this. I enter the room and see him again. Except he's different.

Daniel is sitting in a chair, staring back at me like he's seen a ghost. His hair is white and thin, his eyebrows wiry, but beneath them are the same pale green eyes that always made my heart flutter. The skin around his neck is loose, his milky white complexion wrinkled, but it's still him. And it's also not him, because my Daniel always radiated with the innocence of youth.

I can't get any words out. All I can do is go to him, get on my knees, and lay my head in his bony lap.

"I'm so sorry," he says as he strokes my hair. Even his voice sounds different. Huskier. Drier. "I still remember how bad it hurt when I lost you."

"You didn't lose me," I manage to say. "I'm right here. I love you, Daniel."

"And I will always love you," he replies.

I lift my head, taking one of his hands in both of mine and noticing how gnarled it feels. "I'm going to fix this," I promise him. "I'm going back for you. I already have a plan."

His expression is sympathetic. And sad. "You can't," he says, shaking his head. "And you don't. I would know. You never came back, Reggie."

"This is just an alternate timeline," I say. "Like in—"

"*Back to the Future*? I might be old, but at least I get your references now."

I grip his hand tighter. "Then you know. I can go back and change things."

"I don't want you to."

I stare at him in disbelief. "How can you say that?"

"You should get some rest," he says. "I have the guestroom ready for you. We can talk about this in the morning."

"The guestroom? Why wouldn't we share a bed like we always do?" A thought occurs to me. I look down at the hand I'm holding and see a gold ring on his finger. A wounded sound escapes my throat. "You're married."

"I was." Daniel swallows. "Until I lost him too."

I look around the room for the first time, noticing a fireplace mantle with framed photos above it. Most of them feature two men together. I don't want to look any closer. None of that matters.

"Help me solve this, Daniel. We need to be together. Don't you feel that anymore?"

His expression is apologetic. "From my perspective, our story ended decades ago." He takes a deep shuddering breath. "But yes, Reggie, on occasion it all comes back to me, and I feel you in my heart just like I did back then, and I want you back. I want *us* back. But that's not possible. Our time has passed."

I get to my feet while shaking my head. "You're not him. He wouldn't say these things to me."

"You're right," Daniel replies. "I'm not him anymore. Not exactly. I've changed. You will too."

"No. I'll never stop loving you."

"I won't either. But that doesn't mean we can be together, then or now."

One song comes to an end and another one begins, Chet Baker crooning out a line precious to us both. *My funny valentine…*

"My apologies," Daniel says, pushing himself to his feet with some effort. "I was feeling nostalgic. If I knew you were about to arrive, I would have chosen a different record."

He shuffles toward an old turntable, as if intending to stop the music, but I grab his hand as he's passing me. He's shorter than I remember when I take him into my arms. He resists at first, trying to pull away, but I won't let him go. He finally relents, placing his head against my chest as he begins to cry, and I know he's still the same. Daniel would have carried the pain with him for a lifetime. He never would have gotten over me, just as I could never get over him.

The song is tragically short. Just like our time together. When the music ends, he has another excuse to pull away from me, but he only does so physically this time. I watch as he walks to the record player and lifts the needle.

"You're so handsome," he says, turning around to face me. "I'd nearly forgotten."

"You didn't though," I say, my throat tight. "And you won't. I swear it's not too late. You just have to trust me."

He studies me a moment before hobbling over to a box of tissues. He gestures for me to follow him to the couch, where we sit and take turns blowing our noses. "There's something I need you to see," he says. "I know it will be difficult, but it's important."

He reaches for a memory album that's resting on the coffee table and hands it to me. I open the cover. The first page contains a few photos of him when he was young, but his hair is different from what I ever saw, shorter and styled to the side. Next to this is an employee ID for an aeronautics company I've never heard of.

"This is after I graduated from college, when I got my first job," Daniel says, trying to turn the page.

I put my hand flat on it before he can. "I don't want to see your life without me. This isn't how it was meant to be."

He searches my eyes before reaching for the cover to close the album. "This isn't the right time. I only want you to know that I had a wonderful life, even though I missed you terribly. College wasn't a happy experience for me. I lost myself in my studies. Thinking about you hurt too much. I would anyway, but it exhausted me emotionally. Books were my only escape. After graduating, I forged a new life for myself and learned to be happy again. And I fell in love. I kept my promise to you. Do you remember? It must have been the second time you tried to go home. We were at the gate with Gloria and you were about to leave, but you pulled me aside. You made me promise to find love again."

"I remember," I say, swallowing against the ache in my throat.

"I thought of you, when I first met him. I almost walked away because of it. But then I heard your voice, telling me to try again. In that way you never truly left my side, Reggie. I did so many brave things in your name. You became my moral compass."

"I should have been more."

"What we had was beautiful," Daniel replies, placing a hand over mine. "We were lucky. Let's not mourn that."

I won't, because I haven't given up yet. I just wish he was willing to fight alongside me. "Don't you have any regrets? Any at all?"

He thinks about it and nods, his chin trembling just like it used to. "That final day at the gate. I should have let you kiss me."

"Then I'll prove to you that it's not too late." I lean over and press our lips together, and it's the magic solution I'd been searching for, because I have him back again. I'm sure I do, especially from the way he kisses me in return. But when I pull away, his eyes are filled with watery reluctance instead of fresh fire.

"We shouldn't have done that. I'm old enough to be your grandfather."

"You've always been sixty-five years older than me," I counter. "Nothing has changed."

"We both know that isn't true," Daniel says patiently. "You never used to take your eyes off me. I was the same way. But now you can barely look at me."

"Only because I'm still getting used to it," I say, intertwining our fingers. "And because it hurts, knowing how much time we lost. I'm not giving up though."

"I didn't think you would," Daniel says, gently pulling his hand away from mine. "It's past my bedtime. I'm tired. I know you must be too."

"Back in nineteen fifty-eight, it's only three in the afternoon."

"My goodness," Daniels says, getting to his feet. "And I thought international flights were bad. If you find yourself unable to sleep, you can read this." He picks up the album and holds it out, but I don't accept it. Not until he says, "Please. Look through it. For me. I think you'll understand."

"I don't want to leave yet," I tell him, the idea filling me with panic. I never want to let him out of my sight again.

"You can stay here," he says. "In the guestroom. This whole experience has already been strenuous. Sharing a bed with a nineteen-year-old might kill me."

I shrug. "Sure, but what a way to go."

Daniel smirks. "I should have known you wouldn't make this

easy on me." For a moment, those pale green eyes look me over just like they used to. He even licks his lips nervously. "Come on. I'll show you to your room. Bring that along."

I tuck the photo album under my arm and follow him. The guest bedroom is next to the kitchen. He was prepared, the sheets fresh and already turned down.

"We marked the date," he says when seeing my expression. "Gloria and I figured it out, which is harder than you might think with leap years and such. We did a lot of second-guessing, but we got it right in the end. Your family must be worried. Are you sure you want to stay here tonight?"

"Would you have made the bed if you thought otherwise? You still know me."

"And you still know me, it would seem. Sweet dreams, Reggie."

I stand there, waiting for him to kiss me goodnight or invite me to his room. His expression is apologetic before he leaves, but I'm not discouraged. I love him. Enough to turn back the clock and change history.

— — —

I'm unable to sleep, but it has nothing to do with the time shift. My mind keeps obsessively searching for a solution. I'm unable to come up with anything more hopeful than rebuilding the gate and tearing it down again. I can't exactly do that on my own. I wouldn't be able to lift a single stone block. Maybe there's something Gloria can tell me, even if she doesn't realize the significance yet. I plan on talking to her in the morning, which is still hours away.

I sit on the bed, attempting to ignore the photo album on the nightstand. Curiosity wins in the end. I grab the album and open it on the comforter. I begin on the first page. Daniel is a few years older than when I saw him last, his expression joyless. That changes when I turn the page. I see him standing with his chin held high next to a blueprint of some sort of engine. The white lab coat is doing him all sorts of favors. I would have grabbed the lapels each night he returned home and pulled him in for a kiss. Then he would have bored me during dinner while talking about all sorts of technical mumbo jumbo, and I would have savored each and every word he spoke regardless.

Someone must have had similar thoughts, because on the next page he's joined by an attractive Asian man. He's shorter than Daniel, his dark eyes twinkling with mischief, one corner of his mouth always pulled upward, like he's trying not to laugh. Maybe he had a good sense of humor. Daniel certainly seems happy in the photos. They stand close together without touching, but there's no doubting the intimacy of their relationship, thanks to a handwritten note on the next page.

I find it difficult to read and impossible to tear my eyes away from. It could have been written by Daniel and addressed to me, since the guy is talking about an awakening of emotions inside his stupid little heart. Ugh. That isn't fair. I'm only jealous, feeling like Daniel moved on even though it hasn't even been twenty-four hours since we last saw each other. From my perspective, anyway. The letter is sweet, thoughtful, and probably funny, judging by a few lines that seem like an inside joke. The signature at the bottom reveals his name. Charlie.

The next page includes souvenirs from their dates and more love notes from them both. I only read Daniel's to see if he mentions me. And he does. Sort of.

I never thought I would love someone again. I thought it was impossible.

That he was able to move on is bittersweet because I always wanted Daniel to have a happy life. I just wish it could have been with me.

I continue turning the pages, impressed when I see a patch from NASA and a photo of some sort of control room. Men stand between rows of primitive electronic equipment, expressions somber as they face the front, presumably looking at a screen or readout that I can't see. I scan a dozen of the tiny heads before I find Daniel. He's wearing a dress shirt with rolled up sleeves, his face even less boyish than before. He makes a handsome man. A caption beneath the photo reads *Apollo 11 Mission Control*. As if that wasn't impressive enough, on the next page is a photo of him standing in the middle of three smiling astronauts.

I feel like rushing from the room to congratulate him, before I remember that he's old and probably asleep. I force myself to press on, turning page after page, the photos changing from black and white to colors that get richer as the years fly by. Charlie is always with him, more outgoing in the way he expresses his affection. Soon they are always hanging off each other or hugging. Daniel is kissing him on the cheek in one image, his smiling eyes focused on the camera, as if he's looking right at me.

I laugh in surprise when seeing a photo of Gloria with a full afro and feel sad again when I realize that the man standing next to her with a mustache and shoulder-length hair is my boyfriend. It's a fun look, but I don't like that I almost didn't recognize him. Daniel is clean-cut again on the next page and standing in front of an altar. His tuxedo is white. Charlie is dressed in black. I notice Melody with her arms around two women who bear a passing resemblance to her. Sarah and Lizzie, all grown up. Dr. Parker, his hair now white, stands next to his son while smiling proudly. As stupid as it might sound, this makes me cry. Out of relief, I suppose, but part of me wishes that I could have been more. Even though we didn't always see eye to eye, I still would have liked being their son-in-law.

I feel emotionally exhausted as I continue turning pages, seeing pets and children, friends and vacations that I have little context for, but I understand why he wanted me to see this. No matter how much styles change or how many years go by, Daniel always looks happy. Up until the very last page, which only contains a single black-and-white photo of an old stone archway. The shadows are long, the branches of the trees bare. Daniel stands to one side of the gate, a palm pressed against a pillar. His head is turned toward the archway, as if he expects to see me reappear there at any moment. Beneath this, in his handwriting, are the words:

Thank you for everything you gave to me.

My heart aches with the realization that I'll never take it away from him, no matter how much I might be tempted to. There's no guarantee that his life would have been as happy with me. This is what I wished for. I wanted Daniel to be safe. I wanted him to be loved. And he was. I push the photo album aside and curl up in a ball, longing for everything that I lost while slowly crying myself to sleep.

Chapter 23

I wake the next morning with a start, disoriented by the surroundings until my memory kicks in along with the heartache. I slide out of bed, needing to see him again, no matter what he looks like or how hopeless it has all become. I follow the smell of frying onions to the kitchen while blinking against the light. An old man stands at the stove, wearing a blue bathrobe. Daniel glances over his shoulder at me and smiles.

"It's going to be a gorgeous day," he says. "By the afternoon, it should be warm enough to finally melt this snow."

I pad over and wrap my arms around him from behind. Daniel tenses before he sighs and his muscles relax. As for me, I start crying.

"You're going to break my heart," Daniel says, his voice warbling. "Again."

"I'm sorry," I say when pulling away. "It's just too much. I looked at the photo album."

"Oh. Why don't you have a seat? Breakfast is almost ready. I hope you still like scrambled eggs."

"You just made them for me on Sunday. When we stayed up all night talking. That was the last time we were at the apartment together. Remember?"

He turns around and I can tell that he doesn't.

"You can leave the salt here," I say, rubbing at my eyes. "I'll use my own."

"I'd cry too, if I weren't so old," Daniel says. He hands me a plate and leads me to the table. "They don't tell you this when you're young, but past a certain age, instead of tears all that comes out are puffs of dust."

I look up sharply. Then I laugh when I see him wink.

"That's better," he says, settling down in a chair across from me. "Eat up. I refuse to talk until you get some food into you."

I make a big show of shoveling eggs into my mouth, bulging out one cheek before moving them to the other. It is, quite frankly, a gross feeling, especially when I have to swallow it all, but it's worth it to make him laugh. I don't realize how hungry I am until the first few bites land. I clear my plate in no time and lean back.

"So... Apollo 11, huh? Were you there on the big day?"

"I was just one of hundreds of people who worked tirelessly to make it happen," Daniel says humbly. "But yes. I had the honor of being there for one of mankind's greatest achievements."

"That's bragging rights for life. I hope you brought it up at every dinner party you went to."

Daniel smiles. "Only the boring ones."

"When did you get married? And did you explain to him that, technically, you never broke up with your first boyfriend?"

"Charlie knew about you," Daniel says. "I didn't tell him the full truth until we were together... My goodness, I don't know how long. Twenty years maybe? I didn't think he would believe me. I'm still not sure that he did. But he at least humored me. He's the one who took the photo at the end of the album. Charlie was quite the photographer."

"And he was always good to you?" I ask, maybe a little gruffer than I intend to.

"Yes. He was gentle, honest, and kind." Daniel's expression is sorrowful before he remembers me and smiles reassuringly.

"How long has it been?" I ask.

"Almost ten years." Daniel swallows. "I used to fantasize about walking through the gate and ending up in the future, where they would have a cure for cancer. I even tried once."

"I'm sorry."

"Don't be," he says with a shake of his head. "We had forty wonderful years together. To wish for more would be ungrateful and greedy."

I shrug. "We'd be getting close to our seventieth anniversary by now. And I know that still wouldn't be enough. Not for me."

I don't understand the hesitation I get in return. Daniel clears his throat, picks up the plates, and carries them to the sink. When he turns around again, his expression is softer. "We've had more time together than you realize."

"What do you mean?"

"I was with you on your first day in this world. I stood next to Gloria in the maternity ward when you were finally born and we alternated between laughing and crying, seeing you in your crib." Daniel returns to the table, his eyes sparking when he sits across from me. "I burped you when you were a baby and took you to meet Santa Claus when you were a toddler."

"Please tell me you never changed my diaper," I say, trying to mask how emotional I'm getting.

"No. To be honest, it was a bit surreal, and probably similar to how you feel now. To be madly in love with a baby... I wasn't attracted to you, of course. Not at that age."

"I can't relate," I say, staring meaningfully at him.

He looks uncomfortable before pressing on. "I was even in the audience during your first recital."

"Really? How'd I do?"

"You were terrible," Daniel says playfully. "I couldn't tell if your parents were smiling or grimacing. I thought you'd be a child prodigy, to be honest. Very disappointing."

I toss a cloth napkin at him, which he manages to catch. "We all have to start somewhere. How long was it before you started getting the hots for me again?"

He shakes his head. "I wasn't around much after that. Most people only have limited memories from the first grade. A handful at best, so it felt safe to be around you until then. The older you got, the greater the risk."

"For what?"

"Changing the timeline." Daniel wrings the napkin absentmindedly. "When we met in the past, you never mentioned a family friend who looked like me. Surely you would have made the connection if you had. It seemed I wasn't part of your life, and I wanted to make sure you would still become part of mine. So I kept my distance."

"And decided to buy a house three blocks from me?"

"That was a more recent development. I needed a change of scenery after Charlie died."

"So you moved super-close to your old boyfriend."

"Closer to my best friend, actually. Truth be told, I still saw plenty of you. Gloria would send me photos and videos when

I lived in Florida. And I came to see you play at Fitzgerald's a couple of years ago. It was a lovely show, even from the back of the room. I felt like I was eighteen again."

"I bet I could make you feel that way now."

He studies me before answering. "You're still determined to change the past."

"No." I hate to say it out loud, but it's true. "I understand what you were trying to show me with the photo album. I love you too much to take Charlie away from you. I won't be that selfish. I'm here now though. And so are you. We can still be together."

"I'm old, Reggie."

"Yeah. I noticed. I don't care."

His eyes fill with hope, so I'm confused when he shakes his head. "I wanted you to see that album for two reasons. You already figured out the first. The other was to show everything you still have to look forward to. Buying your first house with the man you love, exploring the world together, navigating the ups and downs of growing old together... I've already done all that. You should as well, with someone who hasn't experienced it yet."

"I don't want to be with anyone else," I say, crossing my arms over my chest. "I want to be with you."

"No." Daniel's mouth becomes a flat line. "You love me too much to take away the good life I had. I love you just as much. I won't let you do this to yourself. I know it will hurt. Believe me. I've been through it already. But beyond the pain, you will find someone lucky enough to catch your eye. You'll still miss me on occasion. You might always wish it could have been different. But you'll also be happier this way. I'm certain."

"So that's it?" I ask in disbelief. "We both travelled sixty-five years to find each other, and you think I should just pack up my feelings and move on?"

"That's what I did," Daniel says.

"Are you happy now?"

"I'd be foolish not to be."

"That's not an answer."

He swallows and looks away. When he addresses me again, his voice is terse. "You need to consider your family. I know what you're going through is difficult, but you've been missing for nearly a year. Think of how they must feel."

I shake my head. "Can't we just—"

"No. This is it, Reggie. No more dwelling on the past or dreaming about what could have been. I'm truly sorry, but it's over."

These words tear through me. I'm lightheaded as I stand. I stare him right in the eyes, jutting out my chin in an effort to stave back tears. "Are you sure?"

He nods. Just once. I don't know how he manages to, because I could never do the same. Maybe I'll feel different after loving some other guy for forty years, but right now, I despise the idea of being with anyone else. My heart belongs to Daniel. I can't believe he's handing it back to me.

I walk away from the table without saying another word. When I look over my shoulder, I see him turn his head away. I return to a guestroom that I never should have been asked to sleep in, collect my things, and leave his house, praying with each step that I'll hear him call my name or feel a hand on my shoulder to stop me. That doesn't happen. I guess it really is over. For him, anyway.

— — —

My family gathers around me while weeping tears of joy. I'm pulled in one direction for a hug before being yanked away into another set of arms. I cry along with them, but not always for the same reason. They fuss over me, offering me food and anything else I could want. Under different circumstances, I would be thrilled.

At the moment, I'm emotionally exhausted. I didn't give any thought to how I would explain my disappearance. One of my brothers mentions grandma's crazy story about how I ended up in the past. Then he asks me what really happened. I look to Gloria for guidance. She shrugs like she doesn't care either way, so when my other brothers asks if I ran away with some guy, I nod, feeling it's close enough to the truth. That's the reason I didn't come home. I wanted to be with him. I still do.

Half the day passes before I'm finally allowed to be alone. I think my parents are worried I'll disappear again. I get away from them by explaining that I need a shower and a change of clothes. Once I'm in the bathroom, I stand unmoving beneath a steaming blast of water, but nothing can wash away the pain. Especially when I return to my bedroom and feel disoriented as

I walk through the door, because I expect to see Daniel's things there instead. I stretch out on a bed that's in the same corner as his was and stare at the ceiling, aware that if I could cross the veil of time, I'd probably find him occupying the same space as me, both of us nursing a broken heart.

My mom knocks on the door soon after, wanting more of an explanation, but she barely listens before begging me to stay in contact with her, no matter where I feel the need to go. When she's finally gone again, I wait until the hallway is unoccupied before sneaking down to the one part of the house that won't remind me of the past—because it didn't exist then—and where I'm the least likely to be disturbed.

My grandmother's room.

Or more like her apartment, since the extension built onto the house also includes a full bathroom and a large sunroom. That's where I find Gloria, reading on a couch drenched in sunshine. She sets aside her book when she notices me and pats an empty cushion. I already feel better as I curl up next to her. At least she understands what I've been through. And what I lost.

"How did it go last night?" she asks.

I tell her what happened. She's perfectly sympathetic, wrapping an arm around me when I become emotional and not falsely promising that everything will be okay. She only reaffirms what Daniel told me. "He had a fulfilling life. I was there for most of it. You would have been happy for him."

"I'm trying to be now," I say. "I just wish we could be together."

I hadn't yet gotten to the conversation Daniel and I had over breakfast. Gloria misunderstands me and thinks I still intend to return to the past.

"I can only tell you what I learned about the gate," she says, "but I don't think it will be helpful. I spoke to someone who was there while it was being built."

"Really?" I ask, sitting upright. "How old is it?"

"Turn of the century," she says. "As in nineteen-hundred or so. That was around the time a strange woman came into town with a dowsing rod. Do you know what those are?" She explains after I shake my head. "I've seen drawings of a single stick split partially down the middle or two separate bent rods. Traditionally they were used to find water underground, so people would know where to dig a well. This woman used them to find what she called time holes. She claimed that she had fallen through one as a child and ended up twelve years in the past."

"Was this also in Churchill Woods?"

"No. I've heard conflicting reports of where she came from, but it was never from around here. The woman made it her personal mission to locate other such holes. She claimed she was sensitive to them and could find them when the sticks began to hum."

"Similar to what I experienced!"

"That detail caught my attention too," Gloria says, "or I wouldn't have pursued the lead as much as I did. At some point in this woman's history, she made the acquaintance of a freemason who had a passion for the occult. I never learned much about him, but he was wealthy enough to enable her travel, and when landowners granted permission, to build the stone circles she claimed would seal the time holes."

"You mean like Stonehenge?"

"She actually disapproved of Stonehenge. She felt it was an attempt to seal a time hole, but that it wasn't tight enough, which is why strange occurrences are still reported there. She decided it made more sense for the stones to be connected, but of course not many people will agree to have part of their land sealed away forever behind a circular wall. So she got creative and turned the circle on its side. I wasn't able to confirm this until decades later, but the gate isn't an archway. It's a loop. We just can't see the part that's buried underground."

"Our gate? Really?"

"Yes. I've had a survey done with underground mapping technology, and later, I had a crew dig deep enough for me to see for myself. Oh. I own my own construction company, by the way. I've been keeping that from the family for years."

I pinch the bridge of my nose. "Wait. What?"

"I thought I would need it to repair the gate. Do you remember Leroy? He wanted to start a building company with his son. I provided the startup capital. Your grandma is very rich, thanks to you."

"Me?"

"Of course. By the time the eighties rolled around, I was tired of working my fingers to the bone. Daniel and I were finally starting to see some of the things you referenced. I wrote many of them down, wanting to see if they would ever make sense or come true. So I had a good idea of what to invest in. Don't tell your brothers. I know that you'll still make the most of yourself, despite the golden carrot of your inheritance dangling in front of you, but I'm not as sure about them."

"So what you're saying," I grumble, "is that it's okay that I traveled back in time and changed things enough to make you rich, but I can't go back so that Daniel and I can be together again?"

"I've thought about that," Gloria says, pausing to take a sip of iced tea. "Maybe there are alternate realities. I don't know. But in this one, you always traveled back to the past. There was never a version where you didn't. How would you have grown up in this house if you didn't inadvertently tell me what stocks to invest in?"

"Maybe you would have figured it out on your own."

"Could be, but I've never cared much for the tech industry, or the stock market, so it seems unlikely."

"Wait a minute, are you saying you own this house?"

"Yes." She smirks. "Funny how your parents never seem to mention that."

I take a deep breath and exhale again, trying to process it all. "So you bought this house, knowing that I would need to grow up here?"

"Not exactly. My mother was getting old and needed to move in with me. I was searching for homes when I saw that this one was for sale. Daniel's family didn't live here anymore by then, but I liked the idea of giving her the house that she used to clean for a white woman. That's my version of progress. So I bought it, knowing that it would remain in the family for at least another generation."

I think of my great-grandparents and feel their loss like never before. "I wish I could have seen them again."

"You did."

"I know. But as I am now. I'm so glad I had the chance to really get to know them."

"They missed you terribly when you left," she says. "I gave them the letter you wrote. They believed you returned to

Alabama to take care of your mother, who had fallen ill. But they always hoped to hear from you again."

I swallow, thinking for the first time of the other people I left in the past who I'll now miss. "How did Mama react?"

"She compared every piano player she hired to you, and not favorably. I'm glad you finally got to meet your grandfather though, considering that he died before you were born."

I shake my head, not understanding.

"Grandpa Al?" Gloria asks. "You haven't figured that part out yet?"

"You don't mean... No!"

"Strange how these things happen." She pats my hand. "But they do. Love is always unexpected. That's what you need to keep in mind. You'll find someone new, even if that seems impossible or undesirable at the moment."

"I already found who I belong with."

"There can be more than one. I know you don't want to hear that now. Not when you're still mourning your time with him. Oh! Speaking of which, I have something for you."

I think I know what she means as we get up and walk into her bedroom. A lump is already in my throat as we approach the dresser. The photo I was so fascinated with as a child is still there, in the frame that I would eventually buy from a department store in the past.

"I took this from Daniel," she admits, "back when your photo was the only thing in it. I know that sounds cruel, but he obsessed over it. We'd be in the middle of a conversation, even years later, when his eyes would dart to it and he'd get upset all over again. I wanted him to move on. By the time he finally did, he asked me to keep it. Daniel would still look at it when visiting me, but he would smile, or simply say hello to you. It was sweet instead of sad. I hated seeing him so heartbroken."

"What happened to my photo?"

"It's still in there. Around the time you were born, I thought it was a good idea to cover it up, and I still had the matching photo that Daniel gave me. You can keep it to remember him by. I figure you don't have a photo of the two of you together."

"I do actually," I say, but only once the frame is safely in my hands. "On my phone. I took it right before I left."

"You have a photo?"

"And a video. Yeah."

"Thank god," Gloria says in exasperation. "Your mother thinks I'm insane. Once everything has calmed down, please show those to her as evidence."

"I will," I say with a laugh before looking down at the frame. I like knowing that my photo is hidden behind his. In a way, we've been together all this time. I only wish it could still be true. "What are you going to do about the gate?"

"Have it rebuilt. I don't know if that will do the trick. It all sounds like a bunch of mumbo jumbo to me, but I don't want anyone else getting lost. We still don't know how it works. Not really. Promise me you'll stay away."

I want to shake my head, but I can't. I keep thinking of the photo from Daniel's wedding and all the happy faces on display. I would be burning that to the ground by returning to the past. So I won't. But I do need to figure out what I'm going to do with my future.

Chapter 24

Over the next couple of days, I struggle to find any sort of normality or routine. I don't have a job that demands my attention. I miss playing at The Silver Rattle. After searching online, I discover that the club closed its doors decades ago. I'll finally attend Columbia College, but not until the academic year begins on the other side of summer. I have plenty of people to catch up with, starting with my best friend, but that doesn't go as well as I'd hoped.

After a tearful reunion, Hannah and I discuss the day I disappeared. From her perspective, I seemed to vanish as the stone gate fell in front of me. I'm honest with her about what happened, even opening the framed photo of Daniel to show the image of me behind it from long ago, but such a thing wouldn't be difficult to fake these days. A simple image filter would do the trick.

Showing her the footage of Daniel and me together doesn't help either, since the background only reveals trees, and there is something undeniably contemporary about a digital high-definition video recorded on a phone. People rarely imagine the past with the same vivid color and detail as the present. I wish I'd taken the opportunity to record more evidence. Then again, if it's possible to deep-fake the president's face so it appears seamlessly on a dog, then there is very little that couldn't easily be explained away. I can tell that she tries to believe me, but I'm not sure that she really does.

"He must have really been something," Hannah says, as if I came up with an elaborate story to justify running away with him.

"He still is," I say. "I'd introduce you, if he was willing to see me."

She changes the subject soon after, talking about people and pop culture that used to matter more to me. Maybe it will again, given enough time. For now, Daniel is all I can think about, so I'm relieved when she leaves. Not because I love her any less. I'm simply looking back despite needing to move forward. Try as I might, I simply can't imagine continuing on without him.

And I don't. Instead I gather up the pieces of Daniel I still have and surround myself with them. I'm sitting cross-legged in bed at night, his framed photo staring back at me, the affection in his eyes never wavering. I watch the short video of us on my phone, wishing that I'd asked him something significant, or that we'd taken turns telling each other how we feel.

I'm really fond of this guy here, so thank you for sending him.

I replay the clip over and over, because it's the closest I can get to hearing Daniel say that he loves me. And I obsess over the only photo I have of us together. I zoom in on his eyes, my own filling with tears. I see the way my cheek is touching his and wonder why I didn't notice it in the moment. I'd give anything to feel that now. It doesn't matter if his cheeks happen to sag more than they used to. At least, I don't think it does, but I need to find out for sure. I've always been willing to confront reality.

I send a text to my grandmother, asking her for a recent photo of Daniel. She sends it without question. I don't feel any sense of loss when it comes to her. If I want to go thrifting with Gloria again, I can. Wealthy or not, she always appreciates a bargain. We can still gossip or grab a burger and see a movie. Nothing has changed, aside from her age. Why can't it be the same with Daniel? That he's nearby and yet so impossibly distant is maddening.

I study the photo she sent of him—a full body shot in his backyard. Daniel is wearing a floppy brimmed hat to shield himself from the sun, a gloved hand resting on the handle of a shovel stuck into the ground. He looks younger when he smiles, but I don't attempt to take solace in that. Instead I focus on all the different ways that time has changed him. White hair and wrinkles mostly. He aged well, all things considered. I might be biased though because I still love him. I grab the framed photo and stare at it, feeling my heart swell for him like it always does. I also do this for the more recent photo, and the result is exactly the same. When I see Daniel, I feel adoration. The details of his appearance are inconsequential.

Wanting to be certain, I calm myself down again. I wait for the intensity of my feelings to subside. Then I pick up my phone and look at a photo of a smiling old man. And I'm absolutely sure.

— — —

Meet me on the bench. Please.

I send the text while still in the house, which is blissfully empty, thanks to my grandmother. She requested help with some shopping. My parents are now on the longest trip to Costco of their lives. I hope their suffering isn't in vain. They're soon forgotten as I check myself in the mirror once more. Then I step outside, cross the street, and walk around the lake to a cluster of trees that offers privacy. Enough for two boys in the fifties to kiss for the first time.

I fidget while waiting, wondering how long it takes an eighty-year-old man to walk three blocks. I refuse to consider the possibility that he might not show. What we had was too special—too intense—for him not to. I stare at my shoes, the grass around them still wet with morning dew, but the shining sun will soon cause it to evaporate. The snow is gone. Ducks have returned to the water. Spring is finally here, reminding me of when we walked through the woods to find a missing backpack. I close my eyes and pretend I'm still there with him, my chest tight with anticipation.

I hear footsteps and the rustle of clothing as someone sits next to me. I'm so excited to see him again that, when I open my eyes, it's like my dreams have come true.

"Please tell me those are happy tears," Daniel says.

"Yeah," I say, wiping them away. "They are."

His expression remains somber. "I'm not sure we should see each other like this. Not so soon."

"But you want to see me again?" I ask.

"Yes. I want us to be friends."

I put my hand over his. "I don't."

He doesn't pull away from me, thank goodness, but he does shake his head. "We can't."

"Why not?"

Daniel sighs. "You know why. These years are precious. You'll understand when you're older. I want you to spend them with someone your own age."

"I want to spend them with someone I love," I counter. "And yes, I know that I have a lifetime of experiences ahead of me, and you don't want to cheat me of that, but how much longer do you plan on being alive?"

He looks over at me sharply. "That's a very direct question!"

"Of course it is. We're always that open with each other. We share everything. I know it's been a while for you, but this is who we are. It'll all come back. I can be patient and let it develop naturally again, but I don't want to be without you. And I don't want you to be alone." I squeeze his hand and turn to face him. "How long do we have left? Five years? Maybe ten?"

"I hope I don't live much longer than that," Daniel says. "I've never wanted to become a centennial."

"I'd be in my thirties by then."

"Still a baby," Daniel says dismissively.

"Plenty of time to experience the rest with someone else. I'll keep my promise. But not until I have to."

"The choice isn't yours alone."

"I know," I say with a swallow. "But I'm hopeful."

His gaze lingers on me, and I can tell that he still loves me just as much. "There's so much you don't know," he says gently. "Getting old isn't pretty. I have to trim the inside of my ears now. And shave the outsides."

"And they look fabulous," I say affectionately. "Although I don't remember them being quite so big. Did anything else keep growing?"

"Let's talk about that," Daniel says. "Do you really think you can have an intimate relationship with someone who looks like me? Gravity is relentless, the results unforgiving. Everything sags at my age. Imagine me naked. Go on."

"I already have."

"I'm not kidding!"

"Neither am I." I take a deep breath. "I get what you mean. If you were some random senior citizen walking down the street, I wouldn't even think to look at you in that way. But you're not, Daniel. You're someone I love and who I've slept with countless times. So yes, your body is going to look different, but I'm still familiar with it. No matter your age, it's still you, and that changes everything. Do you know what I mean?"

He looks me over again and nods. "You're practically a child to me. I won't pretend that young people never catch my eye. Youth is inherently beautiful. But I've always preferred men around my own age, even now."

"I can dye my hair gray if that helps."

"Don't you dare," he says with a laugh. Then he shakes his head ruefully. "What would your parents think?"

I shrug. "We never let that stop us before."

"Would we be a secret?" he asks. "Do you want people mistaking me for your grandfather when we go out to dinner together?"

"I'm pretty sure they won't make that assumption," I say with a chuckle. "And no. We'll be even less a secret than before. That was the entire point in us coming here. You just took the long way around."

He stares at me wistfully, and I'm certain that our relationship is going to begin again in the same place that it did before. Except age must bring caution with it because his expression is reserved, and those lips of his don't come any closer to mine.

"I'm willing to give the idea some thought," he says. "You should too. We can discuss it again once we have, but I don't want you to get your hopes up. I can already think of too many reasons why this is a bad idea."

"I can think of one big reason why it isn't, and it's the only one I ever needed." I slip my hand free from his. "But I understand. If you need time to think it over, that's fine." I nod across the lake. "When's the last time you saw the house you grew up in?"

His eyes light up with curiosity. "Not since shortly after Gloria bought it."

"Come take a look," I say. "The house is empty. It'll be that way for a few hours."

"Really?"

"Yeah! Come see."

I ask what happened to his sisters as we walk together, happy to learn that they're both alive. Sarah still plays the piano, mostly at her church. I'm thrilled that she stuck with it. I have such fond memories of them. And this neighborhood.

"Remember when we used to go skinny-dipping in the lake?"
I ask.

"We did not!"

"Yeah we did. All the time. Your memory is going."

He stares at me, expression concerned before I start laughing.
Then he shoves me away, but I come right back again. I'm still
grinning when I unlock the front door. I step aside so he can
enter first. Then I watch him look around in awe before he begins
pointing out all the things that have changed. He watched me do
the same thing in his living room that first fateful night.

"You must have thought I was insane," I say after mentioning
this to him.

"I thought you were casing the joint," Daniel says with a
laugh. "And I'd already decided that I'd help you carry anything
you wanted out the door."

"Oh yeah?"

"You were very handsome," he admits.

"That was less than a year ago, so what you're really saying
is that I'm… Go on."

"Stop," he says, swatting my arm.

"Never."

He's especially interested to see Gloria's part of the house,
and the new garage. I'm patient with him during this but relieved
when we finally enter the former dining room together. Now it
appears more like a library, with shelves lining the wall and a
grand piano in the center. I sit down as he joins me on the bench,
just like we always used to.

"Any requests?" I ask.

"Anything but the songs that were special to us," he says.

"You know all my old tricks, huh?"

"It's not that. I'm simply not sure I could handle it at the
moment."

"As you wish. Let's see… Anything but our greatest hits."

I begin playing a song, looking at him to see if he recognizes
it. I never played it for him before. Why would I when we were
still together? Although he might be familiar with it, since the
song could have been on the record he was listening to just the
other night. Good ol' Chet Baker. I sing the first line, which is
also the title of the song. "I get along without you very well…"

The lyrics are about someone who insists they are doing fine without the person they once loved, but then they go on to list the endless exceptions. I know the feeling. When you let someone into your heart, they haunt your entire world. I can't walk through this house without seeing him fidgeting on the couch, eager for his parents to leave so we can have privacy. I can't eat without remembering the meals we cooked for each other. I can't even look at myself in the mirror without remembering how he would come up from behind and kiss me on the neck. He's part of me, inside and out, and I know that it must be the same for him, because he leans his head on my shoulder and begins to cry.

"I do love you, Reggie," he says when the song comes to an end. "I never stopped. Part of me was always waiting for you to return. Especially during the difficult times. I'd often turn toward the door and hope to see you there, arriving just as suddenly and improbably as the first time."

"I'm here now," I say. "You just have to let me be with you."

He places a hand on my cheek, his pale green eyes full of adoration, and when he leans forward, my lips smile against his mouth as we kiss.

"Is that a yes?" I ask.

He nods. "I must be insane. Or senile. That's what I'll let people assume when they find out."

"I won't have that excuse, and I won't need it." I tilt my head, taking in the joy on his face, and my heart is made whole again. "Are you curious to see your old room?"

"Reggie!"

"I had to ask. Mostly because I wanted to see you blush again. I was beginning to think you forgot how."

"There are a few things I might be a little rusty at," he admits.

"So do you?" I ask again.

He shakes his head ruefully, but it's not his answer. I don't get that until he stands up and offers his hand. I take it, glancing back as I lead him up the stairs, and all I see is the boy I love. Our relationship has survived hardships and weathered the decades, but age could never touch what we have together. Our song isn't over yet. Not by far. We've only just begun.

———

Author's Note

Dear Reader,

You are powerful! Reviews and word-of-mouth are what truly make a book successful, and I need your help more than ever. I'm an independent author, which means I don't have the backing of a publisher. That's by choice. My stories are unabashedly queer. I don't want to compromise my vision in the name of marketability. Providing you with an authentic experience is too important to me, especially as a gay man who writes from the heart. So if you enjoyed spending time with Reggie and Daniel, please consider writing a review, sharing a link to the book on social media, or contacting a friend to express your excitement. You can also become a patron to the arts by joining me on Patreon where I offer exclusive content. Thank you for the support you've already shown when buying this book!

With love,

-Jay Bell

I love him. And I'm pretty sure he loves me back… even though he's straight.

When I first met Carter King, I knew he was something special. I imagined us being together, and we are, but only as friends. Best friends! I'm trying to be cool with that, even though I know he has secrets, and there have definitely been mixed signals. I don't want a crush to ruin what we already have. Then again, if there's any chance that we can be together, it's worth the risk, because Carter could be the love of my life. Or he might be the boy who breaks my heart.

Straight Boy is Jay Bell's emotional successor to his critically acclaimed Something Like… series. This full-length novel tells a story of friendship and love while skating the blurry line that often divides the two.

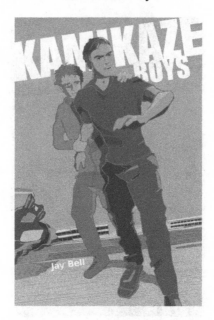

Hear the story in their own words!

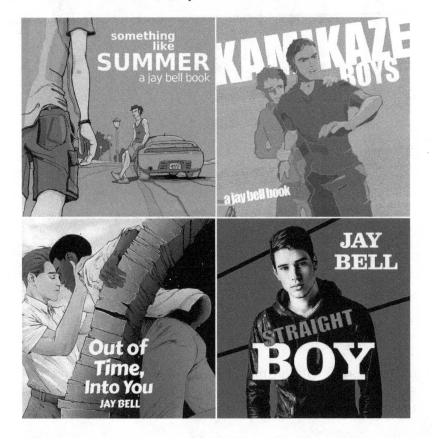

Come chill with me on Patreon! Not only will you empower an indie author through your support, but you'll also gain access to special content that includes:

- Never before published books.
- Exclusive short stories.
- Sexy and sweet illustrations of your favorite characters.
- Early access to upcoming novels.
- The inclusion of your name in my new releases.
- And other stuff too!

Learn more here:

WWW.PATREON.COM/JAYBELLBOOKS

Who makes that gorgeous art?

Cassy Fallon discovered a knack for art at a young age when her drawings were so popular with classmates that she started taking commissions. Since then she's won a prestigious Congressional Art Award before going on to earn her associate's degree in fine arts, although Cassy insists her education is far from over. She intends to hone her craft further as she pursues her dream of becoming a fulltime artist. When not juggling pencils and paintbrushes, she enjoys thrifting and getting caffeine fixes at late-night diners. If you'd like to join Cassy on her artistic journey, you can do so by visiting: www.cassyfallon.com.

Who the hell is Jay Bell?

Jay Bell is a proud gay man and the award-winning author behind dozens of emotional and yet hopelessly optimistic stories. His best-selling book, *Something Like Summer*, spawned a series of heart-wrenching novels, a musically driven movie, and a lovingly drawn comic. When not crafting imaginary worlds, he occupies his free time with animals, art, action figures, and—most passionately—his husband Andreas. Jay is always dreaming up new stories about boys in love. If that sounds like your cup of tea, you can get the kettle boiling by visiting www.jaybellbooks.com.

CPSIA information can be obtained
at www.ICGtesting.com
Printed in the USA
LVHW110447090522
718236LV00005B/233